MA
WAR

DMC SHAW

INVALUABLE FICTION

Shaw, D. M. C., 1975-

The maker war / D. M. C. Shaw.

p. : ill. ; cm.

ISBN-13: 978-0-9891936-7-2 (pbk.)

ISBN-13: 978-0-9891936-8-9 (e-book)

LCCN: 2019920386

First Edition

Printed in the United States of America.

Published by Invaluable Fiction, an imprint of Invaluable Press, Salt Lake City, Utah, USA

Cover design by George Sellas

Interior formatting by John Arce

For the three young Makers in my family

PROLOGUE

The speed of the print is determined by 1) the quality of your Ozmium device, 2) your proximity to a source of starks, such as the Quantum Bank or a local quantum wallet, and 3) the complexity of your blueprint. Make wise choices in battle to avoid finding yourself unprepared due to too slow of a print!

Global Maker Corps Fieldbook

"Oz: Ultralight ramp: three meters!" Zandrie shouted, pointing with her right hand.

Just in time, her Ozmium-55 printed a graphene slope in front of her. Zandrie ran toward the ramp and slid beneath its shadow, barely avoiding a painful and somewhat odd death as a bright yellow antique sports car hit the ramp and jumped over her body. She felt the wind brush her face as the Lamborghini flew overhead.

Or is it a Ferrari? she wondered. *My kid brother would know for sure. He's the one interested in the old wheel-style cars.*

It was a strange choice for a combat vehicle. The Ripper driving it could have chosen from hundreds of thousands of more practical options for a battle, but some people preferred to print obscure or nostalgic objects on the battlefield. If not for personal tastes, then for the effect it had on your opponents, causing them to hesitate for just a split second.

Just like I'm doing right now, Zandrie noted.

She preferred the more practical approach.

"Oz: Light Minigun: juiced rounds," she said, holding out her hands.

The Oz clipped to her right forearm hummed, and from beneath her palm flowed a black, oily substance the consistency of liquid metal. The raw matter flowed quickly and consolidated into the shape of a large rotary machine gun. While the printing process would take only a handful seconds, it wasn't fast enough for Zandrie's liking.

"C'mon, c'mon," she whispered, as her enemy began turning his brand new, one hundred and forty-year-old sports car around for another pass.

The tires on the Ripper's car began to screech as he throttled the engine and began to once again accelerate toward her. That's when she noticed the car's tires were wrapped in aggressive-looking snow chains. A harpoon gun poked through its front grill.

"He's gonna spear me like a fish if this thing doesn't print faster. Come on!" she screamed. "Now, now, now, now, now, NOW!"

In a snap, the shape in her hands blinked from black sludge to completed minigun, the familiar tightness and texture of the carbon-fiber trigger in her fingers. The weapon, while visually hefty and gigantic, was nearly light as a feather. She had spent hours over the last year carefully tweaking and engineering the blueprint stored in her Oz. Underneath the carbon fiber exterior of the minigun was a titanium wire frame, sturdy enough to take the massive kick of such an aggressive weapon. It made her feel epic.

The bullets…well, those were something different entirely.

Zandrie let out a primal scream as she sprayed the front of the oncoming vehicle with hundreds of large-caliber bullets. As they impacted with the streamlined hood of the car, they instantly expanded into silvery grapefruit-sized spheres, sticking to the car's hood like chewing gum. Hundreds of twenty-centimeter spheres glommed onto the windshield, hood, wheels, and grill.

The spheres blocked the windshield so the driver couldn't see, covered the front hood in silvery glue, and slipped in through the grill. They expanded into a collective mass that jammed the harpoon gun, blistered the tires, and buried the entire engine.

Then, they exploded with a jolt of electricity.

Individually, each jolt might have been an inconvenience, but together the effect was immediate—and painful. The old-time-tech of the car's engine shorted as miniature bolts of lightning danced from front to back. Behind the wheel, the Ripper's eyes bugged out as his body jerked, then he slumped forward in his seat like a ragdoll. The momentum of the vehicle, however, continued speeding directly toward Zandrie. She rolled to the right, narrowly missing death by sports car for the second time. The car clipped the side of a nearby building and came to a halt.

After pausing for a breath and chuckle of relief, she spoke. "Comms, Ranjit: one Ripper to bring in, on my location."

"Got it, Zan," Ranjit's voice came back through her aural implant. *"Was that a vintage 2028 Lamborghini Audace I saw? Pretty sweet. Wrong color, though."*

"Don't know what it was, Ranjit. Don't care. All I know is that it tried to kill me…multiple times. And I hate it."

"Aw, c'mon, Zan. You got to admit that the Ripper has style." Ranjit laughed. *"Our job's tough enough. Sometimes you gotta appreciate the little things. Spice things up a bit!"*

"I'll leave the appreciation to you, Ranjit. I've got more Rippers to knock out. They're tearing this city apart. Bring Delaine and pick this guy up. Comms out."

Zandrie paused to take in her location. In the heat of battle, it was easy to get turned around. The Federation of Las Vegas was a big place. *Too* big. Too easy for Rippers to vac matter from just about anywhere. Too loud. Too bright. Too…everything. But most of all, too many people. And she was worried someone would get caught in the crossfire.

Like her little sister, Zoey, had been seven years ago.

She walked over to the yellow gum-covered antique car…whatever it was…which was still smoking from fried old-time electrical circuitry. She opened the door to check and make sure the Ripper was wearing his VacGuard. The telltale purple light pulsed on his left shoulder, indicating that all matter on his body was being shielded. She scoffed.

"You protect yourself, but you don't care if you take everything away from someone else."

Suppressing a moment of bitterness as she thought of her dead sister, she pushed the car's door down and closed it.

Zandrie paused. *Maybe Zavier would want a scan of this thing. Can't hurt.*

She pointed to the car with her right hand and spoke. "Oz: Scan object: atomic. Check database for…Lamborghini Audace 2028. Ignore foreign objects."

She waited a few seconds as her Oz created a blueprint of the vintage sports car's atomic structure. "Scan complete," the familiar voice of her Ozmium-55 soon reported. "Atomic blueprint added to database. Projected accuracy 99.1 percent."

A vidcube popped up and displayed a rendering of the exact car in its current state—minus the globes of electrified glue she had shot it up with. It had some damage, but she was sure her little brother would figure out how to repair the blueprint…eventually.

She flicked her left wrist in just the right way and pointed her open palm toward her target. The QuantVac clipped to her left forearm began ripping matter from the sports car into her squad's local quantum wallet. Technically, vac'ing matter like this from an object you didn't own was illegal. Stealing starks, the building blocks of matter, was the kind of thing Rippers did. But the Global Maker Corps had a license for ripping matter on the battlefield. In fact, it was often necessary, as porting matter from the distant Quantum Bank to the battlefield was usually slower than reusing what you stored locally. Waste not, want not.

As the subatomic particles were stripped from the back of the car, she brought up the vidcube with a flick of her right wrist to check her location. The fine details of the city appeared inside the transparent box with crystal clarity, a small flare of light within it from the tracker indicating her location.

The QuantVac continued pulling matter as it moved from the middle to the front of the car. The unconscious Ripper dropped to the ground as the steel and plastic surrounding him disappeared—or rather, was re-purposed—into Zandrie's personal quantum wallet stored at the command center.

Behind her, a voice yelled, "Oz: Claymore!"

Zandrie spun quickly around at the cry and saw another Ripper. It was a woman wearing grey camo, vac'ing matter from the corner of a building. The concrete and brick were nearly instantly recombined and printed by the Ripper's Oz into a wicked-looking steel monstrosity. Sharp tangs feathered out on either side of the blade, and the large crossguard at the base was modded with razor-sharp blades on each end.

The Ripper brandished the blade like she was a Highland warrior.

Going medieval, huh? Zandrie thought. *Now we're talking.* "Oz: Morning star and kite shield!"

The Ripper lifted her sword and approached quickly, making her way over the rubble accumulated from weeks of street-fighting. Again, the printed weapons appeared in Zandrie's hands just in time to raise the shield against the claymore with a loud clang.

Thank goodness for the latest Oz upgrade, she thought. *Another second and I would have been skewered.*

"You don't own this, *Taker*," the Ripper shouted. "You don't own any of this! You're a GNA puppet. You think the Maker Corps is noble? You're just a tool. You're keeping corporations like OzTech fat and happy."

The Ripper pulled back, changing direction quickly, then slashed at Zandrie's legs. Zandrie leaped straight backward to avoid the blow, holding her shield low and forward.

"I couldn't care less about the Global Nations Alliance…or OzTech. I'm here to protect *people*, not power. Stop and think about what you're doing! You think you're right to take homes away from people? You think you're justified in killing people? In the name of…what? Some deranged utopian crusade? You have nothing. You *are* nothing. You're the 'Taker.' You're a leech, and you need to be put down."

"All of it for all of us!" the Ripper half-chanted, half-shrieked.

It was a familiar mantra to Zandrie; the pseudo-morality rallying cry of every Ripper Zandrie had ever arrested. To her, all it sounded like was anarchy and apocalypse.

The Ripper grunted, this time slashing high. "*All* of it for *all* of us!"

Zandrie raised her morning star with a snap of her wrist, wrapping the claymore in chains. The Ripper's eyes went wide with panic, then Zandrie stepped forward and turned sharply, sending the Ripper tumbling to the ground while stripping the sword from her hands.

"If you're going to make a weapon, Ripper," Zandrie spat as she tossed the sword behind her, "learn how to use it."

The Ripper rolled to the side and quickly up to her feet, backing away while still facing Zandrie.

"I know enough not to bring a morning star to a gun fight," the Ripper shot back. "Oz: Mega-flamethrower!"

A device with a pregnant-looking barrel appeared almost instantly in her hand, giving Zandrie barely enough time to raise up her shield in defense against the wave of fire that surrounded her. The heat licked around the shield, leaving scorch marks on her light battle armor, while the sudden oven-like temperature forced her to step backward.

That was fast for a print that large, Zandrie thought. *Where are they getting that level of tech?*

The tang of burning fossil fuel assaulted her senses as a cloud of smoke enveloped her. She began to feel light-headed. "Oz: Medical oxygen mask."

As the mask printed around her face and provided sweet relief, she backed up while crouching behind her shield, occasionally glancing backward to see where she was going. The Ripper continued to advance, and Zandrie knew her time was limited before she was burned to a crisp or asphyxiated. Her thoughts raced for a solution...and found one.

Zandrie dropped her morning star and whispered into her Oz, "Oz: Liquid Nitrogen Cannon."

Based on the blueprints Zandrie had created and loaded months earlier, the Oz printed what looked like a water-cannon, but with a variety of tubing and insulation wrapped around it. She dropped and rolled to one side, then threw her shield directly at the Ripper, who hesitated and released her flamethrower's trigger for just a moment.

It was all the window Zandrie needed.

With a shout, she pulled the trigger on her cannon and a deluge of supercooled liquid engulfed the Ripper, who tried desperately to fight back by firing her flamethrower. For a tense moment, there was a puff of steam as fire and ice collided in midair, but the nitrogen has already reached its target.

The Ripper cried out in fear as her weapon became so cold it was impossible to hold any longer. She let go of it, which allowed the cold to cover her shoulder, chest, and thigh, creating immediate frostbite. She fell onto her back, then huddled into a small ball as a pained groan escaped her lips.

Zandrie removed her oxygen mask and paused to see if her

foe was dispatched. Seeing no movement, she turned and began searching her surroundings for any stray enemies.

"Comms, Ranjit: got another one."

"Gotcha, Zan," Ranjit replied. *"Delaine and I are almost at your location for the first one. Busy day, huh?"*

"You know how it is…Wait!"

Zandrie caught the sound of movement, and she whirled around to look behind her. The Ripper was gone.

"I lost her, Ranjit," Zandrie said. "Hold your position."

Suddenly, Zandrie heard the familiar sound of matter being vacuumed, followed by a loud crack from the building next to her.

"You want this city, Maker? Here, you can have it."

She looked over to see that the Ripper had pulled in the lower corner of the building, including its supports…a building that was now about to fall directly on top of Zandrie.

"Oz: Exoskeleton!"

But it was too late. Before Zandrie's Oz could begin printing the protective outer layer she had asked for, the building fell on top of her, crushing her legs instantly. Her right arm was also pinned, smashing her Oz in the process.

Zandrie realized she could not feel her legs and started to panic. She found that she could move her left hand around her waist, but touching the ground around her only increased her worry. It felt sickeningly moist. She knew she was losing blood, fast.

In a daze, Zandrie heard the muffled sounds of a fierce battle outside her coffin of concrete. After what seemed like hours, she began to feel the pressure on her chest lessen. Soon, she saw the wall that was crushing her dissolving as both Ranjit's and Delaine's QuantVacs ripped into it.

"No. Oh, no," Ranjit whispered, then tried flashing an unconvincing smile. "I'm going to get you out of this, Zandrie!"

She had no energy to reply.

Ranjit and Delaine clawed away at the remaining rubble, trying to clear up their view of Zandrie's mangled legs.

"I've got your body scan in my Oz," Ranjit said as calmly as his training would allow, but Zandrie could hear the emotion creeping into his voice nonetheless. "I'm going to reconstruct your legs. You'll be okay. Oz: IV: synthblood: A-negative. Stay with me, Zan."

Sweat beaded on Ranjit's forehead as he began the complicated process of medically printing over her wounds.

Zandrie returned his concern with a weak smile.

Ranjit is a genius, she thought to herself. *If anyone can help me…*

She didn't finish the thought, as cold darkness consumed her.

CHAPTER 1

> *Your squad will become your family, not just during your time at the Academy, but for many years afterward. Prioritize spending time with them and getting to know them. Familiarity leads to synergy of thought. Close bonds forged every day can be the difference between success or failure on the battlefield.*
>
> Maker Corps Academy, Combat Squad Orientation

So perfect, Zavier thought. *So seamless.*

He held up his arms and turned his wrists back and forth as he analyzed the tiniest details of the world-altering devices strapped to them. The lightweight pieces of metal that sheathed his arms were the result of decades of engineering. There were no joints, connections, or openings that he could notice. Smooth. Endless. For a moment, Zavier got lost in his imagination as he saw scores of Makers from decades past collaborating, testing, and retooling things until they achieved the result that he had just clasped on at this moment. He had put them on thousands of times, yet it never got old.

Fluid.

On the right arm was his Ozmium-61, or "Oz" as most called it. Over the last ten years, he had been gradually filling it with blueprint after blueprint, design after design—most of his own making…or, rather, modifications of designs others had made. He rarely created something new.

But I can always make something better.

Around Zavier, other young Makers were also strapping on

their Ozes, trading jokes, boasts, and the occasional trash talk. But he was oblivious to it all. There was only him and his Oz.

"Oz: Hall of Fame," Zavier said as he stretched out his right arm. Upon hearing the verbal macro command, his Oz printed a sphere with the appearance of metallic tar. In a blink the dark orb converted into his favorite test-print: an exact atomic replica of the 1939 baseball signed by eleven of the greatest baseball players in history. He picked up the ball and looked at the signatures of Babe Ruth, Ty Cobb, and more.

He had little idea who they were. Zavier could care less about a two-hundred and thirty-year-old sport that had died long before he was born. And yet he chuckled at the irony that something that used to be priceless was now worthless. Anyone in this room could print the same thing in a moment, and no expert in the world would be able to tell the difference.

Just like paper money, the moment the first Maker scanned the blueprint into their Oz, it had lost its value. Forever.

He set the ball down and lifted his left arm. With a flick of his wrist, the once-priceless ball was stripped of atomic stability as raw matter deconstructed into the absolute smallest quantum unit, the stark. In an instant, it was all gone, returned to the Maker Corps quantum cache until he called upon those raw starks again.

Zavier smiled as he thought of the early Makers making an infinite jest by naming the most significant quantum element in the world after a comic book character. Sure, they had claimed it was a mashup of "strings" and "quarks." But he knew the truth: they were geeks.

Like him.

"Oz: Hall of Fame." He repeated the process again. And again. Creating the baseball, vac'ing the baseball, repeat. Repeat.

Print. Vac.

Repeat.

Repeat.

Repeat.

And repeat again.

Print. Vac.

Print. Vac.

Zavier only became aware of the mental loop he was stuck in when Coover yelled out, "Hey gas-for-brains. I think your Oz is working, eh? Give it a break!"

Zavier broke from his trance and looked up. Coover smirked as the surrounding members of his rival squad, Overdrive, began laughing uncontrollably.

Hunter Granholm was from Micronation—or "Micro"—Vancouver, hence his nickname. Vancouverites were known for being the politest people in the world, which is why Zavier secretly believed that Coover had failed a citizenship test and been exiled before joining the Global Maker Corps.

Zavier searched desperately for some intelligent response, but none came to mind. This caused Squad Overdrive to laugh even more.

Suddenly a muscled mountain of a man stepped between Zavier and Overdrive. Tobias Montero.

Toby was perhaps the most massive guy Zavier had ever known—which was saying a lot, considering Toby was seventeen like the rest of the squad. Even though they'd only been together for a few semesters, Toby was fiercely loyal—and valiantly protective—of the rest of Zavier's squad. But it was more than that. Zavier had seen the Guadalajaran insert himself several times when younger or weaker cadets were being bullied. So it was fitting that Toby's chosen discipline at the Academy was to be a "Shield"—a Guardian who specialized in the defense of his team.

Zavier sometimes suspected Toby took this role a bit too seriously. Not just because of his protective nature outside of combat training, but also due to the shield-shaped mark on his left cheek that Zavier assumed was a tattoo. It seemed a bit too… literal.

"Enough," Toby said. "Save it for the arena."

Coover's face turned red and he started to reply when his squad captain, a teen known only as "Grandmaster," stepped forward. He was a smug, skinny kid with a few zits on his face that kept reappearing, despite the latest in medical face-printing treatments.

"Agreed, Toby," he replied. "We will save our words. You may be big, but you are slow…and stupid. Dominating you in battle in front of all the new recruits and their parents will be enough."

Zavier felt a hand on his back and turned to see his friend and squad leader, Kojo Solomon. Kojo was from Micro Accra in West Africa and was a brilliant tactician. Zavier and "Koj" had bonded over the years through their mutual love of all things engineering—and nerdy pop culture. As Koj replied, he flipped up the screens of the vidglasses that had become almost a permanent fixture to his face. Kojo had a bit of a tech addiction, but he was so good at what he did that no one begrudged his near-constant vidglasses use.

"I look forward to your opening move," Kojo said. "I hope it's better than last time."

"Oh, be assured of that," Grandmaster replied.

"Hey, Koj," Coover jumped in, "what's your squad name *this* week?"

"It's a work in progress," Kojo said absently. "We're keeping our options open."

A small girl with short, bright red hair and an abundance of swagger jumped into the conversation. Texas. Jenny Hatchet was from the not-so-Micro Texas—hence the all-too-obvious nickname. She was the Blade on Zavier's squad. Quick, fast-thinking, and a crack shot at using a vast array of her engineered firearms.

"We were thinking of either 'Overdrive's Demise' or 'Kiss My Ozmium.' What do you think, Coover?" she said.

A few chuckles escaped the other team. Coover pursed his lips and blew a mock kiss at Texas.

"Good luck on the match, Kojo," Grandmaster broke in. "I'm sure the best opponent will win, which of course is—"

"Normally I'd feel bad about having to beat you, Grandmaster," Toby interrupted, "But since this isn't real, I'm all for your complete destruction."

Grandmaster smiled and shook his head as if he were a father watching small children misbehave. He gestured to his squad and they turned to continue to their preparations.

"Guys…" Zavier began.

"You *are* going to make sure we win this time, right Z?" Texas asked with a good-natured punch to his shoulder. "I can only cause so much mayhem. A little help from our Edge would be nice. Whaddya say?"

Zavier knew she was teasing, but there was an element of truth that still stung. An Edge's job was to be a squad's Swiss-army-knife—to come up with solutions to complex problems and see things others did not. To be an Edge was to embrace the whole reason the Maker Corps existed: the creativity of the human mind, in the moment, in the moment of need, could always outperform the calculations of a bot.

Yes, some of Earth's more brutal, largescale wars were still fought from a distance with overwhelming force and the mindless actions of a bot. In most cases, though, this kind of reckless destruction had been outlawed through the GNA accords. There were far too many human casualties when nations settled their differences with bombs and bullets…or things far worse.

The Global Nations Alliance founded and funded the GMC— Global Maker Corps—to protect the greater good and provide what each independent state cannot: security and defense at the human level. Zavier embraced the Maker Corps ideal of being a first responder and law enforcer, especially against the continual Ripper threat against order, property, and government.

And he worked hard. As an Edge, he excelled in the blueprint creation. His mind was ever dancing between ideas and adaptation of what was and what could be. His dreams were filled with engineering, and every morning he awoke with frantic urgency to pull up a vidcube and make a mod, or two, or twenty.

And yet…when on the battlefield, it was all noise and confusion. So, Zavier knew all too personally that Texas was speaking the truth. He felt the depressing weight of it on his shoulders.

But all that came out was, "I'll do my best."

"We know you will, *hermano*," Toby said with a gentle slap on the back. "We believe in you! Right, Min?"

In the corner of the ready room sat a young Medic, engrossed as she flipped through her Oz's vidcube and the atomic maps of each squad member's physiology. She wore a set of earbuds that were turned up so loudly that everyone could hear the ear-bleeding-yet-oddly-catchy metalpop music that she used to find focus. Min was from Micro Yanbian, making her both Korean and Chinese—something like that, at least.

She was Zavier's girlfriend…sort of. They hadn't defined it yet. They were more than friends, at least. They had briefly kissed once, if that counted for something—and to Zavier, it did. How much it had counted to her…well, that was a discussion they'd yet to have. Whatever she was, Zavier was in deep with his feelings for her, and he knew it.

So, he waited, hanging on her every word. What came out was…

"I'm sorry, Toby, did you say something?" she said, pulling out an earbud.

Toby laughed and spoke louder. "I said: We. Believe. In. Zavier!

Right?" he added with a wink.

"Oh sure, Z. You're the best!" She said with an absent-minded thumbs up as she put the earbud back in an got to work.

Zavier visibly deflated. Kojo must have seen it because he sat down next to him and took him by both shoulders. "Absolutely, my friend. You *are* the best. You've been prepping for this exhibition for weeks, and the stuff you've made…!" He whistled in appreciation. "Can't wait to see it in action!"

"Thanks, Koj."

"I mean it, Z," Kojo said, and then announced to the rest of the squad. "Five minutes, everyone. Make sure you're prepped and ready to put on a show for the recruits. Vac any molecule of dirt or lint off your full-dress uniform. Brigantine wants us spotless and perfect for these kids."

Zavier popped up the vidcube on his Oz and pulled up a real-time image of himself. Average height, average—scratch that—*somewhat skinny* build, and a bit too much of a slouch. He stood up a little taller and tried to organize the unruly crop of bright-blond hair both he and his sister, Zandrie, had inherited from their Norwegian father. He sighed as he realized he was fighting a hopeless battle. The hair was going to stay where it wanted to stay.

He made a gesture over the map of himself and changed the setting to "target foreign elements." As usual, it found a plethora of unsightly smudges on his clothes. With a flick of his wrist, the QuantVac instantly removed every stray particle, putting his outward appearance back in perfect order.

He stood a little taller and double-checked his image in the vidcube. At least for the moment, he looked the part of a Maker Corps cadet.

Too bad he knew the feeling wouldn't last.

CHAPTER 2

All children who join the MCA receive a world-class cross-discipline education, unlimited access to the latest OzTech innovations, safe and comfortable living conditions, and the very best in medical care. In addition to the monthly ingot stipend they will accumulate, all of your family's material needs will also be taken care of through an open account with the Quantum Bank.

Letter to parents of potential Maker Corps Academy cadets

Lieutenant General Brigantine stepped toward the podium, cleared his throat, and looked over the vast audience of children and their parents.

"We welcome you to the Global Maker Corps Academy Prospect Week." He paused, then cleared his throat again. "Each of you made a long journey to reach us at our orbital facility so you can explore a career in the GMC. Thank you for coming.

"You have already been tested and found to have the brain patterns necessary for success as a Maker Cadet. As you know, every one of the 833 member-micronations of the Global Nations Alliance provides voluntary tests, at age seven, for any parent wishing their child to be considered for the Global Maker Corps. For a variety of reasons, your parents agreed to have you come here. You have passed the first test...so...congratulations." Brigantine raised his arms stiffly in a clearly scripted gesture and was met with silence.

"In a way," he continued after lowering his arms, "Prospect Week is as much about you evaluating the Corps as we are evaluating you. While we're going to test some of your basic aptitudes for creativity and physicality, you're going to be deciding if this is a lifestyle you want to live. And make no mistake about it: this *is* a lifestyle. A commitment to the Corps is a lifetime commitment that begins with a choice to help others. This choice is exciting and rewarding, but comes at great personal sacrifice from a young age. No one can make this choice for you. Not us, not your parents. *You* must decide."

The General shifted a bit on his feet, took a deep breath, then continued.

"As you know, the advent of OzTech's stark-based technology transformed the old way of life. Suddenly, almost anyone could print almost anything they wanted in perfect detail. Starvation disappeared. Life expectancy skyrocketed. Climate imbalances were corrected as we converted waste to valuable resources and reprinted the air and water to perfect quality. Homelessness was eliminated, as we could easily provide safe shelter for anyone.

"But soon, money had no value. Why would it be worth anything, when anything you want could be printed in a moment? The Shattering quickly followed. Almost overnight, the old world governments broke apart, and what was once 200 nations became the 1513 we have…this week. Many of these 'Micro' nations recognized that, while they were divided by philosophy, politics, and culture, they needed a set of international laws to keep the peace among them, and this became the foundation of the Global Nations Alliance. Not long after the formation of the GNA, the peacekeeping force known as the Global Maker Corps was formed.

"Since then, the republic-state members of the Global Nations Alliance have depended upon the Global Maker Corps—or GMC—to protect the greater good and provide what each independent Micro cannot: security. They fund our operations. We are their police force. We are their emergency responders. We are their protectors, especially against the continual Ripper threat that seeks to remove all property ownership and any form of government…"

Here we go again. Zavier thought. *Same speech every year. Same awkward LTG Brigantine.* The cadet stood on the stage along with his squadmates, trying his best to pay attention as the Academy superintendent's voice droned on. He was tempted to simply look up and enjoy the spectacular view of Earth outside the orbital HQ, but knew that would be a bit too obvious.

A textlens message flashed in front of his eyes.

>>**Texas**>>**Here he goes again!**<<

Zavier glanced ever so slightly down and to his right. Texas stared straight forward and gave no sign of the mental text she'd broadcasted to the squad.

Good thing, too, since it was an Academy infraction to use textlenses during training hours. Just wearing them during an important ceremony like this was a punishable offense. But considering it made Brigantine's speech a little less painfully boring, it was worth the risk.

>>**Toby**>>**He looks like he's going to pass out. Get ready to catch him, Z!** <<

That message came from the guy to the right of Texas. Toby was less skilled at keeping his expression steady, and he smirked almost imperceptibly.

Only another twenty minutes to go, Zavier thought. *Then we're on!* Immediately, the words flashed on his eyes-only display, along with everyone else's. He was careful to think *End thought* to make sure no random thoughts were accidentally sent to his squad, which would be beyond embarrassing.

>>**Koj**>>**Minutes that feel like weeks…**<<

A vidloop of a man crawling through the desert also flashed up briefly.

Zavier glanced over at Kojo, who still stood at perfect attention.

An image of a cartoon baby crying gallons of tears flashed on the screen.

In response, Koj sent another animated image of a baby sticking his tongue out.

Knowing he would soon start laughing if this exchange didn't stop, Zavier responded by sending a vidloop of a cyberball referee holding up his hands in a timeout.

Stealing a quick look past Kojo, Zavier glanced at Min and his thoughts took a detour. In Zavier's love-drunk mind, Min was perfection inside and out. Kind, gentle, yet incredibly intelligent. Tough in battle. And beautiful, of course.

Brigantine's voice suddenly broke through the haze of his thoughts about Min.

"…and now to introduce you to the values of the Maker Corps, I'll have Captain Zandrie Vik come up. Captain Vik has neutralized hundreds of Rippers in battle and saved hundreds of more lives. She also received the titanium heart medal for permanent injury received in battle. Captain Vik teaches incursion classes to upcoming Blades and is one of the finest instructors we have here. Captain Vik."

Zavier watched as his sister approached the podium. Her steps had an almost imperceptible hitch to them, noticeable only to someone who knew she had a synthetic leg. She looked far more confident and comfortable than the General, and the crowd quieted at her approach. She scanned them all, then gave a firm nod as she began.

"There are two tools necessary for a Maker to fulfill his or her duty. The first is the Ozmium ultralight wrist printer, or 'Oz' for short. It is the tech fixed on the Maker's right forearm that can create anything physical, in most any state of matter."

She held up her right hand, and printed a fluffy, bright

pink toy Wishwump, a kid-favorite vidcube show. The children laughed in delight.

"The Oz is there to assist the Maker in any way possible," Zandrie continued. "But to do so, the Oz works in conjunction with the Maker's second tool on their *left* forearm. Which is what, potential cadets?"

She eyed the children right below her, and all at once they responded. "The QuantVac!"

"Very good," Zandrie said with a slight nod of approval. "These devices are created and developed by OzTech, who generously shares their advancements with the GMC to help us in our peacekeeping missions for the GNA.

"Together, the OzTech Ozmium and QuantVac work by deconstructing matter..." she said, vac'ing the Wishwump into her Quantvac as the children groaned in disappointment.

"...And reconstructing matter," she continued, printing a Wishwump again, this time in bright green. The children giggled. "All this is done by breaking things down into their absolute smallest quantum unit, which is the..."

"Stark!" most of the children yelled.

"Good! As you all know, the 'starks' let us build *any* sort of device or material. The clothes you're wearing, the food you ate this morning, even this beautiful orbital station—they were all built by OzTech devices recombining this little, tiny building block of everything. We get all the starks from our account in OzTech's Quantum Bank. Every GNA member contributes to that stark account, and we use it to create anything we need to keep the peace."

"The cadets you see behind me take it further," she added. "Using their own blueprints, they print whatever they need to help the Maker Corps do its job in keeping the peace around the world."

Zavier watched in admiration as she continued. He was proud of his big sister and wanted to be like her. Part of the reason why he'd joined the Maker Corps was because of her example. Well, that and Zoey.

Zoey. That thought took Zavier to a dark place for a moment. Their little sister was the reason why Zandrie had joined—forced her way, really—into the Corps at such a young age and become one of the most decorated Blades in GMC history. For her—and for him—it wasn't about keeping the collective international peace. It was personal.

"If we can stop one Ripper from taking one life, it's all worth it," she'd told him the day she'd left for the Academy. "If we can do that, then we can save someone else the pain our whole family has gone through."

Zandrie's amazing, Zavier thought to himself. *But I'll never be a leader like her. I'm not disciplined enough. Not focused enough. But at least I can do* something *for Zoey.*

"…being a part of the Corps isn't *just* about protecting people's property—the very matter that they possess," Zandrie was saying. "But we do protect it, so they have shelter over their heads and food to eat. Do you like to eat food?"

A few random shouts of "Yes!" broke out from the group, causing the children to laugh.

"It isn't *just* about catching the bad guys. Although we do… catch…the bad guys." Zandrie punctuated her words with her fist, smiling as claps broke out from the prospective cadets.

"And it isn't *just* about saving lives. But we do…save…lives." She emphasized the last words again as the children clapped and cheered.

"It's about hope. It's about helping the GNA keep the world safe, just, honest, and fair. We set an example through our actions. We show that, even though the rest of the world may be divided, as Makers we are united in giving the world hope. Do you want to be someone who gives the world hope?"

As she reached a crescendo, most of the children shouted "Yes!" They jumped to their feet and cheered.

>>**Koj**>>**See, folks, now that is how you give a speech!**<<

>>**Min**>>**Yes!!!!!**<<

>>**Toby**>>**Preach, sister!**<<

Zavier sent an old-time vidloop of people at a rally cheering.

Texas sent a vidloop of cowboys dancing.

>>**Koj**>>**Captain Vik has a really nice leg.**<<

There was a pause.

>>**Toby**>>**Wut?**<<

>>**Min**>>**Uh...**<<

Texas sent a vidloop of a woman trying to stop herself from laughing.

Well, okay, that's weird, Zavier thought-texted to everyone. *Did you forget to end-thought? She's my sister, Koj.*

>>**Koj**>>**I meant her synthetic leg! It's well constructed and balanced. You can't tell the difference between that and the real thing.**<<

Oh, was all Zavier sent in reply.

A torrent of vidloops of various people laughing uncontrollably assaulted Zavier's eyes. He flinched as Zandrie returned to her seat. Catching his lack of decorum as he barely held in his laughter, she flashed him a disapproving look.

Brigandine now returned to the podium, as uncomfortable as before. "And now, I would like to introduce our chief educator on staff, Dr. Eduardo Oliveira. He has consistently been voted the most effective instructor by cadets at the Academy. Many of the most decorated Corps members ever to rise through our ranks have done so under his tutelage."

Brigantine smiled nervously. "I recognize that I'm not the best with children; however, I believe you will find Dr. Oliveira more to your liking. Dr. Dado."

Zavier smiled as a smallish man in clean but unremarkable

clothes rose to the podium. As he did, he winked and gave Zavier's squad a small grin. "I am Dr. Eduardo Oliveira," he said, turning his attention to the children in front of him. "But please, call me Dr. Dado."

With his middle-aged appearance, no one would have guessed Dado had the wisdom of eighty-plus years of life on Earth. Thankfully, it was likely Dado would be teaching for another eighty years with current medical practices. That thought was comforting. Dr. Dado wasn't just a good teacher; he was something of a mentor to Zavier. Every time Zavier had felt like he didn't belong in the Corps, or wanted to quit, Dado had been there to pick him up and get him back on track.

Mentor—more like friend. A friendtor, maybe, Zavier thought. He'd never felt patronized by Dado, even though he knew they weren't equals. He still had a lot to learn from his instructor, and he *wanted* to learn from him. Dado made everything interesting and enjoyable. Even now, Dado held Zavier's usually scattered focus. Whenever Dado spoke, he listened, just like he could watch his favorite vidcube movie over and over.

Dado rubbed his hands together. "I am originally from Covilha, which is right on the border of GNA members North and South Portugal. Do you know where those Micros are?"

Several of the children raised their hands. One of them shouted, "I'm from South Portugal, too!"

"Wonderful. It's good to have a familiar face here," he said. "I would like to talk to you about something *maravilhoso*: your brains!"

Dado gestured to the giant vidcube overhead. Inside the crystal-clear box, a fully three-dimensional image of a human brain, accurate to the atom, appeared and rotated slowly for all to see.

"Woah!" the children all exclaimed in unison.

Zavier smiled in nostalgia, remembering the first time he had heard Dr. Dado speak.

"Not just any brains, though," Dado said. "*Special* brains. Brains like yours. Brains that make a Maker a Maker. These are brains that can be *fluid*."

The vidcube brain suddenly began a lightshow of activity, causing some of the children to gasp and cheer.

"Our brains are much like the matter we vac and print from an Oz. Matter is our life, is it not? Now, we've all learned from a young age that there are infinite states of matter. However, there are three *primary* states that we encounter every day. Who can tell me the three primary states of matter? I'll help you, there's solid—"

The children echoed Dado, "—liquid and gas!"

"Very good. Now, did you know that brains can similarly operate in three primary ways, too?" Dado gestured overhead again. "Consider the material state of gas for a moment. A brain that thinks like a gas is completely unfocused. It is out of control, too scattered, and not very useful. It causes a person to make unwise decisions, or perhaps no decision at all."

The activity in the vidcube brain became even more chaotic and sparse. Next to it, a cartoon man appeared and wildly chased butterflies through a field, catching none of them. The children laughed.

"On the other hand, a brain that thinks like a solid is organized and orderly."

The brain activity in the display slowed down and concentrated in one area almost entirely. Next to it, the same cartoon man sat at a desk, doing nothing but staring at a piece of paper.

"Most people in the world think in a solid state. This is a common way for a brain to operate, it helps most people stay focused for a long time and do good work. While this has value for many jobs and situations, it's not quick enough for the needs of a Maker. No, Makers must be liquid or *fluid* in their thinking."

The brain image returned to its original activity, while the cartoon man became dressed in the Maker Corps uniform.

"The problem is: brains that can be fluid are often scattered in their thinking, like a gas. For centuries, brains like these were considered a problem, a challenge, a difficulty. Obstacles to be overcome or suppressed. We gave brains like these labels such as ADHD, or bipolar, or dyslexic. Do those sound like happy words?"

"*Noooooo*," the children said, Zavier's squad joining them.

"No, indeed. People created these words because they didn't fully understand what a brain like this was capable of. What we now know is that these brains can do things and see things that other brains cannot. Instead of being stopped, brains that can be fluid should be harnessed. Like horses! Do you like horses?"

"Yes!" several children shouted. As they did, the brain in the vidcube went to one side as a running stallion appeared, wild and unruly. Some of the children laughed and pointed.

"A wild horse is a beautiful animal. It is interesting to watch. It is powerful. It is, however, not very useful. At least, not without a little help and guidance. We must train the horse; we must help the horse. We must guide it so it can ultimately serve and help others."

Images of a horse trainer gently and kindly working with the wild horse appeared. Over time, these were replaced with images of the trainer putting a bridle on the horse, then a saddle, then finally riding the horse through a beautiful mountain scene.

"At the Maker Academy, we do much the same thing—but with your brains! Each of you was tested previously and found to possess just that kind of capacity for 'fluid' thinking. Your brains are very powerful, but untrained. We can help."

The image of the horse was replaced by cadets at the GMC being trained in classrooms, working with their Ozes while creating weapons and defensive structures, and practicing in battle. The pattern of the brain in the vidcube began to slowly transition from wild fireworks to fluctuating streams of unified activity.

"A Maker is special and serves a special purpose. The advancement of Oz technology allows someone who is quick of thought to respond to any kind of danger—in an instant!" Dado snapped for effect. "Using your Oz, you must imagine what does not yet exist and print it into existence. You must create new ways to solve new problems. You must use that beautiful brain of yours to make decisions that no drone could ever hope to make. Robots are not enough in our world. Why? Because often, you will be facing other humans with fluid thinking."

"Rippers!" one girl cried out, and the rest of the children booed. The vidcube switched quickly to a vivid battle between a Maker and a Ripper. Of course, the Maker had the upper hand.

Dado nodded and smiled. "Yes, the Rooster Rebellion, or *Rippers*, as we often call them, are one of our adversaries. We talk about them the most right now because they have been causing so much…trouble…as of late.

"But fighting battles is not all we do. As members of the Maker Corps, you can serve the world in so many ways."

As various images of Makers building bridges, acting as doctors, and rescuing children from poverty rotated on the vidcube, Dado continued. "All of our services require instant, on the spot, reactive thinking that well-trained brains with fluid thinking can handle best."

Dado turned to Zavier's squad and raised one hand. "This is why I always tell my students…say it with me…"

"Stay fluid!" they yelled out.

"Stay fluid," Dr. Dado repeated. He turned back to the children. "Can you say that with me? One, two, three…"

"Stay fluid!"

"Say it again."

"Stay fluid!" everyone in the room yelled.

"Louder!"

"Stay fluid!"

Dr. Dado smiled and nodded as he looked into the children's eager eyes.

"*Exatamente.* This is your chance, my young friends. You can do something that few get the chance to do. You can create what no one before you has created. All it takes is for you to harness the power of that marvelous, fluid brain of yours."

He let that sink in, leaning forward and scanning the audience for a moment. Then a smile grew on his face. "And now for the best part of Prospect Week. It's time for you to see the fluid thinking of our Maker cadets in action. It's time for our mock battle!"

The children cheered.

And with that, he returned to his seat. "Put on a good show today for these kids," he whispered to Zavier's squad. "We're counting on you."

CHAPTER 3

Each of the five disciplines serves a distinct and essential purpose. Logisticians or 'Sticks' keep the squad organized and supplied. Commandos or 'Blades' instigate and attack hostiles. Guardians or 'Shields' defend and protect the squad and innocents. Medics heal squad members and innocents in need. Innovators or 'Edges' look for unique ways to help the other squad members succeed.

The question is, which discipline will you choose?

Maker Corps Academy, New Cadet Orientation

The Arena had been revamped for the Prospect Week demonstration game, with the cavernous main floor built to parody a small city. Large, empty, box-like edifices stood several meters tall with generic signs on each, such as "Warehouse," "Bank," or "School." Other random obstacles like walls and shipping crates were sprinkled around. At the center of the small urban maze was a large open quad, in which the opposing squads had gathered.

The seating of the cavernous chamber was nearly filled. High above the center of the Arena, on a small railed platform hanging down from the domed ceiling, was some special seating for teachers and administrators of the Academy where they sat to judge the event—in particular, LTG Brigantine.

Zavier's squad stood together at one side of the open quad, their opponents at the other. Grandmaster's team wore silver, while Zavier's team wore white. He could hear the other squad getting pumped up, following the voice of a big, Native American guy everyone called Dakota.

"Team Overdrive!" he shouted.

"Win!" the rest cheered.

Rounding out Grandmaster's team were two others: Hilla, a girl from Central Finland, wearing the green triangle of the Medic discipline, and their yellow-triangled Shield, Samesh, known to his friends as "Sam."

"If I may have your attention," the General's voice boomed throughout the Arena.

The Arena quieted down as parents hushed their children and the cadets came to an immediate silence and strict attention that only many years in the Academy could teach. It wasn't long before the General was the focus of the entire Arena.

"Before you witness our little war game," he began, *"I'm going to explain how a given squad is laid out. As you may have heard, there are five disciplines in the Maker Corps, and a squad consists of one from each such discipline. Today, we have Squad Overdrive—"*

A cheer went up from the Overdrive squad, as well as a scattering of fans throughout the Arena seating.

"—and their opponents, a squad with…no name, led by Cadet Kojo Solomon."

A somewhat halfhearted cheer came out from the spectators on their behalf, accompanied by what sounded like a growl from Texas.

"Besides their team colors, each member of a squad is wearing a colored triangle on their shoulder corresponding to his Discipline. Red for Incursion, yellow for Protection, green for Medicine, blue for Logistics, and the white triangle for Innovation. These serve another purpose," the General continued with a nervous attempt at a smile, which fortunately no one below caught. *"They help the cadets to not forget what they are supposed to be doing, because, well…ahem… Cadet Solomon, let's start with you."*

His attempt at a joke having been stillborn, the General let out a faint sigh of relief as attention now fell upon the squads down below him. Without hesitation, Kojo took a step forward and flipped up the visor on his vidglasses long enough to address the gathering.

"My name is Kojo, and I am a Logistician—or 'Stick,' as we call them. It is my duty to handle in-field logistics, combat strategy, and allocation of raw matter. Matter itself is often a matter of life and death. In every battle, we have a limited amount of matter we can draw upon from the GMC's Quantum Bank account. While we can rip more starks from a battlefield, sometimes there isn't enough. I have to see that our available resources are well-spent and our team is well-coordinated. Because of this, a Logistician is often the leader of a squad, like me and my counterpart in team Overdrive, a cadet we call Grandmaster."

The scraggy teen briefly stepped forward and gave a cocky nod to the stadium, then stepped back in line. Kojo then nodded to Texas, who stepped out for her own introduction.

"Cadet Jenny Hatchet, but I'm called Texas to anyone who wants their lips to remain attached to the rest of their face. I'm a 'Blade,' or Commando, as you can see from the red triangle on my shoulders. I'm the one who gets to run in and wipe the grin off Overdrive's face."

A short round of laughter circulated the Arena, and Zavier smirked. He had grown to appreciate Texas' attitude, even if it had annoyed him at first.

Texas continued. "That big Sioux over with Overdrive is my counterpart, Dakota. But before you start rooting for him, just remember that his size also makes him a pretty easy target."

"And you make a better bug for me to squash," Dakota countered.

Texas scoffed and, for a moment, Zavier thought the two might get into it right then and there, but a glance from their respective leaders sent each back into line. Toby stepped forward next.

"Tobias Montero; Shield. Call me Toby. I'm the guardian for my team, and my job is to do whatever it takes to protect them. Overdrive's Shield is Samesh; we also call him Sam."

The Punjabi stepped out for a brief nod, then both stepped back. Min came out next.

"Cadet Min Yu, Medicine. I'm the squad's Doc, and it's my job to keep these boys alive while out in the field."

"Hear that, Texas?" Coover called out with a grin. "You need babysitting."

"Come closer and say that again," Texas retorted.

Before it could go any further, Min quickly broke in to finish her presentation. "Since this is a demonstration, there will be no serious injuries during the battle—hopefully. So, I will be assisting Toby as a Shield. Team Overdrive's Doc is Hilla, and she will be performing in the same capacity for her team."

Finally, it was Zavier's turn. He stepped forward with what he hoped was his best swagger…and nearly tripped over his own foot, earning a slight laugh from Min. Zavier felt the blood rush to his cheeks.

"I'm Cadet Zavier Vik; call me Z. I'm what they call an Edge because, well, it's my job to find the slight edge our squad needs to win. The Edge's color is white because it represents all the disciplines and none of them at the same time. Basically, that means I'm an innovator that studies each of my squadmates' ways of doing things so I can come up with some unusual ways of saving the day. That's what makes Edges the best, in my opinion."

Texas grinned. "If you like second-rate Shields with delusions of being a Blade."

"Nah," Dakota rang out, "no one that skinny could be a Blade. A rug to wipe my blade *with,* maybe."

"Or a pawn," Grandmaster chimed in.

"Don't worry, Z." Toby grinned. "I'll protect you while you…

Wait, what is it you do again?"

"Funny, guys," Zavier scoffed. "Anyway, the Vancouverite blowhard on the other team who's actually *not* making fun of how crucial an Edge is, is Overdrive's Edge, Coover."

Coover briefly stepped out, gave a quick two-finger salute off the top of his head, then stepped back into line. Zavier gave one last smile to the audience at large, then retook his own place as Dr. Dado stepped up to the edge of the observation platform in place of the General.

"Now that the introductions are finished, the rules of this game are as follows. Besides the usual GMC fieldbook guidelines, there will be no lethal or violent force used. Only plastics and light metals may be printed, and no sharp edges used. No conventional bullets. Each team has a limited number of starks they can use. Each team can draw no more that twenty-five hundred elemental osmium ingots per person to recombine into anything you want. For our young guests, that's a lump of matter about the mass of a transport shuttle per person."

Zavier could see a few of the younger ones draw wide-eyed looks at the thought of such a large lump of matter coming out of the simple-looking devices at the cadets' wrists. Dr. Dado continued.

"Additionally, any of these mock structures you see in the arena may be ripped except those printed bright red. It's off-limits to siphon the ceiling, walls, and floor of the Arena itself. They couldn't if they tried anyway, thanks to the VacGuards that blanket this arena. We wouldn't want to accidentally space ourselves, as that would defi-nitely be bad for recruiting numbers."

The jest got some titters of laughter, which Dr. Dado gave a few seconds to fade. *"The goal is to incapacitate the other squad members by disabling their Oz. You do that with the OzLock. You have each already been given several of these bands to use. Slap this* onto the Oz on the wrist of your opponent, and you'll remove them from battle.

"The winner will get patrol duty at a high priority location down Earth-side, while the losing squad will have patrol duty here in the Academy."

The prospect of some time Earth-side earned excitement from both teams.

"Oh, let it be down in Dallas," Texas remarked. "I'll show you guys a *real* city."

"I haven't been back to Punjab in a long time now," Sam sighed.

"Easy there, Samesh," Dakota told his friend. "I'm hoping for some open prairie myself."

"If it's close enough to my home turf," Coover quipped, "it's good enough for me."

"Hey, Min," Zavier said to her, trying to sound casual, "maybe if we're stationed someplace near Micro Yanbian you can…show me around."

"Maybe," she replied with a demure smile.

"You guys need to win, first," Dakota called out.

"We already have," Texas called back. "You just don't know it yet."

Dr. Dado's voice boomed over the Arena once more. *"Cadets, check your equipment, then begin when the battle horn sounds."*

As the professor stepped back to his seat, the cadets from both teams immediately dropped the trash-talk in favor of more professional demeanors to check their array of OzTech-designed equipment.

>>**Koj**>>**Comm check.**<<

The textlens message flashed across the eyes of everyone on the team, each of which quickly replied back with the usual ready-message. The communications check had no sooner finished when a short blast of sound filled the vast arena.

"That's the position signal," Kojo called out. "Come on."

As young ones covered their ears from the blast of sound, both teams ran away to their respective sides of the maze of mock-buildings. Zavier knew that while the teams were hidden from each other, everyone was still in full view of the vast ring of seats surrounding them. As soon as they were out of Overdrive's sight, his squad immediately took up positions.

Toby shimmied up the side of one of the mock buildings, putting himself in a position to best survey what would happen below, while Texas took a more forward position behind a large trash dumpster as she quickly scrolled through the menu of options in the vidcube display above the Oz on her forearm. Min, acting now as a second Shield, took up position at an adjacent building from Toby's, electing to remain on the ground as they set up their crossfire. Kojo and Zavier took center, taking cover outside a red-painted building labeled "Bank" while Kojo called up a quick area-map on a corner of his vidglasses.

All stood silent with anticipation, but not for long.

CHAPTER 4

Your QuantVac has the ability to siphon or "vac" matter from an object at a distance of up to five meters away. Be careful to ensure that you do not siphon 1) organic matter or 2) matter that clearly is the property of an innocent, as doing so would be a violation of the GMC Code.

Siphoned matter will be stored in whichever is closer of 1) your squad's local quantum wallet or 2) the GMC's account at the Quantum Bank in Prosperita.

Your New OzTech and You, Global Maker Corps Edition

A second, longer, blast of sound filled the Arena and the crowd cheered.

The cadets on both sides went into action, conjuring forth equipment from their respective Ozmium devices. A large rifle printed into Toby's hand, with a muzzle one could stick a fist through and a stock that sported an additional port, which he then hooked directly into the output of his Oz. For Texas, it was a pair of modified handguns, still quickly printing as she dashed out to the next available cover in the direction of Team Overdrive's side of the Arena. Over at her position, Min already had a rifle in hand that looked somewhat like what Toby held, aiming it out across the quad to cover Texas.

Zavier printed nothing, preferring to arm himself as the situation presented itself. Beside him, Koj squatted down by the building, looking out around the corner.

>>**Toby**>>**Got some movement. About thirty degrees to your right, Texas, and moving fast. Looks like Samesh.**<<

>>Koj>>Grandmaster is setting up his defense first. He plans his attacks the way he likes to play chess—very conservatively.<<

>>Texas>>Then I say we give him something to defend *against*.<<

Even as she sent this, the first shot came at her from behind a wall across the quad. It was Sam, wielding a small gun firing out rubber pellets.

>>Texas>>He's trying to pin me down. Like *that's* going to stop me.<<

With his other hand, Sam was focused on printing some additions to the wall, extending it wide around to face Texas. At the same time, a twenty-centimeter hole appeared in its center.

>>Texas>>He's adding to that wall pretty quickly.<<

>>Koj>>The signal I see on my map is a lot more than just from Samesh's work. No way he's doing it alone.<<

Fortunately, from his perch high above the others, Toby had a better angle to see exactly what was going on behind that wall.

>>Toby>>He's not. Samesh's with Hilla. They're working the wall. Wait...I see Dakota coming up behind them. Texas, look out.<<

"Classic opening chess move, like everything else Grandmaster does," Kojo said out loud. "Fortify, then take out the opponent's big gun, then they'll power their way through our Shields."

"But Texas is tough to catch," Zavier remarked. "Wouldn't Min make for an easier target? She's not normally a Shield."

"That's what I would think, but all the heavy hitters are accounted for. Unless you count...Min!"

He switched quickly to his textlens and resent his message.

>>Koj>>Min! Take cover, Coover's coming up on you.<<

>>Min>>Tell me something I *don't* know. He's already got me pinned.<<

>>Koj>>Toby, cover Texas. Z, go!<<

>>Zavier>>On my way!<<

Zavier ran quickly away from the building, leaving Kojo to

coordinate the battle plan. Min was a great healer and competent Shield for purposes of this game, but against an Edge like Coover, he doubted her chances.

Meanwhile, Team Overdrive's shield-wall had been finished. Dakota took cover behind it, using a large gun that looked much like the one Toby had printed. He was sighting on Texas, but she had been using the time to run from one cover to another, and was now no more than ten meters away from them.

"Gotcha, Texas," he called out.

Texas was beginning to charge out with her handguns from behind a red-painted building when Dakota pulled the trigger. Out through the large hole in the wall, he fired not bullets or heavy weapons, but an equally large beanbag—straight on a course for Texas. For a split second, the crowd cheered when they saw what appeared to be the first kill of the game.

A moment after Dakota let off the first shot, however, another large beanbag came down out of nowhere and intercepted Dakota's beanbag mid-air.

"Huh?" Dakota yelled.

"*That's* how you shoot!" Toby replied.

A cheer erupted from the crowd as Texas' charge against the three Overdrive team members suddenly looked a lot less fool-hardy than before.

Zavier came around the adjacent corner as Min was firing off her weapon at someone standing in front of a building labeled "Store." Her gun shot out an odd-textured rubber ball that quickly expanded in flight to become a small octopus coated in self-sealing rubber. It flew through the air as her opponent dove behind a fake hover-car, only to end up sticking uselessly to a light post.

Her opponent was Coover, and he had something shaped like an old, oversized submachinegun with a drum magazine in his hand. It was firing off something not very dangerous but severely annoying: extreme-speed ping-pong balls.

Zavier saw a steady stream of them hit Min in the face and chest as she fired her gun, the rubber octopus landing wide to the left of Coover.

>>Min>>**Would someone get this guy off me so I can** *see* **something?!**<<

Coover took advantage of his opening and started creeping out from behind the car, his pong-gun keeping a steady stream at her while his other hand produced a silver-colored OzLock that he snapped open with a quick flick.

"Got you now, little Min," Coover called out. "Say, how's about after Overdrive wins I take you out for a date Earth-side?"

Min loaded in another freshly-printed sticky rubber octopus, trying to take aim through the hail of small plastic balls bouncing off her face. The crowd, meanwhile, was someplace between laughing and cheering.

"I would rather date a cockroach," Min shouted back. "Now, hold still."

For a moment, Zavier was gripped with indecision. A hand-to-hand weapon wouldn't work, Coover was too far away for him to reach before he'd get to Min, and she was already bending down to her knees trying to use one arm to shield herself from the barrage of projectiles.

Coover laughed. "Looks like I got first casualty."

Min's next shot did little more than trip him slightly, as the self-sealing octopus wrapped around his foot. Coover broke into a run. Min was already printing another octopus round, but couldn't lift up her face long enough to aim for anything higher than his knees.

"Min!" Zavier yelled as he suddenly snapped out of his confusion and made a quick, if unorthodox, decision. He held out his right hand as he called out his command.

"Oz: Foursquare."

Instantly, a bright yellow playground ball popped out into his waiting hand, and he threw it overhead with both hands as hard as he could. It sailed straight past Coover's ear, but then, that's not what he'd been aiming for. The ball hit the car behind his opponent, bouncing off it and directly into the back of Coover's head.

"Ow!"

He pitched forward with a cry, but before he could catch himself, Min got off her next shot, aiming for the one target she *could* reliably see despite the barrage of ping-pong balls: his knees. The rubber octopus wrapped completely around both knees, drawing them together and sealing tight as the arms stuck to one another on the back side of his legs.

Coover's forward tumble turned into a complete faceplant. Zavier leaped across the remaining distance with his own white OzLock in hand. The crowd roared with approval at the unexpected save, while Coover found Zavier kneeling on his back as Min came over to squat down in front of him with a smile.

"I'm afraid I won't be needing that date to see Earth-side, friend."

While Zavier snapped his OzLock open, Min reached over to pluck Coover's machine gun from his fingers. Her smile grew wider as she shot out a single ping-pong ball, right between his eyes.

Dakota had his gun barrel sticking out through the hole in the wall, shooting another beanbag as he voiced a battle cry. But this time, several beanbags came out from Toby's position to crash into the wall and spoil his shot. In fact, it seemed like a never-ending barrage of beanbags.

"Hey, what gives, Toby?" he called out. "Since when can you do rapid fire on that thing?"

"Since I programmed my Oz to print ammo directly into the magazine. It's a little trick our Edge came up with."

Texas ran right up to the wall and leaped, one hand catching its top while her foot came down on top of Dakota's barrel and used it as a springboard.

"Thanks for the lift," she shouted.

The sudden weight coming down on the end of his rifle sent its other end slamming up into Dakota's chin, bowling him back on the ground with a pained cry while Texas finished her vault over the wall. She came down feet-first not on Dakota, but on a pair of large kite shields that Samesh and Hilla had printed to cover both themselves and Dakota from just such a maneuver. She finished her leap with a foot landing on each kite shield.

"Don't worry, I don't weigh much."

From somewhere beneath her, she could hear a female voice cussing in Finnish.

"Out of my way!"

Dakota rolled out from beneath the shields and up to his feet, a large plastic club printing into his hand. He immediately turned around, only to come face to face with the barrel of one of Texas' handguns. She smiled and pulled the trigger.

What came out covered his face in a splotch of white, blinding him.

"I thought you could use some new team colors," she quipped.

She started pulling off several more rounds of both guns as she leaped forward, just as the pair beneath her siphoned away their own shields and ducked quickly out from under her. Dakota suddenly found his face covered in white paint, his club flailing around blindly as she landed on him.

Sam and Hilla, though, were directly behind her.

>>Toby>>Texas is going to be in trouble real soon. Going in.<<

>>Koj>>Got that. Min, how are you doing?<<

>>Min>>Their Edge is down, thanks to Z.<<

>>Zavier>>Any time. You know, as long as your 'date' is out of the game…<<

>>>Min>>Jealous?<<

>>Koj>>Z, get over to see what you can do for Texas.<<

>>Zavier>>On it.<<

Zavier broke into a run, Min on his heels. He wasn't nearly as athletic as his sister, Zandrie, but good enough to outrun Min as they hurried around the intervening walls and blocks of plastic and wood. When he came around one corner into view of the battle happening at the other side of the quad, however, he stopped cold.

What would Zandrie do? he thought rapidly, *Not this. She'd be smarter. She'd see other angles. All angles. This is all wrong.* I'm *all wrong.*

"Z," Min said as she came up to him, "are you okay?"

"I…I don't know. Something I'm missing, I just can't—"

"Not again," she sighed.

Wasting no time, she passed him by, running quickly across the quad with her octopus gun aimed and ready for the instant she got within range. She was several yards away when Zavier realized what was bothering him.

"Wait, we haven't seen Grandmaster yet."

>>Zavier>>Koj, I think Grandmaster's up to something.<<

Texas, meanwhile, dropped one pistol to slap a white OzLock around a blind Dakota's wrist, her other hand unloaded a round of paint straight into Hilla's eyes. Suddenly, Sam came at her from the side and tried to slap a band of his own around her extended wrist. She punched his hand away, causing him to drop the band, but he countered by dropping to the ground and sweeping her legs out from under her.

Texas let out a yelp as she fell on her back. Before she could recover, Sam shot a small pistol that covered her in a sticky spiderweb.

"Aargh!" she raged at Sam, glaring at him defiantly.

"Sorry, Texas," Sam said smugly as he opened a new OzLock. "End of the road for you."

>>**Texas**>>**Team, I need help!**<<

Zavier was still trying to work out what was wrong with the layout before him when a set of bolas came whirling through the air from out of nowhere. They wrapped themselves around both of Min's knees, bringing her to an immediate halt as she crashed to the ground with a surprised cry, her gun spinning away out of her grasp. A skinny figure with surprising speed and dexterity followed, running out from behind the wall of a red-painted building labeled "Church." Grandmaster was approaching her with a ready wristband.

"No," Zavier screamed out. "Min!"

He started to move, then hesitated as he saw Sam standing over Texas. Texas was the squad's Blade and key to their victory, but Min was…well, Min. The prettiest girl in the Academy.

Unable to decide, he watched dumbly as Sam first cuffed Texas, followed by Grandmaster slapping a cuff around Min's wrist.

Seeing Zavier frozen with indecision, Grandmaster brought out a second silver cuff and bolted for him as well.

"Z, snap out of it!" Min called out.

The crowd was going wild. From somewhere behind him,

Coover was mocking Zavier's indecision. He stopped, though, when a brightly glowing boomerang hit Grandmaster from behind. Kojo tripped him up long enough to create a window to run straight for Grandmaster.

>>**Koj**>>**I'll deal with Grandmaster. You go help Toby!**<<

Zavier finally snapped out of it as Grandmaster hit the ground not a meter before him, with Kojo grabbing him around the waist.

"Right," Zavier said to himself. "Z, *move!*"

He broke into a run across the open quad area. Texas was out, but so was Dakota, which left the Shields time to reinforce their position with barricades. They were already working on printing them from their reserves and, in part, from some available plastic crates left as part of the mock city's obstacles.

On the Overdrive side, the new barricades looked like man-sized fanciful creatures with long tails shaped like lightning bolts, glowing with a mild electric charge. One in particular was sticking out a tongue in Zavier's direction.

Well, that's mature, he thought.

Another roar rose up from the crowd, and Zavier quickly turned around to see Kojo and Grandmaster's hand-to-hand martial arts fight. It stopped abruptly when both cuffed each other at the exact same time.

"Well, this isn't something that happens all the time," Kojo said.

"The kings checkmating one another? Indeed," Grandmaster agreed.

As Overdrive's menagerie of barricades went up, their original wall came down, siphoned quickly away by someone on the other side of it. Sam and Hilla spun around just in time to see the center of the wall melting away before the imposing figure of Toby. While his left arm was busy with the siphoning, his right hand held his beanbag rifle, which he now aimed straight at Sam.

"Sorry, Samesh, but the lady's already blinded."

Two quick beanbags to the gut put Sam on the ground. As Toby advanced to try and cuff him, Hilla wiped the paint from her face and quickly slapped a palm-full of paint across his eyes. Toby whipped around to use his rifle as a battering ram against her if necessary, but found the barrel getting shorter by the second.

"*Oye*," he called out, "you can't siphon off my gun while I'm still using it!"

"Your fault," she called back. "You forgot to VacGuard it."

"Payback time," Sam now called as he got back up.

Toby shoved Hilla away, but by the time he got a hand up to wipe the paint from his eyes, he discovered a new problem. Sam had shouted "Oz: Freeform cedar!" and was printing layer upon layer of wood around Toby's legs. It was already up to his knees.

"Hey, what're you trying to do?" Toby growled.

"Makes a nice statue, don't you think? Now, do you want me to cuff you or do you want to be civil about this and save a little dignity by cuffing yourself?"

As big as Toby was, he found himself trapped and unable to move, faced off against the two remaining Overdrive squad members.

Zavier saw Toby's situation and began running toward him, siphoning matter with his QuantVac on the go. He raised his right arm and whispered, "Oz: Saltwater delicious."

Overdrive's Shields turned just in time for a spray of airborne liquid taffy to hit them, coating them from head to toe. Zavier stood a few yards away, his left hand pointing out at the barricades they had just projected up around them as his QuantVac siphoned the matter to the device on his left arm. With his right hand, he held a narrow rifle with a cone-like muzzle, shooting out a continual flow of fresh taffy.

He grinned. "Just thought you'd want to stick around."

Hilla tried bringing up her right hand to project something out, but it was too covered in a sticky mass now to be useful, much like her mouth. The best she could do was mutter half-intelligible expletives in Finnish.

"See what I did there?" Zavier quipped. "*Stick* around. You're sticky because I used taffy. Get it?"

As he spoke, he continued to fire on Sam, who was trying to make his way around Texas and Dakota.

"That's our Z!" Texas yelled.

"This is *so* embarrassing," Dakota grumbled.

The barricades disappeared as Zavier continued to siphon, adding ammo to an increasing sticky mass of people and candy, He advanced until the remains of the Overdrive team were covered and effectively helpless.

"Beaten by *candy?!*" Sam exclaimed.

"Squad name!" Toby yelled out, followed by several other textlenses from the squad saying the same thing.

>>Koj>>"Squad Beaten-By-Candy" Really? Okay. Adding to the database, guys. Option…212.<<

Zavier slapped a cuff around Hilla's wrist while Toby reached out for Sam's.

Dr. Dado's voice boomed above them. *"The winner is team 'Squad Name'…I mean, the team led by Cadet Kojo Solomon!"*

The cadets who weren't stuck in taffy rejoined their teams as the crowd cheered. Kojo and Min stood to either side of Zavier, the latter giving him a light peck on the cheek.

"See?" she whispered to him as Ozbots equipped with industrial-sized QuantVacs came out to clean up the mess. "You did good after all."

"Only after losing you. If this had been a real battle, you'd be dead. Once again, I'm indecisive when it counts. I'm not a leader like Koj here."

"Don't bring yourself down, man." Koj grinned. "You just need a little confidence."

"Yeah. Maybe," Zavier said with a shake of his head. "I'll never match up to Zandrie," he muttered to himself.

As the game came to an end, Zavier looked over to see Dr. Dado with a hand on Grandmaster's shoulder, presumably providing a teaching moment to the visibly angry young Maker. Dado then turned to see Zavier looking at them and gave him a warm smile and nod of approval.

CHAPTER 5

While the prospective cadets and their families were treated to a tour after the Arena battle, the two teams hustled into one of the classrooms for a debriefing of the event. It was a small room with enough seats for thirty people, where the rows of seats slanted down to the instructor's area. At present, the two teams were seated in the front couple of rows, looking at a replay of events in the vidcube that hung down from the ceiling.

Complete three-dimensional scenes of solid matter were continually created and uncreated by the same technology as their Oz devices. It was an animated diorama, complete with audio from each cadet's sound feeds and their textlens messages scrolling by.

Three instructors stood at the front of the room, watching the vidcube with the cadets. One was Major Panefield, a man with aging hair cropped into a short, military-style haircut and a glare that could wither the bravest of cadets. Another was Professor Friedrich, a younger brown-haired gentleman who looked as if he would be more at home in a library.

The third was Captain Zandrie Vik.

Zavier's sister.

"Right there." Zandrie made a gesture to pause the vidcube. "Cadet Vik, you froze, and as a result Cadet Yu was killed. If this was out in the field, you would now be without your Medic for the trip back."

Zavier swallowed hard. "I know Zan—Captain. But I just—"

"A mission is not over until you're back at base," Major Panefield snapped. "There could be others waiting to ambush you after you *think* it's all done, and *that's* when you'll need every person on your team you can get—*especially* Medical."

Zavier had nothing to say; they were right. But while certain members of Team Overdrive now had cause to grin at his expense, Professor Friedrich gestured to the vidcube to change the display to a different time-frame. It froze on the shot of Texas using Dakota's gun barrel as a stepping stone, slamming it up into his chin.

"As far as Overdrive is concerned," Professor Friedrich said calmly, "that gun barrel is what brought you down. If it hadn't been sticking out like that, Texas would never have been able to use it on her way over the wall."

"But, Professor Friedrich," Dakota argued, "how was I supposed to know that she'd actually—"

"Apparently you need a little refresher in my Military History class," the professor replied. "Battles have been lost on the smallest of details."

Dakota fell silent. Professor Friedrich had an amicable enough manner and a soft voice, yet when he corrected you it felt like you'd been caught kicking a kitten.

Zandrie gestured again to move the vidcube to another point. Zavier watched the replay of Min getting ambushed by Grandmaster while he stupidly stood by. He was already feeling uncomfortable.

"Cadet Vik," she snapped, "this is where you got *two* people killed. You *knew* something was wrong; we can see it on your face and in your textlens communications. Yet you stood by and let

Cadet Yu advance, then even after Grandmaster had her down, you *still* didn't move. Cadet Solomon had to come out and save your rear, which got *him* killed as a result. Now, what the *shatter* was going through your mind?"

Zavier was lost for words. It always seemed that his sister singled him out more than any other cadet. That was the problem with being the younger brother of a legend: higher standards. He opened his mouth, but nothing came out, so he ended up with a shrug and a sigh. *It won't do any good to say anything.*

No longer under the spotlight, Dakota let out a faint sigh of relief, while Coover smirked and Grandmaster managed a sly grin.

"You've got to stop freezing up like that," Zandrie continued. "Seconds count in the field. You're *better* than this."

"I know," Zavier sighed. "I just. I dunno…"

She glared at him for a moment, then scowled at Team Overdrive when she noticed their smiles and smirks. The room seemed to drop ten degrees and their amusement disappeared.

"And Cadet Yu," she then addressed Min, "you could see that your Edge had spotted something wrong. You should never have gone charging out without first getting his opinion as to what that might be."

"Yes, Ma'am," Min replied.

Her point made, Zandrie now turned her attention to the leader of Overdrive. "Grandmaster, you like to equate everything to a game of chess, so why did it come down to a king-to-king fight when there were still other pieces on the board?"

"Well," he began, "when Coover got cuffed—"

"And whose strategy was it to have Coover fail to defeat a Medic before the other team's Edge got there? No offense, Min, but your skills are more toward healing than combat. In fact, I'm not sure whether to be more impressed with *your* performance, or disappointed with *Coover's*."

Before Min could respond, the white-haired major jumped back into the conversation. "Cadet Coover, you are an *Edge,* and you were fighting their weakest combative link. Where was your creativity? You should have been able to easily overwhelm Cadet Yu and had a trap ready for when Cadet Vik arrived. Or do we need to rethink your discipline choice of being an Edge?"

"No sir, Major Pain—uh, Major Panefield," Coover replied in a subdued tone. "I guess that…I was showing off for the recruits. I wanted to make a real show of it."

"There is no place in the field for showboating, Cadet," the Major snapped. "You were *supposed* to be showing them how efficient you can be in combat, not how well you can dance and carry a tune."

Coover looked up to make a reply, but dropped his gaze back down, along with the rest of his team. Seeing Team Overdrive humbled made Zavier feel a little better, though he caught a side-long glare from Coover to Min; it was one thing to be beaten by another Edge like Zavier, but to have it pointed out that his defeat started because he couldn't beat a Medic quickly enough? That was almost as embarrassing as Zavier's freezing up.

After a prolonged pause, Zandrie swiped her hands to turn off the vidcube and the display fell away to a waterfall of glittering sparkles, then vanished entirely.

"That's it for the debriefing," Major Panefield said. "Now, I want you all to shake hands before leaving. You were opponents in the Arena, but you're still fellow cadets. Dismissed."

The cadets stood up and began shaking hands, starting with Kojo and Grandmaster.

"Well played," Grandmaster said, then added quietly, "in an amateurish sort of way. Overdrive will beat you into the ground next time."

"Possibly," Kojo replied. "If you learn to start thinking several moves ahead."

"A big ball?" Coover said as he shook Zavier's hand. "Seriously? That's as creative as you could get? What a lead-head. I can't believe how lucky you were."

"And a taffy gun?" Hilla added. "What kind of a *child* thinks of something like that?"

"Hey," Zavier replied, "it worked, didn't it?"

"Ever the credo of an Edge, eh?"

"Hooking the Oz output directly up to a weapon's ammo feed," Dakota said. "I'll give you points for that. Personally, I'd go with heavier ammo…"

Toby shrugged as he returned the handshake. "Certainly saves reloading time."

"Zavier," Min addressed him quietly, "if there's anything you want to talk about as to why you freeze up like that—"

"No, I'll…be okay."

Zandrie dismissed the teams with a final command. "Okay, off to the lab. I'm sure you've all got plenty of ideas for new designs to program into your Oz projectors."

Zavier rushed out the door, eager to get his mind off the verbal hammering he'd been receiving and on to the safety of theoretical engineering.

"Hmm…what about if the knife hilt can shoot out blades? No, need something less pointy. Stunbolts?"

Zavier glanced over at Texas' workstation. At Texas' bench, one vidcube displayed a three-dimensional rendition of one weapon design while another vidcube showed the blueprints for what she was working on. Above her on the wall, a sign with the OzTech logo declared, "Got your VacGuard? Safety first!"

At the edge of her tabletop was a row of icons permanently etched into the surface. She touched one these and the surface of the table rippled once, changing from what had looked like a simple wooden surface to lines of text. With a stab of her finger, a third vidcube popped up at the center of the table, displaying another blueprint design. She pushed it over next to the first blueprint.

With another tap, a model in the new vidcube appeared. It looked like a small pistol with an attached knife hilt, empty of any blade. "Naw, looks ugly. And unwieldy," Texas muttered, smashing the third vidcube into the table.

As both the vidcube and knife-pistol idea disappeared, Dakota leaned over. "You should keep the knife, Texas. Shooting out a stream of blades? That's seriously *fluid*."

"It could also be *fatal*," Texas snapped back. "Or did you miss the repeated lectures about how we're not supposed to actually harm anyone if we can help it? 'Makers are peacekeepers,' and all that slag."

"When some Ripper is after your hide with real bullets and a cutlass, it's not time to worry about niceties," Dakota scoffed.

From the front of the room, Professor Friedrich gave Dakota a frown. "Dakota, cadets do *not* use lethal weapons in the Corps."

"We could save it for when they get *really* mean," Dakota suggested. Zavier eyed him, wondering if he was joking. His tone was light, but Zavier had a feeling Dakota wouldn't hesitate to put down a Ripper on the battlefield—or anywhere else. He understood the feeling, the temptation to want to take out all his anger and frustration and repay the group who had killed his little sister. *Justice brings closure, but vengeance never ends*, he thought. *At least that's what Zandrie keeps telling me.*

"Not under *any* circumstances, is that understood?"

"Yes, Professor Friedrich. I was kidding." As soon as the professor had turned back to the instructor's workstation, Dakota leaned in again. "If you don't think killing Rippers is the best way to fight them, ask your own Edge. His sister lost her leg because of that shattered thinking."

Zavier kept his eyes trained on his table. He'd heard jabs about his sister's injury before. She was an easy target for a coward to pick on, especially when she wasn't in the room. He could feel the anger rising, but he reminded himself that Zandrie could whip anyone in a one-on-one fight—even with a synth leg. So, he tried to ignore it like he usually did.

Texas, however, didn't. She whipped around and grabbed hold of Dakota's arm, giving it a twist as she brought herself as close to his face as their height difference would allow.

"Don't you *ever* go there, lead-head," she hissed. "You know how close they are."

"Hey, easy. I was just using her as a convenient example." He glanced at Zavier. "No offense, Z."

"None taken," Z lied.

While Texas and Dakota exchanged angry looks, Min was at her own bench working at a frenetic pace. She had five holo-displays hovering above her bench, rapidly moving a component of one to another with a swipe of her finger, interjecting with the occasional press of a bench icon to update the vidcube display, then flicking her finger to send the display rotating slowly around for a full view.

Trying to take his mind off his frustration at Dakota, Zavier wandered over to her bench and thought about resting a hand on her shoulder. He quickly killed the idea, though, both out of some uncertainty about their relationship and absolute certainty that she would not appreciate her thought process disrupted. So, he just stood as an interested party—a respectful and healthy distance away.

"Oz: Load design and store under Macro 'Bodyscan,'" she said as she lifted the Oz on her right arm.

A split-second later, a confirmation displayed both on her Oz and the surface of the bench. She pressed down on the vidcubes to disperse them and continued.

"Okay, next," Min said to herself. "If Coover showed me anything, it's that I could use a better means of defending myself… something that neutralizes, but doesn't do any lasting damage."

Try this, Zavier sent through the textlens as he jogged back to his worktable. Then he pushed a vidcube from his worktable toward Min's.

The answer suddenly appeared on Min's worktable in the form of a new vidcube with a three-dimensional model. Zavier waited for her to take in the details of his design and was rewarded by a slight nod of approval and smile in his direction.

>>Min>>**A mini-mega speaker?**<<

>>Z>>**Latest in audio amplification. It's the equivalent of a vidcube theater Realsound system…times ten. Plus, small form factor makes it easy to carry anywhere.**<<

>>Min>>**I like it. Thanks.**<<

Min's smile was all it took to help him get over his hurt at Dakota's thoughtless words. Whenever she was around, things were always better. Now, if he could figure out how to be around her more…

He pulled his attention away from his lovely squadmate back to his worktable. He had a vidcube sporting the suggestion of a quarter-circle metal tray attached to a pistol stock. Coover had the bench next to his and couldn't help but pause for a curious look over.

"What you got there, Z?"

"Oz," Zavier said into his device, "store design under macro 'Banana Peel Gun.'" As the device blinked its confirmation, he looked over at Coover with a smile. "Answer your question?"

"Seriously, *real* banana peels? Why not an oil slick?"

"Oil can catch on fire pretty easily."

"Hmm, you have a point, but…banana peels?"

"Something wrong with throwing food at people?"

"Well, no. I mean…" The Vancouver native gave it a moment's thought, then broke out into a grin. "Actually, I like it. But I think I'll make mine coated in olive oil for that extra slickness."

"That's still oil," Zavier said.

Coover shrugged. "You worry too much. Besides, even if it did and a couple Rippers got fried, I'm still not using anything inherently lethal."

Zavier's instinct was to shout Coover down and try to prove his point. He felt his teeth clench and his fists ball up. He realized, though, that he was less angry about Coover's desire to hurt the Rippers, and angrier at *himself* for secretly feeling the same way. *You're a hypocrite, Z*, he thought as he shook his head and returned to work.

That design done, Zavier grew bored and looked around to see how each of the others were doing. Toby had made a schematic of a large and nasty-looking rifle of some sort. Both Kojo and Grandmaster were hiding in opposite corners of the lab, blocking the view of their vidcubes so no one could see what they were working on. Sam seemed to be putting the final touches on some sort of handheld cannon, while Hilla was almost as busy as Min, loading up medical programs.

>>Z>>Hey, Toby. What's with the big gun? That looks like a pretty ancient design.<<

>>Toby>>Insane rate of fire, *hermano*. Combine parts of it with the beanbag gun, but mini beanbags. Spit them out at a hundred rounds a second…<<

Toby sent a vidloop of a bear running for cover as hundreds of bees attacked it.

>>Z>>Fluid. Try some alternatives for ammo. Marbles for harder targets, then cherry tomatoes.<<

>>**Toby**>>**Tomatoes?**<<

Zavier sent a vidloop of children in a frantic food fight, then added:

>>**Z**>>**I'm into food this week.**<<

>>**Toby**>>**Last week it was vehicles.**<<

>>**Z**>>**Hey, it's always vehicles. Anyway, look at this…**<<

Zavier tapped his table and a new vidcube schematic appeared. He pushed it in the direction of Toby's table, where the vidcube resurfaced for him to view.

>>**Toby**>**Rapid fire cuff gun?**<<

>>**Z**>>**Min's octopus gun gave me an idea. Too slow, though.**<<

Their discussion was interrupted by a pair of loud voices coming from the other side of the lab, where Texas and Dakota's argument had gotten into something less verbal. Texas was holding a freshly-printed pistol aimed at Dakota, whose head was covered in sticky marshmallow along with the barrel of the large rifle he now held in his hands aimed back at her.

"Lot of good your lethal weapon would have done you then, wouldn't it?" she yelled. "You can't fire it off if it's gummed up, now can you?"

"How would you like a stun round right in your—"

"Cadets!" Professor Friedrich hurried across the classroom, printing an old wooden ruler into his hand. He smacked Dakota's fingers away from the trigger of his rifle, followed by a second quick smack at Texas' hand. Dakota let out a short yelp of pain, while Texas said nothing as the Professor addressed them in a calm, admonishing tone. "There is never any good reason to come to blows in this classroom. Now, what is the problem?"

"Texas is afraid, is what's the matter," Dakota said. "Team Chicken-Slaggers."

"I'm afraid of *nothing*," she shot back, "but the gas-for-brains here doesn't get the *non-lethal* part of our training."

"Hey, I didn't say I'd use any of it! I was just preparing for... just in case."

"And in that, he would be correct." It was Grandmaster, walking across the room to defend his teammate. "A good strategist should be prepared for any eventuality, even that which we may view as repugnant."

"There's some truth here," Professor Friedrich said as he tried to calm things down, "but as Cadets, you are not permitted to use any form of a potentially harmful device. Ever. Even if—and I emphasize *if*—you graduate to full Maker, the use of potentially lethal weaponry is only a matter of last resort. We expect you to use your creativity, your minds, to solve problems. You are peacekeepers, not soldiers. You know the rules. Delete anything with a sharp edge or explosive round immediately."

While Professor Friedrich was handling the angry eruption, Zavier turned back to his own work. Just a typical day of sharing the workspace with Team Overdrive. He'd much prefer to work with other cadets, but "getting used to working with people you don't agree with is part of the job"—or whatever it was Zandrie always said.

"Okay," Zavier said to himself, "next design. Maybe I can modify my old net-gun into something involving synthetic tar...and feathers. Might work better than the taffy."

He was about to start when a new message scrolled across the inside of his eyepiece. A textlens message, but not from anyone in the lab.

>>**Dr. Dado**>>**Zavier, I would like to speak to you in my office immediately, if you please.**<<

>>**Z**>>**Dr. Dado? But why? I'm sorry, I mean I'll be there as quick as I can.**<<

>>**Dr. Dado**>>**Thank you.**<<

Zavier touched an icon at the end of the table to save his work and shut down. All his displays vanished, leaving what looked like a normal flat wooden tabletop once again, with only a single icon carved into its surface at the center. With a deep breath, he glanced over to find Professor Friedrich still calming the fighters—not to mention vac'ing up the residual marshmallow syrup splattered across the floor. Then he headed for the room's back door and was quickly on his way to Dr. Dado.

CHAPTER 6

When parents look at a young child and see them misbehaving, they often feel that they must place controls on the child to get them to align their actions with expected norms. Children require boundaries to keep them safe, it is true. Protecting children from themselves is a duty of any adult who has care for a child. This must always be done in love.

Yet, there is a wide gap between protection and repression. Within that open space lies the opportunity to discover who we truly are and what we may achieve. We must allow for and protect that opportunity, just as much as we protect the child.

Dr. Eduardo Oliveira, *Harnessing the Young Mind*

Dr. Dado's office was printed to look like an old study, with ancient tomes filling the wall-shelves, a large mahogany desk, plush leather seats for himself and visitors, and mementos sprinkled liberally around. There was a large globe on a floor-stand to one side of the instructor's desk, like something that some ancient mariner might have used, but with fragmented national borders drawn to post-Shattering specifications. Small figurines nestled in-between the books—one of a unicorn, another of a pair of gnomes with pointed hats, and what Zavier guessed were odds and ends taken from a variety of periods in history. On a small stand to one side of the room was an ancient Chinese vase; or, at least, an Oz-printed replica of one.

The wall behind where Dr. Dado sat was adorned with something far more personal. Framed pictures of past cadets hung upon the wall, each labeled with a name. Each frame showed two pictures side by side—a picture of the cadet when first he or she had entered the Academy, and one taken upon becoming a full Maker. Some had personal notes scrawled across the bottom of the photo, while a couple had a wreath encircling them and a date at the bottom of the picture.

There was another section as well. Way off in a corner of the wall was another series of cadet pictures and names. Some of the names Zavier recognized; others, he didn't. The ones he recognized he knew to be traitors—those who had left the Makers to join the Rooster Rebellion…the Rippers. Zavier had never figured out why Dr. Dado kept those pictures, but never had the courage to ask.

Their reasons for turning traitor had varied, but—as Zavier understood things—it usually came down to some perverted sense of freedom. *Part of the risk of recruiting fluid minds*, Zavier mused. *None of us are great rule-followers.*

It was a familiar story. Somebody disagreed with some command some leader gave, or some rule that kept them from doing whatever the slag they wanted, and they bolted. The Roosters prized the precious *liberté* preached by their leader, known simply as "the Parisian," which was probably why they'd adopted the national symbol of the pre-Shattering nation of France. But what they saw as "liberty," the rest of the world saw as lawlessness.

Anarchy isn't freedom. It's foolishness. I want to be free to do what I want, too, but there's got to be a balance.

Zavier turned his attention to a standard issue OzBot quietly siphoning the floor for any errant dust or other stray particles. The OzBot was scanning and printing every surface with any needed micro-repairs, while also scanning the air and printing perfectly reconditioned air into the room. The ever-hovering, ever-vac'ing, ever printing OzBots had always been a part of Zavier's life, so he was always surprised at how uneasy they made him feel. Perhaps the dark, eyeless, expressionless lens that circled the tops of their "heads" made them look like they were secretly planning his doom.

The OzBot ignored Zavier and quietly continued its work of maintaining an immaculate environment.

"Come in, Zavier—have a seat."

Zavier sat down in one of the leather seats, still wondering why he'd been called in. He was nervous, but Dr. Dado greeted him with a smile.

"Oh, don't worry. I'm not here to scold you, though I did notice the hesitation you showed in the mock battle."

"Half the Academy noticed it." Zavier sighed, looking downward. "I'm really sorry and I'll try better next time."

"No apologies, Zavier. I just want to help. Will you allow me?"

Zavier quickly thought about the many times Dado had helped him learn and grow, so he quickly agreed. "Of course."

"*Muito bom.* There is a reason why it occurred, and it's important. What was going on in your mind at that moment? Was there…something you wanted to tell me?"

At first, Zavier was silent. He knew very well why he'd frozen, and it was not something he liked to talk about. Not even with Zandrie, even though she had been there and understood. Not even his other squadmates knew the full story.

"It's…pretty painful," he admitted.

"Then it will only get more so as time goes on if you do not deal with it now," Dr. Dado replied. "Freezing like that in the field could get your whole team killed, and you wouldn't want that."

"No, sir."

"Then I would like to help you, Zavier. I believe I can. Not a word of what you say will escape this room. Would you please tell me what happened?"

It was difficult for Zavier to talk about, but outside of his own sister, Dr. Dado was the one person he trusted the most. Over the years, he had proven to be more than the Academy's head administrator, but a trusted friend. *Maybe it's time to tell him,* Zavier thought.

"I…I had a younger sister. Her name was Zoey…"

Zavier could remember everything as if it was still happening, just like he'd remembered when he'd frozen in the Arena.

The Rippers were attacking the Micro of New York in the battle of Manhattan. It had been going on for a long time. Four-year-old Zavier had heard about the Rippers coming and taking things and hurting people, but he had never actually seen a Ripper. He'd heard that they liked to take people's homes away from them, especially people who had big nice homes like the Vik family. He heard they sucked the homes into their hands like they were some kind of hungry monster. It was all very confusing, and kind of exciting.

One day, Zavier was playing with his building blocks when he heard the alarms in the city. Mom and Dad had told Zandrie and him to keep their heads down. They should stay with their little sister, Zoey. Keep her quiet so the Rippers wouldn't hear anything.

Keep her quiet.

Zandrie and Zavier shushed her, sang her a quiet song, rocked her, and got her to sleep. He was a good big brother. Baby Zoey was quiet, just like Mom and Dad had asked. Very quiet and peaceful.

Then, the loud sounds happened. He heard ripping and printing happen all around their home. Ozes were so loud back then. It frightened young Zavier, so Zandrie kept him safe by taking him away from the outside walls, where it was a bit quieter.

Away from where Zoey was sleeping.

Despite all the noise, Zoey remained still and so quiet that even Zavier had forgotten about her. He was so scared of the monster Rippers coming.

But Zoey wasn't scared. She was quiet when the Rippers began vac'ing the outside of their home. She was quiet when they saw the furniture in their house broken down like a river of dust flying into the mouth of the Ripper's hacked QuantVac.

To Zavier's horror, she was still just as quiet as the wave of disappearing matter approached her small bed. Zavier wanted to run and snatch her up, but Zandrie held him back. It was too late, and his sister had to protect him. All that he and Zandrie could do was helplessly watch as his sister was siphoned into the Ripper's QuantVac, her body reduced to a stream of the most basic building blocks of everything.

Had the Ripper known he was killing a baby? Probably not. He'd probably thought the crib was a piece of furniture and nothing more. At least, that's the conclusion Zavier had come to after years of therapy.

"…It was during a Ripper attack right in our neighborhood. Zoey was sleeping and didn't have her VacGuard on. We—Zandrie and me were too young, and scared. We weren't thinking. The Ripper started vac'ing part of our apartment and…"

He couldn't finish the rest, but he didn't need to. Dr. Dado dropped his head for a moment and wiped a tear from his eye. "*Meus pêsames.* You have my deepest sympathies, Zavier. As I try to imagine what it would feel like to lose your sister like that, I am horrified. So much pain…I do not want to imagine how this felt for you—how it *still* feels for you. No one should have done this to your family. No one should ever do *anything* like this to another person's family."

"It was even harder on Zandrie. She was in her teens at the time and probably felt more responsible. It's why she enlisted late and forced her way into the Corps."

"And why she worked so hard to become our most decorated graduate," Dr. Dado finished for him. "It's also why *you* enlisted as well, is it not?"

Zavier nodded. "And why I freeze the way I did in the battle," he admitted.

"That's because your mind goes from fluid to gas."

The curious statement got Zavier's attention; he looked back up to the man to see what else he would say.

"Whenever you allow your thoughts to dwell too long on that horrible day, or any time you have a negative experience, then your mind becomes scattered. Like gas."

"I can't help it. Anytime I think about Zoey—"

"Feeling an emotion like this is perfectly normal," Dr. Dado reassured him with a raised hand. "Is it not? Is it not normal to feel sad at the loss of your baby sister?"

"Yes."

"Of course. But what's not normal is the *degree* to which you feel it. What you need is to learn to dial down the intensity of your emotions."

"But, how do I do that?"

"Well, by turning down the emotion dial in your mind. First, picture in your mind a giant dial with numbers around it, from one to ten."

"Okay…" Zavier closed his eyes briefly. "Got it."

"Now, on that scale, how much emotion did you feel in the Arena battlefield when you found yourself immobilized?"

"About an eight or a nine," Zavier admitted, opening his eyes back up.

"And, all things considered, what do you think would have been a more appropriate emotional response in that moment?"

"To keep my calm in battle and be useful for my team…probably about a two. But any time I think of Zoey—"

"Easy Zavier," Dr. Dado said, "that's what we're working on. Now, the next time you feel such overwhelming emotion, picture that dial in your mind and turn it slowly down from that nine to a two. Each number you turn it down by, take a deep breath and release it. When you get it to two, you'll have regained control and can be useful to your squad again."

Zavier shrugged. "Anything's worth a try. I can't keep freezing up like that."

"You want to visualize the dial and turn it down any time you feel your emotions getting out of control. It must become a habit. Will you practice this at least once each day so that the habit becomes automatic?"

"I will."

"Now, I believe you have some Earth-side work to get back to, and a trip to prepare for. You may have frozen up, but you still won the day for your team."

"That's right." Zavier stood up from his seat and reached a hand across the desk. He even managed to smile. "Thanks, Dr. Dado."

Dr. Dado returned the handshake, then added a wink. "I expect someday to see your picture up on my honor wall behind me, Zavier. You have the potential."

Zavier paused at this remark. "Dr. Dado...about those pictures—what about that corner? Why do you keep those traitors? Why even remember them? They've hurt so many people. They've left the cause. Wouldn't it be better to forget them?"

Dado smiled sadly and nodded at the darkened corner of the honor wall. "I understand your concern. Why keep them there? Because they serve as a reminder, Zavier. To forget them is to forget the potential in all of us. Think of your own story. Does remembering what happened to you and your baby sister make Zandrie and you weaker—or stronger?"

Zavier paused. "Well, it made Zandrie and me join the Makers.

It made us want to do more. Is that possible? Something as awful as losing Zoey made us...stronger?"

"*Exactamente*," Dado said. "Even though it was a horrific event, it made you stronger. It helped you become who you are today. I keep these pictures, Zavier, because they remind me that we all have a choice. When something horrible happens to us, we can choose how to respond. Will it make us stronger, or weaker? It is never too late to make the right choice...or the wrong one. Even me. I have a choice every day. I must always be vigilant. I must always look for the right opportunity to choose the best path. I must not let the dark moments of my life destroy me. I must allow them to make me stronger.

"The same is true with every Cadet here at the Academy; everyone has a choice to make. Some will choose wrong because of the very power they have at their fingertips—power like that can corrupt, if you aren't careful. Do you understand?"

"I guess."

"I'm sure when the time comes, Zavier, you will make good choices. I've always seen that in you. You'll continue to choose to be among the very best on my honor wall. I really believe it."

Hearing that meant a lot for Zavier. Dr. Dado only posted pictures of his favorite students on his office wall. To realize that he might someday be one of those brought Zavier's mood up considerably. He left the room holding his chin a bit higher than when he'd entered.

Zavier was walking distractedly back to the lab when he bumped into one of the teachers. Recognizing an officers' uniform he automatically snapped to attention with a salute. "Captain."

Finally looking up, he realized it was Zandrie. She waved off the salute and wrapped her arm around his shoulders to pull him off to the side. "I'm not here to speak to you as an officer, Zavier, but as a sister."

He relaxed his stance and let out a breath of relief. "I really slagged it today, didn't I? I froze again, Zandrie."

"I saw that and we both know why…it was never your fault."

"But how do *you* get through it? You don't freeze up in battle like that."

"You were a lot younger than I was at the time, so it was a lot worse for you. But you're wrong if you think I don't have my own issues. With you, it's paralysis. With me, it's anger. Why do you think I became a Blade? Every time I'd think of Zoey, I fight harder."

"I've seen your medals," Zavier said. "You must have thought about her a *lot.*"

"And I still do; I use it. That's why I know you can get past this and why I'm stricter with you than anyone else."

"Because you don't want to be embarrassed by a failing kid brother? Or you don't want to show nepotism?"

"A little bit of the latter, I'll admit. But mostly, it's because I know you can do *better* than me."

Zavier scoffed. "Better? But you're the single most decorated—"

"My career in the field got cut short because I was sloppy," she interrupted. "I push you harder so you won't make such mistakes, Zavier. You can have a longer and far more brilliant career than I've had, *if* you apply yourself. Get what I'm saying?'

Zavier paused, then nodded. His sister loved him and he knew it, but sometimes it seemed as if she never expressed her love. At least, not in ways he usually saw. "I guess so."

"Good. Now, get back to the lab and finish up your design work. You're going Earth-side soon."

"Okay."

Realizing that the last of what she'd said was more of an Academy matter, he snapped to attention and saluted. This time, she returned the salute in kind. "As you were, Cadet."

He finished the salute and left, walking quickly back to the class lab, his rapid-fire thoughts sifting and stirring. Both Dr. Dado and Zandrie were looking out for him. Well, in Dr. Dado's case, he looked out for every cadet, though he did seem to be a bit more fatherly to him. That, or Zavier was simply the only cadet with a problem severe enough to warrant his personal attention. He hoped it wasn't the latter, because that would be pretty depressing.

I know Zandrie loves me and is looking out for me, he thought. *Sometimes, though, she goes too far. Hasn't she learned that the more pressure she puts on me, the worse things get? I wish she'd just—*

He almost thought "get ripped" out of slang muscle memory, but then realized what that truly meant.

No! Never, he mentally yelled at himself. *Never think that about anyone, no matter how bad they're treating you! Especially not Zandrie.*

It was just that there were times when he wanted to…be left alone. Sometimes, it was easier to deal with everything when no one else was around, no matter how helpful other people were trying to be.

When he entered the lab, the first thing he set eyes on was Min. There she was—perfect as always—working with five displays popped up at once, cataloguing new designs and streams of verbal macros for printing. She'd showed him her catalogue once, and some of her macros even had macros. She had a beautiful brain to match that face.

He paused in the doorway only briefly, but it was long enough for Min to take notice and glance up to beam at him. In that one action, she managed to dispel his worries and leave him feeling far more hopeful. He quickened his pace over to her workbench, then remembered himself and slowed down to try and make it look more casual. Across the room, he noticed Texas rolling her eyes before getting back to work.

"Got everything ready for our little trip, Min?"

She already had her attention back on her work by the time he reached her table, her hands dashing from one display to another.

"Just loading up a few new verbal macro combinations." Her words came out quickly, but apparently not as quick as her mind wanted. "I need to make sure I've got these commands memorized so I can be fast telling my Oz what to print. A split-second can be the difference between survival and…something else. I'll also need to do some fresh scans of everyone before we go dirt-side. Everybody is growing so fast right now, so the bodymaps are probably out of date. I also need to wrap up some new protein-based healing sequences they gave me in Medic class. Lots to do."

"You make it all sound so…amazing."

She was about to reply, then paused. Zavier realized he may have made it all too clear he wasn't talking about her work, and blushed. She pursed her lips and smiled.

"Sorry for getting you killed earlier," Zavier said.

"Oh, that."

Zavier caught another smile before she turned back to her work.

"I'll have to remember to listen better. My problem was, I didn't have my music on like I normally would. Figured it being a demo and all…"

"You wanted to set a good example for the kiddos. I get it. Oh, that reminds me. I found an old archive of a metalpop group from like thirty years back. Plasma-Rip? Pretty intense stuff. Figured you might like a copy for your collection."

"I've heard of them. The lead synth programmer is a genius and the melodies are memorable, if a touch predictable. The vocalist isn't aggressive enough for—" She stopped and turned back to Zavier with a smile. "I mean, I'd love a copy. That's very thoughtful. Thanks."

"Uh, okay…fluid," Zavier replied. "You're…*welcome*?"

"So, what'd you get called away for?"

"Dr. Dado giving a few words of encouragement. Nothing special."

"He's always doing that. Helped me out the first month I was here. I was really missing my family—especially my *halmeoni*, my grandma. Dr. Dado is a special man."

"Yeah, I agree. Dado is fluid. You know, if you ever need someone to talk to, I'm always here for you…"

For nearly a full second they held their gaze, which in teen-time felt about an hour too long, so Min broke it off by quickly turning her attention back to her workbench and her circle of displays. "Say, uh, Toby told me you were working on some sort of jumbo blunderbuss?"

"Still tinkering with it," Zavier admitted with a shrug.

"Well, when you're finished, could you send me a copy of the schematics? That could go a long way to helping me out with, you know…"

"I know how you don't like hurting anyone. That's a good trait to have in a girl…uh, healer. Girl healer. Person. Medic. Yeah, I should probably stop talking now."

Zavier was starting to see that dial in his mind rise up toward an eight, but a light giggle from Min instantly dropped it back down to three. "You're funny, Z."

"Shh. Don't let Team Overdrive hear you. They think I'm hovering death. I have a reputation to keep up, you know."

She laughed again. Zavier thought that he'd do anything to hear her laugh some more like that. Then, he briefly panicked before checking to see that the transmit light in his textlens display was currently turned off.

The moment of discomfort was finally interrupted by Kojo's

voice calling out. "Everyone who's not Team Overdrive, start wrapping up." He glanced over toward Grandmaster, who replied with a sour glare before getting back to his own private work. "We're five minutes from suiting up for our trip Earth-side."

"Right," Zavier said by way of breaking off from Min. "I've got a few things to finish up with my Oz before we go. Catch you in a bit."

As he turned away from Min, he briefly caught Texas staring in his direction. Not knowing what to do, he gave her a double thumbs up sign. She rolled her eyes and turned back to her workbench.

Up at the front of the class, Professor Friedrich made an announcement for the benefit of the other half of the room's occupants. "Team Overdrive: you have another twenty minutes to finish your designs before you have patrol duty around the station. Remember that we have a station full of recruits and their families around today; show them our Maker Academy best."

Texas returned Dakota's scowl with a grin and superior lift of her chin, Sam tried to hide his own disappointment behind a veneer of detached unconcern, while Toby refrained from any displays of personal pleasure…but the corners of his mouth were hinting at the smallest of smiles.

Zavier touched the icon on his table to quickly return all vidcubes back to the way he'd left them and went about rapidly finishing up his work. He had something to focus on now, and that helped. But in the back of his mind, his thoughts raced about the trip to Earth, wondering where they would soon be off to. Except for holiday visitations to families and field exercises, it wasn't often a cadet got to shuttle back dirt-side.

I wonder what our assignment's going to be.

CHAPTER 7

> When those carefree, naïve students at MIT used our first Ozmium prototype to print that pile of money, the world economy collapsed in moments
>
> Then matter, in whatever form it could be found, became the only currency of value. The more dense the matter, the more valuable it was. Suddenly piles of trash and graveyards of ancient, unused equipment became more precious than gold.
>
> Helen Lo, OzTech co-Founder and Author, *The Prank that Broke the World*

"Australia?" Toby asked. "What's in Australia?"

The cadets were seated in the back of the shuttle, strapped in place with their safety harnesses. Dressed in standard issue battle gear, they each wore bulletproof armor-cloth with chest plates, knee and elbow pads, helmets with their comm-gear, and jump-boots.

The jump-boots weren't exactly standard issue. Just a little modification that Zavier had come up with for his squad.

Outside the viewports, they could see the atmosphere rushing past them as the outline of Australia grew. Zavier was sitting between Min and Texas, with Kojo at the far end of the row of seats paying more attention to what he saw displayed across the inside of his helmet than what his team was currently doing.

"Looks almost as big as Texas," Texas said.

"Naw, she looks a lot bigger if you ask me," Toby laughed.

"*Texas* is bigger," she replied. "And if you contradict me with facts, you'll be wearing that beanbag gun of yours as a garter belt. Got it?!"

"Yes, ma'am," Toby said with a smirk. "Texas is certainly the biggest thing in this shuttle."

Before she could reply any further, Kojo called out. "Dropzone is Alice Springs."

"Alice Springs?" Zavier remarked. "What the shatter is in Alice Springs?"

"If my graphic is any indication," Min said as she flipped her face-guard down into place to consult her own display, "nothing but empty desert."

"Not quite empty," Kojo corrected. "Alice Springs, Micro NorAustralia, is home to a massive graveyard of ancient airplanes and transport shuttles. Anything from a couple hundred years ago all the way up to current day is stored there. If it's flown or gone into orbit, one of them is here."

Through the viewport, Zavier could see the vast Australian desert now swallowing up their entire view, the center of which was a quickly expanding view of hundreds of old flight vehicles.

"Oh, so this is babysitting duty, then. Who cares about a bunch of scrap? Sounds like a big waste to me." Toby shrugged. "Why don't they scan everything down there and decombine them into starks? Save a lot of space they could use for something else."

"Like storing your ego?" Texas snapped with a grin.

"What? I try to maintain a very humble ego," Toby replied. "I can't help it if I really *am* the best Shield currently in the Academy. To deny that would be lying."

"Toby," Texas began, "You are so full of—"

"Just like you're the best Blade in the entire Academy," Toby added. "Despite your size."

The statement stopped Texas cold as she tried to tease out compliment from insult, which had the effect of giving Kojo some time to finish his quick briefing. "The government here is a bit overly cautious when it comes to original copies. They prefer to

74

hold onto physical backups of their designs just in case their databases get hacked or otherwise corrupted."

"I thought hacking into a database was pretty much impossible," Min said.

"It is," Zavier said. "Quantum encryption keys can't be broken with anything short of a good century of computation time. Data links are by way of quantum entanglement links which can't be tapped into—as there is not really any physical link or broadcast transmission to tap—plus all the servers are mirrored, so if you even had a way to hack into one, you'd need to hack into *all* of them at once. Short of setting off an EM pulse bomb right inside the server room itself, there is no possible way of getting the system to even blink."

"Nevertheless," Kojo countered, flipping his visor back up out of the way for a direct look at the others, "Alice Springs is where they store everything that's ever flown. That's the paranoid NorAussie government for you. But they pay the GNA their Maker Corps ingot dues like everyone else, so to Alice Springs we go."

"Who cares, anyway?" Min asked. "We're on Earth and get a chance to go to NorAustralia. How often does *that* happen?"

"Min's right," Zavier agreed. "This is a sightseeing trip. Out in the middle of the shattered desert, but a sightseeing trip."

"We should be landing shortly," Kojo announced, "so get ready to disembark."

Texas spared another quick look out through the viewport, gazing at the vast yard of dead ships stretching from one horizon to the next. "Texas is still bigger."

The shuttle came down to land at an open strip near one edge of the graveyard. An ancient electrified fence marked the border. The only break in it was the one entrance, which had a squat one-story building labeled "Reception Center"—that, and a dusty old sign that read, "Got your VacGuard on?" About every three hundred meters of the fence's length, there was a post that stood at least twice as tall as the rest, topped with an Oz projector and a sensor set to continuous sweep; security, fuel supply, and cleanup all in one.

The shuttle was a sleek military model that came straight down and landed gently. They had barely touched down when Kojo set up their makeshift headquarters and local quantum cache in the back of the shuttle before allowing anyone to even step foot outside. This gave the team a fast, albeit limited, stream of starks to pull from.

Zavier and the rest of the team walked out of the shuttle's rear chamber for their first look around.

"Almost looks like outside Guadalajara," Toby was first to remark. "Only not quite as lively."

"If this was Texas, they'd have the decency to have a football stadium or two," Texas remarked.

"If this was Texas," Toby put in, "I'd be halfway to Guadalajara and some *real* off-time."

"Okay, gang, I know this might be a bore," Kojo said. "But remember, we *are* on patrol. Weapons printed and ready, but only load up on *my* word."

"That should be a long time in coming," Zavier quipped.

Nevertheless, each used their Oz device to print up what they considered their own personal "standard issue." With Maker cadets, that often spanned a wide range of options and varied with the day. For Min, it amounted to a medkit strapped to her belt, an octopus gun remodified for rapid reload, a vidcube on her belt set to a music app, and earbuds in her helmet that didn't *quite* keep the loud refrains of her choice in music to herself. Kojo held a micro-crossbow loaded with a variation on a bolo, and Toby had a fold-shield clipped to his belt and the modified bean-bag gun he had been working on earlier in the lab. Zavier only had a couple of his special pistols strapped to his belt—"Just keeping it fluid," as he often said.

Texas took the longest to fully print everything she wanted. By the time the team was walking past their first aircraft, she was loaded up with a ring of miniature grenades at her belt, a pair of pistols, and a large rifle that had a triple-width barrel and slingshot mounted on top.

Toby laughed. "So, Texas, got enough hardware?"

"Three stun grenades, a couple of flash-bangs, smoke grenade, a pair of my marshmallow pistols, and my special Burp-Gun that I call 'Baby.'" She brought the rifle up to her lips to kiss the barrel before continuing. "Since this looks like such a nothing patrol, I thought I'd keep it light."

"So, what's heavy?" Zavier asked.

"I'm from Texas," she said by way of answer. That, and a grin.

At first it felt exciting to be back on Earth—to kick up actual dust beneath their boots instead of hearing the soft step of booth-eels on pristine carpet floors; to feel a real breeze instead of temperature-controlled air conditioning; to have the sun's rays caress your face unfiltered through viewports. But, as they wandered through the maze of metal behemoths, it wasn't long before Zavier and the others realized something.

The dust was choking, the breeze was hot and dry, and the sun could bake a lobster.

"Is it just me, or is this place completely dead?" Kojo remarked.

"Not completely," Toby replied. "I could print some ghosts to haunt the place if you want. Hey, Z, got any idea how to do that?"

Min tapped her vidcube to dial down the volume in her helmet—much to the relief of Kojo's sense of music appreciation, Zavier thought—and offered her own suggestion.

"We could play spot-the-creature. I hear Australia has all sorts of interesting animals."

"None of which are here," Texas said. "And how many of them can kill you?"

"Well, uh, a surprisingly large number of them. But they're still very interesting. And I have a full range of anti-venom on me just in case."

"Don't worry, Texas." Toby grinned. "If some scary snake comes at you, I'll vac it."

"Don't you dare," Min suddenly snapped. "Deadly or not, it's still a living creature."

"Okay, sorry, *hermanita*," Toby apologized. "Just kidding. I know how you are with animals."

"Yeah," Texas said with a smile, "even ones like you."

As they bantered, their wandering steps brought them around an old fighter plane, past a beached patrol ship, and next to an old shuttle.

Zavier let out a whistle of appreciation, pointing to the shuttle. "Hey, guys, do know what that is?"

"Uh, old-school beyond belief?" Toby deadpanned.

"I'll have the info in a second," Kojo offered, his eyes already scanning across his helmet display.

"Don't bother, Koj," Zavier told him. "That's a second gen space shuttle. They came out after the first station went up into orbit. That thing must be more than a hundred years old."

"And it's not all rusted apart?" Texas remarked.

"Ceramic hull," Zavier quickly explained. "It doesn't rust. First model to be built that way."

"He's right," Kojo started reading off his display as they walked around the large craft. "Built one hundred and twenty-one years ago, ceramic composition, and if I got the serial number scanned off that hull correctly, this one flew twenty missions before it was grounded. Got replaced by the next model."

"I'm impressed," Min said as she smiled at Zavier. "You knew that off the top of your head?"

"Part of my hobby." He shrugged. "I'm better with old cars, but this particular design sort of sticks out at you. It was the first one that started looking less like flying breadboxes than its predecessors. Too bad there aren't any cars out here; wheeled or hover, I know them all. I even have this scan of a vintage 2028 Lamborghini Audace that my sister got for me a few years back. Took a few weeks of tinkering to smooth it out and get it looking really fluid. You should see the specs."

They left the old shuttle behind them and wandered through the maze of rusting metal as Zavier used the excuse of talking about his collection to keep a conversation going with Min. Except for their own discussions and the distant sound of some unnamed animal crying out, not to mention the faint, jarring music coming out from the little speakers in Min's helmet, the place was empty of life. Empty as far as anyone could see. Empty as far as anyone's device could *scan*.

Their patrol went on like that. They spent another hour walking through dry, dusty terrain, boxed in by dead planes and grounded transports. This reward for victory over Overdrive had turned out to be a very lonely patrol.

At the two-hour mark, they found a place to take a break. They settled down under a transport with a mouth like some biblical whale that stretched up for at least three stories, its back end open to the elements to provide an opening to its much-welcomed shaded interior.

"What'd they use this thing to transport?" Texas asked as they walked up the ramp. "Other planes?"

"Pretty close," Zavier said. "Imagine a scaled-up modern version of this thing and what it could do."

"Okay, ten-minute break," Kojo called out. "Min, rations for everyone."

Field rations had come quite far with the advent of quantum stark technology. Gone were the days of MREs and ration meal packs with the density and taste of a warm brick. Min simply scanned quickly through her Oz's popup menu, made a couple of selections, and aimed her printer out onto the metal floor while the rest took seats in a scattered circle.

"Oz: Lunch for five."

Her Oz perfectly printed prosciutto canapés, crackers and humus dip, hamburgers topped with nearly everything, and a bowl of fruit. All undoubtedly created with Min's Medic-eye for healthy sustenance, Zavier assumed. She also printed goblets of cold water, plates, and cutting knives for the fruit. Thanks to OzTech, no meal was ever dull...or sparse.

"Dig in, people," she said. "The burgers are a traditional vegetarian alternative I found."

"I thought that old religion was dead," Texas said. "Never find one in Texas."

"No sodas?" Zavier complained.

"Not in the middle of this desert heat," Min told him.

"Speaking of heat, thank you for the Ghanaian pepper-sauce," Kojo said as he doused his meal liberally with a small red bottle.

"I know you aren't happy if you can't pour that stuff on everything," Min replied.

It wasn't long before everyone was eating a hearty lunch in the shade of the ancient transport plane, in the middle of the Australian desert.

"You're a good cook, Min," Zavier remarked as he bit in.

"Yeah," Kojo quipped, "your Oz should be on a gourmet cooking show someday."

Min stuck out her tongue and rolled her eyes.

I like it here, Zavier thought to himself as he leaned back. *There are lots of better places to be assigned dirt-side, but it's still a lot closer to civilization than up in orbit.*

"So, Toby," Zavier said by way of being conversational as they ate, "I've never heard you cuss once, yet you come from a pretty tough neighborhood."

"Just trying to be respectful," Toby shrugged.

"Didn't that get the other kids to teasing you, though?" Min asked.

"As big as he is," Texas pointed out, "who'd dare?"

"Actually, I was teased quite a lot as a kid. Bullied, really," Toby said. "I used to have a port wine stain on my face. The kids in my *barrio*, they were brutal. Later on, I finally had it removed, but left part of it…here." He pointed to the small red shield on his left cheek. "It's a reminder to myself of the promise I made to always defend people who need help."

"And that's why you became a Shield," Min said, smiling. "I think that's sweet."

Toby replied with a quick flicker of a shy grin, then put his attention more fully back to his meal.

"Fluid story, Toby," Zavier agreed. "And I thought that was a tattoo. After all this time together, we're still learning things about each other."

He was just adjusting himself against the bulkhead when he felt something poking him in the bottom. Reaching around, he held it up for a quick inspection. "A peach pit?"

"I don't think I printed any peaches," Min said. "Did you want one?"

"No, I found a peach pit."

Min got a curious look then held out a hand. "Toss it here."

He handed it over to Min, who gave it a quick visual inspection.

"Just an old piece of fruit," Toby said with a shrug.

"Except that it's not all that old," Min said. "It still has pieces of fruit pulp on it. Can't be more than an hour old."

"Then…maybe the regular security people left it?" Toby guessed.

"But today, *we're* the regular security people," Texas said.

"I was afraid you'd say that."

"We'll have to assume the worst. Clean everything up and ready weapons," Kojo commanded as he rose. "Communication by textlens only. Min, you'll have to completely douse the music. We have intruders."

It only took seconds to vac all sign of their lunch. They left the transport, with Toby taking the lead as they came to the edge of a more modern-looking hover-jet. He held up a hand to stop.

>>**Toby**>>**Boot tracks and they're not ours.**<<

>>**Koj**>>**Number?**<<

Toby took a slow step forward to peer around the edge of the craft before replying.

>>**Toby**>>**Three sets that I can see. Passed by the other side of this thing. Headed deeper.**<<

>>**Z**>>**This place is kilometers across. Can you tell how old those tracks are?**<<

Min pointed the Oz on her right forearm at the tracks and scanned.

>>**Min**>>**No more than an hour, I guess. Could be the same ones that left the peach pit.**<<

>>**Z**>>**Any chance they are Rippers?**<<

>>**Toby**>>**No way to tell. Heavy boots, that's all I can tell you.**<<

>>**Koj**>>**Assume hostiles. Toby, lead on.**<<

He wasn't skilled in tracking, but Toby followed the trail as best he could. At the same time, he unclipped the fold-shield from his belt, held it out in his left hand, and thumbed the stud on its back. It expanded swiftly and quietly, stacked layers sliding out again and again until it was a full-sized body-shield. With a final click, the lines marking out its various sections faded away and the shield became a single solid mass—ultra thin, solid, and transparent. He held it by a handle that had formed over the button and kept it in front of himself while everyone else walked in a single-file line directly behind him.

The tracks went on for another thirty meters before being swept clean by the winds, so Toby followed the last general idea of direction. Meanwhile, Zavier was quietly mouthing into his own device, bringing his wrist up close to his lips in a whisper.

"Oz: Ping-scanner."

A second later, he was holding something that looked like a fat digital compass mounted on a glue gun. He swept back and forth while looking at the display in the compass section.

>>Min>>Z, what is that?<<

>>Z>>Mated your med scanner with a small radar gun. Not much detail, but will look for heartbeats. Range of about 150 meters—enough for our needs. Toby, try 15 degrees left and 100 meters on.<<

>>Toby>>That puts it on the other side of that old patrol boat up ahead.<<

>>Z>>They called it a destroyer, and it was a ship, not a boat.<<

>>Toby>>It's still rust.<<

Toby led them around, while Zavier kept an eye on his hand-scanner.

>>Min>>Z, any way of telling how many there are?<<

>>Z>>Too close together. Could be two, could be twelve.<<

When they came to the end of the hover-jet, Toby paused. Ahead of him was a large open space they would have to cross before reaching the old ship.

>>Toby>>Wide open space between us and our target. Perfect for a sniper.<<

>>Koj>>Can we stay on the edges?<<

>>Toby>>That depends. Z, where are your readings?<<

>>Z>>Skirt left. We should come out within sight of target at the back of the ship.<<

>>Koj>>Do it. Toby, does that shield of yours have any blending ability?<<

>>Toby>>One-way projected blending. Like a shimmer-suit. I can see out, but they see a projection of what's behind me. Why do you think I printed a full-body size?<<

>>Koj>>Then approach with caution. Single-file behind Toby.<<

Toby performed as instructed, leading the team around the left edge of the large clearing until they were near enough to the leading edge of the old ship to risk a dash to its shadows. Once there, he peeked around the corner with his shield leading him.

It was a group of people, armed and armored, standing around one of the newer vessels while aiming their right arms at it.

>>Toby>>Rippers. The ship they're scanning can't be more than a decade old.<<

>>Z>>I might be able to figure what they want if I can see what they're scanning.<<

>>Texas>>Just ambush 'em, knock 'em unconscious, then question them.<<

>>Koj>>And be ambushed ourselves by their friends? Stay cautious. Sneak in and learn what we can.<<

>>Texas>>Spoilsport.<<

>>Koj>>Stealth mode.<<

>>Min>>Squad names?<<

No one replied to Min's interjection. Each person readied one of their weapons. At a nod from Kojo, Toby led them all carefully along the side of the ship under cover of its shadows.

Zavier kept his hand-scanner at the ready for signs of any other lifeforms, trying to ignore how much his hand was shaking.

CHAPTER 8

Makers shall only use force that is reasonable, required, and relative to the moment in question. A Maker's goal should be to end an incident or bring a person under control, while protecting those around them.

As the use of lethal force is to be considered a last resort, Makers shall focus their blueprints, modifications, and corresponding prints to ensure an effective resolution of conflict with the least probable risk to life.

Global Maker Corps Code

Together, the squad crept behind Toby's shield, staying in the shadow of the old ship. As they got closer, Zavier could see that the Rippers were ringed around an orbital shuttle of some sort, one nearly as large as the destroyer next to his squad. There were six Rippers that they could see, all spaced in a semi-circle around the front of the craft, talking as they were scanning.

>>Koj>>**Anyone make anything out?**<<

>>Toby>>**Bits and pieces, but nothing yet.**<<

>>Z>>**Activating recorder.**<<

Toby led them closer, careful to keep his camo-shield positioned between himself and any direct view of the Rippers. The rest bunched up behind him. They were close enough to hear snatches of the Rippers' conversation.

"…Big ship to scan. Still take a while longer."

"Just hurry up…out of here before…"

"Piece of space junk…"

"…As long as it makes it into orbit…can carry lots of weaponry…"

Oh, this does not sound good, Zavier thought to himself. Weapons? Orbit?

>>**Koj**>>**Can anyone make anything out?**<<

>>**Z**>>**I heard "weapons" and "orbit." Not good.**<<

>>**Koj**>>**Agreed. Toby, get us closer.**<<

>>**Toby**>>**Just stay on my six.**<<

Toby led the team further along the side of the old ship, his fold-shield before him blending in with the large hull. He crept up until he was nearly in a straight line with the Rippers, and had a clear view of them no more than fifty yards away. Every ear on the team strained to hear what the Rippers were saying.

"…for the assault."

"…place won't know what hit it."

"…bloody Makers…serve 'em right."

Now that they were closer, Zavier had a better look at what they were scanning, not to mention the Rippers themselves. Six individuals, two looking to be women—each in light body armor with a picture of a rooster emblazoned on their chests. Additionally, one of the women also had a picture of a large red and yellow symbol spread across her back. It was a drawing of a devil figure standing beneath a ship, with a pair of soccer balls to either side and the words "Manchester United" emblazoned across the top and bottom. One of the men was tall, built like a Viking with a braided beard, shaven head, and a large broadsword strapped across his back. He stood guard while the rest aimed their scanners at various points of the craft.

Zavier made a quick visual study of the ship's outline before reporting in through his textlens.

>>**Z**>>**That's an old construction shuttle. They use those to build orbital stations like our academy. Solid as a tank.**<<

>>**Koj**>>**Getting data on it now. It has separate fixtures for about a dozen different tool attachments.**<<

>>**Z**>>**Or maybe weapons?**<<

>>**Texas**>>**This is serious slag.**<<

>>**Toby**>>**Language, Texas.**<<

>>**Min**>>**What would they need it for?**<<

>>**Toby**>>**Let's find out. Stay close.**<<

Toby was about to take a step when another Ripper came out from around the other side of the craft. He walked like he owned the ground, eyes sharply fixed on anything he surveyed. He was swarthy and tall, with no hair on his head. His upper lip supported an almost ridiculously long, slender mustache that hung like a curtain-rod beneath his nose, and his chin bore a short goatee to complete the picture. He was dressed head to toe in black leather. The picture of the rooster on his chest wore a small crown, and Zavier could hear his heavy boots stepping across the gravel and sand as he walked into view.

Zavier recognized the figure immediately.

>>**Z**>>**Guys, that's the Parisian! The head Ripper himself.**<<

>>**Koj**>>**This ain't no normal Ripper incursion.**<<

"How soon?" The Parisian snapped out his command like a whip.

Zavier checked the audio on his recorder just to make sure he could hear what they were saying, ready to report to the others what he heard just in case they couldn't pick them up. The feed that he got was a jumbled, garbled mess of sound. Jammers. The Rippers were using jammers. All he could do was listen and hope he could remember what they said.

The lady with the Manchester United shirt responded as she continued to slowly pan her right hand across the area. "Almost done, guv. Just got a little bit of interior scans left to go. No more than a moment."

"Get it done, quickly. The scans on the transport are already finished."

>>Z>>**Sounds like they've got others who've already scanned another ship. A transport.**<<

"This one's got a lot more technical detail to record," another Ripper replied.

"No excuses," the Parisian said. "We have a schedule to maintain. I want the assault going off without a hitch. Then, after tomorrow, we won't have to worry about the Makers ever again."

Zavier's eyes widened.

>>Z>>**Guys, they're planning to attack the GMC facility in orbit. Our home!**<<

>>Texas>>**Maybe. They're scanning for a fleet, for sure. We've heard enough.**<<

Along with her transmission she sent a video loop from an old space opera movie, where fighter craft were just starting to ready for an attack run.

>>Koj>>**Not our fight, Texas. You heard Z; they were scanning some old transport. Let's ghost so we can transmit.**<<

Min was last in line and, on hearing Kojo's order, started stepping back so the others would have room. She stepped on a small piece of scrap metal, which gave off a soft "ping." The squad stopped and held their collective breath.

The Viking with the large sword snapped his head around and squinted in their direction. He took a couple of steps toward them, then pulled out a pistol and took aim.

"We got visitors," he called out.

He wasted no time and pulled off a shot as the Parisian snapped out a command.

"Perimeter!"

The shot hit the ship's hull right behind Min, narrowly missing her leg as it expanded into a one-meter-wide sticky, acidic mass that began slowly eating into the old metal.

Toby took a quick look at his shield, then stared back at Min, realizing what had happened.

>>**Toby**>>**Min, you stepped out from behind my shield.**<<

>>**Min**>>**Rookie mistake!**<<

"Too late now!" Texas shouted. "I'm gonna go all Houston on them!"

Upon the Parisian's command, three more Rippers emerged from behind the craft, each raising a weapon. Of the ones already in view, the Manchester United girl kept scanning while the rest quickly broke off and started printing their own weapons to join in with the rest. The Viking, meanwhile, reached a hand back to pull out his ridiculously large sword while his Oz printed over his pistol, converting it into a larger rifle.

"All of it for all of us!" the Viking called out.

Texas had already leaped directly into the battle. She plucked one of the grenades off her belt and gave it a strong throw just as the Viking pulled off a shot from his rifle. The grenade bounced off his chest and detonated as the rounds left his barrel.

A deafening explosion of sound and blinding flash of light blanketed the area. The Viking was thrown on his back, along with a couple other Rippers.

The explosion nearly deafened Zavier's team as well.

>>**Texas**>>**That flashbang should keep them busy for a while.**<<

The rifle the Viking had been firing continued to go off, but now on its own errant course. It angled across the ship's hull in a line high above their heads. The rapid-fire pulse left a wide hole deep in the hull with each shot that hit. The closest one just missed Min's head, and another blast sent debris flying, coming straight down for Texas and Zavier.

>>**Toby**>>**Watch out!**<<

Toby dove through the air, holding his shield overhead to protect the other two from the raining shrapnel. The move, while successful, removed all cover from the rest of the team, exposing them into full view. As Toby made a mad dash toward him, Zavier watched as two Rippers and the Parisian touched a spot on the sleeve of their suits and faded from view. They became little more than a shimmer against the background of the space craft, then less than that as they ran out into the open.

"They've got shimmer-suits!" Zavier shouted.

The other three Rippers not involved with protecting the one woman leveled their weapons and proceeded to fire. From one of them came a stream of bullets, but no ordinary bullets. Two of them hit the ground with an explosion of lightning, one slammed into the hull to send electrical fingers rippling along its length, while another hit Toby in the leg as he was completing his dive.

The other two Rippers were apparently still recovering from Texas' flashbang, because their shots went wild, missing by several meters. The first was a focused sonic pulse that left a large dent in the hull behind the team, the other a small bloom of fire that exploded high above them.

The rubble bounded off Toby's shield just as the bullet hit him in the leg, sending an electrical shock through his body that caused his every muscle to tighten up and his teeth to clamp down as he hit the dirt. His shield flew out from his hand to skid across the ground.

"They're cadets," the Parisian suddenly called out. "Non-lethal only! No deaths. Hear me!"

Zavier had ducked just in time to avoid Toby's crashing body, while Texas whipped out another grenade. This time, an explosion of smoke erupted from the middle of the combat zone, though not before Zavier's quick eyes spotted a shimmering form diving quickly away from the expanding fog.

"Toby!" Min cried out.

Texas recoiled as a heavyset shimmer slammed into her and an invisible fist crashed across her chin. She reeled back into the ship hull behind her, gritting her teeth. Quickly, she pushed off from the wall and swung her triple-width rifle in front of her.

The smoke from her grenade ended up serving a dual purpose. It didn't just make seeing difficult, but appeared to be just a little bit stuck to the outline of the invisible Ripper. Zavier could see the rapidly moving form heading straight toward them.

>>**Z**>>**Watch out!**<<

>>**Koj**>>**I see it.**<<

Kojo immediately whipped out his micro-crossbow and shot off a bolo toward where legs might have been.

Texas was fighting a foot away from Zavier, who managed to push Toby off himself. He caught sight of the wound in his team-mate's leg. His calf had a long bloody gash, while miniature electrical arcs still danced off the bullet imbedded into his leg as the rest of his body twitched.

Zavier also had a clear view of the Viking, who had been pointblank for the flashbang yet was already getting back up to his feet, looking very angry and with sword in hand. *That sword's big enough to cut me in half,* Zavier thought.

Kojo, meanwhile, tried to get a message off.

>>**Koj**>>**Got some interference. Headquarters, do you receive? Have found Rippers and need backup immediately!!!**<<

"Get this inviso-guy *off* me," Texas called out as she swung the butt of her rifle around.

>>**Koj**>>**Headquarters, repeat: Under attack and outnumbered. Koj to shuttle: get this message through and protect our Local Cache.**<<

Apparently recovering from the flashbang, the other armed Rippers quickly went about reprinting their weapons in favor of something less lethal, as per the Parisian's orders. The Viking charged through the smoke.

>>**Koj**>>**They got up way too fast. They must have protection. Z, we need a little something.**<<

Too much, Zavier thought. *Too much, just like before.* He couldn't move.

Min was quickly responding to Toby's needs, printing a med-scanner as she tried to roll him away from Zavier. Texas was having a melee fight with an opponent she could not see. But all Zavier could do was lay there and stare.

Always too much. What do I do first? They're coming from all directions. What's wrong with me?

In contrast, Min was a professional, quickly kneeling beside Toby with her back to the firefight as she worked.

"Tesla round. Too small to VacGuard." She raised the QuantVac on her left arm and it hummed to life. She flicked her wrist, and the electrified bullet vanished into a stream of dust, flying into the device on her left wrist. Her right hand held the scanner she passed across Toby's leg. "Tissue damage in the calf, peripheral damage in the nervous system. Handle the tissue first. Oz: Program Regen: Medical file 'Tobias.' Scan leg and repair."

While Min worked to repair Toby's injuries, Texas got a lucky hit on her invisible opponent. An imprint appeared in the dusty ground before her, corresponding to the rough outline of hand-prints and a fallen body, accompanied by an "Umph." Texas immediately shifted her rifle to one hand while whipping out one of her pistols with the other, firing off a shot in nearly the same action.

Suddenly her invisible opponent was covered across chest and torso with a blast of marshmallow goo. It didn't stop him from getting back up to his feet, but at least she could see him now.

>>**Koj**>>**Backup's coming, but won't arrive in time. We're on our own.**<<

"Just the way I like it," Texas yelled. She dropped her pistol and swung her large rifle around just as the marshmallow-man sprang back to his feet. "Baby needs burping."

"No swords," the Parisian called out to the Viking with the

large sword. "We don't kill cadets!"

The Viking, though, was lost to the thinning smoke and apparently on a mission of his own. Zavier could just see him charging in the direction of Texas, but still he could not move. Then, Texas fired off her burp-gun; the one she called "Baby."

What came out of the triple-width barrel did indeed sound like a baby burping…if the baby was about ten meters tall and had a *really* bad case of indigestion. The sonic pulse was accompanied by flying strands of sticky string, which randomly wrapped around the Viking from head to toe. No single one of them was strong enough to bind, but taken together, they were a definite problem. The pulse was strong enough to launch the other figure off his feet and back through the air with a cry…

Zavier looked away just as the Viking's blade pierced through the Ripper. He saw the horror in Texas's eyes as she looked down at her burp gun in disbelief. Her jaw dropped and the gun nearly fell from her grip as sick realization spread across her face.

"I…I killed him. I've never…"

And then, Texas did something she *never* did in battle. She stood still and did nothing.

>>Koj>>**Worry about that later or you'll be joining them, Texas. Come on, snap out of it!**<< Then, in another message: >>**Z, wake up. We need a solution!**<<

Min, meanwhile, nearly had Toby's leg mended, the new tissue printing directly into place, but he was still paralyzed from the electrical shock. "I'll need an ampule of paralytic reliever and something to reset the nervous system. Oz: When finished, print electrical stim package."

From the Rippers now came a collective barrage, one shooting a lower-level sonic pulse. It was strong enough to send Kojo off his feet and reeling. Another Ripper sent a wall of BB-gun sized pellets; they did no real damage themselves, but the force of impact was just enough to cause each one to detonate in a tiny fiery spark. The small flares blinded the entire team with sparkling flashes and short-lived micro-fires dancing off their armor.

Texas quickly shielded her face with one arm, unable now to accurately aim at anything. Another Ripper fired out an expanding net that Texas was quick to counter by firing her burp-gun at it before it could make it to Min's unprotected back. An inexact shot, thanks to the constant barrage of fiery pellets, but good enough to send the Ripper whipping back through the air and, conveniently, into the other Ripper in a shimmer-suit. The Ripper found himself enmeshed in his companion's net and sent out a string of Germanic-sounding expletives.

All of this happened as Zavier sat dumbly and watched.

"Z," Texas cried out. "You've got to snap *out* of it!"

She kicked him in the leg with her foot, but he barely noticed it.

"Z, we're about to *die,* if you hadn't noticed!" Texas shouted.

She was readying another shot for her burp-gun, but the assault was leaving them all blind as well as exposed. Her shot hit nothing but air.

"What would Dado tell you?" she called down, with another kick to his leg. "Focus!"

Hearing the name of his mentor brought Zavier's attention back. Yes, Dr. Dado! He'd told him to do something in times like this. What was it? Something about…Yes, a dial. Picture a dial. What was it set to right now?

About an eleven, he admitted to himself. *Okay, got to dial it back down. Take a deep breath and picture it going down to a ten…*

Kojo was getting back up onto his feet, vac'ing his crossbow in favor of quickly printing a rolling mantlet shield large enough for himself and one other. He pulled it behind him as he scooted quickly over to Min.

"How's Toby looking?" he asked.

She was just applying a small patch of foil to the back of Toby's neck, the effect immediate. A small, electrical spark traveled from the foil to his neck and Toby's body finally relaxed, a sigh of relief escaping his lips. Once his spasms stopped, she removed the patch and answered.

"Just finished up. Toby, you'll still be a little dizzy for about a minute more, so just keep lying there for a bit."

"We don't have a minute," Kojo told them. "We're really out of our depth here."

"I'll say, *hermano*," Toby said, managing a slight grin for Kojo and glancing at his rolling shield. "You're doing my job for me."

As something else ricocheted off Kojo's shield, Texas was practically standing over Zavier, trying to get his attention while she fired off another shot of her burp-gun. This time, she managed to connect with the large Viking—except that now, he was ready for it. The man braced himself, then wiped one hand across his face to remove the sticky strands once the pulse had ended. He began moving once again. He had no sword now, but somehow his bare hands and angry disposition looked good enough. He printed a round metal Viking shield into his left hand as he walked, complete with Nordic runes and a large black bird spreading its wings across the center. He was not more than ten meters away.

"Zavier!" Texas screamed.

The dial in his mind continued to move down, low enough now for him to start talking. "Four…Three…" He saw the large figure approaching, silhouetted against the continuing barrage of flash pellets, and made a quick decision. "Good enough."

He rolled up into a sitting position, whipped out his two pistols, and fired.

One pistol had a quarter-circle metal tray on top of it, while the other had a slightly flared muzzle and a two-centimeter-wide pellet loaded into the back of it. From the second came a shot that exploded into a wide puddle of white cream, while from the other a banana peel.

Actually, *several* banana peels, one right after another, all aimed at the man's feet. A large foot stepped on one and managed not to slip, but the other foot stepped on a pair of banana peels well soaked in the cream all around.

"Texas!" Zavier cried out.

She raised up her gun at the slipping silhouette. "Come on, Baby, *burp.*"

With a lack of traction at his feet, the large man slipped, falling onto his back from the pulse and continuing in a mad slide back to crash into a couple of his companions.

"Looks like I picked up a spare," Texas deadpanned.

Zavier realized he'd barely come out of it in time. But as he sat there panting and wondering what they were going to do next, his eye caught the Manchester United woman as she brought down her arm and gave a nod to the Parisian.

"Good," the man shouted out. "We're done here. Call in our taxi!"

"I'll flag down a good one, guv." She aimed her arm out toward an open space on the other side of their shuttle. "Oz: Print shuttle-one."

"Send the Takers a goodbye present, then everyone bug-out," the Parisian shouted.

It hit just as Toby got up and Texas took another aim at the Viking. Someone on the other side threw a grenade. Texas saw it and immediately switched targets.

"Heads up!" she cried out as she pulled the trigger, but instead of the pulse pushing the grenade far away, it detonated it. An aerial burst of light and sound caused everyone to drop whatever they were holding to slam their hands over their ears as they fell to the ground.

It was an amplified version of Texas' flashbang, and Zavier's team wasn't as prepared for it as the Rippers had apparently been.

For what seemed like several minutes, Zavier could see nothing but white, and hear nothing but a loud ringing that dropped down into a low-throated roar over the course of a minute. When his vision cleared enough to at least see shapes, he saw a very *large* shape about the size of the construction shuttle the Rippers had just been scanning, only it was hovering five meters above the ground with no sign of any Rippers.

Toby was first to lift himself up onto unsteady legs, followed by Texas as she retrieved her burp-gun, but by then, the reason for the roar was clear. The shuttle hovered briefly on its jets, then rose more rapidly up into the sky. By the time Zavier and the others were back on their feet with their vision fully recovered, the shuttle was shooting away off into the distance.

"Slag, they got away," Texas swore.

Kojo looked distracted for a moment before reporting to the others. "Backup will be here in sixty seconds."

"Doesn't matter," Zavier realized. "The danger isn't here."

He stepped away from the bulkhead behind them, gaze fixed on the point in the sky where they'd seen the old shuttle vanish from sight. His voice sounded just as distant. "I know what I heard. They have to be warned. The Rippers are going to attack the Maker Orbital Headquarters."

CHAPTER 9

Cadets are Makers-in-training and lack the expertise and technology to engage in real-life combat. As such, if a squad of cadets encounters a hostile situation the squad leader must immediately call for backup and retreat to avoid enemy engagement.

Maker Corps Academy, Combat Squad Orientation

Zavier and his squad stood at strict attention, facing a panel of officers—specifically, the Maker Corps leadership. They were deep within the headquarters of the Global Maker Corps, in a room apparently meant for debriefing, but Zavier felt more like it was meant for criminal sentencing. The bench before them was a semi-circle with its open mouth aimed toward them, the benches raised just high enough to allow every leader to glare down at the squad at a rather discomforting angle.

Dr. Oliveira was there, as was the station commander Lieutenant General Brigantine, along with several other highly decorated officials who made Zavier uncomfortable. But there was one person present that made Zavier especially uncomfortable: his sister. She fixed her angry gaze on him, looking down at him as if he was a young child being scolded by his mother.

Of course, a scolding was exactly what they were getting.

"The *second* you spotted them, you should have called it in," a woman with Colonel's stripes raged. "You aren't fit to handle something like that."

"No, Colonel Gwon," Kojo replied.

"We could have had the Parisian," another Colonel snapped.

"All you had to do was stay out of sight and wait."

"With respect, Colonel Feist, sir," Kojo began, "we didn't spot the Parisian until we'd crept closer. We were trying to see what they were up to."

"And what good did *that* do you?" Lieutenant General Brigantine asked. His tone sounded in control, but the tension in his mouth suggested otherwise.

"Sir, if I may," Zavier began, "I heard them—"

"Quiet, cadet." Colonel Gwon glared at him. "You will speak only *if* we let you."

"Your duty was to simply patrol," Colonel Feist told them. "If something were to come up, you were to call it in immediately."

"Which Kojo did," Zavier reminded them, trying again to make himself heard. "But then, when we got closer, I heard them speaking about—"

"*But* your biggest mistake was in getting spotted in the first place," the General interrupted. "Cadet Yu, letting yourself be seen outside the cover of your Guardian's—Cadet Montero's—shield? That's a first-year mistake."

Min looked like she was about to say something, but under the combined glare of all the officials before them, she closed her mouth and remained silent.

"Sirs," Zavier tried once again, "we made mistakes, yes, but we heard something *very* important if you'll just let me—"

"Cadet Vik," now it was Zavier's own sister browbeating him, "you will shut your mouth and remain at *silent* attention until such time as you are allowed to speak…or I will see that you are assigned to every lowly duty I can think of for the remainder of your time at the Academy. Am I understood?"

Zavier relented with a nod and said nothing more. He knew his sister, and she would keep to the very letter of what she promised if he pushed it.

"Cadet Yu," Zandrie now began, "it was your slipup that got you all spotted. You're lucky you didn't get your entire squad killed. It's obvious you need a bit more discipline, so after you are all dismissed here, you will stand out in the Communal area of the Academy for one hour at strictest attention. Do not move a single muscle, do not blink, no matter what *anyone* else does to or around you. Bat an eyelash, and it'll be another hour."

Before Min might reply with a, "Yes, ma'am," Zandrie went onto the next victim.

"Cadet Montero. You weren't even involved in the entire sequence. What happened?"

"I fell, then was hit, ma'am," Toby stiffly replied. "There was some falling shrapnel and I was trying to shield Cadets Hatchet and Vik from it."

"And you didn't think to come up with something a bit better for shielding *all* of your companions with in the first place, Guardian?" Colonel Gwon snapped. "You're Makers—*make* something!"

"Yes, ma'am, Colonel Gwon," Toby said.

"And Cadet Solomon," Zandrie now cut in, fixing a withering gaze for Kojo. "Ultimately, it is your leadership that makes or breaks this team. The instant you saw the Parisian, you should have sent a message back up to Command via textlens, or at least to your shuttle pilot, then not moved a muscle. You weren't seen and were in the perfect position to collect intel, so why did you order the retreat which exposed Cadet Yu and then the rest of you?"

Kojo was silent at first, then wet his lips as he carefully worded his response. "It *was* ultimately my responsibility, ma'am. I should have better coordinated our withdrawal. But I wanted to get into a position to better see what they were doing. We only saw the Parisian once we were closer. Unfortunately, that put us close enough that I was afraid to transmit anything, in case they had a way to—"

"So, you allowed your squad to hide behind a shield that

was just large enough to hide one, maybe two people," Colonel Gwon stated.

"We were in a line, sir," Kojo replied. "I figured if we were careful that the one shield could—"

"They caught you *broadside*," General Brigantine harshly reminded him. "From your own reports, that straight single-file line of yours ended up being parallel to half the Ripper force. The only real thing hiding you was the shadow of that old destroyer you were walking alongside. I don't care how closely packed you were; you would have been discovered sooner or later. It didn't occur to you to print some sort of wide-area camouflage device? Or, better yet, some binoculars, a rifle-mic, silent drone…*something* so you didn't have to expose yourselves!"

"And, Cadet Hatchet," Colonel Feist snapped. "You *are* aware of the number one credo of the Makers, are you not?"

Texas hesitated for a second, then threw back her shoulders and returned the officer's attention with a direct look. Zavier knew her well enough, though, to see the pain in her eyes. "I fought my best to protect my team. In the process I…I got someone killed. My shot threw one opponent onto another's sword. It wasn't my intent, but I accept full responsibility."

Here, the officers glanced from one to another, then the General gave a nod and replied himself. "That, at least, was the one honest mistake any of you made. The rest was sheer incompetence."

"Cadet Hatchet," Dr. Dado finally spoke up, "'Texas,' I believe they call you? Report to my office an hour after this debriefing is at an end. I believe there are some things you may want to discuss."

"Yes, sir," she replied.

The moment of sympathy, however, was short-lived. All eyes fell on Zavier.

"And that brings us to Cadet Vik," Zandrie said, taking the lead. "On patrol, in the middle of an encounter with the Rippers, *including* the Parisian himself, and you just…panicked? Didn't we *just* talk about this?"

"A team is only as strong as its weakest link," Colonel Feist reminded him, "if that link freezes up in the middle of combat, then the entire team is compromised. It's only by the slimmest margins of luck that any of you survived. No doubt they figured out your Logistician had called in their position and weren't ready for a protracted battle with *real* Makers. They got out of there before they could clean up after themselves."

With the focus now on him, Zavier couldn't figure out a better time to make himself heard, so he spoke up quickly and more than a little loudly. "With respect, sir, but I think there was more to it than that. That was the second vessel they'd scanned, and from what I heard them saying, they have some pretty big plans. Sir, I believe that this very facility is going to be attacked. I'd put it at tomorrow at the latest."

The colonel cocked his head to one side, then exchanged looks with the other officers, each of whom replied with expressions of doubt. "That's a big leap in logic. Explain."

"Well, sir," Zavier began after quickly wetting his lips with his tongue, "I heard the Parisian himself talk about an assault, and how after tomorrow they won't have to worry about the Makers ever again. The type of shuttle they scanned was an old construction shuttle—big and well armored, with fittings for a large number of weapons. Commanders, the only thing they'd need space-worthy craft for would be for something in orbit, and the only thing up here that would bring down the GMC would be this very facility we're standing in. General, you have *got* to get ready for an all-out Ripper offensive!"

"Watch that tone, cadet," Colonel Gwon warned him. "We don't *have* to do anything on the say-so of a nervous young man."

"But sir, I *heard*—"

Before the scolding could go any further, the General put up a hand for silence. "Cadet Solomon, can you confirm any of what Cadet Vik just told us? Did you hear the Parisian talk about attacking this facility?"

"Well, General, sir," Kojo began, "I didn't hear *exactly* what Zavier—er, Cadet Vik, said he heard. He was in a better position, then later I was busy trying to get a message out. Apparently, they'd set up a low-grade comm interference field around their locale, effectively ruining our recording. Nothing I couldn't have gotten past, of course, but it did take my attention away from other things for a moment or two."

"Did you hear anything or not?"

"Well, that is…no. Not exactly. But I believe him if he says he heard what he heard and stand by him completely."

"I see."

The General sat back in his chair for a moment, the others falling into silence as well. From their distracted stares, Zavier guessed they were occupied with their own quick textlens conversation before the General leaned forward. "Cadet Vik, it is obvious that you have nothing but the best interests at heart for the Maker Corps, and for that very reason will no doubt make a fine Maker one day. That day, however, is not this day. We agree that the Rippers were obviously scanning some armaments for a new offensive, but we have no credible evidence to support the theories that their offensive will be this station and that it will be anytime soon."

"But, General, the Parisian said—"

"What you *think* he said from a great distance is not evidence. As Makers we are creative, yes, but we are also *logical*. Your guess is emotional as it's missing the bigger picture. You are a cadet, Vik, and as such, not privy to the larger matters happening around the globe. There are any of several battlefronts the Rippers are currently engaged in that would make for far better targets than all the way up here in orbit. While we will take this encounter under advisement, there is scant evidence to suggest what you are saying."

"But, sir—"

"*Cadet*," Colonel Feist commanded, looking at Zavier as a teacher might look at a misbehaving three-year-old. "Are you a commanding officer?"

"No, sir."

"Are you a tactician of any sort?"

"Well no, sir, but—"

"Are you even a Stick?"

"No," Zavier said, now sighing in defeat.

"Then leave the analysis to those far better qualified to engage in it than yourself. Dreaming up fantasies may be fit work for an Edge, but it has no place in military planning. We do *not* make key tactical decisions based on the word of a cadet who was too afraid to take decisive action in battle, let alone be sure of anything he'd heard. Is that clear?"

Why does it feel like they are all out to get me? Is this what it's always going to be like in the Corps? He looked to Zandrie for help, but she locked eyes with him and gave the slightest shake of her head. He was alone.

"Yes…sir."

Zavier felt like he had a million ingots of osmium pressing down on him. In moments, his perspective swung from righteous indignation to self-flagellation.

Isn't that what I heard? It seemed so real. But maybe I'm wrong… it wouldn't be the first time. This is just like you, Zavier. Delusional. Manic. What are you even doing here?

"Now that that's done," the General picked up, "we have some tactical analysis of our own to engage in. This debriefing is at an end. You are all dismissed."

The team saluted, turned heel, and exited quickly. Only when they were out in the plasteel corridor outside and the door hissed shut behind them did anyone feel relief.

"Slag! I blew it," Zavier swore. "I'm pretty certain I know what I heard, I just couldn't seem to convince them of it. Locking up in combat didn't help my case, either."

"You'll do better next time," Kojo told him. "We all will."

"I'm just surprised they didn't chew me out about turning my back to the enemy while I was working on Toby," Min said with a sigh. "That was rookie mistake number two."

"We all made mistakes," Toby stated. "We're still learning."

"Well, mine'll have me standing in place for the next hour," Min reminded them. "I'd better go report for that little duty now, before someone sees I'm not where I should be. See you all later."

"Bye, Min," the rest said together.

"And I have to get ready for a session with Dado. Later," Texas said as she turned to leave in a hurry.

"Hey, Texas." Toby gently grabbed by her shoulder. "On the way back up, Kojo told me what…happened. I'm sorry. If there's anything you need to talk about—"

"I'm good," she replied sharply as she brushed him off. Then, sighing, she added, "Thanks, Toby. I'll be okay. 'Texas Tough' and all that. Catch ya'll at dinner time."

"And I've got some articles on tactics and world politics to catch up on," Kojo said, as he too started to follow Texas away. "Zavier, don't worry. The General's probably right, but I'm going to do some quick reading up on what might really be going on in the world in the way of Ripper attacks, just in case. Catch you later."

Zavier sighed. "I suppose."

"Which leaves me to hit the gym for a quick workout before working on some new designs," Toby decided. "Hey, Z, you want to work out with me? Great stress reducer, get some of this stuff off your mind for a bit."

"Naw, I know your idea of a quick workout, and it's my idea of bench-pressing an elephant. I might join you later."

"Anytime you need me, *hermano*. Later."

Zavier watched his friend retreat down the hall. Then, with no particular destination in mind, he started to take a step in the other direction when he heard someone address him.

"Zavier, my boy."

He turned and was a little surprised to see who had now stepped out of the room. "Dr. Dado? What are you doing here—I mean…Listen, I'm really sorry about the trouble I caused."

Dr. Oliveira dismissed the concern with a kindly wave of one hand and a brief smile as he fell into step alongside Zavier, directing the youth with a hand lightly on his shoulder as they walked together. "I know you are committed to the Maker Corps. You try your best, and your best is very often exceptional. You are a very intelligent, creative person. All you lack is experience. You're no worse off than anyone else was at your age."

"I appreciate the support, but…I don't know. I know what I heard. At least I think I heard it. I just seem unable to get any of it across. It all just gets jumbled up and stuck in my head."

"Do you think you're the only young person who has trouble expressing himself? What you're experiencing is quite normal. That's sort of what the teen years are all about. And don't be so quick to dismiss your intuition. I've seen moments of brilliance from you. The commanders should have given you more time to make your case. I certainly would have."

"It's so frustrating," Zavier admitted, his head dropping as he spoke. "*Everything's* frustrating—the chain of command that won't listen to me just because I'm too young; myself, because I'm always going lead-headed when it matters most. And then there's my sister…"

"I happen to know that Captain Vik believes in you. When you can't see it, she stands up for you."

"I know, but I keep letting her down."

"In what way? For trying to file a report on a suspected Ripper attack? For coming to the rescue of your teammates when you needed to? In your report, you mentioned identifying the type of craft they were scanning. Don't you think that detail will be of use to the higher powers?"

"Maybe."

"And who saved the rest of your team at the last minute?"

"Well, yeah, but that was only after nearly getting them killed in the first place from my inaction. I let down my team, I've let down my sister, and it's obvious that the GMC has no reason to trust me at all—and I can't blame them. As often as I've failed both them and myself, I could drag the Parisian in by his ear and *I'd* still doubt me."

"Zavier, you are being far too hard on yourself. Give yourself permission to make *progress* while you are still *imperfect*, even if others do not. Let me ask you this: You said that you'd managed to snap yourself out of your mental lockdown. How were you able to do that?"

"I…I used what you said about dialing it down," he admitted. "And it helped, it really did."

"*Bom trabalho!* Good job! You're working your way through your problems. That's progress. Do you see that?"

"I guess." They walked a few more steps before Zavier followed up with a shake of his head. "But by the time I work my way *all* the way through my problems, I'll have gotten my entire squad killed off. No, I…I'm a danger to my team. I'm not even sure I belong here."

"Zavier, please, do not berate yourself like this. Remember: focus on progress, not perfection. Being an Edge is about finding solutions. You have the power to find solutions to your own problems."

But Zavier just shook his head, nearly oblivious to the professor's presence and concerned look. "Maybe that's my *real* problem. I don't deserve to be an Edge. I probably shouldn't even be a Maker at all."

Before Dr. Dado could say a word more, Zavier quickened his pace and stormed off, leaving his mentor behind.

CHAPTER 10

Repairing human tissue is the most intricate print an Ozmium can perform. The variety of matter being printed, the ever-changing nature of the human body, and the potentially devastating consequences of a misprint require precision. It requires both a special mobile medical Ozmium, and the steady mind of a disciplined student of human physiology.

Global Maker Corp Medic Handbook

Zavier wandered around the station, thinking about what he and Dr. Dado had spoken about. His aimless steps took him into the Cadet Commons, where the conversations of a dozen different squads helped to drown out the noise in his mind.

The Commons was a large communal gathering area of couches and tables, with styles changed monthly by non-military Makers. Currently, one corner sported a set of furnishings inspired by Louie the XIV's ancient French styles. The ceiling rose up for three stories, covered with a moving display of designs reminiscent of shooting comets or expanding auroras. Here and there hung a vidcube displaying calls for one squad or another, updates to various class schedules, and other news of the Academy—even a few programs from Earth.

At the center was the largest vidcube Zavier had ever seen, nearly two stories tall. At first, it displayed a beautiful, colorful fountain, with so much detail and such perfect sound that Zavier could have sworn he felt droplets splash onto his skin. At other times, its display switched to images of happy and proud Makers serving around the world, beautiful scenery from exotic locations, and thrilling views of planets and stations around the solar system.

Younger cadets hurried along with their arms full of books. Older cadets relaxed in lounge chairs or around small tables eating gourmet—or nutritionally-boosted junk food—lunches printed to specification by the OzChef dispensers lining one entire wall. Alone or in groups, there was not a time of day when someone wasn't in the Commons. Including one stiff-legged Cadet Yu, nearing the last few minutes of her hour.

Zavier passed by a dozen conversations on his way over to Min, snatches of which he managed to catch.

"…I'm telling you, it's true. The officers on the other side of the facility are getting ready for an attack…"

"…supposed to be some big assault on Earth…"

"…Rippers are going to be attacking some place in Africa, so the Makers are going to head them off…"

"…wish they'd let us go…"

"…you're a senior cadet. You should be down there..."

"…no cadets allowed, not even senior…officers only…"

The Rippers really were going to attack someplace Earth-side. Zavier felt even more like a fool, and his depression deepened.

"They're doing it all wrong," came a big voice. "The Makers should just get it over with. Start using some *real* weapons instead of this kiddy stuff."

A side-glance showed Zavier that the remark came from a table where Team Overdrive had taken residence. He'd thought he'd recognized Dakota's voice.

"If they can have a cuff that deactivates an Oz device," Coover replied with a shrug, "why can't they make one that turns off a VacGuard or something? That'd bring the Rippers down *real* quick."

"Tactically speaking," Grandmaster spoke, "it would be far more expedient, and no doubt bring their movement to a rapid endgame."

"What do you think, Z? No response? Oh, that's right, you prefer to just sit in a corner and hide while all the real fighting is going on," Dakota said, followed by the laughs of Overdrive and other cadets within earshot.

Pretending not to hear, Zavier changed course, weaving around in a direction away from Overdrive's table. He didn't want to listen to anything else they had to say. Thankfully, he soon passed by a vidcube displaying some news program from Earth that was turned up loud, and he paused for a brief listen.

"...earthquake in North Chile that trapped dozens of people and wounded many more. Maker squads were sent out to assist with the relief. They were able to vac out the rubble to free those trapped, while Medics helped to quickly repair the injured. At last report, not one life was lost. The town's Maker-assisted reconstruction was on schedule to be completed by sundown, local time.

"In other news, Ripper forces attacked a military post near London three hours ago that left twenty dead, including three civilians that were there as part of a tour group. The fallout of the attack spilled into nearby civilian areas, causing peripheral damage, including damage to a popular three hundred-year-old pub. The patrons who were there at the time..."

The news was pretty typical, so he started meandering again. His steps soon brought him over to Min, who made no sign of looking at him or acknowledging his presence. She was stiff as a statue.

"Hey, Min. You still on the punishment detail? Sorry about that, it must be pretty boring."

She said nothing, but then Zavier noticed something else: a pair of tiny ear buds hidden deep in her ears. That got a brief flicker of a smile out of him.

"Don't worry," he promised, "I won't tell."

Still no response. He started walking away when a red light

started flashing on Min's wrist. Only then did she let out a breath and relax her stance as she popped the buds out of her ears. She put a hand on his shoulder to steady herself as she stretched her legs.

"Whew! One hour exactly," she sighed. "Of course, no one said I couldn't get a little something else done at the same time."

"Like play your music?"

"What? Oh, that was just to help me concentrate." Min fell into step as Zavier started making his way across the Commons. "I was using my textlens to interface with the design computer. Got an idea I need to try out immediately."

She broke into a brisk walk, which, out of habit, Zavier found himself keeping pace with as she set a course straight across the center of the Commons, muttering some technical half-phrases to herself that Zavier failed to catch. She led toward a large doorway, where an engraving in the wall high above their heads declared it as being the "Engineering Annex: Advanced-Class Cadets Only."

"…But to see if any of this is possible, I've got to do some quick hands-on testing. When I was standing around out there I saw the others drift in here as well. Toby tried making faces at me to get me to blink, but of course I never—there they are."

The Annex was similar to the Commons—but smaller, not as high, and a perimeter of large lab-booths surrounded the central area. Some of the labs had other teams at workbenches fleshing out one design or another, while some were empty. Min and Zavier headed for their squadmates' booth.

Texas was at one bench, working on one of the guns they'd seen the Rippers using, Toby seemed to be tinkering with a larger fold-shield, while Kojo was sitting off in a corner staring into his vidglasses and waving his arms around as he controlled what he was seeing.

"That Ripper had a pretty good idea with those miniature flash pellets," Texas muttered, half to herself as she worked on her latest blueprint. "Kept me from aiming straight, that's for sure. Near as I can figure, it just takes a little mercury fulminate and the right flash powder."

"Hey, Min," Toby called over, "finally off your statuette detail?"

"No time, move aside," she said, shoving her way past to one of the other workbenches. "Got an idea I gotta catch while it's fresh."

Toby stepped to one side as Min rushed past and quickly plugged into the bench and got started. He was turning back to his work when he glanced over at Zavier, who was hovering by the booth's open doorway. Toby was not the first to break the ensuing silence, however.

"Zavier," Texas snapped, "could you have *been* any more of a useless third arm at that debriefing?"

"Gotta admit, *hermano*," Toby agreed, "you could'a said the sun was shining and drawn as much disbelief."

"It's hard enough being a cadet and having to report something to the higher-ups," Texas continued, "but you sounded like some kid crying to mommy about a lost cookie."

Kojo even offered his opinion over his shoulder. "Presentation is everything. Gotta do it with the full military protocol thing, or they can't even see that you exist."

Zavier listened to their criticisms and found himself nodding in grim agreement, face flushing.

"You're right. All of you," he finally said. "Our first real fight in the field and I blew it. What's worse, I couldn't even get the point across to the General about what I heard. I'm a danger to the squad. I know it. And those are just a few of the many reasons why I don't belong in the Makers."

The silence that followed was deafening. Texas paused in her work and snapped her eyes to Zavier, Toby nearly dropped what he was working with, and Kojo's eye-screen flipped up as he suddenly stared at him in shock.

"What?!" they said at once.

Min was the only one without reaction, her back to it all as she worked furiously at her bench.

"You're all right," Zavier restated. "I don't belong in the Maker Corps. I let you down on so many levels. You'd all do much better without me."

"What? No, that's not what we meant at all," Texas said.

She immediately rushed over, pulling Zavier fully inside the lab booth, then thumbed the button to slide the partition door closed behind him. She looked up into his eyes. "Zavier, we weren't saying you shouldn't be a Maker."

"No, *compa*," Toby agreed as he came over and Kojo got up from his seat. "We're just trying to give you constructive feedback. Help you become the best Maker you can be."

"I'm not a Maker," Zavier said with a sad shake of his head. "Not even a good Edge."

"Not a good Edge?" Kojo said as he joined the circle. "Z, you're one of the best at the Academy."

"Nah, Coover's just as good as me. And Coover doesn't freeze," Zavier replied.

"Coover is too busy copying *your* designs to be a good Edge," Texas shot back. "So, you couldn't get the Brass to believe you—they can scare just about any cadet."

"Even you?"

Texas hesitated. Then she shrugged her shoulders as she replied, "Well, I'm from Texas, and the only people I might find scary are other Texans. Especially ones on the Arkansas Confederacy border. *Them* Texans is *real* scary."

"And, Toby," Zavier continued. "I saw you present yourself bolder than any of the rest of us. You faced up to your mistakes head-on, while all I could do was just…sound like a kid screaming for a cookie."

Toby immediately stepped over to grab his shoulder, looking him straight in the face. "*Hermano*, listen to me. That's not how Texas meant it and you know it. Whatever you're going through, we're here to help you through it. We're a team...even if we *haven't* picked a squad name yet."

"Every one of us has significant psychological challenges," Kojo told him. "That's what Dr. Dado was talking about in recruit orientation. We all have 'fluid' minds, which are great for creative thinking and reacting in the heat of battle, but they can be confusing and discouraging as well. The trick is to build upon the natural strengths of our minds while also creating boundaries so their associated weaknesses don't overwhelm us. That means learning from our mistakes. I got too analytical in that battle and it cost us, so now I'm working on a strategic playbook I can use as shortcuts for my brain."

"And I get too excited in a fight, which makes me predictable. So, I'm working on some crazy new weapons to mix things up." Texas added.

"I take things too personally when you guys are threatened, but that much emotion keeps me from doing my job," Toby said. "I've still got a few details to work out to get over that, but that's why I'm here. That's why *we're* here working as a *group*, so we can get ideas off one another."

"Which is why we need you, Z. Like my problem, for instance," Texas said, now pulling him over to her workbench. "I'm trying to reproduce those flying flash pellets of theirs, but I've run into a roadblock. Chemistry's not my best subject, so I can't figure out how to get them to work."

Zavier shrugged. "Just look up holiday fireworks."

"Huh?"

"Yeah. Goes back to the ancient Chinese. Just use some aerial fireworks with a very short fuse. There should be several formulas you can find, then compress the powder into a lot smaller capsule than you think you need. Use aluminum foil so it's easy to detonate, and there you go."

For a second, Texas looked at him with jaw agape, then broke into a broad smile. "Firecrackers, of course! I never would have thought of that. Thanks."

Texas was the one Zavier knew would never lie—in fact, she would tell the truth more bluntly than anyone—so he knew that any compliment she gave was always just as it appeared. He watched as she got quickly back to her work, but before he could back out of the room, he found Toby pulling him next over to his station.

"The Brass was right about my shield. Great for one or two people, but there was an entire line of us and I was a fool for thinking we could all simply hide behind it. I need to prep a better solution for situations like that. Got any ideas?"

"Well, I…I dunno, Toby. I'm just…I'm sure you'll think of something."

"I could do it a lot faster with that fluid brain of yours. C'mon… will you help me out?"

Zavier hesitated, unsure how he felt anymore. In the end, he just shrugged again.

"It's okay, bro. You just let me know when you can. I believe in you."

Kojo then pulled Zavier aside for a quieter conversation. "I meant what I said at the debriefing. I was otherwise occupied and did not hear what you heard, but I believe you because I *know* you— you never lie or exaggerate. Now, the word's all over the station that they're planning a big Maker attack against a Ripper base somewhere in the heart of Africa. But I happen to know a little about that area, and no outsider is going to survive there for long. Heck, they're still finding diseases in the deeper jungles that science doesn't even have names for yet. Command thinks that it's the perfect place to hide a base, but if so, then how did word even get out?"

"A…setup?"

"Exactly what I was thinking. For the last hour, while you were moping around the station, I've been trying to put together a good case to present to General Brigantine. Now, if you could tell me what *exactly* the Parisian said, that would be a great help. Can you remember?"

"I can only tell you what I heard myself. Most of the recording is a jumbled mess thanks to their jammers. But we can start with whatever's left of what my recorder *could* pick up. Unless…no… maybe there's a way to *unscramble* the recording?"

"It's something we could try, at least," Kojo replied.

Zavier pounded a hand to the side of his own head as he turned around once in self-anger, cussing to himself. "I gotta be a gas-head—I could've told that to the General! If we can unscramble the audio feed, then all the evidence I need would be right on that thing. Some Maker *I'm* gonna be."

"Easy there," Kojo said. "Remember that I forgot that as well. Now, where's your helmet?"

"In my Oz," he said with a tap of a finger to his right wrist.

"Which means that by default, any data it recorded will be there as well. We just have to reconstruct your helmet then tap into the data feed."

"It's a start. But let's experiment and make sure it works, first. I don't need another embarrassing chewing out in case we're wrong."

"Now that's thinking like a Maker. You…*are* staying around to be one, right?"

Zavier hesitated before replying with the best answer he had at the time. "I'll…let you know how it comes out."

"That's all I can ask. Send me the blueprint for your helmet after the encounter."

"Sending."

Kojo gave him a smile, then raised a finger to his brow to flip his vidglasses back into place.

Zavier looked up to see Min at her table, a schematic displayed in a popup vidcube before her. Some cables ran between her VacGuard and her Oz as lines of text scrolled down the face of another vidcube.

"She looks pretty excited," Kojo observed.

"Yeah…more so than usual."

Zavier walked over to join her. Kojo came up to her other side as the young Medic nearly jumped off the floor.

"I think I did it. Here, look at this."

She didn't even wait to see if she had their attention as she pressed something on her Oz, at which point a display popped up in a third vidcube—a very detailed schematic of a female human body. It took only a moment for the other two to see what else it looked like.

"Min, that's you," Zavier realized.

"Right down to my white blood cells," she beamed. "Every last atom of my body. At this moment."

"You mean it's realtime? But how?" Kojo asked. "From the cables you've got spread out, it looks like you're doing something with…your VacGuard?"

"The cables are for safety reasons; I'm not doing this wireless," she quickly explained. "What I've done is hack into my VacGuard to get access to the body-map that it creates to protect the object—or me, in this case. Rather than using an outdated map created in the past, I can see atom by atom what a person's body *should* look like…say, just prior to being wounded in a fight. This will allow me to provide medical treatment a *lot* more effectively. Faster too. I can hook my Oz directly up to it and let it create the tissue directly without having to take time out to cross-reference with my medical scans."

"Wait, you *hacked* a VacGuard?" Zavier exclaimed. "Isn't that dangerous?"

"Oh, extremely," she admitted. "That's why you should *never* do this unless you're a Medic like myself using a medical version of an Oz. Hacking a VacGuard disables it while the connection is open. This cable going from my Oz to my VacGuard? That's the way I'm doing it. Direct wired hack from one device to another only."

Her enthusiasm suspended for a moment as she turned around to look them both in the eye with as serious an expression as she could manage. "I can't stress this enough, this is *not* something to be done by anyone but a Medic. The risk is just too great. If your map confuses a limb for a laceration…"

"Then you bring new meaning to the nickname, 'Hopalong Cassidy'," Texas joked.

"Exactly," Min replied. "You could remove parts of someone's body that shouldn't be removed. Or worse."

"What's worse than that?" Toby asked.

"Give them a part of something that doesn't belong there," she replied, causing the squad to recoil in disgust.

"Then why do it?" Zavier asked.

"Because, as great as the danger is, the benefits are equal. This could save precious minutes in the field. What I did down in Alice Springs to fix up Toby? As many minutes as that took me, it would have taken me a couple seconds to have him back up on his feet with this method. Now, imagine even worse injuries, one where the person might bleed out before I could get to him in time. Or a situation where the injury might be considered too much."

"Like," Zavier mused, half to himself as his thoughts wandered to his sister, "if a building were to crush your leg."

"Perfect example," Min said, then turned back around to her work. "The possibilities are positively *fluid!* I've still got some fine-tuning to do, but now that I know what to do, the basic concept is not too difficult."

In the space of a breath, Min was back to her work, muttering medical details to herself and once again ignorant of the two now stepping away from her. Zavier didn't know what to think of this development and looked at Kojo, but he just looked back with his own uncertainty. In the end, neither said a word as they stepped away to the other end of the booth.

"So, what have you decided? You still with us?" Kojo asked after a moment.

"What can I say?" Zavier said with a shrug. "We got Min the budding mad scientist, trigger-happy Texas, a Shield who can't make a big enough shield…Looks like you guys need me. Guess I'm staying for now."

Kojo replied with a smile, then drew his friend over to a free workbench.

"Great, then you can help me go through some of this stuff. We'll start with what your helmet recorded."

"Just gimme a second to connect my Oz up to the bench," Zavier began. "Then the data should—"

A sudden lurch and the distant roar of thunder interrupted him, tossing everyone nearly off their feet. A rocking sensation followed, along with more explosive sounds.

"What the shatter was *that?!*" Kojo exclaimed.

"Just a guess," Texas said, picking herself back up, "but it sure felt like that attack Z warned us about."

Another explosion rocked them. Even Min found it distracting enough to quickly unplug her Oz from the bench and hurry along with the others out from the lab-booth into the confusion beyond.

CHAPTER 11

Ozmiums are designed to operate via verbal macro command only. This is to avoid costly and embarrassing errors that would be likely to occur if accidental thought-commands were given.

Because of this, makers are encouraged to assign unusual verbal macros to blueprints to confuse the enemy and not give them an anticipatory advantage in combat.

Your New OzTech and You, Global Maker Corps Edition

The Commons was in chaos.

Zavier and his squad came out of the lab to see emergency notices flashing across nearly every vidcube, the rest filled with scrolling lists of damage reports, combat conditions, and various emergency notices. The younger cadets were running in panic trying to find a place to hide, while the older ones were clustered around the remaining vidcubes, trying to find out what was going on. Additionally, there was an audio announcement blaring out across the room.

"Repeat: The station is under attack. All cadets report to their emergency locations. Do not engage the enemy. Let the Makers do their job."

The cries of hundreds of voices filled the Commons, as all the cadets around them began speaking at once. Only a few voices rose above the bedlam enough for Zavier and his friends to make out.

"The Rippers are attacking!"

"...officer side of the station."

"...hitting the power core..."

"No…the main dock."

"…straight to the Academy!"

"I want go home! …don't wanna be a Maker…"

Zavier stared at all the confusion, listening to the multitude of voices as the station rocked with yet another detonation. For a moment, he was someplace else. *Explosions outside an apartment, the sounds of ripping, his parents—*

"Hey!" he yelled, as Texas elbowed him in the side.

"Not now, Z," she snapped. "We got a crisis here."

"Yeah…right," he replied, returning her smile. "Thanks."

Kojo was first to take the lead, running over to a free vidcube off in a corner by a food dispenser as the rest hurried after him.

>>**Koj**>>**I can't access the military channel. Let's see what's going on.**<<

Another jolt, and suddenly the lights flickered and the floor was a foot further away than it should have been. Zavier found himself pedaling on air for a few seconds before the floor suddenly slammed up into his knees on his way back down.

"Ouch," Min called out.

"Everyone okay?" Toby asked as they all hurried back up to their feet.

"Peachy," Texas said impatiently. "Now, let's find out what the shatter is going on here."

They reached the terminal after another lurch of the floor. Kojo pressed a palm to the side of the vidcube as he called out a command. "Exterior view; source of the attack."

The message appeared promptly: *Access restricted.*

"They've cut us off," Min realized.

"Probably to keep us little kiddies from panicking," Texas snorted. "As if the flickering lights and sketchy gravity aren't doing that already."

"I can try hacking in," Kojo said thoughtfully, "but that

would take some time."

"Wait," Zavier said, stepping up. "I've got an idea."

He placed a palm to the vidcube as Kojo withdrew his. Then, Zavier gave a command of his own. "Maintenance subsystem, damage control. Visual display."

Immediately, the vidcube's display cleared, replaced with a view of the outside.

"Same cameras, different subsystem," Zavier explained.

The vidcube showed a wide-angle view of the outside as seen from the station's command tower. This maintenance view of the damaged areas happened to also show what was *doing* the damage. A swarm of ships was making passes at the station, shooting out focused beams of energy or missiles from their undersides. Opposing them were the sleeker vessels of the GMC in defense. Just beyond the initial swarm, a couple of large transports hovered in wait, the first of them approaching what was left of the main dock.

"There must be fifty of those things," Toby gasped.

"I recognize them," Zavier realized. "It's the ship we saw the Rippers scanning at the junkyard."

"But modified," Kojo said. "I see about three guns each and a missile launcher. Pretty crudely mashed together, but effective."

"But the station ships are newer," Min said hopefully. "So they should fend them off, right?"

"Too many," Texas responded with a shake of her head. "Looks like the station only had ten vessels ready for defense."

"*Ten?*" Toby repeated. "Who's idea was *that?*"

"We're a police force, gas-for-brains," Texas snapped. "Not a military force."

"Speaking as a Shield," Toby countered, "it still sounds lacking."

They saw a group of the Ripper vessels make another attack run at a point lower down the station's axis, followed immediately by the lights in the Commons going out again, as well as the gravity.

The vidcube paused too, holding within it a still-frame of the battle just as the new explosion went off.

"Main power section," Kojo explained as they started to drift off the ground. "The repair systems should start automatically printing a new generator, but until then, we're on backup."

"Those other ships," Zavier said, his gaze still fixed on the image hovering within the vidcube. "Those must be the transports we heard the Parisian say they'd scanned."

"Looks like they're using them as drop ships," Kojo added. "We'll be up to our ears in Rippers soon."

"Well, I'm not just going to float around while someone takes down my home," Toby stated, pointing out his right arm. "Oz: Hover-bike with sidecar."

The large chamber was still in total blackness, only the sound of scattered cadets calling out giving any sort of idea of who was where. So, while Toby was printing his bike, Zavier printed something else.

"Oz: Mighty torch."

Into his hand appeared what amounted to a compact lamp on a long metal stick, the cylindrical portion on top bright enough to illuminate the area for fifteen meters around them and cast dim recognition on the area beyond. This was soon joined by similar sources of light scattered across the Commons.

Min laughed. "'Mighty torch'?"

"You name your macros what you want. I'll name mine what I want," Zavier replied, then stuck his tongue out.

Toby's bike finished printing and hovered beside him. "I got room for one on back and a couple in the sidecar," he said. "Hop on."

"Squad 'Sidecar.' I like it," Kojo quipped. "Let's get moving."

Texas climbed on back behind Toby, Min and Kojo got quickly into the sidecar, and Zavier…he ended up printing a hover-board and flying alongside, holding his torch aloft like a wizard in some ancient dungeon.

As Kojo climbed into the sidecar, he printed something larger than his normal vidglasses. It was a crude, small metal box that fit over both eyes, held in place by a stiff metal band that wrapped around that side of his head.

"Looks like you have bug-eyes," Min said.

"It's a set of miniature vidcubes with direct uplinks and computer access," he replied. "Allows me to see where we're going a lot easier."

They flew across the Commons, Toby steering them around panicked cadets while Kojo acted as navigator. They could see some of the older cadets working at printing their own devices, from weapons to small vehicles such as their own, though Toby's hover-bike was the first to go sailing through the open archway leading out into the halls beyond. From where he flew alongside on his hover-board, Zavier called out a question.

"Where we headed?"

"The action," Toby replied. "Kojo, where would that be?"

Toby turned a sharp corner, narrowly avoiding a group of younger cadets who hadn't yet printed any lighting of their own, while Kojo consulted the display hovering before his eyes. "Looks like the attacks are focused on the Maker ring."

"The adults get *all* the fun," Texas scoffed.

"We take the main shaft, then," Toby said, making another sharp corridor turn. "But won't the lifts—"

Suddenly, there was light—and gravity. Both Toby's and Zavier's vehicles were set for zero-G, so both plunged to the floor as the extra weight kicked in. Before either could compensate, the bottom of Toby's bike scraped along the floor. Sparks flew briefly before the hover-coils shorted out from the friction and the vehicles skidded to a halt. Zavier hit the ground, then flipped completely over and landed into another cadet running in from an adjoining room.

"Hilla. Funny crashing into you here," he said.

"Get *off* me, you lead-head! I have a fight to get to."

Zavier moved off as quickly as he could. As Hilla leaped to her feet, Toby shot out a question. "The battle's up in the Maker officers' section. Your team joining?"

"Team Overdrive would not miss this no matter *what* Command says. I was just getting a few updates loaded into my Oz before joining them."

"Need a lift, then?" Toby offered.

Hilla took one look at the wreck Toby and the others were currently climbing out of and sneered. "I'd like to get there alive, thank you."

With that, Hilla ran on down the hall to join the distant sounds of combat and screaming cadets.

"Well," Texas said, "bless her heart."

"Never mind her," Kojo ordered. "We need to get rolling again."

Once again, the lights flickered, but while they remained on this time, the gravity did not. Their feet started to leave the floor as Toby started vac'ing up the remains of his hover-bike and sidecar.

"I've got transportation this time," Zavier said, aiming his wrist out before them. "Oz: Tunnel rat."

The squad soon found themselves climbing into a very unusual variation of a jeep. It had 360-degree wheels for the ground, but more sets of ball-shaped wheels projected around the jeep from the ends of adjustable suspension arms. They contracted and expanded to maintain continual friction with the walls and ceiling.

"Fluid build!" Toby said as they all quickly swam their way in. "Good for keeping a steady ride with or without gravity, as well as mowing down everyone in our way. Think we can catch up to Team Overdrive and give them a bump?"

"It's not perfect," Zavier admitted as he climbed in behind the wheel, "but it'll get us there. Just strap in."

Zavier thrust his torch into a cup-holder then hit the acceleration pedal. The strange twelve-wheeled vehicle trundled down the hall, the pressure of the extra wheels against the walls keeping it in place against the whims of gravity or lack thereof. Kojo rode in the seat beside him, while the others huddled in the back seat. Zavier honked the horn as he went, its echo perhaps adding to the confusion of the situation, but at least giving due warning to anyone else that something spanning the width of the hall was coming at them.

Cadets dove out of the way, and when the station rocked once again, the modified jeep remained stable. The gravity snapped back on and it did not crash. They did, however, receive a new passenger falling down from above—a cadet who'd been floating around the ceiling. He landed right onto Toby's shoulders.

"Uh, sorry, sir," the boy quickly stated. He couldn't have been more than ten. "Cadet Hafeez."

"Nice to meet you, Hafeez. Would you mind getting off me?"

"Turn coming up ahead," Kojo said to Zavier. "Can this thing take a sharp right?"

"About to find out," Zavier replied. "Everyone hang on!"

They came to an intersection of corridors. The left-side wall-wheels hit air, and narrowly avoided some quick-footed cadets as Zavier made the turn. That also happened to be when Cadet Hafeez was crawling off Toby's back in the rear of the vehicle. The young lad tumbled off, rolling into another Cadet.

"I'm okay!" they heard from behind them.

"Lift-shaft up ahead," Kojo directed. "We'll have to change up vehicles to—uh oh."

The lift-shaft was there, but missing one vital component. A lift. Or, for that matter, an active light indicating up or down. There was nothing but a dark open shaft.

"No power to the lift," Kojo announced.

"Must have gotten taken out in the attack," Min called up. "We'll have to find another way."

"Not today," Zavier said as he reached for a lever. "There's a reason why I've got wheels all over this thing. Buckle up!"

The lever produced yet another set of wheels popping out from the front and back just as they shot into the shaft. The side wheels popped out farther to grab hold of the walls, while the front and back wheels tilted them up along the facing wall of the shaft. The team now found themselves driving *up* the elevator shaft.

Min looked a little scared, Toby was uncertain, Kojo was too occupied with his vid-display to notice much of anything, and Texas…she was beaming.

"Now *this* is the way to ride!"

"One level up then out," Kojo directed. "This elevator doesn't go all the way to the top ring."

"Can you tell me which side the exit's on?" Zavier asked.

"You'll have to spin around clockwise ninety degrees."

A quick turn of the wheel rotated the jeep as they climbed, and they soon came out onto the floor of another level, right into the middle of a firefight. Two Rippers were holding off some advanced-class cadets with stun rifles, while the cadets fought back with a rifle that shot out high-velocity hockey pucks, another that had already half-blinded one Ripper with red paint, and a third that had apparently constructed a quick barricade of large lead Lego blocks for the others to take cover behind.

Zavier slammed his hand down on the horn. The blast of sound—not to mention the presence of a mutant jeep climbing up out of a lift shaft—caught the Rippers completely off guard. They jumped, spun around, and then dove to the ground just as a hockey puck beaned one of them in the back of the head.

Zavier stopped the jeep a foot away from them. Toby shot to his feet with a pistol aimed at the other Ripper while everyone else leaped out. The pistol covered the Ripper's face in a coating of tar and knocked him to the ground.

"Toby, vac the jeep," Zavier called out as he jumped out and onto the chest of the unconscious Ripper who'd been hit by the puck. "I'll cuff the Rippers."

Before Zavier could print a set of cuffs, however, the unconscious Ripper turned out to not be so unconscious after all. Zavier found himself tossed to the ground as the man surged to his feet, pulling his companion up with him. It wasn't until Zavier hit the floor that he noticed both Rippers had on helmets with visors and body armor. The one blinded by tar simply discarded his helmet as they shoved their way past the other cadets and ran down a branching hallway.

The cadets fired off a last round of hockey pucks at their backs before the Rippers turned out of sight.

"Where we at?" Zavier asked as he leaped back up to his feet.

The answer came from one of the three cadets who had tried barricading themselves against the Rippers. The cadet was bleeding from one ear, his friends equally battered up. "They've got Rippers coming out of all the lift-shafts up to the main GMC levels. Power's coming and going, as well as the gravity."

"So we've noticed," Toby said as he joined them, the jeep now gone.

A quick look at the emblems on their shoulders showed the cadets to be a year behind Zavier's team. That was all Kojo needed to see to take charge. "The worst of the fighting should be in the main shaft up to the Command Level. That should be just ahead, outside the Arena. Follow us in. Keep close and watch your heads."

The Cadets immediately obeyed, vac'ing their barrier and other debris as they came along behind the team with Toby now leading the way. By the time they came to the main lobby just outside the Arena, he had a shield printed that folded out nearly to the width of the corridor.

"*This* time I've got a shield to cover all of us," he declared.

"Yeah," Texas countered, "but there's no way to shoot around it, lead-head."

"No problem. Oz: Mod current shield, pot-shot." And with that, the mega shield altered to create small openings.

"Better," Texas said, as she cracked off a few shots. "What would you do without me?"

"Enjoy the quiet?"

The lobby was a large area, with one wall lined with a dozen lift-shafts across from the Arena entrance itself, which sported a single fifteen-meter-long entry partition that was currently slid aside. Rippers held the elevators while cadets held the Arena.

The Rippers were firing off stun-guns and goo-guns, and a dozen cadets were already on the ground, either unconscious or stuck to the wall or floor in an ultra-sticky mess. Twenty more held their ground by the Arena doors. The Rippers had a line of objects that looked like yellow old-time traffic cones spaced in a line before them as defense, but any time anything came near them, they deflected away as if they had hit something. Kojo was already examining the cones by way of his vidcube eyes.

One of the cadets fired off a stream of heavy-duty foam bullets, only to see them ricochet right back at her the second they tried passing over the cones. Another launched out a foam grenade that ended up hitting a different cadet in the head, covering him in a mountain of bubbles. The Rippers, meanwhile, seemed to have no trouble hitting their targets.

Toby charged out into the open, his large shield looking like a glimmer of approaching distortion. Texas leaped out to one side, her burp-gun once again in hand as she took aim.

>>**Koj**>>**Those are repulse cones. Anything you shoot at them**

will reflect out with the same force.<<

Min saw the incapacitated cadets around the Arena entrance and started making her way over, a med-scanner already in hand. The three other cadets they had led in followed along behind her, while Zavier pictured that dial in his head as he surveyed the situation.

Toby roared as he charged into the Rippers, his cry nearly drowned out by the pulse of the burp-gun in a contained space. The sonic pulse, however, came right back at Texas along with the mass of sticky strings.

"Baby burped all over me," Texas remarked as she picked herself back up.

"The cones," they heard someone shout. "Aim for the cones!"

It was a voice that Zavier immediately recognized. "Zandrie?"

A quick glance showed his sister in the middle of the crowd of cadets, gesturing in the direction of the cones.

Toby nearly reached the Rippers, but then felt the push of gravity working against him and started to slide back across the floor. Only his determination and physical strength kept him going, if very slowly.

"Koj," Zavier said to his friend, "any ideas about the repulse cones?"

"From what I can tell, it's a pretty up-to-date model," he said as he examined his displays. "But it has the same weakness as all the rest. It doesn't cover the bottom eight centimeters, just above the base of the cone."

"That's a pretty narrow gap," Zavier said thoughtfully. "Now what do I have that can—"

>>**Zandrie**>>**This is Captain Vik in command. Shields: put barricades up. Medics: we've got some cuts and bruises back in the Arena. All: stop shooting at the Rippers.** <<

>>**Min**>>**On it.**<<

131

>>Koj>>**There's an eight-centimeter gap at the base of the cones.**<<

>>Zandrie>>**That's our target. Zavier, you've got a good angle. Think you and your Blade could come up with something?**<<

It was only a second before a grin began to cross Zavier's face.

>>Z>>**My fave toy as a kid.**<<

"Oz: Super-duper drencher."

"You're kidding," Texas remarked beside him. "Right?"

She'd just finished ripping the worst of the sticky strings off herself when she found Zavier thrusting a very large water gun into her hands.

"You're a better shot. Just aim for the base of one of those things and knock it over so Toby can get through. And…uh…I modded it to make it a bit more powerful than you remember it."

"You're *not* kidding."

Toby, meanwhile, was still trying to advance, powering ahead a slow step at a time as another gravity field worked against him. Stun rounds were bouncing off his shield, which was already covered in a blinding coating of goo. Texas wasted no time and dropped to the ground, left cheek touching the floor as she lined up her shot.

"Right about…there."

She pulled the trigger, and quickly had to brace herself to avoid being pushed across the floor as a jet of water rocketed out from the gun.

Just as it slammed into the base of the cone, the station's gravity once again shifted. The stream of water started to arc upward. With a lack of gravity to hold her down, Texas found herself plunging back with equal force, her body crashing into Zavier's legs to spin him up into the air.

Toby also began to tread air while the force from the cones immediately slammed him back across the room and nearly into Zandrie.

The Rippers, meanwhile, did not budge an inch. Their boots continued to hold fast to the ground.

>>**Z**>>**They've got mag-boots!**<<

As Toby came at her, Zandrie braced one foot against a waist-high plastic barrier one of the other cadets had just erected and slammed an open palm right into Toby's backside just before he would have hit. The impact shot Toby out toward the ceiling, where he pushed off using his feet.

Texas wedged herself into a corner wall and braced herself using all the strength she had in her legs. She began to line up to take another shot.

>>**Koj**>>**Dead center base and you might short it out.**<<

She pulled the trigger, and like a missile the stream of water hit dead-center of the repulse cone's base and the cone tumbled out of the way just as Toby shot past overhead with his shield still in hand.

That's when the gravity turned back on.

A grinning Toby came crashing down onto one of the Rippers, his shield slamming the man to the ground. With the breech made, the other cadets wasted no time. A barrage of bizarre projectiles from sand bullets to bottle rockets and gigantic peas to caramel bombs made it through the opening in the gravity shield. Someone even tossed in a flash grenade.

The only one the flash grenade seemed to blind, however, was Toby. The Rippers each had helmets with their visors down. Nonetheless, as the other Rippers ducked for cover, Toby leaped back up to his feet, blindly thrashing around with his shield until he knocked a couple other repulse cones out of the way.

One of the Rippers shouted out a command to the others. "Just got the word! Go!"

"All of it for all of us!" the other Rippers shouted.

Under the continuing barrage, the Rippers—some pulling

their wounded behind them—dove into the lift-shafts, just as the gravity turned back on again. The fact that the shaft's power light was off and the interior was pitch black did not seem to deter them. Each jumped in and ran straight up the interior wall of the shaft.

Zavier hurried to his feet alongside Texas, who was both admiring and scanning the water rifle in her hands.

"Not as good as my burp-gun, but not bad. I think I'll call it Esther…or Edna. Yeah, Edna."

The last Ripper Zavier saw dive into the shafts wore a Manchester United logo on the back of her armor-vest. "Zandrie," he called across the room, "those are the same ones I saw back in the junkyard!"

"Don't lose them," she shouted back. "You, cadets over there, secure the Arena. Cadet Solomon, your team with me. There's only room for one team in those shafts, and I want to bring those guys in."

Toby led the charge into the shafts. They were gravity shafts, the direction of force indicated by an arrow on one side, which currently was flickering along with the lights. As such, Toby chose to use the emergency handholds running along the shaft, just in case. Behind him came Zandrie, Kojo, then Zavier, and Texas last. Min stayed with the other cadets, still tending to wounds.

It was a long climb up, but Toby's choice of using the handholds proved wise, as the power flicked off three times before they reached the top. The top, though, was not what Zavier expected to see. There was nothing of the Rippers, nor much of anything else for that matter.

The lift-shaft ended in a flat plain of metal capped by a large, recently created transparent dome. Where the rest of the shaft and the Maker Command sections should have been was little more than open space, tangled lengths of twisted metal, and floating debris. Here and there was a semi-intact section still attached by

134

another lift-shaft or support strut, but there was little in the way of working structures.

With stunned eyes, Zavier regarded the debris and looked for signs of lingering combat around some of the intact sections.

"It's gone," he whispered. "The command section is…gone."

Zavier's mental dial was at a twelve.

CHAPTER 12

The beautiful headquarters of the Global Maker Corps are located in low orbit around the earth. This was a strategic choice made by Global Nations Alliance to allow Makers to be quickly dispatched to member Micros in need.

The orbital facility is equally divided between the administrative wing, the Maker Corps living quarters, and the Maker Corp Academy.

Maker Corps Academy, New Cadet Orientation

When they came back into the Arena, Zandrie took immediate command. A growing crowd of cadets began to gather around her as she stood atop the platform Zavier had printed for her.

"We're using this Arena as a base," she began. "First thing we need is communications. Zavier, I need your team to find the main communications center. We need that restored immediately."

"You heard her," Kojo said. "We're Team Comm now."

"Tell everyone you see to *not* make their way to the command section," she continued to all listening. "It's dust right now. We still have plenty of Rippers around, and it looks like we're the only ones to fight them."

"Where's LTG Brigantine?" someone shouted out.

"What's going on?" said another.

"Cadets, calm down," Zandrie said, raising her hands. "Zavier, get going with the comms."

"Right away, Captain," he replied.

As Zavier and his team were hurrying away, they nearly bumped into one very welcome figure making his way through, with a crowd of children following behind him.

"Dr. Dado! You're still alive."

"I am indeed, Zavier, my boy," he replied. "I gathered up these other cadets and see now that your sister made the same wise choice as I did. The Arena is the perfect place for everybody."

"Dado, can you help us? We can't find—"

"I'm just the head of academics. Zandrie is doing quite well with the military matters. Now, go get those communications back up. And *boa sorte*."

"Right." Zavier chased after the others, pausing briefly when he saw Min tending some wounded. "Min, you coming?"

"I have wounded to help," she replied. "You go. Stay fluid!"

From the looks of it, she had quite a few wounded to fix—children bruised and bleeding, some limping in with broken limbs—so Zavier left her to her work. He caught up to his squad as they left through a different exit, where some cadets were already rigging up stone walls and sling-shots as defenses.

"Min's staying with the wounded," he announced to the others. "Where we off to?"

"As I recall, Communications is a level down and roughly underneath the location of the Commons," Kojo supplied.

"As you recall?" Texas asked.

"I memorized the blueprints for this place a while ago." Kojo shrugged. "Now, shall we go?"

They rushed down the hall through an area with missing sections of wall and exposed power lines sparking madly, then continued swiftly around a corner and straight into a firefight between a squad of four Rippers and some cadets. Zavier saw stun rounds versus badminton rackets, a Frisbee-shooter, and toy jacks tumbling underfoot.

"I don't have time for this," Texas said, not even slowing down as she called out. "Oz: Baby!"

She pulled the trigger and a roar like a lion slammed down the hall, burying one Ripper in a suffocating mass of sticky strings while lifting him off his feet and hurling him away. Kojo launched a set of bolos from his reconstituted micro-crossbow, and a stream of thumb-sized beanbags ripped out from Toby's latest weapons at an unreal velocity.

Toby grinned. "Now *this* is what I call rapid fire."

Much to Toby's joy, the stream of miniature beanbags caught one Ripper across the chest, tumbled another to the floor to join the one covered in sticky strings, and hit another a bit lower in the gut than would be comfortable for anyone.

"Sorry about that," Toby called out to the Ripper who curled up in pain. Looking at his squad, he mouthed the words, "Not sorry."

Amid the distraction, another cadet lifted a rifle with a wide mouth and a foot-long tub for an ammo magazine and fired off another stream of wooden Frisbees for the remaining Ripper. Toby charged right past them, leaping into the lift-shaft just beyond them.

"Go to the Arena," Kojo called to the cadets as he passed them. "Quickly!"

"Oz: Endless bouncer," Zavier said as they ran.

The cadets replied by taking off in the direction the team had come from. Texas covered their escape with another blast from her burp-gun, this time at close to point-blank range, as Kojo went next into the lift-shaft. Zavier made sure he was last as he paused at the shaft and brought out the small black rubber ball he had just finished printing.

"Have fun with the endless bouncer," he said with a grin. Then he tossed the ball at the Rippers and ducked into the shaft.

The ball bounced once off the floor, hit one Ripper just as he was getting to his feet with minimal effect, then bounced again and again, seeming to *gain* energy with each bounce. As Zavier climbed down the shaft with the others, he could hear the cries of the Rippers as they dove for cover.

>>Texas>>**What'd you give them?**<<

>>Z>>**One of my endless bouncers. Modified hyperkinetic rubber.**<<

He accompanied the message with a video loop showing a small rubber ball bouncing faster and faster each time it hit a wall, until it was nearly a blur.

They quickly climbed down the shaft a level and out into another rundown corridor. Doors marked with security labels flanked either side of the long hall.

"Communications should be at the end of this ridiculously long hallway," Kojo told the others.

"In that case," Zavier announced, "it's hover-boards for everyone."

The four of them went tearing down the hall, each on a sleek board that floated fifteen centimeters off the ground. Ahead of them was a heavy-looking door labeled "Communications." Toby simply pointed his Oz at it and seconds later they were inside.

Communications was a nest of controls, display panels, read-outs, and vidcubes. Toby rubbed his forehead. "Anyone know how any of this stuff works?"

"Z, you and me," Kojo directed. "Hurry."

"Toby and me will guard the door," Texas told him.

While Zavier and Kojo went about delving into the guts of the mess before them, Texas vac'ed her gun in favor of a different weapon. This one had three different barrels, each alongside of each other. She gave it a quick kiss before taking her place to one side of the door.

"There you go, Big Mouth."

"Do you always name your guns?" Toby asked.

"Only the good ones."

Down the hall they heard running feet, then caught sight of two burly men wearing rooster designs on their chests. Toby immediately squatted low to fire out his beanbag mini-repeater, while Texas aimed high.

"Time to see what this thing can do on the 'max' setting," Toby said.

A high-velocity stream of the miniature beanbags shot out, forming a solid line across the front man's feet. From Texas' rifle there came a blast from all three barrels at once that filled the hall with what looked like tiny little rocks spraying everywhere at once. The Rippers tried covering themselves with their hands and quickly printed shields, but the debris deflected off the walls to their sides and behind the shields. Of course, worrying about what Texas shot out meant they'd momentarily forgotten about Toby's rounds.

"Rock salt," Texas explained. "A fun variation on what my granddaddy used to use to keep people off his land. Don't really harm you, but it sure does hurt."

"And 'Big Mouth'?" Toby asked.

"Named it after a cousin of mine that talked a lot and had a habit of spitting when he talked."

While the Rippers were outside stumbling around, then running away before another dusting of rock salt could rain down on them, Zavier helped Kojo with some quick and dirty rewiring. Kojo plugged in one of his devices for some reprogramming.

"Rerouting to auxiliary circuit…now," Kojo said.

"Last rewiring complete," Zavier announced as he pulled his head out from inside the equipment. "Comms should be back up."

"Excellent."

Kojo pressed an icon engraved into the side of one of the vidcubes and was rewarded with a quick systems check, followed by the word, "Complete" and the Academy logo.

"We're up and running," he announced.

"Then let's test it out." Zavier swiveled over to another vidcube and touched an icon on its side, calling out a command.

"Connect to Captain Zandrie Vik." Once the prompt appeared, he called into the cube, "Sis, can you hear me?"

The response came both in her voice and face appearing projected within the cube, the view as if from one of the Arena's wall cameras.

"You got Comms back up?"

"All yours."

"Good, then get back here while I call everyone together."

"On our way."

"That's it, then," Kojo stated. "We're out of here. Good work, Z."

Kojo wrapped up his equipment then hurried back to the door with Zavier, where Texas and Toby were giving one last sweep of the corridor.

"Where'd your party-friends go?" Zavier asked.

"They couldn't shake it Texas-style. Go figure."

"Okay, Team Comm, we're vacating," Kojo announced. "Hover-boards all the way."

"Gimme a second," Zavier said. "I'm leaving something behind in case anyone has some ideas."

A quick printing later and the four were off, leaving behind a large metal mat laying just inside the door, with wires hooked up to a battery positioned around the corner and out of reach.

"I also wired the door frame just in case," Zavier added with a smile.

They shot up the lift-shaft on their boards, riding the walls. At the top, Zavier stopped them with a hand. The small rubber ball was still bouncing, now flashing back and forth, up and down, while in a far corner three Rippers lay huddled facing into the wall, trying to cover themselves. A fourth was stretched out on the floor, unconscious.

"So, how do you stop that thing?" Toby asked.

"I've got a magnet buried inside it," Zavier answered. "Oz: Bounce-be-gone."

A large metal plate printed into his hand, which Zavier immediately slid out across the floor. Nearly instantly, the next bounce brought the ball unerringly flat onto the metal plate, where it stopped dead as the plate slid across the floor, landing just behind the cowering Rippers.

"Quick. The battery's only good for about thirty seconds. After that, if they happen to kick it…"

"Yeah, we're outta here," Toby said. "Behind me."

As they ran down the halls back to the Arena, Zandrie's voice came calling out through the facility speakers.

"Attention, all cadets. This is Captain Zandrie Vik. We are under attack by the Rippers. Maker Corps command is down, so it's up to us. All cadets are to make their way to the Arena. Cadets under twelve must take refuge in the Arena for their protection. All others: engage the enemy.

"Remember, everyone *is to equip their Oz and QuantVac devices. If you can't make it to the Arena, then find a secure place and fortify it. Whatever you do, though, do not—repeat do* not*—go to the Command Levels or Maker Ring. They no longer exist. Again, this is Captain Zandrie Vik. Stay fluid!"*

They came running back into the Arena a short time later, where Zandrie had everything surprisingly well-organized. The younger cadets were all clustered at the middle of the Arena, where Dr. Dado was calming them with his words. Around them sat a ring of defense the children themselves had conjured up—a circle of metal shields fixed into the floor surrounded by a circle of grease, then another circle of shields. The older ones amongst them were at the inner perimeter, armed with what appeared to be paintball guns.

To one side of this was another defensive ring—a triage headed by Min and a few other Medic cadets. As each cadet would get healed, they would print up a weapon and join one of the other groups. Ringed around the upper seating level of the Arena were some of the older children, each armed as he or she saw fit. For the rest of it, there were squads of older cadets grouped in their teams, spaced around at every entry.

At the center of it all, Zandrie stood atop a small tower, ringed around with transparent shields and a couple of vidcubes someone had rigged with hoverpads. Some older cadets stood guard around the base.

"Zandrie," Zavier called out, breaking ranks with his squad to go running over to the tower.

She spared a glance down, then cut into his textlens.

>>**Zandrie**>>**We've got Rippers coming in straight for us. I only have partial video feeds, but it looks like the Port entrance.**<<

From the accompanying icons displayed below the message, he knew that the others on his team had got the message as well. He replied with a standard "thumbs-up" icon before racing off across the Arena with his team.

The first shots came in before they were halfway there. Gas grenades assaulted the cadets, billowing clouds of noxious fumes that filled the Arena. Cadets coughed and collapsed to their knees, trying not to vomit. The Rippers walked through this greenish haze, each of them wearing a gas mask. There were twenty of them, all armed, and at their center were three that Zavier recognized.

The Viking, Manchester United—and, between them, the Parisian.

"All of it!" the Parisian shouted.

"For all of us!" the others replied.

To the Parisian's gestures and no doubt textlens commands, the Rippers started as one to fan out. Those on the sides took aim with their rifle-sized grenade launchers for the upper balconies before the cadets there could do anything. More clouds of gas started to roll off the upper walkways, sending the cadets to their knees coughing and choking. Some Medics frantically began printing and distributing gas masks as quickly as they could, while Min and others tried to siphon the noxious air immediate to them and reprint it into something breathable.

"Cadets," Zandrie called out, "fire at will!"

As the cadets began to cut loose, Zavier saw the Parisian pointing a hand in the direction of Zandrie's short tower.

"*No!*" Zavier exclaimed. "Oz—no, cancel that. They have armor and helmets. I need something that can get around that, and quickly."

"Then that's your job," Kojo said from off to one side. "Mine is to guide the team and make sure we've got the starks to survive this battle. Find us a solution."

"But suppose I can't this time," Zavier objected. "Suppose I—"

"You *won't* freeze up and you *will* find us a solution," Kojo firmly stated. "That's not an order, that's a statement of fact, Z. So, get going. But remember, we probably have limited cache access right now, so vac what you can along the way."

"Yes…*sir*," Zavier replied, with an almost mocking nod of his head and a glint in his eyes.

Kojo replied with a quick smile, then flipped his vidglasses down and began to survey the battlefield.

As Zavier started puzzling over how to most effectively take on the Rippers, the Arena exploded in war…not war as regular troops might know it, but war nonetheless. The cadets on the main floor shot a stream of greased ball bearings to the feet of the nearest Rippers. This was accompanied by a rain of hail arcing down over their heads. At the other side of the breached entry, a squad was printing one extremely overpowered wind machine that stood ten meters tall. When they turned it on, the bulk of the gas cloud began swiftly blowing back into the Rippers…not to mention a few of the nearer Rippers themselves, spoiling the aim of a few more.

The Viking, though, was taking aim at Zandrie's tower. A bullet glanced off the side of the ring of transparent shields surrounding her, to which she replied by printing something like an oversized t-shirt cannon and raising it up over the lip of her shields.

It wasn't a t-shirt that slammed into the Viking, but a tightly-wound skein of metallic yarn a meter across. It flew with enough velocity to kick the Viking back into another Ripper.

The Rippers spreading out let loose with stun rounds that dropped cadets on the spot, and low-yield sonic pulses that knocked them off their feet. One inventive female cadet responded with some kind of bazooka married with an ancient kid's toy which shot out just one thing: a concentrated blast of air. She started aiming for whatever physical objects the Rippers were firing through the air to blow them back.

Another cadet in the upper seats above suddenly called down a challenge. "Snowball fight!"

Cadets lifted a hodgepodge of freshly-printed guns. The result was a barrage of high-speed snowballs—and occasionally mudballs—coming at the Rippers from just about every angle. A couple of the muddy snowballs hit some Rippers in the face, knocking their gas masks aside just enough for them to get a good whiff of their own lingering poison.

Toby was charging full speed into the middle of the Rippers with just a single shield in his hands and hovskates on his feet. He made for a bulky rolling target headed on a collision course.

"Toby," Zavier called out, "no!"

"No, what?" came a voice from behind him.

"Huh?"

Zavier spun around to see Toby grinning behind him and did

a double take to also see something that looked like Toby rolling straight into the middle of the Rippers.

"Not a bad facsimile," Toby said. "Don't you think?"

"Wait…a decoy?"

Toby said nothing as his plastic copy exploded into a spray of tar, covering the Rippers.

"Oh," Zavier remarked.

Toby grinned. "Your turn."

The explosion of tar inspired an idea from another Cadet, who shot a miniature missile through their ranks that weaved around like a smart bomb until it found its target: the Viking, who was getting back up to his feet. The missile detonated with an explosion of confetti that covered the already tar-soaked victims.

Including an angry-looking Parisian.

"He never looked better," Zavier said. "Now, what to do…"

While Toby printed a quick wall to shield himself and Zavier, Kojo chose that moment to break into the team's textlens feed.

>>**Koj**>>**I've managed to hack together a tactical map. While a lot are here, there's still Rippers all over the place.**<<

>>**Zandrie**>>**Pockets of cadets are holding their ground, but we need something more.**<<

Then, on a separate private channel, Zandrie's next message came in for Zavier alone.

>>**Zandrie**>>**Z, you stuck again?**<<

>>**Z**>>**Not this time, sis. Just looking for a weakness.**<<

"Toby, let me run something by you," he said out loud as the battle raged around them. "Those Rippers have on some pretty good armor—helmets with flash-visors, and from what we saw, they're wearing mag-boots. Right?"

"Yeah, they came in ready for just about anything."

Another missile shot by over their heads, this one ending in an aerial detonation of powder above the Rippers. Moments later, some of them began furiously itching.

"They knew they'd be hitting the generators, so they knew the gravity would be out," Zavier continued thoughtfully. "And the lights—"

"Yeah, they dove into that dark lift-shaft like it was nothing."

"Those visors must be night-goggles as well—lets them see infrared." Zavier flicked his wrist to bring up a vidcube with a swirling blueprint, then tapped frantically on some settings.

"Heat vision, yeah, great. But what about a weakness?" Toby asked.

Zavier smiled as he tapped the vidcube two more times, then smashed it back down into his Oz. "You'll see. I just loaded a new blueprint. Oz: Flare gun: modified superbright infrared ammo."

As his new gun was printing, Toby said, "But we hit them with bright lights. Those visors protect them."

"From *visible* light, but those things also allow them to see heat sources to get around in the dark. Infrared. You can't have infrared suppressors on that and still get around."

The instant the gun fell into his hand, Zavier raised it up, took aim, and fired. A round like a miniature tin can shot out, impacting into the wall right above the Rippers where it detonated. Nearly everyone saw a dim red glow expanding across the air enveloping that entire section, but all the Rippers—who were equipped to actually *see* in that part of the spectrum—dropped to their knees, grabbing at their faces and screaming out variations of: "I'm blind!"

"Last I checked," Zavier said, "you can't vac what you can't see."

"Z, I'm glad you're on our side."

>>**Zandrie**>>**Z, details!**<<

>>**Z**>>**The visors that protect them against visible light flashes also allow them to see IR. Sending you the blueprint now.**<<

>>**Zandrie**>>**IR flares, got it.**<<

A second later, Zandrie's voice was echoing all throughout the station.

"Attention, all cadets. Use the infrared flash round blueprint I just sent to your Oz. Use it to blind the attackers. Repeat, use these IR flash rounds."

The Rippers who had been charging into the Arena suddenly did not know which way to run. Blinded, they could not see what they were about to trip over or what was coming at them. Some of them started shooting at random, mostly hitting nothing, but on occasion hitting one another.

"Stop that, you fools," the Parisian hissed. "Retreat! We can't fight blind."

"Sir, where are you?"

"I can't see."

"I think I can start to see—whoa!"

One Ripper crashed into several others with an audible *thud*.

>>**Koj**>>**Tactical update: Rippers are scrambling. The blind are trying to lead the blind out of here.**<<

Texas ran up to Zavier and Toby, the latter bearing a zealous smile as he kept firing his beanbag gun on Rippers. She added injury to insult by pulling off several shots of her three-barreled rock salt shooter.

"That was so fluid with the IR flash! Whose idea?"

"Who do you think?" Toby answered her. "Our brilliant Edge."

"Well, it's working over at the other entrance as well," Texas told them. "There's IR flash rounds going off all over the place."

"All they have to do is take off their helmets," Zavier shrugged. "Of course, at that point they'll be vulnerable to normal flash rounds."

"Gotta love it. Z, today I make you an honorary Texan."

"New York not good enough for you?" he replied, but chuckled. That was the highest of praise from Texas.

Amid cries of pain and confusion, a small army of underage cadets laughed and cheered as they pushed the Rippers back to their ships.

CHAPTER 13

> *While the Ozmium device may be used to print any known object of any composition, it cannot provide independent life. Therefore, it is essential that field Medics make clean and precise cellular prints attached to living flesh, to ensure that organic repairs are properly accepted by the host body.*
>
> Global Maker Corps Medic Handbook

From somewhere came the sound of an explosion, gunfire, and screams. People yelling, people running, people…getting hurt. It was horrifying. Min wanted to help people and save lives, yes. But what she hadn't realized before was that saving people— especially in war—meant putting herself in the middle of where so many people were in agony.

Min tensed her shoulders as another sharp report of sound came to her ears, another cry of pain. It was a young voice, which meant another cadet wounded. She paused only briefly then resumed her work on the current patient while the other Medics observed. She was sitting in the middle of the circle of Medics while working on the leg of a female cadet laying on the ground.

"You have to be careful with it," she resumed. "Hacking the VacGuard under any circumstance is dangerous, but as you can see, I can print directly into the wound using the VacGuard's body map and do so a lot faster. There, you're done."

She gave the cadet's leg a pat then turned to the other Medics while the cadet got back up to her feet. "Not too hard once you get the trick of it."

"Amazing," another Medic said with a shake of his head.

"Whatever made you think of this?"

"I had a lot of time just standing around. I'm always trying to think of something new to help heal. Now, are there any urgent questions? Because we have more wounded coming in."

The response was a small chorus of muttered remarks and congratulatory statements, after which the other Medics broke away to tend to the fresh batch of wounded limping in for their help. Min watched at first to see that the others were hooking up their medical Ozes with the given patient's VacGuard before she was satisfied that they had done it correctly. Only then did she glance around for the next patient.

"A brilliant job, cadet."

The one who approached her was not a new patient, but Dr. Dado. Min was about to shoot to her feet and salute, but Dado waved her down and squatted down before her.

"Oh my, but it's getting harder to get down every time," he wheezed. "I need to keep in practice before my body remembers how old it really is. I wanted to congratulate you on discovering such a brilliant technique. How ever did you come by it?"

"Like I told the others, I was just standing around. My punishment earlier gave me time to think."

"Perhaps we should assign you more such punishments, to give you the opportunity to come up with something else? Oh, don't worry, I won't. I just wanted to say 'well done' then leave you to your work."

"Thank you, Professor Dado. It…means a lot."

"Good. Now, if these legs will cooperate…"

As he started pushing himself back up, Min jumped to her feet and offered him a hand, which he lightly waved off.

"Almost got it," he said as he briefly struggled. "Got to keep those muscles moving…There, got it." He stood fully up, a smile of success crossing his face, then offered out a hand to Min. "Keep up the good work, Cadet Yu. I'll let you get back to it while I see to some of the younger cadets."

"Thanks again, Dr. Dado."

As she watched him leave, she realized that his brief visit *had* meant a lot. She was calmer now.

Suddenly she flinched at the next sound of distant weapons fire. The sight of a male cadet limping over toward her with his right hand holding onto his wounded left shoulder, though, snapped her out of it. She was all business once again, bringing out the cable to run between her Oz and his VacGuard as she sat him down on the floor.

"We're pushing them back," the cadet started to ramble, "but I can't believe what's happening. You know? You read about battles but to actually *be* in one…war is horrible."

"I *have* been watching. Now, hold still while I work. What's your name, Cadet?"

"Oh, uh, Cadet Ocampo."

She only half-listened to his response; the question had been mainly to keep his mind distracted while she worked at repairing his shoulder. "Hold very still."

She whispered a few commands into her Oz, ran a finger through some options floating in the display above her wrist, then waited a couple of seconds.

"Is it true what they say? The entire Maker leadership is… gone? Hundreds of people…thousands. Just like that?"

Min kept her gaze strictly down on her Oz, not looking up lest she see the terror in the cadet's eyes and a reflection of her own within that.

"I'm not the one to ask that. And…done."

She unhooked the cable from his VacGuard and finally looked up with what she hoped was an honest smile on her face. The cadet flexed his shoulder a bit, then eased into a mixture of relief and amazement.

"*That* was fast. Doesn't it usually take longer?"

"New technique. Now, get going and stay fluid. I've got some other patients to get to."

"Yeah, sure. Thanks!"

He stood back up and left to rejoin the fight, not hearing the quiet statement Min murmured to herself. "Rejoin the fight just to get hurt again. Maybe next time, I won't be there in time…"

She sighed, then saw another patient approaching and greeted him with a confident smile that, considering how she felt inside, seemed like a dark lie.

Zavier was in the moment, for once not overthinking anything. Blinding the Rippers had given him a new perspective. The Rippers, the same ones who had killed Zoey, were now at his mercy. Finally, here was his chance to get back at them for all they had done, to make *them* feel what he'd felt that one night years ago.

He did take pleasure in watching Toby nearly body-tackle the Viking into a half-working lift-shaft, not to mention pulling off a few shots himself with some more of the IR rounds at nearly point-blank range. And yet, he forced down the temptation to do them any lasting harm. Neutralize them, wrap them up, and maybe break an arm if necessary, but he battled the urge to deliberately hurt them.

"Justice, not vengeance," he whispered to himself as they pushed the Rippers down the hallway. "I'm a peacekeeper. Not a…killer."

It was at that moment that he looked up and saw Texas with her three-barreled rock-salt gun. She was going at it as furiously as ever, but was it Zavier's imagination or was she…pulling back at the last instant? Aiming her shots slightly off-target? Just a little, not enough that anyone but her squadmates would notice. Like she was afraid to…but Texas wasn't afraid of anything, was she?

Suddenly, a Ripper came charging straight for Texas with a cricket bat in hand. He could see, which meant he had apparently avoided the IR flash guns so far. Texas hesitated for a split-second, but that was all it took. As Zavier raised his weapon, the cricket bat came around to the side of her head. At the same time, something shot into the Ripper's shoulder while Kojo's voice called out.

"Texas!"

The object Kojo had shot looked like a swarm of metal bees, but their cumulative effect was that of a continuous stun round, delivering numerous mild shocks to the man. They were potent enough to drop him to the ground and keep him there, twitching.

Zavier shot off another IR flare toward the back ranks of the Rippers, just to make sure there were no other seeing Rippers, then rushed through the confusion over to Texas. Kojo beat him there by seconds. Toby arrived next and immediately started printing a wall to seal off that section of corridor from the Rippers.

"Texas, are you alright?" Kojo asked.

"A little knock to the head, is all," she replied.

"Min can take care of that. I'm asking about why you hesitated."

Kojo was making a quick visual inspection of where she'd been hit, but Texas pushed him away. "I said I'm okay. I just…I'm okay."

She stood up on her own, and as she did, Zavier saw the large bruise around her ear where the cricket bat had hit her.

"You're seeing Min," he insisted.

"And who made you my commanding officer?" she snapped.

"You're seeing Min," Kojo echoed, "and I'm your squad leader saying this. You could have a concussion."

"What, *this*? In Texas we call that a love tap. I'm the squad's Blade and we still got Rippers to fight."

Kojo was still wearing his vidglasses and replied with a shake of his head. "Scanners have them retreating back to their ships. The battle's over, Texas. You've done your job, now get back to the Arena so Min can do *hers*."

Texas looked like she was going to object but Kojo looked determined, so she relented with a gruff snort and started into a fast march back in the direction of the Arena, muttering something about "cowgirl up" under her breath along the way.

Toby had finished his wall and now ran over to join the other two. "What happened with Texas?"

"Dunno," Zavier replied. "I saw her hesitate just a second, but it was enough."

"Might be getting tired." Toby shrugged. "We've been fighting for what seems like an hour or more."

"I can give it to you down to the second if you wish," Kojo put in. "I have the exact time the attack began and—"

"Not now, Koj," Zavier cut him off. "I think Toby's right. I'm exhausted, and I know I picked up a few bruises in the process. We should head back to the Arena."

"What about stragglers?" Toby asked.

"Koj?"

Kojo paused to take in the data flowing to him by way of his eyepiece, whispered a few commands, then answered. "Internal sensors are reading no unauthorized intruders, and the external cameras--or what's left of them—are showing those Ripper transports breaking away from the station. It looks like their fighter craft are only holding defensive positions now, guarding their escape."

"See?" Zavier said. "Now, let's get back. My sister's probably got everything all fluid by now."

Toby agreed with a nod and the three started walking back down the hall, soon to come out at the lobby area with the line of lift-shafts. Underage cadets stood guard by the shafts and around the Arena entrance as Zavier's squad headed across.

"That flash maneuver of yours was pure genius, Z," Toby said.

"I needed something quick." Zavier shrugged it off. "I don't think they'll be taken in twice by that trick. They'll have flash suppressors on their IR goggles next time."

"Think they're coming back?" Toby asked.

"It stands to reason that they would," Kojo replied. "They left their job incomplete, in that we're still around. As soon as they finish licking their wounds, we'll see them again."

Toby grinned and gave Zavier a hearty slap on the back. "Well, by then, our genius Edge here will have thought of something new to hit them with."

One squad of cadets was busy with vac'ing up the remains of the battle, while several others had stationed themselves at various points throughout the Arena. Things were secure enough now that they were vac'ing up the barricades around the cluster of younger cadets as Dr. Dado calmly reassured them that all was well. The Medics were busy with several patients—mostly bruises and cuts—including an impatient-looking Texas being given the okay by Min. Kojo led the way over to their other two squadmates.

"That trick of yours really works," Texas was saying to Min. "That's the fastest I've seen anything healed."

"This was a good field test, I suppose," Min replied. "I've showed it to the other Medics, and the downtime for wounded dropped remarkably. But we can do better. I'm always worried about what I *can't* heal."

Zavier took her by the hand. "You're doing great, Min. Without your help, we'd probably all be dead by now."

"Hey, Texas," Toby broke in as he approached. "Now that your scratch is done with, Kojo says they might be back. Want to start thinking up a few surprises for them?"

She grinned. "Already got some ideas going. What do you think of a rock-salt *landmine?*"

"Hold that thought, cadet." It was Zandrie, approaching in a rapid walk. She had climbed down from her tower and was now making her way across the Arena floor.

"Captain," Texas said, snapping to a salute.

"Yours is the last team to check in," Zandrie continued. "Three other squads are missing, including Team Overdrive. Have you seen any sign of them?"

"Not since this started," Zavier replied. "We were coming out of the Commons and bumped into Hilla, but that was it. She was on her way to join her team in the Command area after getting some supplies or something."

"The Command area. Then you would have been the last to see them," Zandrie stated. "No one's seen them this entire battle. For now, we'll have to assume the Rippers got them."

"No," Min gasped. "They can't be gone."

"Overdrive…dead," Zavier said, his head dropping. "They were a bunch of lead-heads at times, but…"

His words drifted off, and the others lowered their gazes as well for a moment of silence.

"Team Overdrive, Makers to the end. May their souls find the rest they've earned," Kojo said.

"Team Overdrive," the others repeated as one.

Zandrie let them have their moment of silence, then got straight to it. "Listen, from what I can confirm, Lieutenant General Brigantine is dead and the entire Maker Corps leadership is gone. Erased."

"*All* of it?!" Zavier said, eyes widening. "But there's got to be someone left. Maybe an officer Earth-side."

"There were officers in the mission to the Congo in Africa, yes," she replied. "But in terms of this orbital facility, at the moment it looks like I'm the ranking military officer."

"All of it gone," Zavier muttered. "I can't believe it."

"Zavier," Zandrie snapped, "I need you to focus. All of you. I need your squad to come with me to the Academy Admin section. Dr. Dado's going to meet us there as soon as he has the younger ones calmed down."

"Of course," Kojo replied. "But why us?"

"Because of the success of your tactics and the fact that it was your squad who first got wind of something down in Micro NorAustralia. We need your input. There'll be a couple other senior cadet teams there as well. Lift-shafts are unreliable, so we're taking the hall exit at the top of the Arena. Fortunately, Admin's only a level above this one. Let's go. All of you—you too, Min; you can leave the remaining healing to the other Medics."

Not bothering to wait for any response, she led them in a swift march across the Arena and to the nearest set of steps. Zavier knew these led up the stadium seats to the top balcony level. A message flashed across his eyes, a textlens from Zandrie.

>>**Zandrie**>>**Z, sorry about not taking your suspicions seriously.**<<

>>**Z**>>**It's okay. I wouldn't have believed me either.**<<

>>**Zandrie**>>**I'm believing you now.**<<

"The entire upper Maker Corps level was wiped out," Zandrie said out loud.

"Strategically, that would be the first thing they would hit," Kojo agreed.

"But they *only* took that section out. The strike was too surgical. Not so much as a hull rupture in the Academy sections."

"We certainly had enough power and gravity fluctuations," Texas stated.

"Only because those involved systems were physically located in Command section. Not one system in the Academy was touched, except for fallout fire in the corridors themselves, and that's all easily repairable."

They got up to the top row of seats and out into the upper corridor. Zandrie now led them to the Academy Admin section as she continued her explanation.

"The Roosters didn't even need to come in and take it to the corridors. They had enough firepower out there after blasting away the fleet to reduce the rest of the facility to starks. Even while they were pulling out a few minutes ago, they could have fired at us, but they didn't."

"Maybe they didn't want to get caught by any ships returning from Earth," Toby put in. "The minute communications went out, there'd be a small fleet of ships coming up here. They're probably on their way now."

"In the time it takes anyone to respond and get up here, the Rippers could have eliminated all the rest of us. No, this was all far too clean."

"Stated like that, I'll have to agree," Kojo said. "It was like sacrificing a piece in chess to gain a greater advantage. But, then… why?"

"The entire Maker Corps headquarters was destroyed, everyone in it killed or missing. And yet, out of the thousands of cadets within this facility, only a few dozen were killed or severely injured. They could have printed some *really* nasty weapons and been done with us all."

"You know," Zavier said, his face thoughtful, "now that you mention it, back in Alice Springs…I remember hearing the Parisian say something about not killing the cadets."

"Exactly," Zandrie replied. "I think they wanted to leave the MCA intact. Why, I have no idea, but that's part of what we have to discuss. That, and picking up the pieces."

Rippers, leaving them alive? The same Rippers who had killed Zoey? Zandrie's words swirled around Zavier's head, an incomprehensible contradiction he could not make sense of. He was still thinking of what any of it could mean as they approached the archway labeled "Maker Corps Academy Administration" and the doors slid open before them.

CHAPTER 14

An equivalent amount of matter density is required to print an object in its entirety. Thus, one could not use a QuantVac to siphon a cubic foot of liquid water and expect to be able to use that matter to print a cubic foot of solid gold, for they would lack the raw mass to do so. One must either first siphon an equivalent amount of starks or have enough starks stored in their quantum wallet or in the Quantum Bank to allow such printing.

Conversely, one could use a QuantVac to siphon a single cubic meter of a dense matter such as tungsten, and then use an Ozmium to print enough clean air to fill a giant warehouse.

Your New OzTech and You, Consumer Edition

Zavier and his squad found themselves in a conference room in the Admin section. A large oval table occupied the bulk of the room, with Zandrie and Dr. Dado seated at its head. Zavier had spent the last hour restating everything he had heard at Alice Springs, first to Zandrie and then to Dr. Dado once he'd joined them. Then he repeated the story to one of the vidcubes spaced around the table, as Earth officials at the other end sought to pull even a stark of additional information out of him to figure out what else the Parisian and his Rooster Rebellion might have planned.

During that time, others walked into the room, including all that remained of the Academy staff—teachers mostly, and a couple of administrators. They each took their seats at the conference table while Zavier and his squad remained standing around the sides, along with a couple other squads that had been called in as well. All eyes were fixed on a vidcube hung from the ceiling at one end of the long room, where the face of an Earth-side official spoke to all assembled.

"The Global Nations Alliance Council has discussed everything we have heard at this briefing and confirmed by remote satellite views the extent of the damage. First off, let me say that we will not be playing a blame-game here as to who should have done what or listened to who. We must focus on the challenge in front of us. Since the entire upper administration has been wiped out, Dr. Oliveira—"

"Dado, if you don't mind," he briefly interjected.

"As you wish. Dr. Dado, effective immediately, you are hereby given temporary command of all MCA operations."

"I will do what I can to keep things together. Speaking of which—"

"You have been authorized by the Quantum Bank to use all the ingots you require. Print every construction drone and shuttle you see fit to assist in the rebuilding effort.

"Now, regarding the Makers. We have confirmed the severe losses associated with the command side of the facility, and it is indeed a devastating blow."

"Very few up here survived," Dado confirmed. "Only Captain Vik here and three other instructors."

"Additionally," the official continued grimly, *"the force that had been sent to the Congo was met with strong resistance—a trap. Many of them also perished. It has been a dark day for the Maker Corps."*

"Sir," Zandrie broke in, "I have gone through the assignment lists, and there were some that were scattered around Earth-side on other missions at the time."

"And they have been notified of the emergency and are returning to you to assist with the reconstruction and defense. But even so, we have a severe shortage of Makers at present. Based on our estimates, there are approximately five times as many Rippers out there

than there are Makers to fight them. They could put us under any time they wished at this point. We desperately need new Makers and qualified commanders. As such, the Council has decided two things. First, Captain Vik, you are hereby promoted. Congratulations Major Zandrie Vik."

"Why…yes, I mean…thank you, sir," Zandrie replied.

"You have earned this for your valor and continually exceptional leadership. You may be 'ahead' of schedule, Major Vik, but we're confident you can fill the gap we need in this desperate time. Don't disappoint us."

"No, sir."

"Secondly, to fill the ranks with the personnel that we need to combat the Ripper threat, we have decided drastic measures, as necessary. After much deliberation and several dissenting votes, the majority of the council has decided that an interim Maker force must be formed. As such, all cadets aged sixteen and older are hereby promoted to full Makers. Pass my congratulations onto the new Makers."

"I…I will, sir."

"Any means that Maker officers have should be placed at their disposal. We need these young Makers, and we need them to step up the challenge, whether or not they are ready. Part of your responsibility, Major Vik, is to make sure that the council's action in this matter is shown to be a wise one."

Zandrie looked mildly stunned, though not entirely surprised by the emergency measures. But for Zavier and the other squads standing around the room, the news came as a shock. They were skipping one more year of preparation, which Zavier found simultaneously exciting and terrifying. Some jaws dropped, Min looked nervous at the news, while Texas straightened up proudly. Zavier was trying not to sweat.

>>**Toby**>>**It's official, Koj. You're the leader of a full Maker squad now.**<<

The message was accompanied by a video loop of crowds of people bowing in obeisance to a king.

>>**Texas**>>**This means we really gotta come up with a squad name now.**<<

>>**Toby**>>**The Makers-Who-Were-Cadets-Two-Minutes-Ago Squad?**<<

>>**Min**>>**Oh my...I'm a full Medic now!**<<

And if I ever freeze up again, Zavier thought to himself, *then I've got a* lot *more responsibility on my shoulders.*

"Major Vik, based on your familiarity with this young group, you will command this branch of the new interim Maker force."

"Yes, sir. But what about the other Makers coming up from Earth-side?"

"Those veteran Makers will be commanded by Major Damiano Arra of the Sicilian Democracy. He's going up from Earth-side along with the rest. You two will coordinate activities as needed until we can get this mess sorted out."

"Yes, sir," Zandrie replied. "And, sir, what about the Parisian? We need to hunt down the leader and bring him to justice. Is there any idea of where he went? Anyone track his departure?"

"Unfortunately, all of the Ripper attack craft and transports scattered, so unless you can tell us which one the Parisian stepped into before he left, we're out of luck. We aren't even sure where they came from in the first place. There were no signs on your scanner net?"

"No, sir, I would have heard," Zandrie replied. "I think I heard someone say something about a supply transport coming in on the grid a few minutes before, but that's it."

"Hmmm...curious. We'll work on that over on our end; right now, you've a lot of work to do. This is Chairman Pike, out."

The projection in the vidcube immediately vanished and, for a few seconds, there were still some faces left staring at it. So many changes, so much to process. Zandrie appeared to be in control of herself, but Zavier knew his sister quite well, and had no doubt that she was almost as shocked at the turn of events as he was. The difference was, Zandrie recovered a lot quicker.

Dr. Dado was the first to break the silence with a calm word. "Well, there is much to do. Major Vik, your first duty will be to see that the cadets are kept calm and organized while the station undergoes repairs."

"Right," Zandrie said, her face betraying the thoughts racing through her mind. She turned to one of the people seated at the conference table. "We'll need uniforms for our new Makers as well as living quarters…as soon as those are rebuilt."

She didn't wait for a response as she continued. "We'll need upgraded Oz units for them as well. Professor Dado, I know you have a lot to look after right now, but might I recommend some OzChefs set up in the Arena? We have a lot of hungry cadets up there. They could print their own food, but it's better for them to not use their personal allotment of ingots. Also, we need to verify the integrity of the Commons and other places within the Academy."

"Then that will be the first duty of your new Makers, Major," he replied. "I want inspection tours of all Academy facilities and reports as to any damage. I am sure that the crews on their way will be quite adept at finding and fixing things, but there's no reason why we can't help them out a little bit. I want to know as soon as we can which sections are safe, so we can get these cadets back to some semblance of normalcy."

"Yes, Professor. Maker Solomon…"

It took Kojo a second to realize Zandrie was addressing him by the title "Maker." "Uh, yes, Capt—I mean, Major?"

"I realize we both have a lot to get used to," Zandrie interjected, "but this is a critical time to stay fluid. I want you and the other new Maker squads to perform an initial damage assessment patrol and keep an eye open for any stray Rippers as well. If there's a rat hole any of them may be hiding in, I want it flushed."

"Yes, Major," Kojo said, bringing himself into full attention with a snap of his heels.

"I'll pass the news of the new promotion to all cadets and then get you assistance in finding living quarters," Zandrie announced. "With the Dr.'s agreement, this meeting is at an end."

Dr. Dado confirmed with a nod, and thus began the rush of everyone to their emergency duties.

A few hours later, Zavier stood before a large bay window lining one wall of an observation balcony. It was one of many nooks scattered along the halls of the Academy, each with a different view of Earth or the stars beyond, meant as places for cadets to relax or study between classes. The "glass" was actually a very thick reinforced layer of transparent titanium; when you were trying to protect yourself from both vacuum and micro-meteorites, that was the only type of glass to use.

While his mind wanted to continually replay moments of the Ripper attack, he found the view of frantic activity all about the orbital facility to be a mental anesthetic. Construction shuttles held positions all about the station, while OzBots by the hundreds went about everything from vac'ing up the debris from the attack to printing new segments for the base. Even as he watched, shafts, main struts, and entire sections of the station were growing like weeds in a time-lapse vidcube show, a thousand times faster than conventional construction would have been done a century earlier. Soon, it would be as if nothing had ever happened—no sign at all of the chaos and destruction, except for unusually quiet hallways.

Yet it *had* happened. Printing shiny metal and plastic didn't replace the lives the Rippers had taken. Thousands had died.

Thousands more had been wounded, and the horror of that battle would ever linger in Zavier's mind. It was as if the OzBots were trying to sweep it all under a rug and make it disappear—as if the lives lost were of no consequence—and that angered Zavier a little.

Above it all, a larger than normal shuttle hovered like a parent looking over its children. Behind it, a couple military tugs had towed a small asteroid into place.

Zavier stood and watched until the soft padding of a familiar tread came up behind him. He knew without looking that it was Min. She came up to stand next to him and said nothing for a couple of moments, just watching by his side. He was hyper-aware of her presence, and how her shoulder lightly brushed his. It felt electric. The logical part of Zavier's mind understood it to be nothing more than a chemical reaction in his body, yet her light touch still made him feel wonderful.

Does she feel the same way? he wondered.

"It's going up pretty fast," she finally stated.

"They're siphoning off the damaged sections and printing them back out the way they were before," he answered. "According to Koj, they're going on copies of the original blueprints."

"That…would be most efficient. I guess."

Zavier assumed Min was as preoccupied as he was—first with the wreck and ruin, and now with the rapidity with which it disappeared. His anger at the battle's erasure was quickly offset by the rush of endorphins he felt at Min's presence.

"Th…that larger shuttle over there," he pointed, trying not to show how gas-headed he suddenly felt around her. "That's where the architects and astrophysical engineers are directing everything. Koj managed to…hack into their feed and found they're going to be adding all sorts of new layers of shielding—not just around the military section, but the whole Academy. Also, a few gun emplacements."

"That's…good, I suppose. But what if they find…well… bodies? There must be bodies out there. So many…"

Zavier turned to look at her. Min looked like she was ready to crumble at the mere thought of what must be floating around out there, her gaze locked on the field of debris and what it might still be hiding. Thousands of thoughts had been crossing Zavier's mind as well, but seeing Min ready to tremble broke him out of his own contemplation. He slipped an arm around her shoulders and pulled her gently to his side.

"They won't vac them," he told her. "Most of them still have their VacGuards on, so they'll be easy to spot after the debris is cleaned up. Zandrie says Dado's going to check each body against the personnel list until he's verified every single casualty. After that they'll send the remains off to their families for burial."

"That's good, I suppose. They should at least have something to bury."

"Yeah. That doesn't always…happen."

"Oh, Z, I'm sorry. I didn't mean—"

"It's okay, nothing to apologize for. Only the Rippers need to pay."

They quieted again, looking out in silence at the miraculous reconstruction effort going on outside, when Min's eyes narrowed in on something.

"Z, they surely must have enough material from the wreckage to reconstruct the station, so why—"

"Why that big bad asteroid? After what happened, someone realized how much the defenses around here were lacking. From what Zandrie found out, the Council Earth-side has decided to quadruple the number of defense ships, as well as add in a whole bunch of defense drones. This place is going to be *seriously* military in a very short time. They need the extra matter to make it happen."

"Then the Rippers will just print themselves an even bigger fleet." Min sighed. "The destruction will get worse and worse and more people will die. It won't end."

"It will end when we track down the Parisian. Without him, the Rippers have no guidance. They'll scatter like ants. Don't worry, we're full Makers now. We have a chance to make a difference and help end this."

"Cycles never end, Z. They go round and round, pain without end. You can't ever end it…" Her voice trailed off.

Maybe she had a point, but before he could discuss it any further, a voice calling from behind them interrupted the conversation.

"Okay, nice view—but we have to keep patrolling, guys."

Zavier looked back to see Texas glaring at them from the middle of the hall, leaning her weight on one hip and looking impatient, and perhaps a little annoyed. That's when Zavier realized his arm was still around Min. He quickly broke away. "Oh, uh…right. Min was a little—I mean, let's go. I'm sure Toby and Koj have the Study secured by now. What's next, the Commons?"

He hurried out past Texas, his pace brisker than normal. He felt his cheeks growing flush as he jogged.

"Come on, you two," he called over a shoulder. "What's keeping you?"

The repair and reconstruction of the orbital facility was being completed in record time, as were the new ships bristling with guns—though with precious few Makers and pilots to man them. For the time being, at least, they would have to rely on the drones for protection.

Zandrie led the newly graduated squads up to one of the freshly constructed Maker levels. They came out of a row of lift-shafts to a large, circular room peppered with several exits all around its perimeter, each labeled with a letter of the alphabet from "A" to "J." The center of the room was currently empty except for some vidcubes hanging from the walls and ceiling, currently displaying nothing more than the Maker Corps logo.

The former cadets streamed in behind her as Zandrie gave a quick introductory speech.

"This is your new habitation ring, built especially for all you new grads. The veteran Makers are still working on their own area, but for now they are mostly busy with station defense anyway. You'll notice we haven't had time to redecorate, so I leave that up to you. The wings are marked out by simple alphabetical designations. We were going to list it by squad name, but apparently not everyone has chosen a name yet."

A couple snickers came from the other squads, while Kojo tried not to look guilty and muttered to himself. "We're still toying with a few new ones."

"You should have your wing assignments listed in your wrist-coms by now," Zandrie continued. "There, you will each find your new Oz devices, complete with all your old blueprints loaded up into them. Settle in quickly, because from now on, you're on call at a moment's notice—you're *Makers* now. If anyone ever needs me, my quarters are now in the 'C' section, along with any other Command personnel. Dismissed."

She spun around to look them over and everyone snapped to attention, saluting their new Major. For a second, she looked them over—those who had just been cadets, now forced to grow up a little bit faster. To most people there, it seemed like their Major was passing a critical eye over them, but Zavier knew better. She almost looked…*proud* of them.

Zandrie returned the salute, then spun away to head for the "C" section, leaving the rest to mill about and find their own ways.

The gathering broke up into their squads, each talking excitedly as they made their way across the room to their assigned sections.

"We're section 'D,'" Kojo said as he consulted his wrist-com.

"Let's hurry up and get there," Texas said, leading the way. "I feel naked without my Oz."

"They better not have messed up any of my medical programs," Min said, half to herself as she followed along with the rest. "I have some irreplaceable blueprints in them."

They made their way around the other squads, then down the hall labeled "D" along with a couple other squads, Kojo leading the way.

"Hey, I'm sorry I snapped at you back by the Arena after I hesitated," Texas said to Zavier as they walked, her voice quiet.

"Don't worry, I above all people understand," Zavier said with a slight smirk. "I freeze up all the time."

"I wasn't freezing, exactly. It's just that—well, back at Alice Springs…I'd never killed anyone before. I didn't want to make the same mistake if I could help it. It's not like I'm getting soft or anything."

"Don't worry, I won't tell anyone."

For a moment, Zavier thought he saw a look in her eyes that went a little deeper than mere appreciation, then it was gone.

"Look for room five," Kojo read off.

"What about the rest of us?" Toby asked. "Would that make us one through four?"

"No, it just says five," Kojo replied.

"One room for *all* of us?" Min asked. "Don't we get any privacy?"

"I would say yes," Toby remarked, "but this is usually about where Texas would give some comparison about how big her homeland is and how everyone there would have a gigantic room for themselves."

"Truth," she stated with a cocky smile

"I'm more interested in why Z not only hasn't voiced his own opinion on the matter, but why he's grinning like that," Toby continued. "Come on, Z, what do you know?"

"Come to think of it…" Texas began, shifting her gaze slowly in Zavier's direction.

They came to a stop before a single extra-wide door labeled "D-5," and waited with all eyes on Zavier while Kojo hovered his hand before the hand-scanner.

"Nothing, guys, really. It's just that having an older sister in the corps means I grew up knowing how to get the inside info on military life. Privacy won't be an issue. Trust me."

"We're about to find out," Kojo said. "This scanner should be keyed to the blueprint of our hands on file. Let's double check it. Pass your right palms before the scanner and wait for the green light to verify."

One by one, they each palmed the front of the scanner, and one by one, the light turned green before they passed inside. There, they discovered why Zavier had been grinning over their privacy concerns. It was a single room, about the size of a single-squad Commons room, around which were spaced six different door-ways. Each doorway had the printed name of a squad member, with the sixth one directly opposite the entrance labeled as "Lab."

"Each squad gets their own suite," Zavier explained, "which includes one Commons and one Lab room. From what I remember my sister telling me, there should be a fully equipped lab bench in there, along with unlimited vidcubes. The rest is up to us."

When Zavier walked into his room, he found nothing but an empty room with his upgraded Oz sitting in the middle of the floor on top of a neatly folded new uniform. He went over and quickly retrieved the Oz, then clamped it around his right forearm before scrolling through the directory hovering above his wrist. It was lighter and sleeker than the devices issued to cadets, and it seemed custom-fitted to the shape of his arm. The more responsive vidcube was a nice touch as well. He gave it a test print with a bag of potato chips.

Fast. Very Fast.

And tasty, he thought as he sampled the result.

"Everything looks like it's here. Well, I guess decorating is up to us, so with that in mind…"

After first swapping out his cadet uniform for the black suit and white triangle of an Edge in the Maker Corps, he went about redecorating with his new Oz. He scrolled through furniture blueprint options on a vidcube, then printed a bed and a table, after which he found the door that slid aside to his shower and personal sanitation closet. By the time he walked back into the communal section, Toby had already printed a couple couches and a small tub of popcorn atop an end-table, while Kojo was coming out of the Lab room.

They were all dressed in their new uniforms, colored triangles on their shoulders appropriate for their division within the Corps.

"Everything there checks out," Kojo absently stated. "How's everyone else?"

"Fluid, man." Toby grinned, taking a handful of popcorn and plopping himself down on a couch. He kicked his feet up on the end table. "Got my new uniform, room decked out, the latest and greatest in high-end Oz devices strapped to my arm, and I'm feeling just fluid."

Min came out of her room, still scrolling through her own Oz's menu, absently muttering to herself.

"All the subcellular routines look good, everyone's backup blueprints intact…" She barely noticed her surroundings as she sat down on the other couch, one hand reaching for some popcorn and jamming it into her mouth. "My new hacking routines check out and—Yuck! Cheese? How can anyone eat this stuff?!"

She nearly spat out what popcorn she'd eaten as she made a disgusted face. "It tastes like styrofoam and kibble."

"Squad name," Toby and Kojo both said.

"Whatever," Min continued. "Why would anyone want to do this to perfectly good popcorn?"

Texas was entering the room when she saw Min's little outburst and couldn't help but laugh. "I like the stuff, but I think I like Min's reaction even better," she said. "So, I got my room decorated."

"Lemme guess," Zavier ventured. "Three types of guns, a Texas flag, a portrait of Sam Houston, and a framing of your grandmother's chili recipe."

She grinned. "You missed the Texas-shaped bed."

"This is exciting," Toby stated. "We're really into it now. Full Makers and everything."

"Along with the responsibility that goes along with it, I might remind you," Kojo said as he sat down on the couch with Toby.

"Full Makers." Zavier sighed as he joined them. "You guys have no idea how long I've waited for this."

"We get to protect all the little folk now." Texas elected to simply lean against the top of the couch's back as she said this. "I hope I make my brother proud."

"Which one?" Toby asked. "You have a few, don't you?"

"Four that are still alive," she admitted. "The other one was in the Corps until a Ripper got him. He's the one I want to make proud."

"*Five* brothers? Man, Texas," Toby exclaimed. "No wonder you can take on anyone twice your size."

She grinned. "*Three* times if they aren't from Texas."

"Five brothers?" Kojo scoffed. "Try five sisters, plus two more brothers thrown in for good measure! If I had one more sibling we'd be our own Micro. Five brothers…"

The squad laughed, and Kojo continued, "I hope you're all settled in. I know we're all very excited about this, but don't forget the reason why we're here, why we got our promotions a year early. The *real* work begins now."

"He's right," Zavier agreed. "After what we've seen, we need to take down the Rippers…once and for all."

CHAPTER 15

>>Toby>>They're not in sight.<<

>>Texas>>Well, I certainly hear SOMETHING.<<

>>Koj>>Keep it together, people. There's five of us and only two of them.<<

Toby ducked behind the building and quickly siphoned off part of its wall. Then he printed a wider wall, involving heavy quantities of magnesium-carbide alloys, spikes on the outward-facing side, and a couple holes for guns. Texas immediately leaped behind his new barrier and pointed an odd, heavy-caliber rifle through one of the holes. She loaded in a large clip of grapefruits.

"I hear *something* coming, but I don't see anything," she remarked as she looked through the peephole.

>>Texas>>Koj, I need a target.<<

>>Z>>My ping-scanner says there's movement straight ahead of you.<<

>>Texas>>Still don't...Wait.<<

The sound had been increasing rapidly, and now that she looked again, she caught a faint glimmer through the peephole.

>>Texas>>Shimmer-suit, but it's going mighty fast. There's no way he's...Wait, can you put a shimmer-suit on a vehicle?<<

The quiet electric roar was nearly upon them. Suddenly,

an explosion of something white and powdery took space in front of them, thanks to a quickly-printed launcher from Zavier. The instant it hit, the substance clung to the vehicle as it shot off the ground for the wall. It was a hover-bike with the outline of a helmeted rider on it. Zavier could see a fat cannon mounted on the bike with a cable running from the weapon's back end into the rider's QuantVac on his left wrist.

Texas barely had time to pull the trigger on her spiderweb rifle when the bike's gun fired off, but not with any sort of projectile. Instead, there came a backward pulse of energy that reduced both the spiderweb projectile and a large swath of Toby's wall into a stream of particles that flew through the air and into the hovbike. Texas unexpectedly found herself squatting in front of a one-meter hole—with the bulk of her rifle's barrel missing as well—while the bike flew out overhead, dropping a couple cubes between her and Toby.

The cubes exploded in a flash that left the pair stunned and momentarily blinded. A second explosion of tar followed, immobilizing them completely.

Zavier stood across the alley, watching with Kojo and Min. The bike was still in the air when Kojo printed a handgun loaded with a dart and Zavier consulted his handheld ping-scanner.

"They're fast. We need to take the other down before it's too late," Kojo said as he took aim.

"Not picking up the second opponent," Zavier said. "No sign of—wait. Motion about fifty meters behind us. No, fifteen meters up. No, he's—"

A figure dropped right between them and whipped out a pair of pistols. The figure was dressed in a complete bodysuit, jets coming out through the heels, elbows, and back to direct it to a safe landing. Min had her octopus-gun in hand and fired, but the wrap-around rubber arms did little good before the figure got off a shot from the rifle it held. All three found themselves covered in thick tar…then a spray of brightly colored feathers.

A loud buzzer echoed across the Arena in which the training session had been taking place.

"Okay, take five," Major Vik's voice sighed. *"Delaine, tell them what they did wrong. Just watching gave me a headache."*

As the squad got to their feet to gather together in the alley between them, their two opponents removed their helmets for the debriefing. The biker was a man with short blue hair, while the one in the armored suit was a woman with black hair that tumbled out of the back of her helmet.

"So, before I vac you guys clean," the woman said tersely, "would you like to know what you did wrong?"

"Besides getting beaten by a Shield and a Medic?" Texas asked. "A Medic who rode a bike and got past a Shield *and* a Blade?"

"And what's with the vacgun?" Toby added. "Did you actually hook your QuantVac up to your bike? You took out the barrier I made!"

"That's your fault, Cadet Montero," Ranjit, the blue-haired man, said. Then, speaking loud enough to address everyone, he added, "Always print a VacGuard onto any object you don't want the enemy to steal from you. Better yet, add a VacGuard to every blueprint of every object larger than your head."

"I thought I was pretty cool coming up with those jump-boots," Zavier said, changing the subject. "But you got a whole *suit*, Delaine."

"That's *Captain* Macdonald until you ex-cadets get some of the green off your hides," the dark-haired lady snapped. "But yes, my little jumpsuit here was able to confuse your crude ping-scanner so I could land right in front of you in a single-bound. Very mobile, armored, and very much protected against having a rubber octopus wrap around my legs."

Min sighed. "So I discovered."

"You need some better weaponry, Maker Yu."

"I'm a Medic," she replied. "I heal, I don't hurt people."

"You're a *combat* Medic," Ranjit shot back, "which means that you do both or you risk losing a team member."

"Why a *shimmer-suit* on a *bike?*" Texas asked.

"Why not?"

"He's got you there, Texas." Toby laughed. "But, Ranjit—I mean, *Captain* Jha, where does a Medic learn how to ride a bike like that?"

"Growing up on the Gangetic plains of Uttar Pradesh."

"I *knew* it," Texas said. "That's like an Indian version of Texas."

"And *this* was the team your sister worked with?" Kojo whispered to Zavier.

"Two of them," Zavier replied. "Zandrie was the tough one."

"And since you grew up on her stories, Maker Vik," Delaine said, "then you should know better. You're no longer cadets, so stop thinking purely horizontally."

"Time to get vertical. Start using more suits and vehicles like we did," Ranjit added. "Anything that will get you above and behind your enemy, that will make you mobile as well as combative. As Makers, you should seek to avoid harming or killing others, but the Rippers have no such limitations.

"You need all the advantage that you can get. Remember: your new Oz devices can handle much bigger prints at much faster speeds. Stay fluid, but think *big* too. Once, we were hunting down a group of Rippers that were well entrenched in a bunker, when Vik thought it best to get together with our Edge and print a full-sized tank for our team to go charging through. Busted straight through their fortifications and got the job done."

"A *tank?!*" Kojo exclaimed.

"I remember my sister telling me that story while on leave one day," Zavier confirmed. "Nothing the Rippers had could dent it, and they didn't have the time to print anything strong enough."

"But that's regular army stuff," Kojo said.

"Not when the turret's loaded with stun grenades the size of my fist, it isn't," Zavier replied.

"Also, billions of BBs," Ranjit added, "but that's only because one of them was in armor. The point is, you're full Makers now and need to take it to the next level."

"Personally, I'm not sure if any of you are ready," Delaine stated bluntly. "Battle is chaos. We stay fluid. Can you? You're going to have to figure it out, *Makers*, or we're all slagged. Now, vac yourselves clean then take a break and see what new tricks you can come up with. Maker Yu, heal their bumps and bruises. Next round's in thirty minutes."

Ranjit vac'ed up his bike first, before stepping away with Delaine. As a last thought before leaving, he quickly vac'ed the tar and feathers off Min.

"Remember," he said as he vac'ed her clean, "the one advantage we have over you is experience. We have a decade's worth of experience using thousands of different blueprints. Unfortunately, the Rippers have that same advantage."

Once she was free, Min vac'ed Zavier and Kojo. As she stepped over to clean up Toby and Texas, Zavier pulled Kojo a little farther away to speak to him.

"When we have the time, I'd like your help with something."

"New device?"

"More like a new…technology. I think it could give us the edge we need in this war against those shattered Roosters, but I need your help."

"Our new suite's lab space will work," Kojo replied. "Later after dinner?"

"Perfect."

Min, meanwhile, was finishing up de-tarring Toby while muttering to herself. "*Combat* Medic, indeed. What kind of a healer *is* he? I save people's lives, or at least try to."

"Min," Texas said.

"If you want to hurt some people then find a Blade or a Shield. I just—"

"Min," Texas said a bit louder.

"—fix people up so they can go get themselves hurt again."

"*Min!*"

Min stopped what she was doing and looked up to see Texas glaring at her.

"What?"

"Sunshine, I realize how you feel," Texas said, with as kind a smile as she could manage, "but I really think you should pay more attention to what you're doing."

"Huh?"

That's when she noticed. She had not only vac'ed all the tar and feathers from Toby and Texas, but also the remains of the wall Toby had put up, what was left of Texas' gun, and part of the building behind them. Min immediately turned off her QuantVac with a sheepish look.

"Oh, sorry. Distracted, I guess."

"Okay, Team...er, Team 'Get Vertical,'" Kojo said. "Let's start doing as they advised and think bigger and think more...upward. Z, can you could duplicate that jump-suit design of theirs?"

"Not in under five minutes, I can't. I still have my jump-boots, though. Can jump about three meters or so in those things."

"Not as good as what I saw Delaine do in that suit, but it's something," Toby stated. "I'll take a pair."

"And me," Texas said. "Make mine a full *five* meters up."

"Now *there's* an idea," Kojo pondered. "Maybe if we *all* have a pair of those jump-boots, they won't be able to hit us. Not when we're constantly jumping all over the place, they can't."

"We'd need a quick-fire weapon to go with it," Toby added. "Something that will drop when we're at the top of our jump. I've got a few, but they're all heavy weapons that most of you couldn't carry, much less with the springs on those shoes."

"Weight would be limited," Zavier agreed. "But I think I have something. I was experimenting with a grapeshot pistol."

"What good would a gun that shoots grapes do?" Min asked.

"Grape*shot*," Zavier said as he popped up a small vidcube in his hand, displaying the weapon. "Old style cannon-shot from a few centuries back that shot small lead balls to scatter across the enemy. Great for tearing through things. I was working on a scaled-down version of that, but for the ammo I can load it up with a mix of paintballs, tear gas pellets, and fog grenades. That should cover about anything they might try. Good for only a single shot at a time, but it'll scatter across quite a wide swath."

"So, no matter how well they've covered themselves, we'll nail 'em," Texas said with an appreciative smile. "I *like* it."

"We'll try that, then," Kojo decided. "Jump-boots with grape-shot pistols. Z, share the pistol and ammo blueprints with the rest of us so we don't have to depend on you for reloads. That'll be good for an initial surprise, but I want backup weapons as well."

They spent another few minutes brainstorming before time was called and the next round of intensive training began.

This round they did better, tripping up Ranjit once…but they still lost.

After a couple more such sessions, including a battle involving two other newly promoted squads against Delaine, Ranjit, and Zandrie—which they lost—all the new Maker squads were invited to attend a briefing.

The first couple rows of seats were filled with a small group of older Makers who had come up from Earth-side. The newly promoted cadets sat behind them. Dr. Dado sat off to the sidelines, listening, but let those of military rank take control of the presentation. Zavier and his squad sat three rows up, in the center.

Zandrie was presenting, along with a black-haired, olive-skinned man in his late twenties: Major Arra, the new commander of the veteran Maker forces. As Zandrie began, the vidcube on the wall reshaped itself into a map of the world, complete with elevation projections for mountains and blue-colored depressions for the seas. Borders outlined each country, and the land was covered with a series of red dots.

"These red dots represent sites where the Parisian has been spotted personally leading a Ripper attack," Zandrie said. "As you can see, there's a greater density of them in the old European areas of the world than elsewhere. We've run some predictive algorithms and have narrowed their base of operations down to the central section of Paris."

"Given that the man comes from there, we believe he might be hiding in the old Paris underground," Major Arra picked up. "Those sewers are plenty big and centuries old. As you can see from the lines…"

On the vidcube, lines began to appear from the scattered points across the world to France.

"…the density of his personal appearances goes off geometrically with distance. A coordinated strike in the region of Paris should flush him out."

Major Arra then started going over the details of the assault plan, but Zavier heard little of it. His mind flew wildly across the map and dots, his eyes drawing entirely different lines. While the Majors were concerning themselves with drawing each dot to one common point, he saw a different pattern: most of the attacks fell within different *clusters.* A cluster around Sweden that looked to center around Stockholm, a cluster around the Mediterranean countries that seemed to center on Naples, another set of clusters in North America that seemed to be centered around Brazil and Toronto.

Clusters, Zavier thought to himself. *Like someone was using a central base inside each one. So, if you treat the center of each cluster as a single dot instead of the bunch of them individually...*

He popped up a vidcube on his wrist for some quick computations, then saw the result floating inside the cube seconds later. It showed lines drawn from the center of each cluster of attacks to a common locale, but not the same one as was projected up on the vidcube.

"Majors!"

Without warning, Zavier jumped up to his feet. His stunt earned him some unpleasant looks from the Makers and their two commanders below. "Paris isn't where he's at. He's in the Panasqueira mine!"

"Maker Vik," Major Arra said, looking up at him impatiently, "I can assure you that all the best analysis has confirmed that—"

"No, you're treating it like scattershot instead of clusters, and the clusters all focus in North Portugal. The Rippers have a tendency to use mines as their base of operations, because it lets them strip high-density matter for starks." He popped up a vidcube in his hand with a topographical map of North Portugal. "I'm certain they're in the Panasqueira Mine!"

Zandrie pursed her lips and held up a hand to quiet the other commanders, who were outraged at the interruption. "Zavier, please sit down," she warned. "When it's time for questions, then you'll be given your turn. Major Arra, please continue to outline the Paris assault plan."

"But you're wrong!" Zavier insisted. "You're all wrong! If you look at how the points are in clusters, like he was visiting and found a safe-house to operate out of, then—"

"This is what we get for promoting children," one of the veteran Makers below remarked to a smattering of laughter.

"Please...sit...*down*," Major Arra commanded, visibly losing his patience. "Major Vik, he falls under your command. Please do something about him."

"Zavier," Zandrie snapped.

"Not again," Texas muttered.

To the horrified faces of his squadmates and Zandrie, Zavier walked out to the aisle and down to the area below, shouting and pointing as he went. "Look at the way they're clustered. If you use *those* as your dots, then the lines all converge on Portugal. This is the chance to nail the Parisian, and you're all being fools just because I'm inexperienced. But I'm telling you, *that* is where his real headquarters are."

He jogged down the steps and started to point at the giant vidcube map, but a couple of the older Makers got up from their seats and grabbed him from either side. That got Toby instantly to his feet to run down to help his friend, while Texas rolled her eyes.

"We're going to get grounded for life...Oh well, a Texan never turns her back on a friend."

Texas joined the disruption as well, leaving Min to stay out of it. Kojo, meanwhile, had flipped down his vidglasses the second Zavier had mentioned "clusters" and begun working on his own estimates. He then flipped up his glasses, but said nothing after glancing down to see how far out of control things had gotten.

"Koj, tell them!" Zavier shouted. He also shot a pleading glance toward Dado, who sat with pursed lips and slowly shook his head.

Zavier, Toby, and Texas struggled with a small group of buff Makers when an ear-piercing sound nearly sent everyone to their knees. Everyone, veterans and newbies alike, suddenly froze at the noise. They looked over to find Zandrie holding up a freshly-printed air-horn, looking very cross. She didn't even need to say "attention"—she got it with a look.

"Zavier, you and your squad are now 'Team *Grounded*' for the duration of this mission. You will return to your quarters for the rest of this cycle, then remain on the station as security details while the *grown-ups* proceed with the attack on the Rippers in *Paris*. Is that *quite* understood?"

Zavier wanted to say so much more, but from the look on his sister's face, he knew it would get him nowhere now. Instead, he relented with a heated look of his own and two words uttered between clenched teeth. "Yes…*ma'am*."

"Then go. Maker Solomon, you need to keep a tighter rein on your squad."

The Makers they had been wrestling with started to escort them out, but before they could lay a hand on Texas, she backed away, held her head proudly, and led the march out of the briefing room herself with not another word uttered. She was followed by Toby and Zavier, with Min and Koj joining them on their way up out of the room.

Only once outside and walking down an open corridor did any of them speak.

"Well, *that* could have gone better," Toby said.

"They're wrong. It's not Paris," Zavier mumbled.

"Not doubting your opinion," Texas said. "Just the way you presented it."

"You gotta work on your people skills, man," Toby added.

When they came to an intersection of corridors, Min started to go left with Toby and Texas while Zavier turned right, Kojo following him.

"Zavier, we're grounded," Min said, pausing. "Our quarters are this way."

"And the nearest dock is *this* way," he countered. "I'm sorry I got you guys into trouble, but I need to get down there and prove I'm right...to myself, if no one else."

"Wait, what? An unsanctioned mission against your own sister's orders?" Texas brightened. "Count me in!"

"Me too," Toby agreed, joining Texas in changing direction. "You'll need someone to protect you guys, after all. But, Koj, you were already turning this way. Where were *you* going?"

"Oh," Kojo said, as he finally flipped up his vidglasses, "I figured Zavier would be wanting to go down there, so I was going to join him. He'll be needing me to handle the specifics of strategy and logistics. He's right, you know. I ran the analysis myself."

"And you didn't say anything?" Zavier asked.

"It wouldn't have done any good at that point. I would have been a voice in the wind, thanks to Zavier slagging it up. At least *one* of us needs to maintain his respectability to be able to cover for the others in the future."

"Gotta admit, the Maker has a point." Texas shrugged. "Min, you making it unanimous?"

Min hesitated. She was still faced in the direction of their quarters, but her head was looking after her friends. "I don't know. Major Vik told us to stay put."

"My sister says a lot of things."

"Zavier was right before, and look what happened when no one listened," Toby told her. "Granted, he could have handled himself a whole lot better—but do you want the *rest* of the Maker Corps to fall into another trap because they're going for the wrong target?"

"Well...no."

"Min, I understand your reluctance," Kojo said. "You don't like to see people get hurt, but a *lot* of Makers, a lot of our *friends* will get hurt or killed if we don't do this. I don't want that on my conscience, and I believe you don't either."

Min thought about it for a moment longer. Then, she reluctantly turned back and joined her squadmates.

"*That's* the way to operate like a team," Texas said as she slapped Min on the shoulder. "I only have one question."

"How are we going to hijack a ship?" Toby asked.

"That would be the question."

Zavier smiled. "That's the wrong question, team. Didn't you learn from Captain Jha? We need to think *big*."

The main dock was busy and full of crews coming and going, but one of the recently completed smaller docks was not quite as busy. In fact, it only had one shuttle from which a construction crew was just coming off, while the other two berths were empty. Zavier led his team over to one of the empty berths, quietly explaining as he went.

"When I looked through my Oz, I found a number of standard issue blueprints that apparently come with the job. Including…a ship."

He swiftly scrolled through his Oz's menu until he came to a design labeled "Attack Shuttle" and smiled.

"Nice," Texas admitted. "That's thinking Texas-big, alright. But do you know how long it'll take us to print one out?"

"Only slightly longer than it'll take me to hack into a few OzBots," Kojo said as he flipped his vidglasses into place. "Keep a lookout for any officers."

It wasn't long before three OzBots came flying into the small dock. Once Zavier had loaded the blueprints, their ship began rapidly materializing there in the berth. The ship was a sleek shuttle with front and rear facing gun turrets on top. It was nearly finished when one of the technicians came over to their berth.

"Hey, what're you doin' with my bots?"

Without hesitating, Zavier stepped up to answer the man while Kojo finished working with the OzBot. "We're prepping for a scouting mission in advance of the Paris assault. Figured you guys are busy enough getting things flying around here, we'd fend for ourselves."

"You got that right. Got any orders I can see?"

"Really? In the mess *this* place is still in?"

"True," the man admitted. "My last updates came by a runner, of all things. Got a pilot?"

Zavier gestured in Kojo's direction, who replied with an absent nod, his attention once again back on his vidglasses. "Covered."

"Fine by me," the man relented. "I still got a lot of other work to do. But hey, whatever your mission is…give those shattered Rippers one for me, okay?"

Zavier smiled but said nothing. That seemed to be enough for the technician, who then gave him a wink and left to go about his other duties. Continuing his act of knowing what he was doing, Zavier led the way into the shuttle. Only once everyone was inside the shuttle and the airlock access panel closed and airtight did anyone speak.

"My heart was pounding the entire time," Texas exclaimed. "That was *great*."

"I was almost going to throw up a couple of times," Min said, with considerably less fervor.

"Let's get this thing moving before we're discovered," Zavier said as he opened the inner access door. "Just one question. Koj, you really *can* pilot this thing, right?"

"That was just what I was studying up on," he replied, still mostly focused on whatever he was reading in his vidglasses.

CHAPTER 16

Attn: [name redacted]

The time is now. Initiate the Monkey Paw plan effective imme-diately. All liquid assets are at your disposal.

I recommend reaching out to [name redacted] right now and offering him [redacted] for purchase of the [redacted] tungsten mine. Offer whatever price you feel he will take without question. Per the plan, there is no limit.

As a reminder, I've attached a list of the top dense-metal mines throughout Europe. Your counterparts, [names redacted], will be pursuing the purchase of all similar mines on the other continents.

Time is of the essence. Do whatever it takes. I will be available at any time if you need to speak.

From: [name redacted]

OzTech Internal Message, 19 January 2096

"Looks like we're clear," Zavier announced.

"Loading autopilot program," Kojo stated as he worked. "Destination, the Panasqueira Mine."

"Got something coming in on the Comm channel," Texas announced.

"We've been made," Toby said.

Min winced. "We should go back. "Oh, I'll be standing in the Commons for a *month*."

"Don't panic yet," Kojo told them. While his mind-link via his vidglasses interface worked overtime, his fingers also raced across the craft's main panel, calling up a quick selection of menus until he found the one he wanted. "There, that's the one. Mess with the gain a bit…Texas, how do they sound now?"

She listened through her station's earpiece before answering. "Can't tell, too much static."

"Which is exactly what *they'll* be hearing now. The way things are, they'll think it's something else that needs fixing. All we have to do is ride steady like we're not trying to escape and we should be fine."

"Sounds a bit nerve-wracking," Texas remarked. "I love it."

"Texans seems to like a lot of things sane people shy away from," Toby said.

"It's called being fearless," she corrected. "We even love a football team that hasn't won any major titles in the last fifty years."

"Football," Toby pondered. "Is that still a thing?"

"In Texas it is, and you better not say otherwise."

"Okay, people, ease up," Kojo announced. "It won't take us long to get there, and we need to prepare."

Toby grinned, holding up the Oz on his forearm. "I've got everything I need right here."

"Maybe not," Kojo said. "Remember, this is not an authorized mission. We won't have access to a local quantum cache, and from what I've read, that mine is far too deep for any quantum transfers to make it through with any degree of reliability. That means no printing once we're down there."

"No printing?" Texas exclaimed. "That sounds positively… rigid."

"You'll have to print all your equipment ahead of time," Kojo instructed. "Only what you can carry."

Min was already ahead of the game, scrolling through a list of options hovering above her wrist. "Standard med-kit, of course, with a few healing-foam capsules, general antitoxin in case we run into any poisoned weapons, suture kit, pocket medscanner, bone-knitter…what else…"

"Just how deep is deep?" Toby asked.

The answer came up hovering within the cockpit vidcube. A schematic traced out what might have either been a wind chime, cross sectional view of an ant hill, or a *very* deep cave system.

"We'll need to automap while we move," Zavier immediately realized. "I can hook it up to my ping-scanner to minimize equipment."

"Before the Shattering," Kojo began, "the Panasqueira mine was already large, covering some twenty square kilometers of surface area and going pretty deep. But when the Shattering occurred, everyone began digging down to make as much use of their land as possible, and Panasqueira was no exception. The problem here is that after a couple decades of going ever deeper, they hit upon a system of natural caves that allowed them to go deeper still. Latest estimate is that this thing could be *kilometers* deep."

"That's a lot of rock over our heads," Toby said. "Okay, so no local quantum cache access."

Kojo turned toward Zavier. "I'm transmitting all the maps that exist to you, but there's no telling how deep the Rippers or anyone else may have dug since these were made."

"I'll load those into my mapper app to use as a reference point," Zavier replied. "It will track our every movement and maintain an updated map of everywhere we'll be exploring. We'll also need transportation. That's a lot of tunnels to go searching on foot."

"Too narrow," Min replied. She was still printing her equipment as she spoke. "These are mine shafts."

"We'll use hovboards, then. Fast, silent, and quicker than walking. I'll also add climbing equipment just in case. Anyone familiar with rappelling and climbing?"

All eyes turned to Texas, waiting for her to say something about Texas. She did not disappoint. "Sonora Caverns, Bridge Caverns, Cascade Caverns, Fern Cave, and of course the Honey Creek Cave over in Bexar, which is the deepest in all of Texas," she recited. "You just all try and keep up with me."

"Okay then," Zavier said, half to himself. "I'll just have to watch what I say next time. Make sure to print backpacks to carry all this stuff in."

"We'll have to wear *backpacks?*" Min complained. "I'm used to only carrying around my Oz. It has everything I need in it."

"Not this trip," Kojo told her. "Okay, ready up. I'm bringing it down in a little ravine outside the main entrance. We'll have to assume they've got some perimeter sensors around the place, so Z, we need something for that."

"Not a problem. I share a set of blueprints for some shimmer-suits…with my own special modifications, of course."

At that moment, a small red light popped up on the navigation panel before Kojo.

"Sixty seconds to landing, everyone," he announced. "Strap in…"

Their craft landed in a ravine a short climb down from the main cave entrance. Before leaving the ship, they finished printing their equipment, limiting themselves to what they could carry either on their belts or in their backpacks.

For Toby, it was a transparent fold-shield with a gun-hole, grappling hook gun, rifle with a crossbow attachment on top, bolts for the crossbow, and a coil of rope hanging from his belt. Min had her backpack mostly full of her medical equipment, a medi-scanner clipped to her belt, headphones with a music card, Zavier's mini-mega speaker, and a mechanical slingshot with a belt-full of softball-sized ammo to go along with it.

"No octopus-gun?" Toby asked as they exited the shuttle.

"Recent training proved its limits," she replied, "so I came up with this. The ammo is flash-heated as it's shot out, which creates an exothermic reaction that causes it to rapidly expand into a human-sized sticky mass, which then hardens into a shell after it hits. Porous, of course; I wouldn't want anyone to suffocate."

Kojo had a belt-full of assorted electronic and computerized knickknacks, and an air-pistol with a pump-handle loaded with a range of small darts and pellet-shaped ammo. For Zavier, it was his auto-mapper and ping-scanner, a couple of stun grenades, two pistols, a lighter, electric lamp, a small coil of special chemically-treated thread fuse that he'd modded to burn far hotter, and some protein bars and canisters of water.

"Or did everyone forget that we might get hungry or thirsty on our long way down and back up?" he remarked.

"Actually, I did," Toby admitted.

"I didn't," Min spoke up. "I have stim patches, as well as Nutritabs."

Then, there was Texas.

She sported a belt of grenades of various types, two rifles, three pistols scattered around her body, a bandolier of various types of ammo and pellets crisscrossing her chest, and a thirty-centimeter metal stick.

"No hunting knife?" Toby joked.

"After that…accident…at the ship graveyard, I try to avoid anything with a sharp edge," she replied. "So, no Texas toothpicks."

"What's with the stick?" Zavier asked. "Planning on clubbing someone over the head with it?"

She took out her stick in one hand and thumbed something on the side. Immediately it popped out to a pole two meters long. "When I'm not pole-vaulting with it, yes."

Another press of her thumb, and the staff retracted in the

same swift motion back into a small metal stick.

"Ask a silly question…" Zavier said. Finally, he passed out a shimmer-suit for each person, as well as the promised hover-boards.

"Okay, zip up your shimmer-suits," Kojo announced.

"I designed in a flap to toss over your backpack," Zavier said. "And there's a set of IR goggles built into the hood so we can see where we're going without having to light up. They're also how we're going to see each other with the shimmer-suits activated; you'll see the others as an outline overlaying where they are. As long as we remain quiet and avoid any large quantities of smoke, we should remain unseen."

"textlens only," Kojo told them. "No talking, or we might give away our position."

Once everyone's shimmer-suits were sealed up and activated, they faded away against the background as they hopped onto their hover-boards to speed up the slope. The main entrance had no sensors that they could see—just a dusty, ancient security camera.

>>Koj>>That's probably where they're hiding their perimeter sensors: right inside that relic.<<

With that caution taken as a given, they kept their hover-boards as low to the ground as possible as they sped one at a time into the cave. Once inside, Zavier felt more relaxed, but not by much. He was in the lead with his auto-mapper loaded up with what Kojo had found of the cave's tunnels, Toby flew right behind him, ready to intervene if anything came up, followed by Texas, Kojo, and Min.

>>Texas>>Do we have ANY idea where we're going?<<

>>Z>>Deep.<<

>>Koj>>Follow the security. Wherever we see a security measure or guard, that's the right way.<<

>>Toby>>Or an excessive amount of tracks. Hold up.<<

They hopped off their hover-boards while Toby bent to the ground for a better look. The ground was mostly rock, but enough loose dirt was scattered across it to make out signs of where it had been disturbed. Ahead of them, the tunnel split. The dust on the left path looked heavily trampled, while the right one looked fairly smooth.

>>**Toby**>>**I'm no tracker, but that looks like a lot of people.**<<

>>**Koj**>>**Okay, we go left.**<<

>>**Toby**>>**But no hover-boards.**<<

They slid their hover-boards in the slot behind their backpacks, then continued along on foot. The tunnel sloped down gradually, winding down ancient mine shafts, across ground pounded smooth by recent use that was plain for anyone to see.

>>**Z**>>**Activating recorder.**<<

>>**Texas**>>**Lot of foot-traffic around here.**<<

>>**Toby**>>**Be on the lookout for security measures. They probably have sensors all over this place.**<<

>>**Koj**>>**We passed three sets already. I was able to deactivate two of them myself.**<<

>>**Min**>>**And the third?**<<

>>**Koj**>>**Thank Z for the shimmer-suits.**<<

They followed the trail of recent use until they came to another branching of tunnels, this time a choice of three, while the left-hand side opened up into a deep drop over ten meters across. Ancient cables hung from the ceiling, plunging down into the depths and thick enough to carry an ore-laden cart in some sort of primitive elevator. No one could see any signs of recent use, but from the top of the ceiling hung a string of old light bulbs that were lit up.

Before anyone could make a comment about any of this, Toby's arm shot out to pull Zavier back against the wall. The others took the hint and flattened themselves as well. Out of the silence came the growing sound of voices approaching from the far-left tunnel nearest the pit.

"…got them good, stinking Makers."

"I can hardly wait to see what the next phase is. It'll be all of it for all of us soon enough."

"No more monopoly, that's for sure."

Two men came walking out, each with an Oz on one arm and a QuantVac on the other, and a gun and a knife at each of their belts. In appearance, they might have been miners, complete with headlamp helmets—but from their talk, the team knew batter. The pair continued chatting as they walked right past the hidden squad.

Zavier held in his breath as they passed by. The pair of Rippers were walking side by side, one of them passing within a breath of Toby. Close enough that he might feel it if Toby exhaled—so he stopped breathing as he squished his muscular frame against the rock wall.

Texas was small enough that, even with all her equipment, she was an easy fit into one of the cracks in the cavern, while Min was so diminutive she nearly vanished into the rock. Koj was taller and lankier than Toby's musculature, so flattening himself against the cavern wall wasn't too difficult.

Even so, things happen.

"Ouch! Stubbed my toe against something." One of the men stopped briefly before Kojo and glanced down. Kojo held his breath and tried not to shake. "Just a rock."

Kojo's eyes shifted to look down; his foot was resting blessedly behind an actual rock.

"Gas-head," the other one said. "Come on, tough guy, you can lick your wound once we're outside in the daylight."

"You can be a real slagger, you know that?"

"Go rip yourself."

Their voices grew fainter as they left, until they were both out of sight and hearing. Only then did anyone exhale.

>>Koj>>**Close. Okay, continue.**<<

>>Toby>>**Same way they came from. Z, how's the auto-mapper going?**<<

>>Z>>**Should be an old shaft up ahead to the deeper levels.**<<

>>Min>>**That would make it easier.**<<

>>Toby>>**Then let's get going.**<<

A hundred meters on they stealthily crept, until they came to a lift at the end of the tunnel. Not an antigravity lift-shaft such as they were used to, but something far more antiquated. A flat-bed elevator with guard railings, a cable and pulley, and a panel mounted inside the elevator with a couple of buttons.

>>Min>>**Really? We're supposed to ride in that?**<<

>>Toby>>**Too loud. They'll hear us coming long before we even get there.**<<

>>Koj>>**Can we use the boards to get down there?**<<

>>Z>>**Shaft's too steep. Nothing for the hovboards to push against. We'd free-fall.**<<

>>Texas>>**Then it's the elevator.**<<

>>Toby>>**What?! You're crazy. They'll hear us.**<<

>>Texas>>**But not see us. I'm ready for them. Kojo, got sleepy-time darts?**<<

>>Koj>>**Knockout pellets. Why?**<<

>>Texas>>**Get them ready.**<<

They all filed in, Texas standing dead center with one of her pistols in hand, this one loaded with a pellet from her bandolier. Off to one side, Kojo was ready with a dart in his pistol crossbow, while the rest stood against the far side. Zavier pressed the lower button that began their trip into the abyss.

The elevator had a more modern lighting panel fixed to it, but the shaft was still a long, dangling trail of ancient lighting that somehow still worked. The elevator dropped down with a very audible trundle and squeak of gears that had Min shaking and Zavier wondering if it had been such a good idea to come down here after all. The Rippers would definitely be able to hear them coming.

>>Z>>**According to the map, this shaft goes down to the very bottom of the old mines.**<<

>>Toby>>**There a "but" in there somewhere?**<<

>>Z>>**My ping-scanner says it goes a lot deeper than that. Can't tell how far. Out of my range.**<<

Texas sent a vidloop of an old man falling infinitely into a fiery abyss.

They continued to descend for several long minutes, coming to where the ancient light bulbs dropped deeper into the darkness. Far more recent light panels now adorned the sides of the shaft, clear enough for them to get a good look at the side walls as they passed them by. They were smooth—not as roughly cut as the older walls.

>>Koj>>**These walls were cut using laser tools. Not too recently, but newer than the rest of the tunnels.**<<

>>Z>>**We should be getting into the cave system.**<<

The walls around them suddenly disappeared, giving way to a large open pit beneath them. They'd dropped out of a roof straight into the middle of the most spacious cavern any of them had seen. Stalactites hung from the ceiling above them, reaching down a meter or two as sparkling colors flashed along their sides from the reflected light. But soon, the squad travelled to the end of the lighting panels. Nothing but a single dim light glowed far below them as unfathomable darkness crept in.

>>Toby>>**You realize that the only thing between us and a long drop is that thin little cable we're dangling from?**<<

>>Texas>>**Your point?**<<

Texas added a vidloop of a chicken running across the ground.

>>Toby>>**Nothing. Just checking.**<<

>>Min>>Well, I don't mind admitting I'm afraid. What if this thing snaps?<<

>>Z>>It won't. Replaced with poly-diamond fiber when they dug into this cave.<<

>>Min>>How do you know?<<

>>Z>>Wouldn't you?<<

Their journey into blackness finally saw an end. The floor of the great cavern was littered with scattered points of artificial light planted around a maze of rock walls and narrow passages. Throughout the floor were suggestions of a range of equipment, habitations, and generators. It would have been a confusing maze from the ground, no doubt, but was clearly visible from high above it. One large, blocky-looking metal safe caught Zavier's eye, and apparently Kojo's as well.

>>Koj>>They got a cache of their own down here. We definitely found the right place.<<

The elevator cart dropped down between one set of walls, each about twice the squad's head level by the time the cart came to a rest and the gates spread open.

Outside the gate stood a couple of curious guards. They were on their feet, looking into what they saw as an empty elevator.

"Why would someone send down an empty?" the guard on the left wondered.

"Maybe a short in the system," the other guard said. "Let's give it a check."

Both guards took a step in, then no farther. The one on the left was hit by a dart in his shoulder, while the other one took a small pellet to the chest that stuck to his garments and released a small cloud of gas right up into his nose. Both guards dropped straight to the floor of the lift.

>>Texas>>That should hold them for a while.<<

Texas holstered her gun while Kojo quickly put away his air-pistol.

>>**Toby**>>**Hurry.**<<

They all rushed out, Zavier coming last. He stepped out, then reached around to push the other button on the lift before quickly scurrying away. The gates closed and the lift started its long trip back up with its pair of unconscious passengers.

>>**Z**>>**We're out of the range of my map, but the auto-mapper'll keep working so we can find our way back.**<<

>>**Toby**>>**I'll take lead, then.**<<

They walked into the maze. Echoes of other voices came at them from branching stone halls and overtop the walls. Toby led them down into a turn, following a natural passage of limestone formations that had been fused together by Oz prints into full walls. The corridor opened occasionally into rooms—some for private quarters, supplies, a couple of guard stations, and a locker from which one of the Rippers was taking out a few spare Ozes. They quietly followed him into a far more open section of the compound.

The wide-open floor had been cleared of any natural obstacles, and was now filled with a variety of equipment. Some Rippers were calling up blueprints and experimental designs from the lab benches scattered across the area. Zavier saw one cluster of vidcubes around a central raised dais, where people stood watching the display. At the far side, they saw others practicing printing some of their designs, some of which looked rather brutal.

Light panels bathed the area in a daytime glow as people by the dozens came and went about their various chores. They stood in groups chatting, or in one case gathered about a vidcube displaying a recent news report about the attack on the Maker orbital base. Cheers came from that one, along with cries of, "All of it for all of us!" Finally, around the perimeter of the large open area, they could see other entrances back into the maze and other limestone halls leading off into more quarters or supply areas, each with people coming and going.

>>Toby>>We just hit Ripper central.<<

>>Koj>>Z, your recorder still working?<<

Zavier sent a thumbs-up pic.

>>Koj>>Then get of some of those blueprints and tech they're working on. This intel is invaluable.<<

>>Texas>>Spread out a little. If we bunch up too close, we'll be easier to spot.<<

>>Min>>I think I see a lab table with someone working on some medical procedures. I'll look into that.<<

>>Z>>I'm sticking to the guy with the spare Ozes.<<

The team trailed about, each creeping carefully through the maze of people and equipment, careful not to touch or bump. Whenever Zavier passed by a lab table, he recorded what was happening on it. Passing by someone testing out a new experimental rig, he recorded that as well. Not too far away, Min looked over the shoulder of what appeared to be one of their Medics, while Texas examined the weapons testing at the other side.

>>Texas>>They've got a wicked weapon over here. Shoots out a burst of caltrops.<<

>>Z>>I see a self-replicating fifteen-centimeter pyramid with spiked tips. Also a 'scatter-gun' that shoots out a cone of darts.<<

>>Min>>What?! Those are *my* designs! How did they steal my designs? They're locked away in my Oz!<<

>>Kojo>>Did you share them with anyone?<<

>>Min>>Just other Medics.<<

Zavier continued to follow the Ripper with the spare Oz units, weaving through the people and equipment. He occasionally lost sight of his quarry in his effort to remain undetected, then caught up to him again. The man finally came out into an open section around the raised dais that they'd spotted earlier, where a group of people were milling about. The man went straight over to them.

"These are your new Ozes," the man said, holding out what he'd been carrying. "They're unregistered, so transfer all your blueprints over to them then vac your old ones. We take no chances on anything that can be traced."

"Now *this* is more like it. No more limits on what we can do. We can finally get things *done*."

The voice was *very* familiar, yet Zavier didn't dare get any closer. He scooted around the edge of the clearing until he had a better angle, then what he saw made his jaw drop. The one who'd spoken was *Dakota*. Next to him, calmly examining his fresh Oz unit, was the gaunt figure of Grandmaster, followed by Sam, Coover, and Hilla.

"The policies of the *Takers* have done nothing but make things worse," Grandmaster stated. "All it has given us is a new group of oppressors."

"I've got some fluid new designs I'd like to get started on," Coover said as he took his new device. "Nothing they'd ever let me work on back up *there*. Too brutal, they said."

"Our lab benches are open for anyone to use," their guide told them. "Remember to first transfer your designs into the new units."

"There are some bio-weapons I'd like to experiment with," Hilla said. "Nothing that would linger in the environment, of course, but the MCA still wouldn't approve of me working with it. Said there was too great a chance of civilian fallout. It's war; there's *always* a chance of civilian casualties."

"Like they say," Sam added, the last to take a new Oz, "all of it for all of us."

The rest of them laughed in response.

For a moment, Zavier was stunned. His squadmates sent query icons over textlens, asking about his silence. They had scattered around the chamber, so only Zavier had a good view of what was happening. But when he could finally form a coherent thought to textlens, what he told them left even Texas a little speechless.

>>Z>>**Guys, I found Team Overdrive. They're *Rippers!!*** <<

CHAPTER 17

All of it for all of us. We use it as a rallying cry, but do you really understand what it means, my fellow Roosters?

"All of it" means everything. All the matter that OzTech has stolen from every person under the guise of the Quantum bank. The food you eat. The ground under your feet. All that you see.

"All of us" means that it belongs to the people. You. Me. Your brother. Your sister. Your children's children. Your enemy. The person who smiles at you on the street. Not just a handful of Elitist oligarchs hidden far from view on the Moon.

We should be free to make whatever we want from whatever we see, but the law prohibits this. This is because the law is built upon the idea of ownership. It protects the Elitists.

So the law must first be torn down.

All of it for all of us, my friends.

The Parisian, Intercepted Ripper Transmission, 14 July 2156

>>**Toby**>>**Say again?**<<

>>**Z**>>**I'm looking straight at Overdrive, all five of them, and they're with the Rippers.**<<

>>**Texas**>>**Those traitorous shattered sons of slaggers.**<<

>>**Kojo**>>**Easy, everyone, let's find out more first. Z, still recording?**<<

>>**Z**>>**Yes.**<<

>>**Kojo**>>**Then get what you can. The rest of us will make our**

way around. Careful, though, and don't bunch up. We get caught, we're dead.<<

Zavier carefully glanced around. Through the special optics of his shimmer-suit he saw the glittering outlines of the others slowly making their way around the crowds of Rippers, their movements slow so as to avoid attracting attention. Zavier's position seemed okay for now, but that could change suddenly; he needed something better. Spotting an unused lab bench within arm's reach, he slowly stepped over and then squatted down underneath it to get out of the way.

The status display on his shimmer-suit optics told him the recorder was still going, and the visual and audio gain was about as much as he could get from where he was. So, he squatted there and listened, hoping he had somehow been mistaken.

"Welcome to the Rooster Rebellion," the man said to the members of Team Overdrive. They were busy hooking up their old Oz devices to the new ones for the data transfers. "Now, you'll be striking against the *real* enemy."

"Time to get out from under the thumb of the Elitists and put them in their places," Grandmaster said.

Coover was scrolling quickly through his new Oz database as he waited for the transfer to complete. His eyes widened with excitement as he examined it. "This is *so* fluid, man! What I can't do with *these* designs."

"I haven't seen anything more cutting edge," Sam remarked of his own catalogue.

"We get the best of what the Makers have without them even knowing it," the man said, grinning.

"I would never have expected anything like this from what I used to think of as being a bunch of cheap terrorists," Dakota said.

"Well, you're Roosters now, like the rest," the man stated. "And we look after our people. 'All of it for all of us' isn't just a slogan. It's a way of life."

>>Toby>>Traitors!<<

>>Texas>>You know what we'd do with them back home?<<

"I always wondered where Estelle and Bjork went to," Grandmaster said.

"Two of our finest," the man before them said. "Along with Kotori Yakamura, Andrei Popov, Jackie Pipoly, Antonia Tierni, and many others down through the years. All originally cadets like yourselves, then converted over to our cause."

>>Texas>>There's been OTHERS?<<

>>Toby>>How far back does this thing go?<<

>>Min>>My designs...one of the other cadets I showed them to must have taken them. I think I'm gonna be sick.<<

>>Z>>Those names...they sound familiar, but I can't remember where I've heard them.<<

>>Kojo>>If they're recruiting from within the Academy, then they must have a contact—a mole.<<

>>Toby>>Makers betraying us from the inside?<<

>>Toby>>Maybe it's not a Maker. Could be nearly anyone.<<

>>Z>>Those names he rattled off...I know I've heard of them somewhere before.<<

From their hidden places, they watched as Team Overdrive finished the data transfer to their new Oz devices. One by one, they took off their old devices, pulled out the VacGuard circuits, then dropped their old equipment on the ground to vac them into a stream of starks.

"That's it," their guide said once the last old Oz had been vac'ed up. "You're full Roosters now. As far as the outside world is concerned, you're all dead. Just remember to keep your faces hidden when out in the field."

"We will not betray our secret," Grandmaster said. "We have sworn this as a squad. We knew what we were signing up for."

"Finally, all that training's going to be put to some *real* use,"

Coover said. "I've got some devices I've been designing that I can't wait to try out in the field. No more being held back by lead-headed rules."

"I can't wait to get into a ship of our own," Dakota said excitedly. "I joined the Makers for a *cause*, and now I have one."

"Well, you're all just in time for our next big push," their guide stated. "We have a major offensive coming up very soon, and we'll be needing every Rooster we can get. Soon, the monopoly will be broken."

"Then, it's all of it for all of us," Hilla said with a smile.

"Well, I'll leave you people to get familiar with your new Ozmium devices and start customizing the additional blueprints as you see fit," the man said. "I've got a lot to do before the big move."

Zavier watched as the Rooster walked away, while the team members talked with some enthusiasm amongst themselves about one or another new feature or blueprint, and how everything was soon going to change. He squatted in his hiding place listening and wondering, just as he knew the others must be.

>>Z>>Why does it sound like crippling the Maker Corps was *not* their big plan?<<

>>Kojo>>Agreed. It was only an opening move. Their main goal is something much bigger.<<

>>Texas>>They blew up the Corps headquarters and that's *not* their big goal?<<

>>Toby>>Koj's right. The station is already nearly back to one hundred percent; they were only after Maker officers.<<

>>Kojo>>So they'd be out of the way. But of what? We need to investigate further.<<

>>Z>>We've got a maze of tunnels ahead of us. Look for some-place with a lot of traffic. The Parisian should be in the middle of it all.<<

>>Kojo>>Cancel that. Quite the opposite. Storerooms are going to be busy this close to an offensive. But the leader will be finalizing

plans with only a few captains around him.<<

>>Z>>In that case, let me scout around with my ping-scanner for relative concentrations of people.<<

Zavier crawled out from under his table, then ducked back in quickly as another Ripper passed him. As soon as he could, he made his way toward the center of the open part of this stone-walled maze. *The leaders will be far away,* he reasoned. *As far away from the entry as possible, for their own safety.*

He looked across at the various openings scattered across the far wall, picked out what was roughly the center of that wall, and started making his slow and careful way in that direction.

"So, we can finally do a little real harm if that's what it takes?" Dakota asked as Zavier brushed by Team Overdrive.

"Speaking as a strategist," Grandmaster replied, "if killing a few ends this conflict quickly and thus saves many more lives, then it is our duty to entertain even death as a first option. For the good of the world as a whole."

I really hope that Min didn't hear that, Zavier thought to himself, *because she definitely wouldn't like it.*

In an open area, several Rippers were testing new weapons or engaging in mock training exercises, forcing Zavier to circle a long way around before he found a section safe enough to cross. At this point, his suit's optics showed him that the outline of another shimmer-suit had caught up to him. From the slender form he guessed it to be Min, which was soon verified by a textlens transmission.

>>Min>>All of them are talking about a big offensive. More killing. And they're *celebrating* it. They're bragging about all the other casualties they've caused on their raids.<<

>>Z>>I know. You don't want to hear what else Team Overdrive was saying.<<

>>Min>Already did. I have the audio pickups on my suit turned up. It's sick, Z. Nothing justifies murder.<<

While Zavier mostly sympathized with her, he didn't want to get involved in a lengthy debate over the nuances between murder and death in a war. *I'm sure to lose to Min anyway*, he thought.

He opted for simply sticking to the mission. He tugged on Min's arm and started across the opening for the far wall, moving slowly so as not to risk detection. They'd made it to the far wall before Team Overdrive came wandering over, with Sam in the lead.

"Here's a free spot. We can practice here."

Zavier and Min hurried out of the way just in time.

The far wall appeared to be corrugated limestone. Along its length, he could see a few natural openings here and there, made wide from creative use of Ozmium technology. Zavier headed for the one he'd picked out. From here, he could now see that the carving of a rooster marked the top of the stone frame. It wasn't long before other faint shimmers joined him and Min.

>>**Koj**>>**Check in. We all here?**<<

>>**Texas**>>**This is me on the other side from Z and Min.**<<

She sent a vidloop of a woman in a crowd leaping up and down waving her hands frantically, superimposed over a quick snapshot of the place where Texas now stood.

>>**Toby**>>**Right next to Texas.**<<

>>**Koj**>>**Z, what's your ping-scanner say?**<<

>>**Z**>>**Distortion from the walls, but that opening in front of us has minimal activity.**<<

>>**Koj**>>**Then we try that one first. Z, take the lead. Everyone else, be ready for anything. No shooting if we can avoid it.**<<

Zavier was first to creep into the break in the rock wall. It had been smoothed into a round archway, and after peeking around the corner to be sure there would be no one to bump into, he made his way in.

He felt like he was in some weird office building, where the walls were made of rock instead of other materials. The walls were still a little rough to the touch, but the floor had been smoothed out, with no trace of dust or dirt thanks to the OzBots that quietly vac'ed everything to a state of perfection.

>>Texas>>I like this floor. No footprints.<<

>>Toby>>Stick against the walls. If we come to another opening, give it a pause before crossing.<<

Zavier led them on several yards before coming to the first archway-like opening on their left. There were no doors for privacy in this section—just openings in the rock. That made it difficult to duck out of sight if something should happen with their suits. Zavier and the team could hear some voices through this first archway, none of which Zavier recognized. Their conversation was unsettling.

"I don't care how small they say it is; that tax they're charging everyone is way too much."

"Agreed. About time someone brought down the Bank."

Zavier was about to cross when the click of boots approached the archway. Immediately, he fell back against the hallway wall, his right arm flinging back to push Min behind him flat as well.

>>Z>>Hold up!<<

Two men in Rooster-embroidered jackets walked out from whatever room lay beyond, still chatting with each other.

"…just keeps them in power."

"Don't have to sell *me* on it. I'm looking forward to watching it all burn. Bury every last one of them."

Zavier watched the two walk out into the hall, turn to the right, then head back toward the large open area. He waited until they had turned out of sight before signaling to the others.

>>Z>>Clear.<<

He took a quick look through the archway to see a small cave fixed up like an office of some sort. He scurried past the opening and crept a few yards down, then waited for a moment until he felt

Min's light tap on his shoulder.

>>Min>>I'm clear.<<

A second later, Texas' transmission flashed a thumbs-up, followed in turn by Kojo then Toby. Zavier briefly consulted his ping-scanner, then started moving once again. The stone-bound corridor started into a wide curve.

>>Z>>My ping-scanner's bouncing all over the place with these walls. I'm picking up our own echo.<<

>>Toby>>Any chance a Ripper might have something to pick up those same echoes?<<

>>Koj>>I could run countermeasures, but it would interfere with our equipment as well.<<

>>Z>>Do it. My ping-scanner is useless down here. Have to design an upgrade next time we're back up at the station.<<

>>Koj>>Done.<<

Zavier put his ping-scanner back in his backpack, quickly secured the flap to cover it, then continued down the curving hall. He was just in time to flatten himself against the wall at the sound of more approaching steps.

"Boss says to rally the troops," one Ripper, a woman, was saying. "We're moving out soon."

"Any word about that base we trashed?"

The second Ripper was a large man that Zavier instantly recognized as the Viking. That's when he saw the logo on the woman's jacket as they passed; it was the Manchester United Ripper.

"Nearly rebuilt, but we planned for that. The point was to get rid of those Makers so they won't be in the way."

"Yeah, they'll be so busy hunkering down they'll miss the *real* show."

The pair had walked past Zavier and were nearly past Min when the lady stopped suddenly, sniffing the air.

"Something wrong?" the Viking asked.

"Not sure," Manchester United replied. "Smells like antiseptic mixed with a little…perfume?"

"Probably nothing. One of the Medics getting something ready."

"Yeah, well…maybe." She turned around, still sniffing the air, until she was facing the rough direction of where Min hid. "I could swear…"

"No time for you to track down some phantom smell," the Viking impatiently snapped. "We've got work to do."

Another sniff. The woman leaned in close between where Min and Texas stood, from what Zavier saw in his optics. Both were rigid, not even letting out a single breath, until the woman pulled away.

"You're right. Probably one of the new recruits. You know, we gotta tell them to not wear body scents. It'll unveil you every time, no matter how careful you are."

"That's how we lost Liza. Well, come on."

The pair started moving once again, and soon were well past Toby at the end. Zavier let out a sigh of relief then transmitted his question as simply as possible.

>>**Z>>?**<<

>>**Min>>Sorry, I thought I got it all; I cleaned up just before that hearing. That lady's got a very good nose.**<<

>>**Koj>>What were you doing wearing perfume anyway?**<<

>>**Min>>No reason in particular. Guess I need a new scent.**<<

>>**Toby>>'Phantom smell.' Add that to the squad name list, Koj.**<<

>>**Texas>>Let's just get going. Z?**<<

>>**Z>>Right.**<<

Zavier quickly pressed on. The corridor stopped curving and now flattened out into a straight line to another archway at the end. Overtop of the archway, Zavier could see some kind of figure engraved into the stone. It was a few steps more before he could make

213

out what it was: a rooster with hearts and other embellishments carved into it. There were no other exits or rooms that Zavier could see.

>>**Z**>>**Jackpot. I think we found the head Rooster himself. Follow close.**<<

He crept along as silently as he could, one foot after another. A little closer and he could see a light reflected through the archway. A little more and he saw suggestions of a large room beyond. A little bit more and he began to hear voices.

"…ready to execute the final part of the plan, now that the Makers have been eliminated."

"Good. For far too long, the Quantum Bank has been bleeding everyone dry. That tax of theirs is a stranglehold to keep OzTech swimming in starks and their investors in power."

"Agreed. Everything printed or vac'ed, they take a small portion of it. People are fools to not see that they are giving up a piece of their existence."

"It's about economics, my friend. The Oz seems like a godsend, but as long as all matter runs through the Quantum Bank, it is really a noose around our necks…with OzTech holding the rope."

>>**Koj**>>**That first voice. Definitely a French accent.**<<

>>**Texas**>>**Think it might be the Parisian?**<<

>>**Koj**>>**Maybe. Z, see if you can get a better look.**<<

>>**Z**>>**What about that second voice? It sounds *real* familiar.**<<

Zavier crept forward another yard, up to the lip of the doorway, then carefully peered around the corner into the room. At first, he saw a couple of desks, lots of electronic equipment, and several vidcubes—including a giant one that displayed a map of the Moon settlement with a few places indicated with special markers.

>>**Z**>>**Office.**<<

One of the vidcubes in the far-left corner was active. Z could see the Parisian's image projected clearly inside it from where he stood, but whoever was talking with him was out of sight.

>>Z>>**The Parisian, alright, but he's on vidcube. There's someone else here.**<<

"Their control will end once we seize control of the bank, no?"

"Seize control then set the matter free, yes; starks without limit for everyone. Their control will be shattered and the world freed from their slavery. Finally."

"Then, do I have permission to proceed?"

>>Texas>>**Huh? It sounds like the Parisian's taking orders from someone else.**<<

>>Toby>>**Then who's really in charge?**<<

>>Koj>>**A very good question. Z, who can you see in there?**<<

>>Z>>**Bad angle. Let me get inside a bit more.**<<

>>Texas>>**Be careful.**<<

Zavier took one very quiet step inside, then another, until he was standing fully inside the room by himself. As he entered, the figure sitting in front of the vidcube came into view. He was a middle-aged man, short and unremarkable, seated in a chair at a desk with an assortment of buttons and old-style floating holographic controls below the cube. "You have my permission," the man said. "Begin final arrangements."

Z knew that face anywhere: Dr. Eduardo "Dado" Oliveira, head administrator of the Academy and all its cadets...and Zavier's mentor and friend.

>>Z>>**It can't be! Dado?**<<

A flurry of question marks came out to Zavier via textlens. Too shocked to speak, he managed a quick mental command to his textlens to transmit what his recorder was still recording as a live feed.

>>Texas>>**Uh...**<<

>>Toby>>**DADO is the big man?**<<

>>Min>>**No...just, no.**<

>>Texas>>**He helped me after I killed that Ripper.**<<

215

>>**Koj**>>**He's helped everyone, but...I guess that explains how the Rippers are always up on their tech. But...WHY?**<<

Zavier's jaw hung open. There was Dr. Dado, talking to the Parisian on vidcube, giving him orders like he was in charge. "All of it for all of us," Dr. Dado said.

"All of it for all of us," the Parisian echoed from within the cube.

>>**Koj**>>**We've got to get out of here** *now*. **Z, snap out of it! Let's get moving.**<<

It took Zavier a second or two to come back to himself, with a little help from a hand on his shoulder.

>>**Texas**>>**Z, move!**<<

Properly nudged, he started to creep back.

Dr. Dado began to speak as the vidcube clicked off, making the squad freeze. "You know, besides that corridor outside being lined with a number of sensors designed by my people, some of which can even pick up the suggestive imprint of a shimmer-suit, the floor here in my humble little office is layered with a micro-fine conductive powder that records the imprint of any foot that's not my own."

Zavier froze, as did the rest.

"Since the rest of the Makers are getting ready to go off chasing a wild aquatic fowl in the bowels of Paris, I can only assume it's the Academy's most brilliant and most disobedient cadet…since his sister. Zavier, please remove the hood of your suit. I *so* hate talking to empty air. It makes me seem almost senile—which I am not…yet."

Dado turned his head to look directly at Zavier, who glanced down to see an outline in red, marking where his feet stood on Dado's sensor-floor.

Dado smiled.

CHAPTER 18

A wealthy landowner in Barcelos discovered his silver sto-
len. The theft coincided with the arrival of a humble pilgrim
from Galicia, and they arrested the man despite his pleas of
innocence.

At his hanging, the accused pilgrim declared: "It is as certain
that I am innocent as it is certain that this rooster will crow
when I am hanged." The people laughed as they looked at
the whole roast rooster on a platter before the judge, served
for his meal after the trial....

At the very moment when the Galician was being hanged, the
rooster came back to life and crowed loudly for all to hear.
Realizing the man was indeed innocent, the judge ordered the
Galician cut loose. They freed the pilgrim and he continued
on his way in peace.

Rooster of Barcelos – Wikipedia Entry, May 4, 2165

The Rippers came charging down the stone-lined hall behind them, covering all avenues of escape and aiming a variety of
weapons at Zavier's squad—who all stood dumbly in shock. Team
Overdrive was among the Rippers.

"I am going to assume that you did not come alone, Zavier,"
Dado said. "Your squad would not leave you to the wolves, so to
speak. Please, I would like to make this conversation a friendly one."

>>**Z**>>**He's got me pinpointed, but the rest of you can sneak out.
I'll lie.**<<

>>**Koj**>>**No. We stick together.**<<

>>**Texas**>>**We're not leaving you.**<<

With a sad sigh, Zavier pressed the toggle to deactivate his shimmer-suit, then reached up to pull back his hood. The others, still standing in the doorway behind him, followed.

"You were right, Grandmaster," Sam said. "They finally did figure it out."

"So, we gonna be working together?" Dakota asked. "Or do we drop 'em right here?"

Dado held up a hand, to which all the Rippers immediately quieted. He pointed toward Zavier and waited for a response.

"Dr. Dado, what…what's going on?"

>>**Toby**>**Maybe it's some plan of his. He could be an infiltrator.**<<
>>**Koj**>>**Yes, but for which side?**<<

"I understand your confusion," Dr. Dado stated. "No doubt you are wondering if I'm here trying to infiltrate the rebellion, or if have some convoluted plan to which you have arrived just in time to save me. But I can assure you, that is not the case."

"Those names that guy mentioned," Zavier suddenly realized, "Antonia Tierni, Jackie Pipoly, the others. I know where I've seen them before. They're with the pictures of the traitors on the wall in your office!"

"I treasure the memory of their time at the Academy, along with the others of my best cadets," Dr. Dado replied. "They saw the light and rose bravely to the occasion, and so I honor them for joining this struggle I started."

"You…founded the Roosters?" Zavier gasped. "But you run the Academy! You train *Makers*."

"Using the resources of the MCA, I train and recruit future *Roosters*," Dado corrected. "Can you think of a better way of getting a leg up on the latest tech?"

"You've been playing us for fools," Zavier realized. "But why?"

Dado stood and smiled once more, then started a slow,

meandering walk across the room to the large vidcube. "When you figured out that this mine must be the base for the Rooster Rebellion, did you bother to look into its history?"

"History?" Zavier hesitantly replied. "Uh…no."

"I'm surprised Kojo didn't, but then again, you must have been in a bit of a rush after that hearing. I know it was all I could do to get down here before you did—but then again, I didn't have to build my own ship from scratch before leaving. This tungsten mine was owned by my family long before the Shattering. Think of it: the sheer amount of dense tungsten metal, ripe with starks, in this vast mining complex. In today's matter-based economy, that would have made me quite well off."

His steps brought him to the vidcube. He touched a finger to it, bringing up an enlarged family portrait. It displayed a man, his wife, and a young child.

"My parents," he explained. "A picture taken back in far happier times. Yes, my father owned this mine. It had been in the family for quite some time. Then, in 2097, some very rich people offered to pay my father a ridiculous amount of money to buy the mine. Billions upon billions. My father happily took the offer, thinking his family was set for life. *Several* lifetimes."

He took a last look at the portrait, then turned to face the squad members standing in the doorway.

"That was January 23rd of that year. Two days later, the Shattering began. You see, certain OzTech investors—we call them Elitists—knew ahead of time about the potential for their new technology and what it would do to the world's economy, so they began buying up repositories of dense matter from which to strip raw starks. It didn't matter what it was; the denser, the better. Matter—in particular, *mass*—became the new economy.

"Overnight, the money of old became worthless, the world's economy collapsed, and those people the Elitists had paid obscene sums of money to quickly discovered they had nothing. Using inside information, the corporate aristocracy once again seized the reins of power, deepening their oligarchic grasp upon an ignorant world."

Dado paused a moment for reflection, and Zavier finally found his voice. "Your father…he lost everything. Everything your family had worked for all that time."

"*Exato*. The Shattering shattered more than nations; it shattered souls, Zavier. When I was still quite young—not much older than you see in this picture behind me—my father took his own life. By the end of that month, all those billions he had been paid were worth little more than the dirt in his shoes. Driven to despair, he killed himself and my mother and I were left destitute."

"That's awful," Min said with a sad shake of her head. "I can't imagine anything like that."

"Thank you for trying to see my point of view, Min," Dr. Dado said. "The Elitists built their power on the backs of many like my father. Now, they use that power to manipulate the world for their gain. Do you see?"

"No one controls the world," Toby put in. "There's too many nations, especially now."

"Yes, Toby, so many little nations—none of them large or strong enough to hold any real wars on their own. OzTech wants war, because it feeds their bottom line. More starks are used, more devices are created—and taxed—by 'peacekeeping' efforts than from any other industry. So, they support the *one* force able to go anywhere on the planet and wage war on behalf of hundreds of nations. Then OzTech profits from the turmoil."

"The Makers," Zavier said, feeling a little stunned. "But the Maker Corps aren't soldiers, we're just—"

"Just a police force, yes I know. But *whose* enforcers do you think the Makers are? The Global Nations Alliance? Perhaps. OzTech hides behind the GNA because it allows them to appear neutral. But the reality is, war is *good* for business. Every battle means there'll be a lot of printing to fix things back up, and that means OzTech's Quantum Bank gets to take out their tax to feed their coffers. As creators of our entire economic system and the technology that supports it, they benefit from *everything* we do. It's a monopoly. Do you know that one percent of every print or Vac goes to the Quantum Bank? One percent of everything you eat, sleep in, or wear. But war is more profitable—they get one percent of every bullet, shelter, weapon, vehicle, surgery, and repaired limb. All of it for all of OzTech."

"But you're supporting them by waging your war!" Zavier shouted.

"Yes. But it's only to bring it all down upon their heads. A short-term sacrifice for long-term liberty. Both OzTech and their dimwitted accomplice, the GNA, need to be torn down for all of us to be free again." Dr. Dado pressed a hand back against the vid-cube. The portrait vanished, replaced once again by the enlarged map of the Moon and capital city. He strolled a couple steps away from the wall and stood in the middle of the room facing them, the Moon map to his back.

>>Min>>This is twisted.<<

>>Texas>>The Shattering affected everyone. Not just Dado!<<

>>Toby>>Twisted or not, we need to come up with a way to get out of here. We got about three full squads at our backs.<<

"The Elitists own the world, Zavier," Dr. Dado continued. "They look down upon it from their corporate campus—or should I say palace—in the sky. When my father took his life, my mother vowed to take revenge on these Elitists who took our lives away, and the lives of so many others. She started to plan how to overthrow these tyrants and trained me to be the executor of this plan.

"I have spent my life trying to set things right, to bring down these Elitists and unshackle the world. No single individual or organization has any right to control such vast reserves of matter. It belongs to the world."

"All of it," Zavier slowly quoted, "for all of us."

"Exatamente." Dr. Dado beamed. "Still a prize student after all."

"But…why a Rooster?" Zavier asked.

"The theory is that it refers to the Gallic Rooster," Kojo jumped in, "a symbol of French rebellion, thus making the connection to the Parisian."

"A nice little deception on my part, Kojo," Dr. Dado admitted. "It actually refers to the Rooster of Barcelos; the unofficial symbol of old Portugal. Many Portuguese still have one in their homes for good luck. But at a deeper level, it symbolizes the plight of those falsely accused, the struggle of the poor, and how true justice for the common people will triumph in the end."

"Justice?" Texas suddenly burst out. "The Rippers kill people, families—cause chaos."

"We are freedom fighters, Jenny. Something which Texans should be very familiar with, if you study your homeland's history." Dr. Dado started to pace a little, assuming the role of teacher before his students. "Sam Houston, Davy Crockett, James Bowie, and many others fought the much larger forces of General Santa Ana for the right for Texas to be free. This was an impossible overwhelming task that involved the sacrifice of their very lives, but they did it. Hasn't Texas been independent *and* united ever since?"

"And proud of it!" Texas found herself saying.

"So, you can understand my struggle, can you not?"

"Well, I…"

>>**Texas**>>**Sorry, guys, reflex response.**<<

"I desire no less than to liberate the world from our age's Santa Ana and his dragoon hordes, known as Makers. Do you really want Micro Texas under the control of some executives in their mansions on the Moon?"

"*No one* controls Texas," Texas snapped.

"Ah, but they *do*—just as they control Guadalajara, Accra, Yanbian, New York, and every member Micro of the Global Nations Alliance. As Makers, you swore an oath to protect the citizens of the world. But in reality, that is exactly what the Rooster Rebellion is trying to do."

"Listen to him," came the voice of Hilla from behind them. "Finland used to be a united, prosperous nation. Now we are poor, broken, and beholden to others who own all the major mines and material rights. I have seen families vac deep pits beneath their homes to harvest the raw matter they need just to get by."

"India is a nightmare," Sam picked up. "The Shattering divided us into dozens of factions. We have over a billion people to support, but the resources we need to print food and other necessities are nearly all owned by these same Elitists. OzTech promised free food and wealth for everyone—a golden age. But we're as entrenched in poverty as ever before. Yes, our streets are all clean and the people fed, but they are no longer our streets, and the people work for powers we can never see or speak to."

Dr. Dado nodded his head in agreement. "You see? None of my Roosters are here for some pleasure they get in killing and anarchy. Every single one of them has a similar story, a similar desire to free the world. The Quantum Bank on the Moon holds the reins of their power, their wealth. Every print or vac gives them a piece of the world. But why? Yes, their founders created the technology, but the current residents do next-to-nothing to earn that wealth. They're leeching off the hard work of others. They sit back and collect a payment while everyone else lives and dies. It has got to *stop*. And who will stop it?"

"All of us!" every Rooster shouted.

He fixed them with a determined glare, then padded back over toward his desk. "Yes. All of us. That is why I started the Rooster

Rebellion. To free the world."

>>**Texas**>>**Can he be right?**<<

>>**Toby**>>**I don't like the idea of a few people controlling the lives of billions, but there's still something wrong here.**<<

>>**Koj**>>**Ghana used to be wealthy, but now little Accra is a poor country. I've always been afraid of my family going hungry, even with Oz technology. Maybe the Rippers have a point.**<<

>>**Z**>>**Perhaps Dado's using all of this as an excuse for revenge. This isn't justice. He's tearing down our world just to prove a point. The Rippers are making our world worse, not better.**<<

>>**Koj**>>**Maybe that's because for all his talk about freeing us from control, he's just one more person doing the controlling.**<<

"You are no doubt messaging each other right now, deciding whether I should be trusted, or whether I am a raving madman," Dado observed. "Take your time."

Min had remained silent this entire time, her face working through several emotions at once. Caught between Dado's words and what she saw her team saying via textlens, she finally burst out in an uncharacteristic display of emotion. Her small body tensed, face twisting up with anger, then she shouted in a tone that had the Rippers aiming all their weapons at her, ready to fire.

"You *still* kill people! Can't you see? You're worse than the corporate ruling class you're trying to replace!"

"Min," Kojo cut in, "Dado's does have one point. My country is a prime example of what's wrong with the world."

"So, he's going to fix the world through violence?" she snapped. "His actions tell us who he *really* is. The Rippers are trying to bring down the current oppressors, but they'll end up becoming the *new* ones. This cycle will never end. The Rippers are not the kind-hearted rebels Dado paints them out to be! Just ask Z about his sister."

For a second, Min fixed a hard glare at Zavier, as if by force of will she could make him remember that which he could never really forget. Dado looked about to say something, but Min's hard glare caught him short.

"I guess not too many people at the Academy know, except a couple of my squadmates and Dado," Zavier began, "but I had a little sister and she…she was killed by Rippers when they attacked Micro New York when I was a kid. Vac'ed by them in her crib."

For a few seconds, all were silent. Coover mouthed something like, "Oh man…" while even Dakota was stunned. Nonetheless, they still kept weapons up and leveled with the other Rippers.

>>**Koj**>>**I'd nearly forgotten.**<<

"Miss Yu—Min, there has been a certain amount of regrettable fallout over the years," Dado said. "But our goal is a noble one."

"Noble?" she shot back. "Is it noble to kill? Is revenge 'noble' while you pretend that it's another word for justice?"

It was Zavier who noticed two things as Min was debating Dr. Dado. First, she had her headphones in place. That was normal enough for anytime she was on a mission; no doubt she was listening to some very loud music to help her focus. But the other thing was that one hand had drifted down to where the mini-mega speaker was clipped to her belt, one finger hovering absently over a small button on its top.

>>**Z**>>**Everyone, cover your ears! Activate your suit's sound-dampers.**<<

>>**Toby**>>**Our suits have sound-dampers?**<<

>>**Z**>>**After that pounding we took in training, they do. Now, do it! Blue button on the belt.**<<

"The Rippers are nothing more than another type of thug," Min continued. "And I can't be a part of any of that!"

Dr. Dado took in a breath to reply, but Min's finger hit the speaker button. There was no hearing after that. What came out through Min's little speaker was not simply a loud blast of annoying, heavy metal-inspired pop music, but a physically damaging sonic attack that launched Dado off his feet and back into the giant vidcube. The impact shook dust and rocks loose from the ceiling, and filled the room and attached hallway with an audio detonation that had the Rippers on their knees screaming as they dropped weapons to slam hands over their ears.

In such a confined space with such volume, the sound not only shook the room and knocked loose objects from tables, but continued all the way down the hall with little loss of intensity. Inside Zavier's modified shimmer suit it was still loud, yet he had installed enough sound dampening to at least make it manageable and allow his team to operate…which was more than the Rippers could do.

Toby immediately snapped out his fold-shield and started into a charge through the flailing Rippers, tossing them aside like bowling pins, while Texas brought out her metal stick and snapped the button as she followed behind him. Her stick sprang out to its full two-meter length as she charged, holding it across her body to knock anyone across the head that Toby's shield had missed.

Kojo was next, but not before he tossed a miniature grenade toward Dado's desk. It detonated in an explosion of electrical arcs that danced around the vidcube, computer terminal, and anything else electronic in nature.

Zavier grabbed Min by the shoulder and pulled her back with him after the rest, while pulling off a stun grenade from his belt.

>>**Z**>>**The lady can sing!**<<

>>**Koj**>>**No warning?**<<

>>**Min**>>**I knew Zavier would spot me. Besides, who do you think advised him on physiologically safe audio levels when he was designing his ear-dampers?**<<

>>**Toby**>>**Anything else about these suits we should know?**<<

They ran down the hall past the squads of ailing Rippers and around the long curve, Min's music accompanying them as they went. Around the middle of the curve, they found a pair of Rippers already on the ground clutching at their ears in pain, while an attached room showed three more on the ground.

>>Z>>**Your shoes have jump-boots. Give both heels a hard rap on the ground as you flex your knees. Then jump.**<<

>>Texas>>**Nice. You also put a slushie-maker in these things? Cause I'm hot and thirsty.**<<

Min, meanwhile, was readying her mechanical slingshot with one of her softballs, while Kojo pulled out his air-pistol, loaded a pellet into it, and started pumping the handle.

Out into the large open cavern they now came, straight into several Rippers. As the source of the sound came bursting out of the tunnel, the Rippers slapped their hands over their ears. This brief delay was enough to allow Zavier to throw his stun grenade first. It arched out into the middle of the Ripper's semicircle, while a flash-heated round that rapidly expanded as it flew came from Min's slingshot.

A dozen Rippers were stunned from the grenade, while off to the right a man-sized sticky mass collided with another pair of Rippers, gluing them together. Kojo shot a pellet from his airgun, hitting one Ripper in the chest where it detonated in a brief flash. The enemy dropped, rigid with electrical paralysis.

While all that was happening, they had not ceased to charge. Toby slammed another Ripper on the left away with his shield, and Texas swatted one on the right across the knees with her staff. Then they broke straight through the middle.

>>Koj>>**Lift is still on the other side of this cavern. Lots of Rippers between us and it. Not to mention a maze of walls.**<<

>>Z>>**Then let's take this up a notch. Jump!**<<

He led the way up by taking a leap, landing with knees flexed as both heels slamming down onto the ground, then felt the recoil of the jump-boots propelling him up and out. He sailed over a squad of surprised Rippers and landed on top of a workbench. The others jumped a split-second after him and flew several meters above the ground…except for Texas. She stretched herself to gain extra height above the rest while swinging her staff below her to knock another Ripper in the head.

>>**Texas**>>**Wee!**<<

>>**Toby**>>**Min, any chance of getting some good chase music out of that thing?**<<

>>**Min**>>**This metalpop remix was used for the chase scene in the remake of *Fast and Furious: Asteroid Drift.* Did you want something louder?**<<

>>**Texas**>>**Love ya like a sister, but some time we're gonna have to talk about your taste in tunes.**<<

>>**Min**>>**You mean the taste that's saving our skins right now?**<<

They landed on available tables and benches, then leaped again. One long high-flying footstep after another, they bounded across the cavern. Rippers tried desperately to take aim at the moving targets while not falling victim to the deafening music that echoed throughout the cavern. Zavier accompanied his next jump by tossing out his other stun grenade into the thickest concentration of Rippers available, while Kojo tried another shot from his air-gun. The shots were poorly aimed, but they kept the Rippers busy.

A couple of enemy projectiles finally reached them, fired off by Rippers in the distance. One shot deflected off Toby's fold-shield, while the other was intercepted by a swing of Texas' staff as she reached the height of her jumping arc. Toby had a small dent in his shield, and Texas knocked some kind of canister off to land in another group of Rippers. The canister exploded into a cloud of gas behind them.

>>**Texas**>>**Never mess with a Texan in battle!**<<

>>**Toby**>>**I think my shield caught a bullet of some kind. They're getting serious.**<<

>>Koj>>**Almost to the other side. Those corridors are going to be narrow.**<<

>>Z>>**Then we go over them.**<<

As they came to the other side, Zavier led the way by jumping off one last table. He flew up over the six-meter wall to the maze beyond, landing briefly on top of one of the walls before giving another jump. The rest followed in kind, jumping first onto the nearest walls, then over the roofless maze on a direct line for the lift cables in the nearing distance.

They could see the corridor below and a few rooms here and there. Scurrying Rippers tried to get a good shot at them, only to be slammed down by the intensity of disagreeable sound coming from Min's little speaker. By the time the squad's last jump landed them right before the lift, there were no Rippers within sight.

Well, except for the one on the ground by the lift control, who was clutching his ears.

They ran into the lift, Kojo slamming the gate closed behind them while Toby thumbed the control button. To the refrains of Min's music, the lift started to bear them upward. Midway up to the ceiling of the large cavern, Kojo decided they'd had enough.

>>Koj>>**Min, shut off your speaker. We're out of range of anything they could toss at us.**<<

>>Toby>>**And we don't need to rattle the stones loose above us.**<<

Min thumbed the speaker control and stillness returned, though not before one large stalactite broke loose from above and went plummeting down to the Ripper encampment far below.

"I hope that doesn't hit anybody," Min remarked as her eyes followed its course down.

Toby chuckled. "Saved by our Medic's bad taste in music."

"Soon as we're up there," Kojo said, "we make a dead run for the ship. We have got to get this to the Makers before Dado acts on his big plan."

"I still can't believe he's with the Roosters." Texas sighed. "The *founder*, no less."

They rode in silence for a bit. When they started passing up through the narrow shaft, Zavier had a quiet word with Kojo. "Koj, you looked to have some doubts back there."

"I did," he admitted. "The Rippers have some valid points. If there's some secret group of despots controlling everything and profiting from the misery of others, then that needs to stop. But not at the price that Dado's asking. Not with all this bloodshed and destruction. The man's crazy. No, there's a better way. Don't worry, I'm still a Maker."

In time, the lift brought them up to the surface where they had started. Then, it was a mad run back through the cave. At the fork, they surprised a pair of Rippers. Between Texas' staff and Toby's shield, they literally did not know what hit them. After that, it was a straight path out past the hidden security scanner, and directly across to the ravine where their ship was parked.

As their vessel started to lift off and arrow straight into the sky, Zavier sat in silence. He found himself hyper-analyzing everything Dr. Dado had said.

…and what Zavier wished he had said in reply.

CHAPTER 19

Their ship docked in the same small berth as before, which now had a team of guards posted at it along with the construction workers. Zavier led the way out, setting a fast pace.

"Team Renegade—er, renegade team," a guard called out. "You guys went AWOL. The Maker Council wants to see you—now. Come with us."

"Perfect, because we want to see them," Zavier replied.

He marched straight past them, followed by Texas with Min, then Kojo and Toby. Belatedly, the guards hustled along to at least make it look like they were the ones doing the escorting.

When they came to the meeting hall where Zavier had been scolded before, the guards hurried on ahead to precede them with determined looks and drawn stun-guns. The doors flew open and the squad continued into the briefing room they had been in before. Zandrie and Major Arra were directing a meeting that now comprised a greater number of Makers, new and veteran alike.

"Commanders, we've rounded up the squad—"

Zavier pushed past the guard, followed by the others, and started straight down the central aisle. "I'm really sorry to interrupt, but this is urgent."

"Zavier, you were grounded," Zandrie shot back, her knuckles white as she gripped the podium. "You were grounded, then you ran off on a joy ride? You're going to be busted back to cadet for this."

"I would suggest something harsher," Major Arra stated. "Do we have an intact brig yet? Because I want that entire squad tossed into it. We can court-martial them after we finish here."

One of the veterans was starting up to his feet as Zavier reached the podium floor. "I'll toss these kids out myself, so the *adults* can—"

Toby gave him a hard shove to let Zavier pass. Zandrie glared at him, and Zavier knew he wouldn't have long to make his case. Midway across the floor, he stopped and started flicking his way through his Oz's pop-up vidcube while addressing Zandrie and the rest.

"'There's something you need to hear, and after that, you can do what you want with us. But you have *got* to listen. We've had it all wrong this entire time."

"Zavier, you may be my brother," Zandrie began, "but you're also under my command. I will not have any more of your insubordinate—"

"This time I have *proof*. We went to the Panasqueira mine. I was recording everything the entire time we were down there. Not only was the base in Portugal, like I thought, but the Parisian's not even the guy in charge."

"Zavier, are you mad?"

"Just arrest them and haul them out," someone called out.

"Gas-headed children," another said.

The selection that Zavier wanted finally scrolled into view above his wrist. For a moment, his old anxiety flooded his mind once again, but in his head he yelled, *Stop it!* This was too important; he had to push past his fear. He placed a finger to the selection and made a motion to push it in the direction of the room's central vidcube. A second later, the recording started to play.

"This is the external view of the cave," he quickly began. "Now, let me advance it a little…"

The view now shifted to the point when they were coming down in the lift and the extensive layout they saw in the cavern below them as they descended. The sight of so many Rippers and their equipment stopped all objections cold, and moved Zandrie from angry to thoughtful. "Dado should be seeing this," she said. "Where'd he go off to?"

"I'll show you," Zavier said. He lowered his voice a little. "Sis, you may want to sit down."

He sped up the recording to allow them to see their tour through the facility at higher-speed, then brought it down to normal at the point where they first saw the Parisian in the vidcube, then who he'd been talking with.

"…*Zavier, please remove the hood of your suit, I so hate talking to empty air. It makes me seem almost senile—which I am not…yet.*"

It was a stunned audience that watched the rest, several heads shaking "no" as they tried to deny it. But Zavier knew his sister. She would be shocked at first, then analytical and want to see it all out. When it came to where they escaped from Dado's office, Zavier paused the recording and picked up his explanation.

"This entire time, Dr. Dado has been in full control of the Rippers. He's been manipulating all of us; even the way he teaches is just another way of recruiting, making us feel like we owe him or something. He's responsible for everything." Zavier paused, then lowered his voice and turned toward his sister.

"Zandrie, *he's* the reason why Zoey—"

"I get it, Zavier," she said, absently waving him off. She had seemed shocked while the video had been playing, but now she was all military. She looked at her brother, then the rest of his team, and finally nodded to the guards, motioning them away. "We'll deal with your punishments later. Right now, we obviously have more important things to deal with."

Min let out a sigh of relief, while Toby and Texas took on a more relaxed stance.

"Despite Maker Vik's blatant insurrection, I cannot deny what I see," Major Arra stated. "The attack on Paris must be changed immediately."

"No," Zandrie said with a shake of her head. "The first thing we do is change all of Dado's access codes. Delaine get on that immediately. Next—"

Her command was interrupted when the words "Incoming Transmission" formed at the top of the central vidcube, followed by a three-dimensional image building itself out of the wall below it. A head—the face of a man everyone had *thought* they knew well. Dr. Dado smiled out at them all.

"By now, I assume that you all know my little secret."

"Dado, you traitorous…" Zandrie began. "How could you do this?"

"I am sure that the recording Zavier was no doubt making was quite clear on the matter, but allow me to elaborate. Major Vik, the Maker's sole job is to keep the people in charge safe, to secure their holdings and the grip they have on the world. The Roosters are not terrorists by any means, but freedom fighters. Whether you know it or not, you are being played. The Elitists who run OzTech use the 'useful idiot' known as the Global Nations Alliance to maintain both their power and their cut of everything in existence. How many people are even aware that they tax a share of all matter, both printed

and vac'ed? A seemingly small amount, that in totality is enough to maintain control of a planet. Makers are merely pawns of the GNA, which itself is a tool for OzTech and their Quantum Bank, to increase their profits. You aren't peacekeepers; you're security guards for the wealth of corporate shareholders."

"No," Zandrie said. "The Makers have kept the peace of the Alliance."

"Look at your history, Major Vik. Before the Shattering occurred, OzTech investors used their inside information to buy up whatever they could of dense matter stores—like my parents' mine—knowing full well what was going to happen. Their invention of Ozmium technology didn't cure poverty; they created more of it. They shifted even more wealth over to themselves and made the world beholden to them through the monopoly of their Quantum Bank...which sits conveniently next to OzTech's corporate city on the Moon. Everything you do to serve the GNA—all your vac'ing and printing and policing the world in the name of peacekeeping—simply enrichens them."

"And you kill people," she said.

"Any revolution throughout history has had its regrettable fallout. But you have a chance to change that, Zandrie. You can prevent any further bloodshed by turning the Makers over to me. Stop the lie, stop the stranglehold the Elitists have over the world."

For a moment Zandrie hesitated, a flicker of doubt crossing her face as she addressed the image of everyone's mentor there on the large vidcube. "Even if what you say is true, how can anyone hope to move against them? They control it all."

Dado replied with a soft smile, which had others worrying.

>>**Toby**>>**Uh oh, she's slipping.**<<

>>**Koj**>>**If she turns over the entire Maker Corps to Dado...**<<

>>**Z**>>**Easy there, guys. My sister's a pretty good actor.**<<

>>**Texas**>>**What do you mean?**<<

>>**Min**>>**All this time...Is there anyone we can trust?**<<

Zavier continued to watch, the others in the chamber sitting on the edges of their seats as they wondered which way things were going to come down. Zandrie, meanwhile, continued to hesitate. She shook her head as if in disbelief. "The Alliance was formed to keep the peace, to prevent wars."

"Is that what you believe? I am truly disappointed if you are this naïve, Zandrie. War isn't bad for business—it is the very stuff corporate empires are made from! Consider: the destruction of matter and property means rebuilding, which means more profits for OzTech's Quantum Bank. The Makers innovate new blueprints to help you keep the peace, yet everything you create results in you paying more taxes. Do you think OzTech wants this war to end? Of course not. This war is a game they set up so that the only side that ever wins is them. The benefits people enjoy in this age of stark-based technology are simply a side-effect of OzTech getting what they *want: more profit. But I can end this, and you can help me do it."*

"You can't take down such power…" she countered. "Can you?"

"I can, but not with the Global Maker Corps acting as their guard dogs…at least, not easily. A change is coming, Major, and it will happen with or without the Makers picking the right side. The point is, how much more blood will continue to be shed before that change arrives? My Roosters are better equipped and now more numerous than the Makers and a handful of recently promoted cadets. I do not wish to create grieving parents and widows like certain others did when they broke my father. You know me; you all do. At my core, I want peace and prosperity for all."

Suddenly, one of the newly minted Makers jumped up from the higher back seats of the room and shouted out, "Don't listen to him, Major Vik!"

Zandrie turned and snapped out a command. "Shut up and sit down before I have you arrested! I'm in command here."

"As am I," Major Arra reminded her, "and I don't think we should be listening to this…insanity. Fighting the Rippers is our main duty."

"And why is that?" Zandrie asked. "I'm starting to wonder now. But even if—and I say *if*—we were to believe him and possibly join up, how does that get us anywhere with changing things? You can't take on the Alliance, and you can't change the world."

The expression that Zandrie now wore looked like a cross between angry and depressed. Her shoulders drooped as she faced back to the image of Dado suspended out before the vidcube.

"My child," Dado said, now looking more like the patient, gentle mentor they had all come to know, *"you have always been a brilliant student, warrior, and tactician. So listen to me when I say that they have one significant weakness. If one can get control of OzTech's wealth of starks, spread it out for anyone and everyone that needs it, then they are finished."*

"They have too much," she said. "As much wealth as you say they have, they can simply hire any amount of security to protect it. We'd never get near them."

Dado's face eased into a broad, confident smile now as he spoke—like a cat finally seeing its prey before it pounced.

"In that you are wrong. Rest assured that it is all going to change very soon indeed. It will not be long before no one will ever have to worry about OzTech's Quantum Bank ever again. Those parasites will have their little piggy bank taken away from them for good, then it really will be 'all of it for all of us.' All matter will be free for everyone without any limits.

"Think about it, Major. A world where everyone—not just a privileged few—can have whatever they want. A world where even the poorest most inaccessible parts of the world never have to worry about disease or famine. A world without control from above. A world without kings and queens, where everyone has an unlimited

share of the pie. Think about it, then tell me if you still want to support your Alliance overlords."

For a moment, Zandrie said nothing. She hesitated as her gaze drifted to the ground. She started to pace, first away from the vidcube, then turning on heel and back again.

"This is a big decision," she finally said over the objections of the commanders around her.

"Of that I have no doubt. Your vow was to protect the people of this world, to stand beside them. Will you do that now? Will you stand with the people against their oppressors?"

"I…need time to think. There will be dissenters."

"I quite understand, and you may have some time. Not too much, though, you understand. Plans are afoot, and once sent rolling, the boulder will continue on its way. I will make contact again in…two hours. I hope you are able to convince the rest of the Makers of the legitimacy of our cause."

He ended with bowed head, then the transmission stopped and the vidcube flattened back against the wall. The second it was completely flat, Zandrie's hesitant, confused demeanor changed completely. She spun around, snapping out orders.

"Block all unexpected incoming transmissions like that, so he doesn't take us by surprise again. Major Arra, pass word to everyone on the station to ready up. We'll need as many ships as we can get printed. *Fast* ones, and armed to the teeth. Everyone else, we pull out within the half hour. We need to get to the Moon in force before the Rippers do."

"Wait," Major Arra interjected. "You mean you *aren't* thinking of joining Dado?"

"Of course not," she snapped back. "If he's successful in taking down the Quantum Bank, then we'll be looking at another Shattering; only this time, we may never recover. Now, why isn't everyone moving? We need to get to the Quantum Bank as soon as possible. Arra, I'll need you to stay behind and look after the younger cadets as well as the continued repair of the station."

"You're leaving the station undefended?" Major Arra asked.

"Possibly, but that doesn't matter right now. With the wealth at the Quantum Bank, we can always rebuild, but if those Rippers get hold of it, all is lost. Now get moving, and don't forget to cancel all of Dado's system access."

"Agreed," Major Arra replied. "I'll also notify Alliance Command as to events."

"Not right away," she countermanded. "We don't know if he has any moles there. Ready an information packet for them, but do not send it off until we've arrived at Prosperita on the Moon."

"Right."

As people started hurrying to their tasks, Zavier turned an eye and a grin to his squad. "See? Told you."

"Your sister *is* quite the actor," Kojo agreed. "She had me convinced."

"Maker Vik! What are you standing around for?"

Zavier turned immediately back to face his sister, coming to attention as she glared at him.

"Get your squad equipped for the mission! All hands for this one. You can start designing what new equipment you might need on the trip over. Remember: even though you're full Makers now, and even though we're headed for war, lethal force is only to be used as a last resort. Understood? Now, *move* it!"

"Yes, Major."

Zavier spun around and rejoined his team. Everyone else in the room was already running out on one errand or another to comply with Zandrie's commands. Soon, word would be spreading throughout the station of a major offensive forming against the Rippers, as well as the incredible news of who was behind that most hated enemy. What remained of the Maker Corps was now on the move.

CHAPTER 20

Thanks to the very best in terraforming technology, Prosperita metropolis-on-the-moon provides the richest experience available. Featuring designs by master engineers, chefs, artists, and artisans, OzTech's corporate living campus is second-to-none...

All OzTech executives receive their own acre of land* and a free customize print of the latest in luxury estate plans...

Prosperita living—only the very best.

*Siphoning below the surface prohibited. Other terms and conditions apply.

Excerpts from OzTech recruitment brochure

Zavier's squad was in one of two-score Maker Corps ships burning their engines to reach the Moon in time. Older craft of a century or so might have taken weeks to get there; now, it would only be a matter of hours. Even with that, though, every minute was crucial with the looming Ripper threat.

Every Maker available, veteran and newly promoted, was crammed into the vessels. Zavier was there with his squad and two others, everyone furiously going through the pop-up vidcubes on their Ozes, quickly tweaking blueprints and readying up macro programs for immediate use. In the cockpit section of the ship, beside the pilot, sat Zandrie. She hadn't stopped communicating with one person or another since before they'd left the station.

"We're on final approach," she said into her comm. "I don't know how far behind us the Rippers are, but we need to start... Yes, they really *are* going to attack the Quantum Bank. Did you watch the council replay, or were you multitasking while playing vidcube games? That was a joke—now, listen. My Makers are going to start printing defenses the second we get down there. So, I'll need a way cleared and recommend that all nonessential personnel be immediately evacuated…Yes, just whoever you need to keep life support systems running. No…Certainly not…If you don't want our help, we can always turn these ships around…Okay, we'll be landing shortly. Major Zandrie out."

She deactivated the comm with a thought then leaned back in her chair with a sigh. "I hate dealing with those people. How soon?"

"Prosperita coming up now," the pilot stated.

"Then let's get this started."

She pressed a control before her and the walls along either side of the passenger section faded into transparency as she made an announcement.

"I know pretty much none of you have been to OzTech's headquarters on the Moon before, so get the gawking over with now before the fighting starts. We'll be passing over Prosperita first, then the Quantum Bank is past that—near the dark side."

She sent a private message via textlens to Zavier.

>>Zandrie>>Heck, I have a bit of gawking to do myself. Only seen vids of the place.<<

The Moon came into view swiftly. At first, OzTech's corporate campus looked like a large glittering splotch stretching tendrils across half the lit-side of the Moon. Silvery arms reached out from a circle that spilled out from the edges of the Sea of Tranquility.

As they came closer, details of a world only possible through OzTech printing began to resolve. Zavier saw atmospheric domes kilometers across and several stories tall. Highways crisscrossed between each dome and continually flickered with the movement of high-speed trains. OzBots by the hundreds flew on one errand of repair or another.

As they drew closer, Zavier found the domes were transparent enough to see what lay within. Gleaming glass towers filled the domes with colorful art, arboretums, and parks with trees, grass, and even rivers.

Zavier touched Min on the shoulder and, pointing to a park, said, "That might be a nice place for us to visit sometime...when all this is over."

Min turned from her battle prep to look at Zavier with confusion.

Toby snorted. "Bro. Seriously? Did you just ask Min on a *date*? Just before we're about to fight in the biggest battle of our lives? I love you, *hermano*, but the timing...wow. After we win, you and I will have to have a little conversation about crafting some blueprints for being smooth."

Zavier blushed but still laughed at himself as the squad laughed as well. Out of the corner of his eye Zavier caught Texas her rolling her eyes and then turning back to her work with a scowl.

One dome covered a farming complex situated within one of the larger craters. Elsewhere, Zavier could see reproductions of several historical Earth sites—museums from around the world, monuments from a dozen cultures—all together under the same dome. He also saw places of amusement, contemplation, art, business, and industry. In short, OzTech's Prosperita was a world in miniature, perfect in every detail.

Nearer now, he could make out another feature. At the center of the sprawling city he saw one gigantic dome connected to many smaller domes. It a deep crater filled with a saltwater ocean, where originally there had been nothing but a sea of grey dust.

It boggled Zavier's mind to consider the ingots of raw matter required to print habitats of this colossal scale. He was not alone in his wonder, as every Maker on board also pressed their faces up against the transparent hull of the ship for a better look.

"That's some large pond they got there," someone from one of the other squads on board remarked. "I can even see fish in it."

"Check that," Kojo corrected. "That little pond is about a hundred kilometers across, and from this distance, those little fish you see have to be whales…those had to have been imported since printing lifeforms is impossible. And grav-tech—they must have enough gravitronic emitters to keep the water from floating up to the ceiling."

"It's so fluid," Texas marveled. "Prosperita looks near as big as Texas."

"Bigger," Toby corrected, "not that you'll ever admit that."

Texas didn't object.

"Coming into low orbit," the pilot announced through the intercom. *"We'll circle over Prosperita, then over to the other side where the Bank's located."*

They had dropped low enough now that they could see details through the more transparent domes. OzBots were keeping the avenues clean and tidy, trimming plants and gardens, making sure that everything retained its glimmer. Some of the taller buildings looked to be well over a thousand meters tall, while others seemed to plunge down into the bowels of the Moon itself.

"I see a lift shaft large enough to carry this shuttle. It drops down below the surface," Toby said. "How far under did they build?"

"According to records," Kojo said, flipping his vidglasses over into place, "about a kilometer or two. They also have some mining projects, but they put those on the dark side."

"Probably so it wouldn't spoil any resident's perfect view," Texas remarked with a light snort. "Look, we're about to pass over one of the arms. The whole thing looks sorta like a sunburst."

The arm they were passing over was a long, covered extension many kilometers long. It was filled with tall, artfully designed buildings, extensive parks and gardens, and a self-contained city in a single structure many kilometers across and a kilometer tall. Above it all rose a glittering white castle with towers and parapets, topped in gold and silver leaf.

"I wonder what that section's for," Min asked, breaking her silence.

"It's…someone's house," Kojo said after a moment. "Wait, re-checking. Yeah, that palace is home to one of the OzTech investors Dado was talking about."

"A person's *house?*" Zavier exclaimed. "The entire complex? We're gonna have to have a long talk with these people when this thing's finished."

They quickly passed beyond the city, then over several kilometers of terraformed terrain that had changed the bulk of the Moon to more resemble a large park, occasionally marked by a covered transport tunnel or outlying dome. At regular intervals, atop mountain peaks mostly, they could also see tall, slender towers topped by red blinking lights.

"What are those?" Min asked, pointing.

"From what it says here," Kojo said, reading from his vidglasses, "those are grav-field pylons. Just enough of a pull to keep the atmosphere in place without domes, but not enough to significantly alter the Moon's gravity. They've actually terraformed about one-half of the Moon over the years."

"We're headed straight for the Quantum Bank," Zandrie announced. "That's what the Rippers are after, so that's where they'll attack. By necessity, it's located some distance from Prosperita, so that should minimize the risk of civilian casualties."

It was nearly a minute before something else came into view, accompanied by another announcement by the pilot. *"Coming into Quantum Bank airspace. You should be seeing the perimeter fence below us."*

The perimeter fence looked to be fifty meters tall—solid, double layered, with a combination of security-cams and perimeter lasers every hundred meters. The fence was broken only by a gate connected to a transport-tube, the gated entrance having even more weapons aimed around it. Within the gate the land was completely flat, more resembling a desert. Overhead, the thin atmosphere faintly glimmered.

A few minutes later, the small fleet could see a large structure on the nearing horizon. It was a few moments before its scale sank in and jaws started to drop. The structure was a dark cylinder—like a water tank, but it stretched for over a hundred meters up and to the horizon in either direction.

"Fluid," a young person from one of the other squads exclaimed. "Is that the Bank?"

"Actually," Kojo said, quickly consulting his vidglasses, "that's the cap. The Bank reserves stretch for...a hundred *kilometers* down?"

"That's some big cap," Texas remarked. "Almost as big as—"

"Actually," Kojo interjected, "it's as big *as* your country."

"And all of it pure starks?" Toby said, then let out a whistle. "I'm surprised that thing doesn't throw the Moon off balance or something."

"Grav-tech," Kojo said. "They probably have the whole rock filled with gravity stabilizers. Without them, that dense of a collection of starks would probably suck half the Moon right in and throw what's left all over the Earth."

"Sounds something like what they used to call an 'Extinction-Level Event,'" Toby remarked.

"Worse, probably." Kojo shrugged. "The Moon would be sucked into a black hole and the Earth would become an asteroid field. But don't worry—I'm sure they have safeguards on their safeguards, or we wouldn't be here talking right now."

The fleet passed over the cylinder, below them an array of antennas and conical structures dotted the Bank's metallic horizon. They also saw more OzBots, hundreds of them buzzing like insects across the top of the vast structure, making little repairs where needed, fine-tuning the antennas, and even making quick passes around the ships before zipping off again. They flew for another couple of minutes before the pilot's next announcement came. *"Ready for landing. They have a landing strip up ahead on top of this thing."*

"You heard him," Zandrie snapped. "The minute we touch down, I want all of you breaking into a run. There's supposed to be an atmospheric field over this area, held in place by grav-tech, as well as something vac'ing out any hard radiation and micrometeorites, but I want everyone in envirosuits just in case. One hit on the wrong thing and you're sucking on vacuum. Now, move it!"

As the squads hurried about equipping themselves, the landing zone finally came into view. Above them loomed a solid ivory-white tower nearly two kilometers tall and three hundred meters across at the base. Zavier could see several neat rows of equally spaced docking spaces, each with tall thin posts topped by a light and navigation signal. The nearest lay far enough away from the main tower that vehicles were already waiting by the edge of the landing spaces to ferry passengers across.

"We're not parking that far away," Zandrie decided. "Zandrie to fleet; we're touching down right around this tower. Pilot, land us right in front of those people. I'm not wasting time."

Much to the obvious dismay of those waiting, the fleet descended directly in front of the tower. Forty ships came to a sudden halt, hovered for a moment, then drifted straight down to land. The second the hatch opened everyone hurried out, with Zandrie in the lead.

The envirosuits everyone wore looked like little more than

silver-tinted jumpsuits adorned with the OzTech logo, but they were truly a feat of incredibly complex engineering. With the exception of the heavy boots and sealed helmet, there was no bulk to them at all, nothing to encumber movement. The fabric was woven—or rather, printed—of impenetrable material. The OzTech employees standing before the tower entry wore something similar, but theirs were designed with fashion in mind as well—the helmets completely transparent, and in some cases currently open in front to take advantage of the artificial atmosphere.

Toby led the run behind Zandrie and was the first to discover one little thing they didn't have to worry about back at the station. Lack of gravity.

>>**Toby**>>**Whoa!**<<

>>**Texas**>>**Activate your boots, fool.**<<

A moment later, Toby came back down, taking much slower steps and without as much gusto.

>>**Z**>>**Only the city proper has a continual gravity field.**<<

>>**Koj**>>**The grav-boots will keep you weighted down, but you have to turn them on first. If you want to take a good flying leap, *then* you can turn them off.**<<

Zandrie approached the welcoming committee with a quick salute before launching into things. A dozen people were dressed in fashionable envirosuits, with at least as many bodyguards dressed in far more heavily armored battle-ready suits. The pair who stood at the front of the rest was a man and a woman. He had golden-colored hair cut to the latest trends and stood more than two meters tall, while she was a svelte figure with long black hair, looking like she'd come straight from an ancient and beautiful Chinese painting. Both looked young, or at least well-kept, and sported a superior attitude in their every movement.

"I'm Major Vik," Zandrie said, opening her helmet to speak to them. "I gathered as many Makers as I could. We have to work fast."

"Major Vik," the man said, his voice an odd combination of exaggerated bass with a touch of nasal arrogance. "The first thing you need to do is move these ships. There are spaces clearly marked. I do not need these unsightly beasts crowding in around me." His pace of speech was agonizingly slow for such an urgent time.

"Yes," the woman agreed. "I'm already starting to feel a little claustrophobic. Please move them."

"Sirs," Zandrie snapped, "I don't know if you're aware, but this place is about to become a war zone once the Rippers get here. Which means we're about to put up a whole *lot* of unsightly defenses to protect this place."

"Then please, be a good soldier and do it a little farther away," the man insisted. "Besides, your printers and QuantVacs may have trouble working this close to the main transmission antenna."

He indicated the antenna with a haughty glance at the tower behind them.

"*Sir*, the battle is going to be right *here*, because this is where the Rippers are going to attack. Now I've got to—"

From within the crowd of other noble-looking figures, a third, much older person now stepped forward. Her envirosuit was black, her posture relaxed, and the tone of her voice impatient and annoyed. She wore old-fashioned glasses on the end of her nose, and looked vaguely familiar to Zavier, but he couldn't explain why. "This is Ryan Pedigrand, President of the Quantum Bank, and Ci Xi, Chairperson of the Board of OzTech. They prefer that you address them as 'President' and 'Chairperson.'"

Zavier wanted to laugh at the titles, yet deftly squashed the impulse. Zandrie looked like she was ready to explode at the "President" and "Chairperson," and Zavier remembered what his sister had told him about her anger issues. He decided to step in and move some of the heat to himself. He came up with a quick salute to his sister and didn't wait to be given permission to speak.

"Major Vik, permission to start constructing defenses. Estimates are that the Ripper fleet might be under an hour behind us."

"Print away," Zandrie ordered, then with a glance at President Pedigrand, added, "Make it a fifteen-kilometer radius. Will that be sufficient...*Mr. President?*"

"There should be little interference at that radius," Pedigrand replied.

"Then in that case," Zandrie said, "President and Chairperson, I've got your *assets* to protect."

Without so much as saluting or waiting, she turned on her heel and began to leave. Zavier quickly joined her.

"Well," President Pedigrand huffed quietly, yet enough for Zavier to hear, "I would expect a bit more respect from these Makers, considering all we do for them."

"Oh, let them play soldier," Chairperson Xi whispered loudly. "We can watch from the inside. It should be rather entertaining."

"I suppose..."

With that, the group turned and started walking back inside their tower. Zandrie sealed up her helmet again and made a quick textlens to Zavier.

>>Zandrie>>Nice save. I was ready to feed the stuffed shirts to the Rippers myself.<<

>>Z>>"Justice, not revenge," right? I seem to remember some wise person telling me that.<<

Zavier's squad was already printing their defenses, as were all the other squads, veteran and newbie side by side. Toby and Texas were together, printing an old howitzer-sized gun emplacement, while Kojo was already on his third hovbike. Min quietly printed a defensive wall to provide cover. Across the surface of the vast cylinder, other squads were working as well, everything from hovtanks and mortars to an entire ship bristling with weapons.

>>Z>>Need some help?<<

>>**Koj**>>I've got some blueprints from the mine I managed to swipe. No time to look at them, though.<<

>>**Z**>>Transmit them.<<

A quick swipe across his Oz, and Kojo's stolen blueprints appeared in Zavier's unit. Seconds later, Zavier was already making his selection and aiming out his wrist to print.

"Oz: Modified plasma gun: scale to three times design size."

As Zavier started printing, a message came in from Zandrie to all Makers.

>>**Zandrie**>>Everyone, automate as much as you can and delegate printing to any OzBot you can grab. We've been given authorization from the QB. We have a large perimeter to protect and few personnel.<<

Kojo finished printing his last hovbike—one with twin guns mounted on the sides—and stepped over to Zavier's side. "They came up with a *plasma* gun?"

"Which means we need some better shielding."

"Right." Kojo looked over at the first stretch of towering ceramic-composite shielding that Min was erecting and shook his head. "Not enough."

>>**Koj**>>Min, triple the thickness of those shields. They've got plasma cannons.<<

Min said nothing, but sullenly commenced thickening the wall.

As Zavier printed his two-story gun emplacement, Kojo saw what some of the other squads were printing and decided a change in scale was in order. He went from hovbikes to a tank. Texas and Toby, meanwhile, had finished their emplacement and gone onto a sort of boomerang launcher two and a half meters tall and large enough to launch out two-meter razor-tipped metal boomerangs.

"Koj," Zavier said as he was working, "we haven't really had time to unpack that conversation with Dado."

"I know," Kojo replied. "And I could see his point, to a degree."

"I respect the man and love him like a father, but the way he's doing it isn't right. Is it?"

"Z, the one reliable export of Accra after the Shattering has always seemed to be poverty. OzTech didn't change that; it just changed who the rich and the poor were. So, Dado does speak some truth. I know many who would side with him if it meant a change in their lifestyles."

"And you?"

"Me…I'll admit I had a moment there…but then I realized it would only trade one form of poverty for another. These Ozes we have on our wrists created a different kind of wealth, but they didn't make poverty—or greed—go away. What Dado offers is complete anarchy as a solution to complete oligarchy. Do you think that would protect people like my family any better? Without law of *any* sort, my people would simply get run over by the biggest and the strongest…*again*. That sort of chaos is far worse than the rule of an imperfect system. It's not right, but it is *true*."

Kojo paused, deep in thought. "But what finally made me see the light was when I realized that what Dado's been doing is no different from any given African warlord over the past hundreds of years."

"How so?" Zavier asked.

"Well, your average warlord would abduct the children of a village, manipulate them, brainwash them, and turn them into soldiers. Once they had control of the kids, they'd wipe out the adults, and repeat the cycle. Sound familiar? Dado had influence over all the kids at the Academy, but he used words to manipulate the young and vulnerable instead of the barrel of a gun. He followed that up by wiping out all the adult Makers. He's no better than any of the hundreds of warlords Africa has seen over the years. That's what finally decided me against him: history."

"I see." Zavier was silent for a moment, then his Oz beeped and a few OzBots huddled around him as the printing job was finished. He scrolled through for this next selection. "Oz: Modified mega rail-gun: fixed emplacement: destination twenty meters."

He aimed his wrist and the printing commenced with the help of the bots. Even considering the extra help, print speed was shockingly fast, largely due to their immediate proximity to an endless source of starks.

"I guess you're right," Zavier decided. "I don't mind people finding a way to get rich and all, but the poor need protection from greed, too. New technology doesn't change the struggle between right and wrong; it just amplifies it. It's been that way since the beginning of time. Someone needs to stand the middle ground and protect the balance of law. And I guess that's us…we keep the balance."

He considered his own words for a moment, while Min came walking over to join them, listening in on their conversation.

Zavier continued, "Something Zandrie told me is still true, and it's that acting out in pure vengeance is not the way. I don't think Dado ever learned that lesson."

"So, you're not focused on avenging your sister?" Kojo asked.

"What would be the point? No, it's already happened. I need to be there to make sure that no more Zoeys get killed. It's about simple justice. We're the Law, Koj, and when you get right down to it, that's the only thing holding this world together."

"Agreed. Laws aren't perfect…but they're far better than the alternative. And, hopefully, they improve over time."

Their printing jobs were nearly finished, but Min had been standing beside them not printing anything, remaining silent and thoughtful. So silent, they'd nearly forgotten she was beside them until she spoke. "Order versus chaos, right and wrong, power and powerless. All of this fighting results in death and misery. There has to be another way. A third option."

Zavier nearly jumped when she spoke, then offered a grin at his own foolishness. "There's no other option...just balance. We keep the balance, Min. We're the ones that are entrusted to enforce the laws that protect *both* sides...protect *everyone*. Dado's way won't work, because people will still be greedy; in the end, his Roosters will end up like those stuffed shirts over there, strutting around like they own the place."

"We're the ones who unstuff *everyone's* shirts." Kojo grinned. "Okay, anti-ship cannon next, I think."

He had started printing his next selection when a message came in to everyone from Zandrie via textlens.

>>**Zandrie**>>**Heads up, Rippers incoming!**<<

Kojo immediately swung his vidglasses into position for a quick look, then let out a long slow whistle. "That's a *lot* of dots. Okay everyone, helmets sealed. This is going to get messy."

Zavier glanced around, then spotted it on the horizon: a cloud of fast-moving vessels skimming across the surface of the Quantum Bank's cap, headed straight toward them.

"Min, I know how much you hate death and violence, and so I know how hard this is going to be for you. I hope you know how grateful we are to have you here—to keep us alive, keep us fighting," he said. "Get ready."

They closed the front visor on their helmets, but Min did so very slowly, a breath of a sigh escaping her lips as what would be unavoidable suffering came into view.

CHAPTER 21

As no printer can create life, it is similarly illegal and unethical for a member of the Maker Corps to print a replica of another human being. Printing of human flesh shall be prohibited except for in cases of reasonable medical needs.

Global Maker Corps Code of Conduct, 2113

>>Zandrie>>**Makers, to your craft!**<<

The Makers had spread their fortifications around a solid fifteen-kilometer radius of the central ivory-white tower, with a few drones equipped with VacGuards already in the air. Drone craft that resembled mini-jets shot out at super-sonic speeds. Other drones swooped in that were full-sized craft with little more than a large gun, a guidance system, and an engine. Manned craft shot up into the air as well, anything from standard space-worthy fighter jets to designs inspired from popular classic movies, television shows, and anime features from the last two hundred years. They included delta-wing designs, fighters shaped like a large "X," designs based on old World War II classics but greatly updated, something that mimicked a miniature battleship with grav-jets, and many more. There was even a vessel that looked more like a pirate ship hovering above the ground, with cannons that fired far more deadly ammunition and sails filling with a phantom breeze.

Entrenched along the surface of the Quantum Bank's immense cap was an array of defenses that included large anti-ship guns. These shot out anything from explosives to beams of focused energy. There were kilometers of quickly-printed fortifications, manned by a scant few hundred Makers—most of them teenagers fresh off a rushed graduation. The defenses varied widely and included something that resembled a tall mechanical trebuchet, a giant self-cranking crossbow twenty meters across, firework launchers, magnetic rail-guns, plasma cannons, and of course Texas' two-meter boomerang launcher.

Past those, encircling the very outer perimeter, were the barricades the Makers had constructed. There were thirty-meter-high ceramic composite walls punctuated at intervals by tall Tesla coils that towered two more stories above them and emanated an intense electric field along the entire perimeter. Joining that, awaiting any landings by the Rippers, were a wide selection of hovtanks and hovbikes ready for action. A short distance away, Zavier could also see the suggestion of a very tall flagpole that Ranjit and Delaine had constructed.

The Rippers' imagination was not lacking either. The craft coming in had the same degree of variety, accompanied by some much larger models. There was one immense craft that resembled a large black tanker flying behind its escort of fighters. It was a three-hundred-meter-long black cylinder with an engine at the rear, and its bottom bristled with rows of guns and launchers. As it came into view, hatches opened up along its top, from which sprang out dozens of speeding hovbikes shooting toward the surface of the Bank. There was also another craft that looked like a flying saucer, a sharpened circular disc was fixed along its rim— essentially a spinning razor blade. A large array of armed drones accompanied the manned fighters.

Look at all that, Zavier thought. *Is there anything they aren't throwing at us?*

One craft was notable, not for its size or weaponry, but for the picture emblazoned across its hull of a rooster standing next to the Eifel Tower. The craft was the size of a small cruiser, atop which was projected an enlarged image of a tall, dark, and bald man with a long mustache and goatee. The Parisian. He gestured and pointed with gusto, like a mad orchestra conductor.

>>Texas>>**It's the man himself—or rather, his puppet.**<<

Flying through the ranks of both sides, the ever-present OzBots continued to go about their routine operations, ignorant of the impending destruction that was about to make their jobs a lot harder.

>>Zandrie>>**The best defense is a good offense. Time to be offensive, Makers!**<<

The drones launched out first, preceding a wave of Maker fighters that slammed into the enemy's face. The swifter ones shot out toward the Ripper fleet, diving and twisting as they shot out focused bolts of energy and charged bullets of hefty caliber. They ate up the intervening distance in seconds, their weaponry doing little to damage any hulls—but this was only the opening salvo.

>>Z>>**Soon as something's within range, we start firing.**<<

>>Zandrie>>**Makers, focus on that large cylindrical craft. I don't want that thing getting anywhere near the tower.**<<

Not one Ripper ship fired on the drones. The smaller ones were free to fly into their ranks unopposed. The larger drones flew high, trying to gain ground above the Ripper assault force on their way toward the large black tanker.

>>Koj>>**Something's wrong. They're not engaging.**<<

>>Toby>>**Maybe they're not afraid of the drones. At least the smaller ones.**<<

>>Koj>>**No. They're baiting us. It's a gambit.**<<

That's when Zavier noticed something else. The newly released hovbikes were either riding above the Ripper ships or on the ground below. Not one of them lingered in the middle of the fleet.

>>Z>>**You're right. Major Vik, they're about to take out the drones!**<<

As he sent off the message, the Rippers' fighter craft started to glow. A bolt of electricity sprung from craft to craft until it had formed a tightly woven net of electricity. The net caught the small drones, frying their systems or ripping them apart. Drones by the score started to fall.

>>**Zandrie**>>**Sentinel drones: Fire!**<<

From the bigger drones hovering above the fleet, a range of missiles and lasers shot out, targeting the nearest Ripper vessels. They had not gotten very far, though, when the electrical net exploded out in a pulse. An electromagnetic wave slammed through the larger drones. Missiles both in flight and still being launched detonated on the spot, taking many of the drones with them. Some of the drones simply stopped working and fell. A few of the larger drones remained, but only those that had been well shielded and firing lasers. The missile drones were completely disabled.

>>**Z**>>**Did I just blink or did they take out our entire drone force in one shot?**<<

>>**Texas**>>**Both.**<<

>>**Koj**>>**I doubt they can do that a second time; the matter requirements are drastic and their resources limited. Operate on that assumption.**<<

The manned ships, meanwhile, came out to meet the assault. Finally, the Ripper vessels began to engage them. Fighters met in the space above the established perimeter as explosions began to light up the sky. Launched from fighter-mounted rail-guns, colorful pyrotechnic explosions, charged rays, jet-propelled ninja stars, and metal lances stabbed into the enemy heart. All of it ripped across the sky in a line where both sides met.

In the middle of it all, the projection of the Parisian's face smiled. His voice rose up over everything. *"You had your chance to join with us. Now, feel the hammer of justice come down upon your heads!"*

Texas rolled her eyes in response, then pulled back her hood to call out through the artificially contained atmosphere. "Z, what distance do you make those Rippers?" she called out, running over to the controls of her boomerang launcher as Toby tended the howitzer.

Zavier too pulled back his hood. "About a couple kilometers past our outer wall."

"Good. The range on this thing should be about twenty-five kilometers."

"The howitzer's more like twenty, but it's all good," Toby put in. "Firing away."

Thunder cracked as Toby's howitzer sounded off, an explosive report that nearly deafened anyone without ear protection within the surrounding twenty meters. The shell shot through the sky, arching up over the line of scrimmage to come down into the middle of the Ripper fleet. It did not hit into a single ship, but detonated above, dividing out into a storm of a hundred mini shells that slammed through hulls and armor, fully penetrating before they exploded in a sonic boom *inside* the vessel.

"Toby, you've been holding back on us," Texas said. "Where'd you get *that* one from?"

Toby grinned. "Did I mention I modified the shells a little bit? I got the idea from the old grapeshot ammo. I call them my 'rumble shells.'"

"Well, let me show you how we do it *Texas*-style." She pulled a lever and the large slingshot launched off the two-meter boomerang, spinning swiftly across the sky.

"You *do* realize," Toby remarked, "that boomerangs are Australian, right?"

"Shut up, Toby, and watch."

The boomerang shot across the sky, directly into a gap through which some Rippers were about to emerge, then cut straight through one fighter without even stopping, followed by two more before it arched high above them and began to circle back.

"Uh, not meaning to disparage your design," Zavier called over, "but don't those things *return?* How you gonna catch it?"

"Patience, Z."

As the boomerang came for a second pass through the Ripper ranks, Texas yawned once, then stepped over to the other side of her launcher. She flipped a panel with one finger, then waited as a simple joystick emerged from the vidcube under the panel. Laying a finger on the tip of the joystick, she moved it slightly to one side.

The boomerang responded, changing its course to curve around down the length of the Rippers, who were now diving quickly out of the way to evade the flying razor. "I *did* say I was doing this *Texas*-style."

"Okay, my turn," Zavier said. "Plasma cannons, ho!"

Zavier reached over to press one control on the first plasma cannon he had made, and *both* of the mammoth guns took aim on the closest targets. Twin globes of plasma shot out, eating up the kilometers in seconds to turn a larger two-man Ripper craft into molten liquid. Instantly, one of the other Rippers changed course to fly straight into the mess, vac'ing up the remains through a front gun port to leave nothing behind.

"They've got industrial-sized QuantVacs," Zavier stated. "Everyone remember to put VacGuards on all their stuff?"

Another Ripper ship came down, speeding through the Maker lines to be the first to engage the outer perimeter. It too had a giant QuantVac, but when it fired, the wall stood firm. As the ship pulled up, it hit the electric field of the Tesla coils and found itself spinning out of control back into the advanced lines, just in time for Texas' boomerang to slice through it.

Zavier shrugged. "I guess someone remembered."

As Texas' boomerang carved through more Ripper fighters, she printed a second large boomerang into the slingshot launcher. She was nearly finished when the razor-edged saucer met against the first one and cut straight through it, leaving the two halves to fall to the ground. The remains were quickly vac'ed up by a passing Ripper ship while Texas frowned.

"That was my favorite boomerang."

The saucer continued on a course toward the wall, dodging Maker fire along the way.

Zandrie watched from her aircraft's perch high in the sky. Several kilometers away, on the other side of the zone of defense, other Maker weapons fired. The tall metal trebuchet lobbed off a large glittering rock that exploded into a small star over the midst of the Rippers, a blinding detonation that sent Rippers scurrying to avoid one another. A row of giant twenty-meter crossbows cranked themselves via remote then fired off hulking, guided metal shafts that pierced through multiple Ripper fighters before arcing out of sight. Fireworks launched out that heated up the horizon with sizzling bits of debris that melted through the hulls of anything passing through them.

Rippers on hovbikes began making their first run across the open metal field and met with an equal number of Makers on hovbikes. It was a hovbikes joust, with mounted lasers replacing lances. While Toby fired another shot from his howitzer and Zavier did likewise with his plasma cannons, the brutal mid-sky duel began.

The Makers on bikes were mostly the newly promoted, as the veterans protected the wall with their tanks. Maker bikes shot out with their lasers, only to see Ripper bikes dodge and weave, fly suddenly up, then come nearly straight down on top of their heads for a point-blank shot with their guns. It wasn't that the young Makers were bad bikers and gunners—they were actually quite good. The Rippers were just a lot better.

If Zandrie didn't act soon, it would be a slaughter.

"Okay, time to get my hands dirty," she decided. "Haven't been in a good fight since I got the new leg."

Zavier and the others watched another Maker fighter shoot straight into the mass of Ripper craft, corkscrewing around one while shooting up two others before leaving the third one behind with a missile coming out from its rear-facing gun. Another passing Ripper ship immediately vac'ed up the debris.

"Who's in *that* ship?" Toby exclaimed. "Did you see that? *Three* shot down at once!"

"One guess, and her last name stars with a V," Zavier replied with a grin, knowing Zandrie had joined the fight.

Kojo, meanwhile, had been consulting his vidglasses, and Min had remained quiet. She was simply standing there with a larger, more complex-looking med-scanner in her hands.

>>**Koj**>>**The Rippers outnumber us and have more experience, but they have limited resources. They'll have to rip anything they want to print. We, on the other hand, have direct access to the QB and unlimited resources.**<<

>>**Z**>>**Sounds like we should be able to hold them, then.**<<

>>**Koj**>>**But something is bugging me. Too easy. I've been pulling video feeds from the security cameras around here, and it all looks normal. Fighters, Ripper pilots, the whole deal, but still...**<<

>>**Min**>>**That's because those aren't Rippers piloting them.**<<

Zavier fired off another pair of shots from his cannons before turning to look over at Min. She was coming over to join them, opening up her helmet for a quick verbal conference.

"Min, I have visual confirmation from the cameras," Kojo said. "There are pilots in those things."

"Simulacrums," she replied. "Empty bio-prints, perhaps, but nothing with a pulse or my med-scanner would have picked them up by now. They're within range for me to at least detect something, but outside the ones on the hovbikes, there's not a single living form on any of those fighters. They're lifeless flesh surrounding bots."

"That's disgusting and unethical!" Kojo exclaimed. "Drones covered in muscle and skin? But if *everything* there is a drone, that means…"

He fired off a hasty message.

>>**Koj**>>Major Vik, those fighters are all drones! It's a diversion.<<

>>**Zandrie**>>Thought it felt too easy. Attention all Makers. The fighters are drones. Be ready for a Ripper attack from elsewhere.<<

She had no sooner made the announcement than explosions came from the exact opposite side of the walled perimeter, over thirty kilometers away from the main front. Zavier could see nothing at first until they appeared in a line of shimmering light. Ripper hovtanks and fighters began attacking the wall.

"Reading life forms," Min confirmed. "They're the real thing."

Grandmaster's voice assaulted their ears. *"What's the matter, Koj? Didn't figure I'd suggest to the powers to try a little bait and switch?"*

"Overdrive's with them," Kojo stated. "Grandmaster wants to make it personal."

"Then let's take it to them," Zavier urged. "We can use that fighter you printed."

"I'll pilot," Kojo agreed. "You got gun. Toby, you and Texas man the fort down here."

"We'll cover you guys, don't worry," Toby assured them.

Zavier turned to Min. "Min, if you're having trouble with the killing—"

"I'll shoot drones and treat wounds," she replied. "Don't worry. I may not like what's going on, but I'm still a Maker."

"Good."

Zavier and Kojo sprinted over to the fighter. By the time they were airborne, the second Ripper assault force had shot up several of the Tesla coils and were working on the wall itself, while several gun emplacements swiveled around to take aim. Plasma shots peppered the sky over the Ripper drone fleet.

As she flew her own craft through enemy fire, Zandrie saw as the Rippers' razor saucer charge straight at the wall. Electricity from the Tesla coils danced across its metallic body, but that only seemed to fuel it. It became a spinning sphere of lightning crashing into the Tesla tower, cutting through in an explosion of sparks sixty meters high and into part of the wall behind it. When the smoke cleared, the Tesla coil was gone—along with a portion of the wall.

"We have a breach," someone announced over the comm-system.

From the other front came a series of explosions and an announcement over the comms by another Maker.

"Make that two. Every one of those tanks behind us has plasma cannons and the fighters are equipped with rail-guns."

"I knew this was too easy," Zandrie muttered to herself, then spoke into the comm. "Get some units over there and seal those breaches before anything gets through."

Kojo brought his fighter in a tight arc around towards the rear front, and Zavier turned away from the devastation to ready the weapon controls.

"What'd you arm this thing with?" he asked.

"Twin rail guns," Kojo replied.

"Sounds good. Line me up."

Kojo was just maneuvering his fighter into position when two things happened. First, they saw the breach the tanks had made.

A thousand meters of wall and Tesla towers were just so much scrap, all of it being swiftly vac'ed up by what they now knew to be the Ripper-controlled OzBots. Accompanying that sight came another broadcast from the Parisian. *"All of it for all of us! You are caught in the grip of the vise of vengeance. Now, suffer the folly of your decisions."*

>>**Texas**>>**Doesn't he ever shut up?**<<

A line of Maker hovtanks arrived to hold the line at the larger breach, accompanied by some of the Maker fighters that managed to break off from the drone fleet to join Kojo and Zavier. There were still far more Ripper craft than Makers, a couple of which broke off to head for Kojo's fighter specifically. Kojo banked the fighter sharply while Zavier pulled the trigger on the rail-gun. The stream of high-velocity metal slugs missed the oncoming pair, but cut across another fighter and into one of the tanks, ripping both open. Kojo's craft, though, was buffeted by a plasma shot and a Ripper's rail-gun narrowly missed it.

"I'm going to assume that's you in there somewhere, Grandmaster," Kojo said into the comm as he pulled the fighter into a sharp upward bank.

"Slow as ever, I see," came Grandmaster's voice over the comm. *"So, do you have Z or Texas with you? I'd love to humble them along with you."*

Kojo ignored the remark. "Coming around the left side," he said. "Z, get ready with the rails."

He started banking left, but Overdrive's fighter was just as quick to change course and intercept, heading right into them but at a slightly higher elevation that put the rail-gun on its bottom side, even with Kojo's cockpit.

"Can't get a shot, he's too high," Zavier said.

Dakota's voice came through the comm. *"Fool. You left your comm open. We heard every word."*

"Yeah I know," Kojo said, then quickly switched to textlens.

>>**Koj**>>**Texas, now!**<<

Kojo banked his fighter in a sharp downward angle, heading straight toward the ground. He'd left the Overdrive fighter in a direct line of sight with the distant howitzer and boomerang guns, which Toby and Texas had swiveled around into place while the fight was going on. They wasted no time in pulling off a shot, the howitzer launching a round that exploded directly in the face of the fighter. Screams came over the comm from what sounded like Dakota and Coover, right before the freshly launched boomerang cut straight through what was left of the craft.

At the same time as the Overdrive fighter was reduced to shrapnel, Kojo was aiming his fighter nearly directly down…straight for the hovtank that had taken aim for them. As the tank tried to aim a gun straight up—which it was not designed to do—Zavier pulled back on the trigger.

"Two weak points on any tank," he said. "Top and bottom."

Twin lines of high-speed slugs ripped down so fast it resembled a laser of metal. The hovtank tried to swerve, but quick maneuvers are not in any tank's design specs. The armor peeled off, and the turret opened like an onion before it exploded.

This time, they could hear the joined, cut-off cries of Sam and Hilla. Koj pulled the fighter out of the dive mere yards from the ground, skimming across the dark grey surface and continuing to chew up anything in its way before pulling back up to a safer elevation.

"Farewell, Team Overdrive," Kojo said.

"Yeah," Zavier agreed, subdued. "I'm not taking any pleasure from it, though—"

"All of it!"

Something exploded at the rear of the fighter, sending them into a spin as Grandmaster's angry words assaulted them from the comm speaker and another fighter zoomed past them.

"Ejecting cockpit," Kojo called out.

A second later, the outer canopy blew off as the entire cockpit section launched out into the sky. Kojo got quick control of the small capsule, activated the jets, and steered it back over the broken wall.

>>**Texas**>>**Covering you.**<<

Theirs was not the only craft to be shot down. As Zandrie watched from above, the Ripper assault force rolled right over what few hovtanks the Makers had left and were now headed for the inner defenses. Most of the Maker fighters were diverted from the front line to the rear, leaving mostly automated guns to protect that section from the drones.

In the midst of this came the Parisian's voice once again over the comm-lines.

"Do not doubt the power of our resolve. The monarchs shall fall and liberté *shall take its place."*

That's when the drone fighters before the large cylinder ship parted, making way for it to advance. Maker gun emplacements tried to take aim on the mammoth vessel, but the drones shielded it by sacrificing themselves to the artillery fire. The ship approached the break that the razor-saucer had made, then slowly swung open like a lid, revealing thick clusters of missile launchers that immediately fired.

With most of the Makers in flight shifting over to the rear front, there were few there to act quickly enough to intercept the barrage. The assault slammed into the perimeter wall, reducing a long line of it to expanding clouds of vapor and blinding flashes of light.

Zandrie dove her fighter into the worst of it and started firing.

Kojo quickly consulted the escape pod's instruments as he brought it in for a landing by the rest of their squad. "Short-lived radiation, blinding flashes—those are old style *tac-nukes!*"

"Slag it, where'd they scan *those* from?" Zavier exclaimed. "How many old designs did they steal from Alice Springs?"

Its payload unleashed, the cylinder led the way in through a gap that now measured most of the thirty-kilometer length of that side of the perimeter. The gap at the rear, meanwhile, had been greatly widened. By the time the escape pod was on the ground and Kojo and Zavier hopped out, there were Rippers coming in from both directions. The Parisian's voice again intruded across all comm channels and over the battlefield.

"And the just hand of righteousness squeezes at last around the throat of its oppressors."

Kojo and Zavier looked at each other in silence. They were tired, they were bruised, and they were short on ideas. Things were beginning to look hopeless.

That is, until a message flashed in front of their eyes.

>>**Zandrie**>>**A month's pay to the Maker who can shut that guy up!**<<

CHAPTER 22

Why watch vapor when you can experience the real thing? Introducing the new Bido "Video Cube."

Based on the latest OzTech advances, the "Video Cube" can display pinpoint-accurate SOLID images inside of a crystal cube. With continually printed and refreshed simulated images at 24 hertz, you'll swear you're right there!

Now available in a gorgeous, affordable twenty-centimeter size.

Wave goodbye to your hologram; say hello to Bido!

Early vidcube ad, 2107

An increasingly distraught Min slammed her hand down repeatedly on the plasma cannon control, tears leaking out from beneath tightly clenched eyes as the noose closed in around the Quantum Bank. She slapped the control repeatedly without looking as Zavier ran from the escape capsule to join Texas and Toby.

"I don't remember designing those like machine guns," Zavier said to himself, pausing to take in Min's frantic state. She barely heard him as she continued to fire relentlessly.

The Parisian's voice came over the comms again. *"With talons like an eagle's, the rooster closes it's—huh? Move it, you fool! No—AAAAHHHHHH—!"*

A stream of plasma globes was on a direct course for the Parisian's ship as the projected image of him above it turned to one of pure terror. His ship and all within it detonated with an explosion that sounded across the length and breadth of the Quantum Bank.

Min continued to fire into the ballooning cloud of destruction. Zavier ran over shouting, the others behind him. "Min! You just shot down the Parisian!"

"Huh?" She looked up, pausing her panicked punching of the control button. "What?"

"The Parisian," Toby said as he came up to her with Zavier. "One of your shots nailed him."

"About five or six is more like it," Texas corrected.

"I…I really shot him down?" Min asked as she shook.

"Shut him up for good," Toby said with a nod. "There's not enough left of him to soak up with a sponge."

"Wait, you mean I…killed him?"

"Without a doubt," Texas insisted.

"I…killed someone."

"Yeah," Texas said in a more subdued voice. "It's not a good feeling, I know."

"But it was the Parisian," Toby added.

>>Zandrie>>**Who do I have to thank for shutting that guy up?**<<

>>**Z**>>**Min.**<<

>>Zandrie>>**You're kidding. Well, a promise is a promise. Hold on a sec…**<<

Zavier watched as Zandrie's fighter narrowly escaped meeting with two fighter drones, instead causing them to crash into each other, she then hit another line of them with what looked like metal pancakes. They stuck magnetically to the hulls of each of the vessels, but did not explode. Instead, they each let off a sudden burst of electricity that had the fighters unexpectedly flying without power or guidance on their last trajectories, which mostly involved them crashing into other drones and occasionally the metal ground.

A dozen such drones went down, the last mine hitting instead into the side of one of the Ripper hovbikes. He too started on an uncontrolled vector, hitting another hovbike while the attacking Maker fighter pulled away. The destruction only deepened Min's intense shock.

>>**Zandrie**>>**Had to handle that. Okay, Min, you got a month of my pay. Now see how many of these other guys we can bring down.**<<

Before Zavier could lend Min any comfort, Kojo broke in with a reminder of their situation. "They're coming at us from both ends. We need to take this in close."

"Right," Texas said, already on her way to one of the hovbikes. "Toby, you ever play with string as a kid? I've got something to show you."

As the two rushed away, one of the many OzBots flew over their heads, apparently determined to start work repairing some of the ongoing damage from the battle.

"That reminds me." Zavier pulled Kojo to the side. "How are you doing with that other project? Think the hack might work?"

"It's possible," Kojo replied. "Haven't had too much time to deal with it, but if I can get access to one of the subroutines…"

Their conversation drifted into the distance as Min put in her earbuds and tried to use loud music to drown out the chaos in her mind.

Texas and Toby shot up into the air. They banked their hovbikes around to the solid row of Ripper hovtanks that fired out in unison with their plasma cannons and reduced everything before them to rubble. Walls shattered, barricades fell, and then they began targeting some of the anti-aircraft gun emplacements, clearing the way for the fighters now shooting past them.

The pair came straight at the first tank, Toby veering left, Texas veering right.

>>Texas>>**Let's find out what Koj loaded these things with.**<<

They both pressed the triggers as one. From the sides of the bikes, slender missiles emerged with a ring of metal teeth on their noses. By the time each pair impacted into a tank, their teeth had turned into a drill, burrowing quickly through the armor of the tanks before detonating. The tanks drifted to a halt. One Ripper emerged from the top hatch, bathed head to toe in the white mass. He tried to jump from the tank when the substance started to harden, and he was frozen in mid-air like a bizarre sculpture.

>>Toby>>**Quick-harden glue? Let's see what happens when we shoot one up the backside of a fighter.**<<

They banked back around, lining up a shot for a passing Ripper fighter. This one had its wings spread apart in the shape of an "X." Texas struck one of its left-side wing jets with a glue-missile, which sputtered out the engine and set the fighter into a quick, one-sided corkscrew. It collided with a Ripper on a hovbike who had been trying to avoid a Maker firing shot-puts with a double-barreled launcher.

That still left quite a few others getting past the duo, including several more on hovbikes.

>>Texas>>**Toby, time to play jump rope.**<<

She brought out a handgun as she came in alongside Toby and fired it at the side of his hovbike. A metal dart—attached to a cable—pierced into the side of the bike. She then reached back and slammed the gun against the side of her own bike, where it stuck firmly in place.

>>Texas>>**Stay about three meters apart.**<<

Toby nodded then banked away, the cable unspooling from the pistol as he parted. At three meters, he leveled out his course. Exchanging a look, they both brought their bikes up to speed, coming right up behind a line of Ripper hovbikes. They didn't bother shooting, but sped right past to either side. The cable was still stretched taught between them, which caught the first Ripper across the back and flipped him off his bike.

…then the second one.

…then the third one.

…then the fourth through eighth bikers as Toby and Texas strafed through their line. The Rippers were tossed up into the air or pushed down, popping and screaming all in a row.

>>**Texas**>>**Huh. They're not very good at jump rope. Too bad.**<<

Zavier was reaching for his plasma gun control when he saw a Ripper hovtank rapidly approaching. He grabbed a still-stunned Min around the shoulders, stomped one heel down hard to deactivate his grav-boots, and jumped. He sailed with Min through the air as the guns exploded behind them.

"Oz: Hovbike: two-seater: hover-mode active." The bike materialized before them. Zavier grabbed it by the handles to draw himself and Min onto the seats. They were no sooner seated than he shot it straight up, looking for tactical options. He saw one and steered the bike straight for it. It was the tall "flagpole" Ranjit and Delaine had built.

"Hang on, Min!" He power-dived straight toward the pole, three hovbikes in pursuit behind him and a small fighter-jet coming into line.

"They're on our backs!" Min screamed.

"Make sure your seatbelt is on."

He got nearly to the top of the flagpole itself, then made a sharp turn straight up. Immediately, something shot up to the top of the pole—but it wasn't a flag. It looked like a gun emplacement mounted on a disc wrapped around the pole. Delaine was seated behind it. The disc spun around the pole in a blur and Delaine fired wide sprays of projectiles from it as she ascended. When her turret-disc hit the top restraining ball, it bounced back down.

Anything in the air within twenty meters was hit, with hovbikes dropping and the fighter finding several sources of electromagnetic energy pulsing out across its skin and into its innards. Delaine hit the bottom, where she had printed a thick resilient pad that bounded her back up again for another round of spinning shrapnel fire, the action of the gun firing providing the push for the spin. Small jets on the underside of the disc controlled her descent, and then she repeated the same bounce-and-fire.

Zavier leveled out high above, pausing the bike for a moment to admire the mess below. "She really looks like she's having fun down there."

"I'm not," Min objected.

"Print a transparent shield to cover us, but make sure it has some holes for guns."

Min took in a breath to quickly collect herself, then nodded and got to work. It wasn't long before their hovbike had a cover, with a selection of small holes perfectly sized for sticking a gun barrel through.

From his position, Zavier had a good view of the battlefield. The outer walls were pretty much all gone, as were most of their outer defenses. The Maker fighter ships had drawn back a few kilometers to circle a tighter perimeter, while those on hovbikes were staying even closer to the tower. Half of the gun emplacements were gone, though most of the hovtanks were still in place.

They were badly outnumbered.

From the rear came the main Ripper force, with most of the drone fleet still intact and hovering close to the large black cylinder ship. As quickly as the Makers could down another drone, a Ripper bot would vac the remains and print another drone to replace it. Explosions rang off the hull of the large cylinder, both from above and beneath, surrounding it with a prismatic halo.

The ship drifted over the thickest Maker entrenchment and the weapons protruding along its underside began to glow, each picking a different target. When they fired, they did so all at once. It looked like a firestorm ringing out through the artificial atmosphere. Weapon emplacements smoldered, Maker tanks were torn apart, and even the thick metal of the Bank's cap started to rupture. Fire fountained up in a display that was no doubt seen from the edges of Prosperita.

Then, panels on the top side of the large craft slid aside, and in a moment of fearful epiphany, Zavier knew what was coming. He took one look at the number of Maker craft, trying to attack it from above. "Look out!" he shouted into his comm.

He gunned his bike and felt Min's arms wrapping around him from behind. He wanted to go over there and do something, but he really had no idea as to what. He knew that vessel was designed to chew up anything near it. Top, bottom, sides—it didn't matter.

>>**Koj**>>**Z, get back here!**<<

>>**Z**>>**Got to stop it.**<<

>>**Koj**>>**How?**<<

That one question got him to pause, and the nearness of Min's nervous, panting breath made him veer away. Suddenly, his sister broke in with the solution.

>>**Zandrie**>>**Everyone, pull away from that death cylinder. Drones only. In fact, gimme every drone we have left, all on my tail.**<<

Zavier saw Kojo coming with his own hovbike, behind him a cluster of Ripper bikes in hot pursuit. He had a transparent shield printed overtop of his bike, but that was quickly chipping away under the fire.

>>**Koj**>>**Got someplace I can put these?**<<

>>**Z**>>**Yeah, follow me. Z to Delaine: Incoming.**<<

Delaine had dropped down on her bouncy gun a second or

two before the two bikes sped on by. She came up to the top of the pole again just as the Ripper force was nearly to her and greeted them with a broad smile…and lots of high caliber electrified exploding shrapnel. Zavier and Kojo quickly pulled up above the level of the pole while several of their pursuers just as quickly hit the ground in multiple pieces.

Clear of that, Zavier spared a glance to see what his sister was up to. A cloud of what remained of their drones was going on an attack run for the black cylinder, but as the copious array of gun emplacements shot them all out of the sky, a single Maker fighter broke off and dove for the still-open front maw that had unleashed all the tac-nukes.

"She's not going *inside* that thing," Min said in his ear. "Is she?"

"It's Zandrie." Zavier sighed. "Of course she is."

>>Texas>>This battlefield does not look pretty.<<

The Makers were few and quickly becoming fewer, while the Rippers seemed to be everywhere. The Ripper tanks on the one side were within eight kilometers of the tower, while the cylinder and drone fleet on the other side was eliminating what was left of the defenses.

>>Texas>>**Koj, how high up does this artificial atmosphere go?**<<

>>Koj>>**About two hundred meters, I think. Why?**<<

The answer came in the form of Texas herself jumping up *past* them, something like a harpoon gun in her grip and grinning widely. Once she was several yards above them, she fired off her harpoon gun at one of the passing fighters, then started coming back down.

>>Texas>>**Our bikes got shot up so I swapped footwear. Do you know how high those jump-boots of yours can do in the Moon's gravity? I think I cleared twenty meters easy.**<<

>>Zavier>>**But a harpoon against a fighter?!**<<

>>Texas>>**Why not?**<<

The harpoon imbedded in the side of the fighter, and a moment later the whole craft exploded, pieces of it racing down to the ground and carving a long black scar into the Bank's cap.

>>**Texas**>>**Of course, I miniaturized and modified the clunky thing.**<<

Through their comm-channels, Zavier and Kojo said two words in unison. "*Texas style.*"

>>**Texas**>>**Squad name.**<<

She sent a vidloop of a Texas Republic flag, proudly waving in the breeze.

Zavier watched as Texas leaped again, joined by Toby in his freshly-printed jump-boots. With perfect timing, Texas landed atop Zavier's bike while Toby landed on Kojo's. They both clung to the transparent shells with their knees. Zavier thought he heard a "yee-haw," but couldn't be sure.

"*I grew up riding a horse,*" Texas said.

"*They shot up all our fortifications,*" Toby said via comm. "*And it doesn't look like they'll have much trouble with what's left. We need a fallback position.*"

"*We'll draw back toward the tower,*" Kojo ordered. "*Hold the line about four kilometers around it so that antenna doesn't get in our way.*"

"Then hang on," Zavier said. "Min, you doing okay back there?"

Her grip merely tightened around his waist. He led the way straight for the ivory-white tower, racing through clouds of fire and swarms of brightly glowing embers. A rising cloud of smoke and debris expanded across the horizon while a hundred ships from a hundred different inspirations battled. For a moment, it looked to Zavier like six classic science-fiction movies, three old television series, and a handful of recent anime cube flicks were duking it out over the supposedly impenetrable fortress of the Quantum Bank.

From the corner of his eye, Zavier was first to see it: a single fighter configured to look like a sphere with flat plates to either side of it. It came barreling straight at them with a single transmission coming in via comm. The transmission was in Grandmaster's voice.

"Ha! You didn't expect the double fake-out!"

Everything happened at once, but for Zavier it felt like it happened in slow motion. First, he saw Toby reach for his belt and throw something.

Then came Grandmaster's shout in the comms, *"You all die now, Takers. Checkmate, Koj."* Texas lifted her harpoon gun and fired just as a small missile shot from Grandmaster's ship. At the same time, Toby's thrown object expanded into what look like another fold-shield, except this one hovered and was twenty meters across. The missile reached it and the shield collapsed into a small box. Suddenly, Texas' harpoon slammed into the front part of Grandmaster's fighter, and it too detonated.

Grandmaster was lost to a blast of fire that ripped completely through his ship.

Toby's box contained the bulk of the missile's explosion, but not all. The box shattered, flinging shrapnel everywhere, most of which bounced off the protective domes they had constructed… the same domes atop which Texas and Toby now clung. Pieces lodged into Toby's side and Texas' back, as well as the undersides of the bikes where the shells ended. The bikes began to sputter as the two outboard passengers cried out in pain.

"Going down for a crash landing," Zavier announced. "Hold on!"

Zavier's bike spun once to the left, straightened out, then dropped several meters before he got it straightened out again. Thanks to Toby's bulk, Kojo's bike was nearly riding sideways.

The hovbikes crashed down before the very doors of the tower and skidded to a halt. Texas and Toby were harshly thrown to the ground, while the riders within the bikes found themselves bouncing off the interior of the domes.

But nobody wasted any time massaging bruises.

"Min, let's vac this thing and get out of here," Zavier said as he extricated himself from her desperate lock around his waist.

By the time Zavier, Min, and Kojo had vac'ed their ways out of their ruined bikes, Toby was limping up to his feet, supporting a gasping Texas.

"She's hurt worse than me," Toby wheezed.

"Let's get inside," Kojo directed. "Can anyone see how?"

The doors seamlessly blended in with the surrounding walls. Zavier rapped a fist on them and demanded entry.

"Let us in! We've got wounded out here!"

No reply.

"Listen," he shouted. "Do you want the publicity fallout from letting a squad of young Makers die on your doorstep?"

The doors suddenly slid open, revealing the elderly assistant with glasses.

"Enter with alacrity, if you please," she said.

They dragged themselves in, the door sliding quickly shut behind them, and entered a very spacious and luxurious lounge with plush couches, a chandelier, and a food printer that came complete with its own butler. Zavier saw several more sliding doors spaced around the place, as well as a sparkling pearl staircase that wound around and up until it was lost to a glare of white.

They dragged Toby and Texas over to one of the couches while Min printed her medkit and scanner, including a cable she was already hooking up to her Oz. Away from the horror of war and death, she seemed focused and back in her element. She knelt by the couch to get immediately to work.

"I'll have to use my new Oz-hack to repair the damage in time."

"Thas…otay," Texas said, barely able to sit up straight.

"I's…Texas tough…"

They left Min to her work, Zavier pulling Kojo over to the far side of the room for a quiet talk. "I need to know if we can hack into those OzBots *now*, because we're sucking on stark fumes here."

"Agreed," Kojo replied. "But what do we do with them?"

"Not entirely sure yet, but we need to—"

"Could you *please* hurry up your treatment? You're getting blood everywhere."

Standing before one of the now-open sliding doors was Chairperson Xi and President Pedigrand, their protective space-suits gone to now reveal expensive business suits in the latest fashion.

"Get working on it," Zavier said to Kojo. "I'll handle the 'board of directors' over there."

Zavier rushed over to the pair and was preparing to chew them out when he saw something that caught him short. The assistant was saying something to President Pedigrand and Chairperson Xi that caused them to look nervously at Zavier and his squad . Behind them, he could see a very large room and several others of their well-dressed crowd, all of them looking as superior and in control as before—but here and there, he spotted a furrowed brow or nervous glance.

But he also saw something else, something that had him pushing his way past them despite the presence of bodyguards.

"You can't go in there," the elderly woman told him. "I demand that you stop immediately."

But before a guard could step up and intervene, Zavier had already seen too much. The room beyond was far larger than the anteroom, towering up for several stories, all of it filled with walls of enormous vidcubes. Crystalline runways and stairs spiraled up before them, while here and there a white-robed technician tended to one of the cubes.

"Is this a control center?" Zavier marveled. "But what could—"

The vidcubes displayed scenes of the battle outside, but what caught Zavier's attention were the angles from which the views came. Not from the forest of security cameras, but moving views—ones taken from the middle of the battle itself from a hundred different viewpoints. They were shots from what appeared to be moving people: Makers fighting and dying.

He saw Zandrie piloting her ship in perfect detail. She was inside the black cylinder ship! He saw her fire a single missile at a weapon stockpile. Then, the view did a complete loop-the-loop as she spun her fighter completely around and headed back out through the cavern like a missile. The explosion set off the entire stockpile. The death-cylinder was gone, along with the drone-fleet, but the Rippers coming in from the other side were still within a few short kilometers of engaging the tower directly.

He breathed a sigh of relief that she was well.

Then two vidcubes unexpectedly caught his attention: They showed his parents.

His mom was in a New York laboratory, surrounded by a variety of equipment used for printing and testing new compounds. It was her workplace. Zavier knew it because he had visited her at work before. Zavier noticed how perfect the detail of her was, down to the color of her kind eyes that he knew so well.

Neither his mom nor the lab workers who surrounded her were currently working. They all were looking up at a vidcube, watching intently as it displayed scenes of the battle of Prosperita—the battle Zavier and the Makers were fighting.

In the other cube, he saw his dad resting on top of a mountain, with nothing but nature and fresh air for miles around. The man looked out across a vast valley, deep in contemplation, a touch of sadness in his face. He looked concerned, as if he knew the danger his son was in but was struggling with the reality that he could do nothing about it.

The mountain was a place his dad went to be alone, to clear his thoughts. Zavier knew it because his dad had taken him there several times before. He also knew there were no cameras or vid signal in that area; it was one of the few truly quiet places left in the world.

Zavier turned to the OzTech executives. "*How* are we seeing this?!"

He glanced back to the cubes and noticed a small timestamp in the corner of each. He was not viewing recordings. These were live feeds.

Zavier marched over to the executives and their assistant. In the doorway, Kojo was coming in with Texas, Toby, and Min, all now gawking at what they saw.

"If you want to survive the next hour," Zavier snapped, no concern for the rank and privilege before him, "then you'd better start telling me what's going on here. All of it!"

"My successors have messed things up enough," the assistant said as she removed her glasses. "I believe it's time we had a candid conversation, young Maker Vik."

CHAPTER 23

"None of this was meant for your eyes," the elderly woman said. "As they say, 'ignorance is bliss,' and it is far better for you to remain ignorant. But I suppose that's part of growing up...something I'm not sure these dimwits here will ever do."

Pedigrand and Xi looked at each other hesitantly, the other well-dressed executives in the room gathering in a loose circle around the elderly "assistant."

Min took a step closer to the woman, studying her face. "I know you. You're—"

"Helen Lo," Kojo interrupted. "One of the three founders of OzTech. But that happened almost ninety years ago. You must be…"

"A gentleman never reminds a woman of her age, Maker Solomon."

"Yes," President Pedigrand said. "She is the former CEO and founder of OzTech. You should show her some respect. This woman helped create everything you see."

"Oh, do shut up, Ryan," Helen said. "The only reason you and Ci have a position here is because I owed your grandparents some favors."

Zavier noticed the looks of protest flash across their faces. Looking around the room, he saw that most of the OzTech executives kept glancing at the vidcubes to check the battle. He followed their gazes, noticing that one bank of vidcubes showed views from the streets of Prosperita as several people looked up in curious wonder at the fiery display in the distant sky above, while yet another vidcube high above their heads seemed to show a view from the Academy. Other vidcubes showed the inside of a café, or a bedroom as a family got their kids ready for school. One view showed a couple of young men on horses, riding across an open plain.

"I don't care who you are," Texas exclaimed. "Those are my brothers back on the ranch! How?"

"That one over there…" Toby pointed. "That's my mom's kitchen back home."

"My uncle's sand garden," Min muttered in disbelief.

"And the detail," Kojo noted, pointing to one of the views. "I can see the sweat on that Maker's face in the cockpit…from *inside* his envirosuit."

"There are views of the battle all over the place," Toby added. "But none of them correspond to the security cameras we saw coming in."

Min stepped out toward the middle, then stopped to pan her gaze around. Her lip trembled.

"What the shattering," Zavier cursed, "is going on here?"

Helen Lo took in a deep breath, raised herself as tall as she could, and then finally spoke. "I will tell you—only because the situation is desperate, and only if you vow never to tell anyone outside this room."

"I promise to broadcast it to everyone if I don't like it," Zavier snapped. "Now, spill it!"

"It's the VacGuards," Helen began. "They allow us to continually track all wearer movements, and all objects, in very fine detail. This gives OzTech pinpoint accuracy of the location of every person and printed object anywhere. A necessity," she quickly added, "for our quants—quantitative analysts—to keep an eye on everything."

"So you can track us?" Zavier asked.

"No," Helen replied with a patient smile. "So we can predict all possible futures and all possible outcomes. Think of quants like investment scientists. They help us make decisions about who to invest in, who to support, and who to cut off. They make sure OzTech profits are maximized for our shareholders."

"How do you even know who we are?" Min asked. "Why track us and our families in particular?"

A man standing in the circle, presumably a quant, offered, "Our algorithms have determined that your choices are pivotal in creating certain results for OzTech and its investors. You are mathematical linchpins, so to speak."

"We're variables in an *investment* equation?" Toby exclaimed.

"What's the range?" Kojo asked, stepping over to join Zavier.

"Thanks to quantum entanglement, range is not an issue," Helen replied. "We can view anyone with a VacGuard anywhere on Earth and the solar system."

"Billions of people," Zavier said slowly, "and you *see* them… all?"

"Anyone—and anything—with a VacGuard, yes," Helen stated.

"But the computational power needed just to handle all that traffic," Kojo pondered, "even with quantum-level circuitry…"

"The mainframe is buried at the core of the Moon," Helen explained. "It's roughly two kilometers in diameter."

"Two kilometers…"

Zavier's mind was spinning. He paced away from the elderly founder of OzTech for a moment, walking across the room where sheets of vidcubes towered above him. This was an ivory tower indeed, the ultimate version of one. He finally stopped and slowly turned to face Helen, a question on his mind. "And…how long have you been able to do this?"

"Since…Oz model ten came out," Helen admitted. "But it's the VacGuard that does it."

"So, that's…" Zavier started doing the math, but naturally, Kojo had an instant answer.

"Fifty years," Kojo stated.

"*Fifty* years?" Zavier exclaimed, fixing all the OzTech executives with an angry look. "You've been tracking everyone for the last fifty shattered years?! Didn't you ever stop to think this was *wrong?*"

Helen looked at him in surprise. "Of course we did, my boy. But then we realized that our success gives us resources to make the world a better place."

"Yes," Chairperson Xi added. "We are the single biggest donor to *every* major non-profit in the system."

"Profitability creates its own morality," Helen concluded.

Texas had to struggle to hold Toby back.

Zandrie's fighter came spitting out from the expanding fireball that had been the large black cylinder ship. She set a changing course across the airspace around the tower to get a better view of how the rest of the battle was commencing. A swarm of OzBots automatically came in to repair the damage done to the surface of the Bank.

She had put a significant dent in the Ripper offensive, but the main assault had always been from the other side, as was proven by the storm of jets and fighter craft now speeding toward the top of the tower. Ripper tanks were trying to roll over the Maker defenses.

One Ripper fighter dove through a maelstrom of fire, wove between a pair of Maker defense drones, and shot something out directly at the tower. The object impacted, but did not explode. Instead, it unfolded like a starfish with a ceramic sheen. Its wide tentacles wrapped around the wall of the tower and then began a slow climb down toward the base.

"It's going to use those arms to pry open the main gate," she realized. "Zandrie to Makers: I want three squads directly in front of that door! I'm going after that starfish myself."

With that, she adjusted her controls and dove straight down toward the tower, guns blazing. Intense pulses of radiant energy guaranteed to roast any one of the small craft there, but the giant starfish's ceramic hide simply absorbed it. Additionally, as the energy sank into its skin, it ran up the arms to collect at the center into an increasing glow.

Zandrie swerved her fighter sharply to one side as she realized the energy of her own attack was about to be shot right back to where she had just been. The shot went off, just missing her and instead hit another fighter in the sky.

"This one's going to be tricky. Good thing tricky is what I get paid to do."

Banking her craft sharply down, she leveled out at five meters above the ground, circled once around the base of the tower, then altered course and shot straight up its side. The bottom of her craft was not more than a foot above the surface of the tower's wall and was about to get closer as she tilted the fighter to one side, brushing the right wingtip with the wall itself. Sparks flew as she shot up the side, her speed increasing to her craft's very limits.

The right wingtip scraped up along the surface, speeding like a bullet underneath the clinging ceramic starfish. It hit at a speed in excess of Mach nine, scraping the starfish loose and popping it out into the air, flipping end over end as it flew apart. Some remnants from the ends of its arms remained fixed to the tower wall, but not enough to do more than spark and cling.

Zandrie shot out off the top of the tower before leveling out her course.

>>Ranjit>>**Every time you do something like that, it makes it harder for us to come up with something to match. Especially with your robotic leg.**<<

>>Delaine>>**Forget it, we're not topping that one. Now, back to the bouncy-gun before they realize all they have to do is shoot the pole.**<<

Zandrie grinned at their remarks, but quickly got back to the task at hand. She could reminisce later, *if* they all survived this battle.

Another explosion caught her eye, as well as the Ripper Ozbots that sped to clean up the debris while another bot finished printing a new drone mid-flight.

"First thing's first," she said, thumbing the comm switch. "This is Major Vik. Priority targets are those Ozbots of the Rippers. Take those out and they can't resupply themselves."

She aimed her fighter toward the nearest one to take it out herself.

The horrified squad took in the sight of the massed vidcubes, the gathered OzTech executives, and the revelation that had just been presented. Toby looked ready to take the world's frustration out on their hides and it was all that Texas, Kojo, and two security guards could do to hold him down as Texas whispered into his ear, trying to calm him down. Zavier was fuming, but in the moment, he was unsure of what to say.

The first outburst, though, came from Min.

"You have been spying on our private lives all this time? *Everyone's* private lives? I have my VacGuard on me all the time, *everyone* does; it's an unavoidable safety measure. How many times have you or your technicians seen me in the shower? How many times have you witnessed someone mourning a lost loved one and watched like it was some soap opera? How many times… how many times have you seen our most private moments? I can't think of anything more disgusting. You people should be… should be…"

Zavier snapped out of his own sickening feelings and raced over to wrap his arms around her and hug her tight, whispering calmly into her ear. "Easy, Min. Don't say anything you might regret; that's *my* job. Calm down."

Her shoulders shook with faint sounds of quiet sobbing as she held her face down into Zavier's shoulder. When she looked up at him, her face was wet, but it was accompanied by a look of gratitude in her eyes.

"I'll find a way to hold them accountable, don't worry," Zavier said.

"I'm fine," she whispered.

With one last hug, he released her, at which point Texas came to take over. Seeing Min's outburst had calmed Toby down enough that they could release him, though his rage was still palpable. Texas took Min aside, talking to her quietly about the sorts of cowboy justice that would happen to people like that back in her home country—suggestions that earned a tearful smile from Min.

Helen remained impassive throughout these outbursts. "The other founders saw OzTech's stark technology as simply a way to enhance the quality of everyone's life. But I saw it for what it really was: a tool for complete economic transformation. The VacGuard tracking ability is key to our—"

"Shut up," Zavier snapped.

In response to the astonished looks of everyone present, two of the security guards stepped up to either side of Zavier. They were twice his build, but at this point he didn't care. He fixed them with a determined glare.

"I represent the legal authority of the Global Nations Alliance and the Global Maker Corps, and I'm better trained than you are in using those Oz units on your wrists—so back off! When all this comes out, there's going to be a lot of people landing in deep dark dungeons with actual live rats nibbling at their ankles. Would you like to be among them?"

Both guards stepped back, leaving Zavier free to face their masters.

"Dado was right," Zavier said, but quickly added, "at least in part. Your choices helped create the monster that Dr. Dado has become. You people have betrayed…*everything* just for your own greed. You don't *need* more profit. You already have more starks than all the rest of us combined. Your rationalization that you're helping others doesn't justify breaking every privacy law in nearly every country. You have no self-control—you just continue gobbling up anything you can, then keep going for more without a thought for anyone else's lives. That war happening out there, the lives the Rippers have taken, are a direct result of what *you* people have done! You have *far* too much privilege, and it's time someone brought you into check."

For a moment, everyone stood stunned, including several of Zavier's own squad. Min stopped her tears and looked in surprise at Zavier; while beside her, Texas regarded him with a grin and what almost looked like pride. Toby squared his shoulders, gave his friend a supportive look, and whispered quietly into his Oz, "Oz: Handcuffs."

Kojo, though, took a more temperate approach. "I agree," he said as he stepped over to Zavier, "but now is not the time. This technology might give us an advantage in this battle. We need to figure out how."

Zavier was suddenly aware of how much attention his words had attracted. His squad, the OzTech executives, the technicians scattered about—all eyes were on him, each filled with some degree of panic. He took it all in a glance. Kojo looked to be asking for his support, Min was still wide-eyed, Toby was symbolically dangling a pair of handcuffs from one finger, and Texas gave him a slow nod.

"Whatever you decide," she said, "we're with you."

He held her look for a moment, then turned back to the huddled owners of the world. "The *only* reason why I don't turn this place straight over to Dado is because people all around the world depend on the proper flow of starks to better their lives. So, you're right in that respect, and frankly, I think Dado's hand on the switch would be worse than *yours*. Now, listen up. Your technicians are going to help Koj here figure out a way to use your tracking system against the Rippers so we can save your miserable hides. We'll worry about the legalities of what you've done later."

"And if you don't…" Toby added, holding up his handcuffs with a wicked grin.

Helen Lo paused, then looked up at one of the technicians on the ramp and gave a nod. "Whatever you need."

In an aside to the OzTech executives, Toby said, "You may want to take notes. My *hermano* Kojo is a pretty bright fellow."

Kojo flipped down his vidglasses and raced across the room up the ramp toward the technician, spewing out tech-speak en route. "We need a way to track the Rippers. No—better yet, make them stand out in comparison to everyone else with a VacGuard around here. Something nice and easy to use. I assume you have search parameters on these things?"

Two other technicians hurried around from different places on the circular ramp to join them as the first one replied to Kojo's query. "With ten billion people to track? Of course we do. We can search by name, unit ID, or nearly any other parameter you'd care to name."

"None of the Ripper units are registered," a second technician said. "They have no history of Bank access that we can track, no user ID. We see shapes and people, but nothing more."

"And that," Kojo said, "is how we're going to track them. I'm assuming you can highlight the Rippers by cross-referencing people who are wearing VacGuards but holding unregistered Ozes?"

"Certainly. Give me a moment," the first technician said as he entered commands into his vidcube. "There."

Nearly all the dots vanished, save for a small swarm of them darting about the Quantum Bank, now colored a bright glowing orange.

"Those would be the Rippers," Kojo stated, "since theirs are the only units left unregistered. Tag the VacGuards attached to those units and we can identify all Rippers anywhere in the solar system."

Texas grinned. "Like fish in a slagging barrel."

"Next, we need to send this tracking data to every Maker." Kojo said. "I want to be able to use this data for every self-guided projectile that we use. How soon do you think you can set it up?"

The first technician replied with a shrug, "About three minutes? Maybe less. The system will run a quantum search algorithm, then verify all hits in a second sweep before—"

"Let's get to it," Kojo told them.

As Kojo and the technicians hurried to their work, pulling a couple of vidcubes up to work through, Zavier activated his textlens for a transmission to Zandrie.

>>**Z**>>**Sis, you need to hold out for the next three minutes. We've got something going here.**<<

>>**Zandrie**>>**Where are you?**<<

>>**Z**>>**Inside the tower. Long story, explain later. Three minutes.**<<

>>**Zandrie**>>**Okay.**<<

Outside, Zandrie was scouting the battle from high above, taking down anything coming at her while trying to avoid getting hit in the process. The large trebuchet below lobbed off another one-ton metal orb, this one exploding at the rear of the Ripper tank lines into a rain of gummy bears that melted into a fruity tar around every exhaust vent and opening, then released a choking gas. Tanks and passing jets were compromised, their engines sputtering from the clogs, and people leaped out of the tanks to get to clean air. A dozen tanks and a couple of fighters fell victim to the hit.

It was a small dent in the battle, and not something they could do for much longer.

"Zandrie to everyone. We're going to have to lay off the area attacks. Our own people are in too close a proximity to the Ripper forces to risk it."

Besides, she thought to herself, *there's no real way of telling which of these things might actually be drones piloted by meat-bots.*

She could see someone printing more giant crossbows. The crossbow bolts were large enough to pierce a passing fighter, but not fast or accurate enough to reliably hit them. They did, however, have the advantage of being simple, brainless projectiles not subject to electromagnetic assaults, computer hacking, or similar countermeasures.

Then she saw it: something new coming in from the rear Ripper ranks. Another fighter, this one wider, the front cockpit resembling a bird's head—perhaps a rooster. Across its bottom side sat rows upon rows of small guns. She started veering course before it began firing.

"That's an antipersonnel craft if I ever saw one."

The opposing craft sped across the surface at high Mach speed, too fast for anything to hit it, while from its bottom hundreds of tiny rounds shot out every second. Not large enough to penetrate any of the armor or fortifications, but easily able to penetrate softer flesh and lighter personal armor. Makers started diving for cover.

"That thing's got to be putting out a lot of excess heat from so many guns," she said.

She pulled a cable out from the control-board before her, snapped it into place on her Oz's output, and immediately called out a command while still keeping her Oz-hand on the pilot's stick.

"Oz: Print heat-seeking mini-missiles into firing chamber."

She brought her craft around in a quick turn, an overhead display now popping up which she used to draw a targeting circle around the Ripper craft before her.

"Target and fire!"

A stream of foot-long missiles shot out from her fighter, but the other ship was quick to react and swerved sharply away as it continued its own barrage of the personnel below. Her mini-missiles, however, were even quicker to react and immediately altered course as they increased their speed. Zandrie, meanwhile, continued to fire missiles while changing course to put herself in pursuit of the Ripper craft.

Her ship rocked from an explosion behind her, while ahead of her the first of the missiles caught up to the Ripper ship and transformed it into an expanding plume of wreckage. Zandrie didn't waste any time and called out another order as she shot through the debris cloud.

"Missile retarget: whatever's on my tail shooting at me."

The mini-missiles immediately changed course toward a new target, and the skirmish continued.

Zavier watched as one entire half of the multistory wall cleared as the stacks of vidcubes sank back, transforming into a single colossal vidcube across which now displayed a map of the Moon, complete with images for Prosperita and the Quantum Bank facility. Uncountable orange and white dots appeared overlaying the map, thick clusters of them changing the view of Prosperita into one brilliant glow, while swarms ran around the area of the Quantum Bank.

The first technician Kojo had spoken with was busy at a vidcube on the ground level. Kojo stood beside him, while the other two technicians stood by at other terminals.

"Search progressing," the technician was saying, "verifying, and…"

All eyes focused intently on the technician and the one screen towering above him; even the President and Chairperson held their breath. Zavier found himself standing between Min and Texas, a hand to each one's shoulder as they watched together. Then, it happened.

"Got it," the technician announced with a sigh of relief. "All unregistered units now fed into the tracking system."

Kojo nodded in satisfaction. A small cheer went up between techs, Makers, security guards, and even the executives.

"*Órale*! *Now* we can nail them to the wall," Toby said. He looked at Texas and his grin grew. "*Texas*-style."

CHAPTER 24

When both Commando and Guardian work together in harmony, your squad can gain a significant competitive advantage.

As their nicknames may imply, "Blades" and "Shields" are meant to synergize their efforts on the front line of conflict. The Maker Blade attacks while the Maker Shield defends. They regroup together, and they attack together. They should create and print blueprints that complement each other.

Consistent communication between each Commando and Guardian pair is essential to both victory and survival.

Maker Corps Academy, Combat Squad Orientation

As the cheers went up, Kojo hurried over to a terminal past the technician, pulling down his vidglasses and thought-activating his comm along the way.

"Kojo Solomon to Major Vik. I have some important information."

He started quickly working on the terminal as Zandrie's voice came back into his ears.

"It'd better be really good, Kojo, because we're about to be pushed up against the wall out here."

"I am patching you into a new tactical map. All those orange dots are Rippers. We have tracking signals on every single one of them."

"You what? How in the shattering did you manage that one?"

"It turns out that the Quantum Bank has been able to track

the precise location of every single VacGuard for the last fifty years and never told anyone. They were watching the battle in real time using body maps. Right now, on one of the vidcubes here, I can see the inside of your cockpit—and the fact that you're making an angry fist while hearing this."

One of the smaller vidcubes did indeed show Zandrie's hand forming a fist ready to pound down on something. When she spoke again, they could hear the gritted teeth she was speaking through. *"And how detailed is the imagery?"*

"Just don't use the bathroom with a VacGuard on if you want any privacy."

There was a pause, during which Zavier decided to flip his own helmet over into place and break into the conversation. "Zavier here, Sis. I got the confession from the founder of OzTech herself. Kojo did his usual wizardry and now we're looking at a map pinpointing every last one of them. OzTech needs to answer for what they're doing, but we've got something more immediate to worry about now. Imagine the *Rippers* getting hold of this."

It was a few seconds before Zandrie responded, during which the view of her fist started to unclench. *"Well done, Kojo. We can definitely use this. Zandrie out."*

"Well," Toby said once that was done, "anyone want to get back into things and see how much trouble give the Rippers?"

Kojo spun around to address his squad, again assuming the role of their Stick. "I'll stay here and help you guys out with a bird's-eye view. Get back into the battle and start knocking heads."

"I'll print us up some new rides," Toby said, starting to turn away.

"I'll handle the weapons," Texas said.

"Pardon me," the third technician Kojo had worked with spoke up, "but not anywhere near the antenna you won't. The antenna would cause too much interference. It's constantly sending and receiving stark streams from all over Earth. Your little wrist units would be overwhelmed."

"But I was able to heal their wounds with my Oz," Min told him. "It worked fine."

"That's because the interior is shielded," the same technician explained. "All quantum signals are piped through the core of the antenna down into the vault. Immediately outside there's a wash of signals. In fact, the cap for about three kilometers across is slightly concave to better focus the incoming signals. I'm afraid that you'll have to go out farther than that before your equipment will reliably work."

"Maybe you could turn it off or something," Texas suggested. "At least until we're through with the battle."

Helen Lo spoke up. "That would be extremely unadvisable and quite possibly insane. Everything is in a very delicate balance that we cannot simply turn on or off. There are strict procedures that must be followed at all times.

"What we're effectively sitting on is a proto black hole. It actually doesn't take much space for the equipment needed to send and receive starks; the bulk of this facility is a containment vessel and the equipment needed to maintain it. Without us to constantly monitor and make adjustments, without this equipment constantly running and the gravity dampers kept online, we'd risk having a containment breach. If that ever happened, you could say goodbye to every piece of matter from the orbitals of Venus to Mars."

"Koj, any of that true?" Zavier asked.

"Sounds about right," Kojo said with a nod. "The only way to store this many starks in such a relatively small space requires something approximating a black hole...a carefully constructed, heavily shielded, continually regulated black hole."

"Simple solution, then," Zavier said with a shrug. "We print everything over in the lobby. Come on, let's get going."

While Zavier led the way into the anteroom to begin their preparations, Zandrie's voice came in a broadcast to every Maker comm. *"Attention, this is Major Vik. As we speak, you are all being linked into a new tracking grid. Every orange dot you'll see on your displays corresponds to a Ripper. Select one and follow the signal. Update all weapons with homing configurations and have fun. Maker Solomon will be coordinating from the tower."*

Zavier and the others wasted no time in printing some vehicles. Min stuck with a red hovbike that resembled a wheeled version from an ancient anime. For Toby, it was a hover-trike with a broad car-like axis and hov-pads in back, the front coming to a point with a single hov-pad, plus a set of missile guns attached to the back. Texas printed a hovbike that bore more than a striking resemblance to the contours of a large black and white horse, with her guns mounted at the back and looking more like large shotguns rather than missiles, and the Texas flag emblazoned across its rear.

"A horse?" Toby asked as they were printing.

"I had a paint horse like this back home as a kid." Texas shrugged. "Meet Trigger."

Zavier's choice was a little bit bigger. In fact, it was a car. A very particular car, with sleek lines and classic stylings from an era gone by.

"What the heck is that?" Texas asked.

Zavier smiled. "Something my sister scanned for me a long time ago. Vintage 2028 Lamborghini Audace. The car of the rich and famous for its day. I've been tinkering with it over the years and designed a hover-version of it."

The car was printed with two long missile tubes along its sides, a gun sticking out from beneath the front hood, and extra thick armor all over carefully molded to maintain the integrity of the design.

Texas had just completed printing her vehicle when she saw the look on Min's face as she stood on her own; Min's lip was trembling a bit. "Hey, you going to be alright?"

"I'll be okay," Min replied. "It's just…so much death and destruction. I never signed up to be a soldier. What about you? Back at Alice Springs when you—"

"Yeah, I know, but I can deal with it. As long as I keep shooting at *things* and don't think about what or who may be in them, I'm good. That first time was a bit too…up front and personal. Maybe you could try that for yourself? Think about shooting at inanimate targets and never mind about the *who*."

"Or I can stick with targeting drones." Min shook her head. "I'd still rather be saving lives than taking them."

Texas ended by giving her a hug, then stepped back over to her vehicle. Once all four vehicles were completed, Zavier spent an extra moment or two synching the targeting computer of each bike with Kojo's tracking signals.

"There," he announced. "Even if you don't select a specific target, it'll home onto the nearest Ripper signal."

"Sounds like it's going to get messy," Toby said.

"That's what I like," Texas quipped. "A precise mess."

Much to the dismay of the OzTech executives, all four started their vehicles inside and sped out through the door the guards held open for them.

Makers were already adjusting both their devices and their tactics by the time Zavier and the others made it up into the air. The trebuchet was loaded with a new type of ammo, while the next line of massive bolts being printed into the twenty-meter crossbows were now tipped by something electronic, with a small jet attached to the back ends. On the side with the Ripper tanks, a line of Makers were nearly finished printing custom missile racks, a large square box atop a swivel mount, with thirty missiles each. There were six such banks, all connected to Kojo's new central control.

Once they were far enough away, Texas was the first to begin arming herself in earnest. "I know what *I'm* going to use. Oz: Modified *Thelma* splat gun: homing rounds."

"Now *that* has me curious." Toby grinned. "For myself...Oz: 'Shields of Faith 2060.'"

"Oz," Zavier said to his own device, "Blunderballs: homing modification."

With his ridiculously wide mouth weapon printing, he glanced back to see what Min was doing. He was worried for her, concerned that the death and destruction had caused her too much trauma. But she was busy printing her own weapon: a two-meter bike-mounted version of her old octopus-gun.

>>Koj>>I have the targeting program running. Lock everything onto the tracking signal and let the computer do all the work.<<

>>Texas>>Sounds like you want to take all the fun out of this.<<

>>Koj>>Not at all. By all means, indulge yourself.<<

>>Texas>>In that case, indulging.<<

Zavier saw Texas speed Trigger out past the rear lines, what looked like a four-barreled RPG now fixed to a shoulder brace loaded with four small missiles. She flew out into the midst of speeding fighters, exploding weapons, and flying projectiles, then hovered in place high above the rows of Ripper tanks. With her right hand on the weapon trigger, she reached out with her left hand and motioned a finger to the Ripper masses. "Come here, you overgrown picnic specials, Mamma's gonna show you how to *really* barbeque."

She grinned as four fighters came at her, two from the front and a pair from her left.

Zavier yelled, "Texas, what are you—"

She pressed the trigger and from her four-barreled gun shot a total of sixteen missiles. She wasn't even aiming—just had her weapon angled a little down because of the weight. The missiles shot out, curled around in the air for a split second, then straightened out and sped toward a definite target—four missiles for each of the four-fighter craft, unerringly directed. They didn't just slam into the fighters, but went directly for the cockpits and the pilots within wearing their VacGuards.

When the missiles detonated, it was not with concussive explosions, but electromagnetic ones. Colorful displays of wildly flailing arms of lightning sent each of the craft either suddenly nose diving, veering out of control, or rocketing straight up through the atmosphere.

None of them ever reached Texas.

She beamed. "Oh, I liked the way that looked."

Left with only the launcher, she undid its brace then dropped it down toward the tanks below, but not before pressing a red button on its side. The launcher hit the top of one of the tanks with an explosion that flipped the tank over onto an adjacent tank.

Toby, meanwhile, had his "Shield of Faith 2060," which consisted of what at first seemed like a small triangular fold-shield, but when he lifted it into the air, it unfolded in all directions and started to spin and shoot off layers of itself—one spinning shield after another, until the space around him was a growing bloom of dozens of speeding spinning transparent shields.

>>Toby>>**Normally this would be dangerous since they tend to hit anything in their way, which is why I never use it. But since we have something for them to home in on…**<<

A hundred spinning shields exploded out from Toby, each heading for the nearest Ripper VacGuard. Several of them sliced into a passing fighter, a few more suddenly angled downward to imbed themselves into an unfortunate tank, while still others started chased Rippers on speeding hovbikes. They dodged, swerved, and climbed into the air, and no matter what the hovbikes did, the spinning shields kept up with them. One pilot ejected, his panic visible as he saw the incoming shield immediately alter course to slam him painfully down to the ground.

Other Ripper hovbikes sped up as fast as they could, desperate looks on their rider's faces. They were barely keeping ahead of the spinning shields when something unexpected came at them from the front: a storm of octopus-shaped rubber masses with extra self-sealing power. They wrapped around faces, wrists, and Ozes— and around the engines of their bikes.

"I can't see!" came one muffled cry.

Their engines stopped working from the rubber shorting out the components, turning their bikes in to projectiles along with the shields. In what looked like a synchronized ballet of demolition, all affected riders hit the ground simultaneously causing puffs of smoke and dust.

>>Texas>>**Your shields truly are faith-inspiring, Toby.**<<

She included a vidloop of Joan of Arc praying before battle.

"Amen, *hermana.*"

Min was on her anime-bike hovering ten meters above the ground, an empty launcher on the side of her bike and an unreadable expression on her face. She hovered there, watching as what was left of the two bikes and their passengers crashed into the ground.

Zavier flew out into the thickest part of the battle in his modded Lamborghini. He dodged in and out of traffic until he passed between two Rippers. The Rippers stopped and appreciatively watched his car as it flew by, then turned and pursued him in earnest. Seeing them in his rearview mirror, he issued a command.

"Launch dice countermeasures: target following Ripper signatures."

Two twenty-side "dice" jettisoned from where the exhaust of his car should have been. The countermeasures swerved directly into the windshields of the two Ripper bikes, then simultaneously erupted into giant lumps of sticky bubblegum. The Rippers and their hovbikes plummeted to the ground.

Zavier sped away, corkscrewing and swerving around enemy and friendly vehicles alike until he realized he still might get hit by friendly fire. He banked a little higher before searching for a shot to take.

>>**Koj**>>**Added a new wrinkle: all weapons will home in on Rippers, but specifically avoid anything NOT a Ripper.**<<

Zavier glanced around to see that the latest barrage of missiles and strange ammunition did seem to be actively steering around him. "Well, that's convenient."

From a couple kilometers away, he heard a loud mechanical snap and saw a row of ten-meter crossbow bolts fly up through the sky to start chasing an equal number of Ripper jets. This was accompanied by the trebuchet lobbing another large glittering boulder into what was left of the drone front, but this time when the projectile exploded something different happened. The boulder detonated into thousands of glittering darts, *each* of which picked a target and sped off. Drones of all shapes and sizes were perforated through and through, not to mention several hovbikes with the riders still on them. Every pierced piece of tech plummeted to the ground.

Then came a thunderous boom as the Maker missile racks fired off—six racks, thirty missiles a rack, each one fitted with a homing tracker and each one hitting a different tank, fighter, or drone dead center.

"My turn," Zavier decided.

Freshly printed to the front of his Lamborghini was his "blunderballs" weapon, an ancient-looking giant shotgun with a wide mouth, attached to a clear plastic barrel of rubber balls.

"*Z, what are you up to with that thing?*" he heard Texas' voice in his ear. "*And why do I like it already?*"

"Well, you remember that hyper-kinetic rubber ball I used to get past those Rippers?" Zavier pressed the firing trigger.

Hundreds of rubber balls exploded out from the trumpeting muzzle at high velocity. They hit fighters, hovtanks, passing Rippers on hovbikes—they hit anything that moved, and where some missed and hit the ground, they bounced back up on a direct course for the closest available Ripper target. Their first hit perhaps only annoyed a passing rider, but after they bounced they came back faster than ever.

And each time, they veered toward another Ripper.

Zavier fired again and chaos dominated the battlefield. A hurricane of small balls bounced back and forth through the air, faster and faster. They spread through the Ripper ranks until their impacts could not be ignored even by fighter pilots. Two pairs of jets found several of the balls pinging rapidly back and forth between them, throwing off control mechanisms. One hovtank was unfortunate enough to have its hatch cracked open when the blunderbuss fired and several balls made it through the seam and assaulted the crew trapped within. The mayhem that had to be happening inside the tank had Zavier chuckling in satisfaction.

>>Toby>>Nice one!<<

The Rippers' solution came in the form of a couple of their Ozbots making a sweep to simply vac up the hyperkinetic projectiles.

>>Zandrie>>Koj, can you run a program to target any Ripper VacGuard signatures that are not accompanied by local life forms—human or animal?<<

>>Koj>>Easily, why?<<

>>Zandrie>>Because I just thought of how to eliminate those Ripper bots that are keeping them supplied.<<

Not long after, Zandrie sprayed the sky with high-speed electrified pellets that seemed to have a specific taste for unmanned VacGuarded Ripper drones.

Back in the tower's control center, Kojo was looking at the display of orange dots relative to the tower icon at the center—watching them pull their lines farther and farther away, much to everyone's relief.

"We're doing it," he stated. "Another couple of minutes and they'll be back at the original fifteen-kilometer perimeter mark."

"You did quite good indeed," came the voice of President Pedigrand from somewhere behind him, "and I shall be glad to reward you when this is over with."

"Bribe me so I won't talk, you mean," he said without even glancing back. "No thanks. I'm a Maker, 'Mr. President,' I protect the law."

"Well, I see you do have some integrity, Cadet Solomon."

The voice came from one of the vidcubes, which promptly moved itself across the wall and expanded in size directly in front of Kojo. It showed an enlarged view of an old man's face staring directly into the VacGuard on his wrist. It was a face Kojo knew well.

"Dr. Dado! But how—"

"You are a very brilliant young man, but I have been at this a few decades longer. Now, I hate to dash your hopes, but I came here to perform what you might call a citizen's arrest of those people in the control room with you."

"You can see…You've hacked into my signal!"

Kojo started frantically working with the terminal and his vidglasses, but it was already too late.

"Attention, Roosters. Time to crow."

Dado's face vanished, while up on the wall-map, things changed. The orange dots suddenly changed to blue, while everything else in the vicinity of the tower changed to orange. Kojo immediately realized what had happened.

"He reversed the targeting program!" Immediately he activated his comm and called out. "Kojo to Major Vik. Dado's switched around the targeting. You are now targeting Makers. Repeat, you are now targeting *Makers*. Major Vik, come in!"

There was no response. Nothing but Dado's smiling face once again hovering before him. *"Mr. Solomon, if I can hack into your targeting program, don't you think I would be able to block your comm signal as well? Oh, not communications in general, since that would get suspicious—just your own. In fact, I've locked you completely out of the system. Good luck trying to undo it, young man."*

From the views on the other vidcubes, he could see the battle change instantly. Missiles launched out by Maker vessels turned right back to destroy the source. Maker drones shot up other maker drones, the trebuchet aimed itself towards the other side of the perimeter, where its next shot detonated well within Maker ranks. Massive crossbow bolts suddenly changed course to pierce into Maker aircraft. Zavier's next load of hyper-kinetic balls started bouncing exclusively off Maker targets, while Min found herself barely in control of her anime-bike as she became covered in a mass of her own octopus rounds. He even saw the view of Zandrie's cockpit as she tried frantically to evade her own missiles.

Kojo, meanwhile, desperately raced through computerized menu options, trying to undo what Dado had done. The technicians tried helping him out on their own terminals.

"He's right," Kojo said. "I'm completely locked out of the entire Maker subsystem. In fact, it says here that—I'm dead? He reported me dead, so the system would automatically lock out all access. How am I going to get a communication out?"

"We have comms in here," the first technician offered. "You can use those."

"Maker security protocols wouldn't let the signal through," Kojo told him. "At least, not in time. Is the search program still identifying the Makers?"

"Correctly, yes," the second technician reported. "It's only in your program and transmission that the information is getting scrambled."

The views continued to show a complete reversal of fortune. Toby was on the ground, behind him his hover-trike was cut up with a few of his own shields, while Texas limped away from even more extensive damage. It was all Zavier could do to land his Lamborghini near Min's anime-bike without crashing, then run over to free her of her own octopus wraps.

Across the field, the large metal trebuchet lay in ruins, the gigantic crossbows in pieces. Combatants for kilometers around limped away from the wreckage of their vehicles, and now, not all of them were Rippers.

Kojo took a breath to steady himself, then gave the problem some careful thought. "Dado has hacked into the Maker system, probably using some backdoor he put there himself long ago just for the day when he would be discovered. But the main system on this end is still correctly identifying Ripper targets. He can't hack into the Bank, or he wouldn't need to attack it…

"You," Kojo told the first technician, "cut the communication link to all Maker feeds, including mine, then clear the targeting program completely. Reset everything."

"Immediately," the technician replied.

Before the technician could completely sever all ties with the battle outside, something came in over Kojo's comm link. It was Zandrie's voice in an urgent announcement.

"This is Major Zandrie Vik. We have been compromised. Take all targeting systems offline. Repeat, visual targeting only!"

CHAPTER 25

The Logistician's responsibility is far deeper than the "Stick" nickname may imply. Field logistics combines the ordered thinking of strategy, analysis, and calculation with rapid-fire decision-making. It might be compared to a game of chess played at lightning speed.

The stakes are much higher, though, because a Logistician's success is determined by the success of their squad. The other disciplines require a "Stick" who can stand high above the fog of war and make instant, objective recommendations.

Therefore, careful planning of outcomes, followed by daily, repetitive simulation of real-life events is crucial to being pre-pared when the real moment of decisions arrive.

Global Maker Corp Logistician Handbook

It took Toby's brawn to get Min free, while Zavier offered the appearance of assistance.

"These octopus-things of yours really stick," Zavier said as Toby pulled Min free. "One...last...there."

Zavier and Toby escorted Min out from her bike's wreckage. She looked hurt, but the first thing she did when she saw Texas limping was jog over to her while printing a fresh medkit. "Texas, are you alright?"

"Sure, once I recover from the embarrassment of shooting myself," she said. "Not to mention losing Trigger. What the heck happened?"

Min sat Texas down on the ground and proceeded to tend

to her, running a line from her QuantVac to Texas' VacGuard to hasten the repair, while Zavier tried to sum up as best he could. The nearest battle line was still a few kilometers away from their current position, but the concussions from the explosions were loud enough, even in the thin artificial atmosphere, that he had to raise his voice a little.

"Zandrie said something about the system being compromised."

"I can believe that," Toby agreed. "My own missiles came right back at me."

"I'll see what Koj has to say...Koj? Kojo?...Nothing on the comms, I'll try textlens."

>>Z>>Koj? Are you there?<<

"Still nothing. Zavier to Major Vik—what's happened?"

The response came on Zavier's comm-link, as well as those of the rest of his squad. *"I was hoping you'd tell me. I can't reach Maker Solomon. The system reports that he's dead."*

"Impossible," Zavier declared. "He's locked away inside the most secure structure in the solar system."

"Agreed, which means that something weird is going on. As impossible as it sounds, the system may have been hacked."

"Impossible?" said a man's voice, *"Your thinking is limited. Haven't I taught you better than that? Stay fluid, Zavier."*

The voice that came in through their comms was not that of Major Vik, but Dr. Dado.

"Dado," Zandrie exclaimed. *"I had all your access codes revoked!"*

"As would be standard protocol," Dado answered back, his voice amiable as always, *"But a long time ago, I hacked into the root system to do a little tinkering of my own. I was a hacker long before I was a Maker, Zandrie. My dear* mamãe *made sure I was well schooled in everything I needed to seize control from the Elitists. You see, I've been preparing for this for quite some time. Long before you*

were born. Long before the Makers existed."

"Dado, don't do this!" Zavier shouted into his comm. "Yes, we know now those people in there are the scum of the Earth, but this isn't the way."

"On the contrary, young Zavier, this has always been the only way. No court in the solar system will try them. They own everything and everyone. Revolution is the only way, just as it has worked time and again throughout history. The old United States began with a revolution. So did the French First Republic. And the People's Republic of China. And on and on. Thus will begin our *new order. Free and unrestricted access to the starks, for everyone."*

"With you in control, you mean," Zavier snapped.

"Ah, but you misunderstand, Zavier," Dado calmly stated. *"I am not here to take control, but to set it all free, like I keep saying. Liberdade! Anything limiting access shall be removed, the starks allowed to run as free and unrestrained as possible. No more controls, no more constraints; we'll shut it all down. Unlimited wealth for everyone, can't you understand that?"*

"No more controls?" Toby interrupted. "That sounds like when those techs were talking about containment!"

"No!" Zavier gasped. "Dado, you have no idea what you're— Dado, the founder of OzTech herself told us. We're standing on a proto black hole that's barely held in check by its containment protocols and gravity dampers. If you do anything to breach that containment, the Moon, Earth, maybe everything from Venus to Mars will be gone—smashed to rubble and then sucked away into a new black hole! You can't let the starks fly as free as you want without risking a containment breach. This won't just be anarchy—it'll be the end of the world!"

"Zavier," came Zandrie's voice over the comms, *"what're you talking about?"*

"It's true," Zavier said. "I heard the technicians explain it all, and Kojo confirmed it."

An elderly woman's voice broke in. *"It's true, Eduardo. While you may be justified in your anger toward OzTech, your calculations are seriously inadequate. You're about to destroy us all."*

"Helen Lo," came Dado's calm voice, *"is that what you've been telling these young, impressionable Makers? I think they are wise enough to not listen to the mastermind behind OzTech's rise to power. Zavier, did she tell you that she was responsible for my family's ruin and, consequently, my father's death? This is what OzTech does. They use fear-mongering to manipulate people for their own gain, don't you see? Of course Helen would scare you with some doomsday scenario, but that doesn't mean it's true."*

"It doesn't mean it's not," Zandrie broke in. *"Dado, you are brilliant, but physics is not your field. If you go in there and turn off those safeguards, that's it! You turn the Quantum Bank into a quantum bomb."*

"What a fantastic nightmare OzTech weaves for you." Dado chuckled. *"But you shall see. When we remove all constraints, then the world shall finally flourish. No more Elitists, no more governments. It will be a golden age."*

"It will be nothing but wreckage, Eduardo," Helen replied.

"You're delusional, Dado," Zandrie snapped. *"A madman!"*

"As is everyone of brilliance called in their own time. Perhaps the same could be said of you, Helen...no? But years from now, the world will see this was the only *way. Now, pardon me while I adjust a few controls here. My program tells me that I've recorded enough samples of your voice, Major Vik, so time for some new orders."*

"Some new what? You can't—"

Zandrie's voice immediately cut off, replaced by...Zandrie's voice. Calm, in command as always, and no trace of her previous anger.

"This is Major Vik. Ripper reinforcements reported coming

from the same direction as the initial drone force. Squads A through D: hold the line against the rear attack. All other squads: pull out to engage the new offensive. Estimated distance, forty kilometers and closing."

"That's more than two-thirds of what we have left," Toby exclaimed. "Why would she—"

"It wasn't my sister," Zavier corrected him. "Dado simulated her voice."

"They're going off on a wild goose chase, while Dado's ready to end the world." Toby said. "We've got to stop it."

He started screaming into his comm, but got no response. Then he tried using his textlens, but nothing of his messaging appeared on anyone's display. Texas was standing back up now, fully healed, along with Min who had tended her own wounds before going over to run a quick scan over a frustrated Toby.

"My comm's dead. Z, what about yours?"

"He's cut us all off," Texas said as she came over, "just like he's obviously done with Koj. Dado is sending everyone away so the rest of us here can get killed."

"And by the time anyone catches on," Zavier realized, "the Rippers will own that tower, then his 'free and unrestricted access' will turn everything into a black hole. There's nothing we can do…"

He glanced across the battlefield. In the distance, he saw the bulk of the Maker forces taking wing and abandoning their fight with the remainder of the drone force and bikers. The few squads left behind to face the army of tanks and fighters would not last long. The great tower was in the distance, then the presence of the OzBots flying around on their orderly duties, but not much else. His gaze lingered briefly on the bots, then moved on.

Overwhelming problems washed over him like a wave, threatening to drown him in their demands on his attention. It was too much all at once. People dying in every direction and more to follow, and all of it seeming to land on his shoulders as the only Edge with a complete understanding of the situation. He could feel his mind starting to lock up again, but if that happened, then all might be lost.

He remembered what a teacher had once told him: Dr. Dado. He might be a crazy, revenge-driven lunatic, yet Zavier knew that the principles of truth remained true—regardless of the source they came from. Zavier closed his eyes, tuning everything out and doing as he remembered. He took a deep breath and once again imagined the large dial in his head. It was shaking angrily as it tried to push all the way past ten and implode his mind. He told his mind that he was in control. He ordered it to turn the dial back to nine. It reluctantly complied. He then urged it one more time to an eight, and again the dial slowly moved. He stopped there, because, given the circumstances, it was helpful for him to have that level of urgency and awareness. All of this happened in mere seconds.

Slowly he opened his eyes, much calmer and able to think. The first thing he saw was the fiery aerial displays. He got an idea as Min came over to examine him.

"You've got a few scratches," she said. "Here, allow me."

"No time," he said, breaking away from her. "Toby—you, Texas, and Min get to printing a four-man shuttle as fast as you can. Make sure it has a little rocket launcher. Quickly."

"A single rocket against all *this?*" Toby exclaimed.

But Texas grinned. "I know that look. He's got an idea."

"That I do," Zavier said, bringing up his Oz. "Oz: Multiple modified signal flares. Letter C, letter O, letter M…"

While Zavier's Oz popped out one flare after another, the other three got to work on printing a new shuttle. They were halfway through when their Oz devices started to sputter.

"Hey, what's the matter?" Toby wailed.

"It's happening with mine too," Texas said.

"There must be interference," Min explained. "Boost the signal gain on the Oz—that should handle it."

The adjustments worked and by the time Zavier was finished with his small mound of flares, he had a ready-made ship.

"Where's the launcher?" he asked.

"Back section," Toby answered. "We had some trouble with the Oz units."

"Yeah, me too. It's the main stark transmitter. We must be just close enough to get some interference. Okay, help me pile these in. The flares are all numbered, and once we get up there they have to be fired out in order."

"Signal flares?" Texas said, eyeing him. "What're you gonna do, spell it out across the sky?"

When Zavier didn't reply, Texas chased after him. "Oh, you have *got* to be kidding!"

Kojo was still in the control room of the tower, watching system messages display across one of the terminals. In the others, he saw the few squads left to face the main Ripper force getting wiped out as the rest went out to confront a new threat that did not exist. He knew Dado was responsible, and had heard the entire exchange through the vidcubes there around him. He could see Zandrie's frustration; he could see Makers dying; he could even see Rippers in their craft gloating as they started to run over the few squads left between them and the tower.

"Comm system rebooted," the technician announced. "Do you want to reestablish connection?"

"In a minute," Kojo said thoughtfully. "I think I'm getting an idea. The germ of one, at least."

"New activity overhead," a different technician reported.

"Main view," Kojo ordered.

More vidcubes sank back into the wall, producing a huge vidcube next to the one with the map.

"Composite image taken from several available sources," the same technician reported. "Coming up."

The new vidcube showed the sky above a portion of the battlefield, directly above and in front of the Maker force currently speeding away from the tower in their quest for a supposed new foe. A single large shuttle was zipping across the sky shooting out flares, each of which exploded like a holiday firework to etch a twenty-meter letter across the sky.

"They're spelling out a message," Kojo realized. "I don't have to look at the vidcubes to know that has to be Z."

He watched as the message completed itself, many of the Maker vehicles slowing down as it did so. The view of Zandrie's cockpit showed her grinning with delight.

COMMS SLAGGED! NOT MAJOR VJK!

Kojo laughed at the misspelling, but got the message all the same. "Way to go, Squad…Skywriters."

He spent a moment more watching to confirm that the Makers had started turning swiftly around, then Kojo hurried back to his terminal with a new idea.

"We can reestablish communications now, if you wish," the first technician said.

"Not yet—Dado will just pull something else," Kojo replied. "We need something…new search program."

He connected to the vidcube terminal and began quickly scrolling through some recent files. "Sub-search within identified Ripper signals. Visual search with facial recognition. You guys can monitor *all* signals up here, and not even he can change that."

"Whose face are we looking for?" the technician asked.

Kojo found what he was looking for—a communication file from which he quickly grabbed a still image, then sent it to the main screen with a dramatic slide of his hand. He turned around to face the vidcube and the image that appeared on it. "*That* one."

It was the face of Dr. Dado himself.

"Did you just misspell you *own* last name?" Toby laughed mercilessly. He was sitting beside Zavier in the gunner's seat, while Min came up with Texas from where they had been feeding out flares.

"I was in a hurry!" Zavier shouted. "Lots going on, Toby! You want to go back and run a spell-check on it?"

Toby raised his hands in surrender, still chuckling to himself.

"That's the last of them," Texas called up.

"…of all the times to make a typo…" Zavier grumbled, then banked the shuttle hard.

"At least everyone will be in the same spot when things go down," Texas said. "Just like at the Alamo."

"You do realize they *lost* that one, right?" Toby said. "Badly."

"Not the overall war. That was the opening. Like this is."

"Yeah, right," Zavier said with a snort. "Tell me, do all you Texans enjoy fighting impossible odds?"

"Now, what fun would *easy* battles be?"

Zavier shook his head.

"Looks like everyone got the message—misspelling and all. Everyone's turning back," Toby reported. "But we still don't have proper communications."

"Then we'll print up one last flare. Something nice and simple. Toby, know how to fly?"

"By flapping my arms?"

"Just hold this stick like this while I go in back real fast."

Toby quickly exchanged seats with Zavier, while the latter ran through to the back portion of the shuttle. He'd nearly finished printing another flare when Min came in.

"Z, can we speak?"

She looked as worn as ever, her face an expression of sadness, but there was no time.

"Later, Min. I've got to get this last flare out. Hold tight and we'll get through this."

The flare printed, and he popped it into the launcher and hit the switch.

Kojo looked up from the search screen long enough to see a new development in the skies above. Starting the floating message was a long fiery line, at the end of which was a very large arrow pointing in the direction the shuttle was flying: the tower. Another fighter immediately came up next to the shuttle, and Kojo knew from the views around him that this was Zandrie's ship. She planted herself at the end of the arrow to draw attention to her position and took the lead of the Maker forces once again.

Fighters altered course, tanks turned around, bikes spun about, and a few of those on the ground started printing new ways of getting about, all of them headed in a race back for the tower and the nearing Ripper forces.

From one part of the battlefield a large globe sprang up, transparent outer shell rolling speedily along while one person inside remained steady at the controls, a second person manning a gun mounted *inside* the globe. From his vantage point, Kojo recognized Ranjit and Delanie.

"Now what are they…" Kojo began.

The globe sped ahead of the rest, hurtling past the tower at a speed that left some of the fighters in the dust, and stopped directly in front of the enemy just in time to rescue a pinned squad that was about to lose out. Delaine fired the gun, and for a moment Kojo wondered if she was insane or suicidal. The gun, however, was a laser. Since the shell of the globe was completely transparent, the beam of focused light passed straight on through, ending at the nose of the nearest hovtank and cutting a line across its front as the globe passed on by....

No, not passing, Kojo thought, *but circling.* It made one quick roll around the tank, the laser firing the entire time, then shot off once finished, leaving behind a hovtank with its severed top now flipped completely off to reveal a cowering Ripper.

"Fluid. A motorized laser-ball tank." Kojo marveled. "Okay, back to business. Establish comm lines, but make sure it's on Bank frequencies only. I'm going to assume that they're pretty much hack-proof?"

"Of course," the technician replied.

"Then link Major Vik's comm directly through the Bank and work on pulling the rest of the Makers in as well. We'll build our own new network, bypassing the Maker network and any other tricks Dado's put in there. Hurry."

As the first technician hurried off, another one called out. "The search you requested is completed."

"On the map."

A new dot appeared on the Moon map, this one colored a bright gold. It was at the far edge of the Bank cap, but fast approaching. "That's Dado. Now, what to do with this info?"

"Comm's up; Major Vik available."

"Great," Kojo replied. "Major Vik, can you hear me?"

"Finally! I've been screaming at this thing for ten minutes. Is this line secure?"

"As secure as the Quantum Bank can make it."

"Good. How's the overall situation look from your end?"

"We lost a squad against the main rear line, and in the brief time it'll take everyone else to get back here, it looks like we're losing another. I should have communications reestablished with everyone momentarily—this time with no tricks from Dado. I also have located the man himself, and he's coming in fast."

"Excellent work! How far have the Rippers gotten?"

"Holding the line at six kilometers, but there's only a few of us over there and so many Rippers that they're simply going around."

"Okay, we'll have to pull back and establish a new perimeter— one we can hold. Recommendations?"

"Hold on."

Kojo gave the map a quick look, compared one set of dots with another, and did some quick mental computations. He took another look at Dado, who was arriving. His craft was large, like a set of old airplane wings joined together, minus the actual airplane.

"At this point, the only perimeter that might work would be within a kilometer of the tower, but Dado's coming in with some-thing big."

"Figures."

"But I should warn you, the specialists here tell me that our Oz devices and other tech may not reliably work when close to the tower. The signal interference from the tower's antenna is just too much."

"No choice."

"Maker Solomon," one of the technicians called over, "full communications reestablished and routed through the Quantum Bank server."

"Good. Major Vik, you now have full comms."

"Good, then stand by."

Zavier's shuttle raced past the tower to catch up to the laser-ball tank. Zandrie's fighter flew on their left, and other Maker craft followed the large arrow in the sky. What was left of the units that had remained behind in the rear lines were nearly surrounded, the rest of the Maker force simply speeding past them on a direct line for the tower. There was one exception, of course.

"Would you look at that ball-tank go," Texas marveled. "It's taken out four tanks already and hasn't even gotten scratched."

"Too maneuverable," Toby said. "Say, uh—Z, now that we're here, what do we do? Most of those tanks and fighters out there may be drones, but there's a *lot* of them. Five times more than what we have left, would be my guess."

"I was kinda going to cross that bridge when we came to it," Zavier replied.

"The bridge is here," Texas pointed out. "What do we do?"

Before he could answer, the comms suddenly came to life.

"This is Major Zandrie Vik. The real Major Vik. All units pull back to the tower. Establish a new perimeter within a kilometer around the tower. Our Oz devices won't work that close to it, but neither will theirs. Make sure to print what you need before we get there. Fighters keep a high perimeter as long as you can; everyone else, shoulder to shoulder on the ground. No gaps. Vik out."

"You heard her," Zavier said.

As he altered course to circle the tower, Texas pointed something out. "Uh, we didn't equip this thing with much more than a flare launcher. At least if we're on the ground we can go inside and print some hand weapons."

"Good idea," he agreed. "Going down for a landing."

Kojo watched as the Maker forces reformed their lines. A hundred varieties of ground craft, piloted and drone alike, came to a circle around the tower, planting themselves right next to one another as ordered. What remained of their fighters and jets patrolled around the tower above. He watched as Zavier landed his craft and ran inside the tower with the rest of the squad to quickly print some new weapons in the lobby, then left again while Min stayed behind.

"I'm a Medic," she told the others. "Send any wounded in here for me to handle."

He also watched as Dado's ship came into view. It was a large flying delta-wing at least three stories thick and a hundred and fifty meters across, carrying a giant cargo box beneath it via cables and grappling hooks. It stopped to hover, then carefully dropped down its cargo to the surface while several more drones launched from the rear of the ship. The cargo unfolded, revealing its contents and a few Rippers who scurried out.

"That's one large Oz factory," Kojo gasped. "Military spec. Really old design, but good enough. Which means those new drones have to be Ozbots."

The flying wing started up again, moving toward the tower at a stately pace. The rest of the Rippers, meanwhile, had been circling around the new defensive perimeter, trapping the tower and the Makers within it.

Zavier burst into the room as the flying wing came within a kilometer of the tower. "How's it looking in here, Koj?"

"Bad. He just dropped a gargantuan Oz factory far enough away to be out of range of the tower's interference. Between that, some new Ozbots, and all the debris out there available to vac up, he can keep adding to his forces while we're stuck with what we have."

"I think I should have stayed outside. What about Zandrie?"

Kojo looked at one of the vidcubes before answering. "Landing her fighter right outside. Guess she's tired of commanding from a pilot's seat."

"More like she's taunting Dado into a fistfight. She's trying to give us some tiny chance of surviving. Well, here's to a good last stand."

He looked up to see the flying wing looming large within the central vidcube. He was awestruck, but not nearly as astonished as the technicians, guards, or the clustered OzTech executives. It filled the entire screen. "How close *is* that thing?"

"About…a hundred meters."

Makers stood shoulder to shoulder in their tanks and other ground craft, weapons ready and aimed while Zandrie stepped in before the tower's entry, pulling out a long sword. Behind her, Toby and Texas stood firm, the ball-tank rolling to a stop to one side. They faced an inexhaustible horde of Ripper forces, the flying wing taking center stage with both its sheer size and the number of gun ports sticking out along the entire front edge.

"What did someone once say about this being a good day to die?" Toby asked.

"The guy obviously wasn't a Texan. A Texan would say it's a good day for the *other* guy to die."

Thousands of Ripper craft rolled up into a tight circle around them. It was clear that the hundred Makers standing around in defense wouldn't last more than a few seconds once the barrage started.

And yet, it did not start. Vehicles came to a stop and soon the only sound was that of the jets from both sides, still flying around the tower as a hush came over the battlefield.

"When the king is surrounded with no place to go," Kojo stated, "it is checkmate."

"I hope you're wrong," Zavier said. "But if so, then why aren't they shooting?"

From the large image before them, they saw something slowly emerge from the underside of the large flying wing. A single platform lowered down, covered by armored transparencies on all sides and carrying three people. The Viking and the Manchester United woman flanked an average-looking man with a friendly face who every person there knew. The platform stopped lowering once it was five meters down, held there by the long metal beams gripping its corners.

Dado smiled, and when he spoke, his voice came amplified from the transparent walls for everyone to hear.

"As I promised, the death of the old world is about to begin."

CHAPTER 26

My dearest Eduardo,

I am so very proud of the man you have become. I have watched as you have grown wise in your young age. You have already changed so many lives for the better, and the world has begun to take notice.

The years we have worked together will now come to fruition. The followers you and I have gathered are becoming leaders. It is time to let them lead.

Remember to be patient. Let your followers work in the open, while you work in the shadows. The covetous Elitists will not see what you and I have created until it is too late. All of it for all of us, my son.

With love, your mother.

P.S. Our cause needs a name and symbol to rally behind. Choose wisely, my son.

Final letter from Leonor Oliveira, 2109 (translated)

"It's over," Kojo stated. "Tactically speaking, we're out of options. Dado's got a gun pointed at our heads."

Zavier looked up at the images towering over him. The massive flying wing played centerpiece to the Ripper force, as the rows of tanks encircling the great tower pressed in on the young Makers. He saw the wreckage of combat littering the sprawling metal field beyond, the ubiquitous OzBots struggling to clean it all up. He looked at the various craft left to the Makers still in the air, who warily circled the tower while Ripper drones kept pace.

Most of all, he saw Dado smiling down at them like an amiable grandfather, holding it all back in his mercy.

"Ever the professor. He wants to talk. He wants to *teach* us," Zavier realized. "If I can just keep him—Koj, remember that little idea we've been talking about?"

"The hack?" Kojo's eyes went wide with realization. "No. We have no way of predicting what could happen."

"It's probably our only way out. I'll see what I can do to stall, but don't take too long."

"I'll do my best." Kojo sighed, then flipped down his vidglasses and called out to the technicians, "Okay guys, I need a mainframe interface."

Zavier ran for the exit into the lush anteroom, where he nearly ran into Min. She was furiously working to print and repair wounds on one of dozens of Makers who'd filled the entryway. Her face was set into as brave a manner as she could manage, but beneath it, Zavier could see the fear in her eyes. She said nothing, but didn't need to.

"I'm scared too," Zavier knelt down to tell her. "But Koj is working on something."

She stayed quiet, continuing her work at a feverish pace.

"If it comes to it," Zavier continued, "and they get through, if you don't fight them, they will probably leave you alone. You're a Medic, they'll get that. Now, I've got to go out there and stall them for as long as I—"

He never finished the sentence. Min suddenly stood up and wrapped her slender arms around him, hugging herself into his chest where he could feel the quiet sobbing break loose. "Don't leave, Z. If we're going to die—"

He raised a shaking hand gently to the back of her head and held it there for a moment, his voice lowering for her ears alone.

"No one's dying, but I've got to get out there."

She drew back with a final sniff, straightened herself out, then addressed him like the Maker she was. "I'm coming with you."

"Min, you don't have to do this. These people need—"

"There are other Medics here. You said yourself, you need to keep him talking for whatever it is you've got Kojo working on. I can help. So, let's get to it."

He gave her a last look, for a moment seeing something stronger than he had expected. He nodded once and hurried across the room, now with Min by his side.

When they got outside, Zandrie was taking aim with a rifle while Dado tried to address the remaining Makers.

"None of us are budging, Dado," she called out. "Which means if you're so intent on starting your new world order, you'll have to do so with mass murder."

She fired, but her projectile was absorbed by the clear protective barrier that surrounded him.

"I'm so disappointed in you, Zandrie," Dado scolded, ignoring the shot. His voice was amplified for all around to hear. "You have no doubt seen what lies within the structure behind you. How can you continue to support that? I wish to liberate, not execute. I want to set this matter free—for everyone!"

"The only thing you'll liberate is a few hundred extra rounds of ammo from my gun as soon as I can—"

"You're a hypocrite, Dado," Zavier yelled as he stepped in front of Zandrie. Min, Toby, and Texas stepped forward with him. "No one is making you do anything. You *want* all of this destruction!"

Dado smiled pleasantly. "My favorite student."

"And you *used* to be my favorite instructor. Now, I know you were a manipulator," Zavier called back. "So, why haven't you killed us all yet?"

"I would think that obvious, *meu rapaz*," Dado began. "I would like to try one last time to dissuade you from your position, to help you to see your error in judgment. You are siding with the wrong people, Zavier. You know that now."

"But does that make you the right people? All I've seen Rippers do is kill."

"Your Makers have been guilty of a little killing yourselves. Ask your friend Texas. She suffers from quite a bit of remorse over the death that she caused, the one whose life she took at Alice Springs. We spoke in great length about that incident and her resultant doubts in being a Maker."

Zavier looked back to see the expression on Texas' face change instantly from defiance to one of betrayal. She had a gun in her hand, but now it slipped from her grip. From the look of her, she was caught in a loop between wanting to hurt her former mentor and fearing to kill another face to face.

"Th—that conversation was private," Texas stammered. "And I didn't doubt, I was just…just…"

Toby reach a hand around her and hugged her to his side. "Easy there."

"The point is," Dado continued, now returning his attention at Zavier, "that both sides kill. The difference is the Roosters do only what we need to do to liberate the world from the tyranny of the oligarchy. Everything beneath our feet, everything that tower behind you controls—it's all about *matter*, the very substance of the universe. It is the food we eat, the comforts we give ourselves, the medicines we need to stay healthy. It is wealth and it is power.

"There is more than enough of it for everyone to live like kings should they wish it, and yet only a few control it. But to what purpose? Does it really gain them anything? Yes. It gains them control over people. Living, breathing creatures—the one thing the Ozmium device cannot create. And for this reason, the Elitists control it. They want to horde their dominance over people, Zavier, and that has ever been the template for some of history's most despicable despots."

"Control? You seek to control us all," Zavier countered. "You are just like them, even though you hide behind your self-righteousness."

"I seek to control nothing. The power to control the flow of all matter in our world effectively makes one a *god*, Zavier. But why them? Why not all of us? The Elitists like Helen Lo want it all simply because they are covetous. They don't want a world where everyone has what they do, because then they would have no way to raise themselves above the rest. They want power. They want people serving them. They want to be able to tell someone to walk off a cliff then watch as they promptly do, just for their own amusement."

Zavier scoffed, but Dado ignored him.

"We are a game to them, but the game must stop," Dado continued. "No one should have such power over anyone else. Certainly not a handful of overlords whose only contribution to mankind is in more creative ways of spreading misery and getting people to cheer about it. You've been a fool, Zavier—*all* of you. You believe that you can help people with this power. That's why you joined the Maker Corps, is it not? To make a difference. But what difference have any of you really made? With all the elements at your feet to shift around and change as you wish, your friend Kojo still has poverty-stricken family back in Accra, people like Min's grandmother still needlessly die of cancer, and people in Toby's homeland still fight one another for reasons that in all my eighty years have never ceased being ridiculous. So, tell me, what difference *have* the Makers made? Like all law enforcers, they enforce the status quo, but the status quo is what is wrong with the world.

"Can't you see that, Zavier? Can't any of you see that? It is time to turn the power back in upon itself, to return it to the people. This power belongs with *all* of us, not in the hands of the privileged few."

Dado paused for a moment to let his words sink in, and from what Zavier could see from the sea of Maker faces, there were a few doubts within the ranks. Doubts that, if he gave them time enough to grow, could lead to desertion.

>>**Kojo**>>**Z, keep him talking. I need more time.**<<

Zavier responded by continuing to argue with Dado.

"You say that this is about the people, Dado, but I know it's not," Zavier argued. "It's nothing more than revenge, plain and simple. You want *revenge* for what OzTech did to your father and your family. I can understand that, because I've wanted revenge too. I've wanted revenge for what your crowing Roosters did to my little sister, Zoey. That was my sole reason for joining the Corps, just as it was Zandrie's. I wanted to push back against who I thought was responsible and see him swing from a very short rope."

Zavier felt Min take his hand and squeeze. He realized that she was caught between sympathy and concern over the direction of his words, but he had more to say. "I see now that my life needs to be about more than simple revenge," he said as his eyes teared up. "Revenge only brings more excuses for someone *else* to be violent in the name of vengeance. No, it is about stability and protecting the law. The same law that applies to everyone equally, or it means nothing."

"On that, my son, we do have common ground," Dado said with another warm smile. "Yet your law has never seemed to apply equally toward those in power. Do you not see? Before you can administer the justice that you seek, you must *remove* those in power. Cut off the head of the snake. It is the only way to reset everything and start clean; otherwise, the cycle continues endlessly."

"What you're talking about is anarchy!" Zavier shouted.

"Some anarchy is necessary, yes," Dado stated. "The slate must be wiped clean, the cycle broken. With all of us in power, we will usher in a new dawn of peace and prosperity. Then, out of the chaos, will come order and balance once again. Then the Ozmium device really will be the glory of mankind."

Zavier scoffed. "Balance? Were your people creating balance when they killed my little sister? Was it for reasons of balance that you leveled the Maker headquarters? What kind of balance are you trying to bring with the deaths of thousands—hundreds of thousands—of people?"

"The death of your sister," Dado sighed, "was...unfortunate. And tragic. As were the deaths of any others like her. But war is often messy, and make no mistake—this *is* a war."

>>Koj>>Z, a few more minutes. I think I can actually do this!<<

"The only reason why we have a war right now is because of *you*," Zavier countered. "Right now, the primary purpose of the Makers is to keep the Rippers in check, because *they* are the ones doing the killing. But it has to end. Someone has to find a way to end the bloodshed, to stop the pointless destruction.

"You say that the lump of matter at our feet is everything, that once it's taken away from the current hands that control it and it's laid free to everyone, that the world's problems will be solved. But *will* they? What is this technology without the people who know how to run it? The people who design and create? Makers are more than soldiers. We're designers, technicians, scientists. This is what *you* always told us! We do things that your average person could never do so that they may benefit from it.

"Are we then part of your 'Elitists'? Anyone with a skill or ability above anyone else's should be knocked down, is that it? The power should be scattered amongst those who have no idea how any of this works or any sense of responsibility, then when someone makes the next Earth-shattering mistake, at least everyone will share in the blame equally—is that it, Dado? Kill the investors, kill the designers and the dreamers, kill the intellectuals. But when you kill people, *any* people, you kill everything and reduce our civilization to the level of warring, grunting animals. *People* are glorious, Dr. Oliveira. *People*, not dead matter—not even technology! It sounds like you've forgotten that. Or maybe you never really knew and were just pretending. Maybe it was something your father never had a chance to teach you before he died."

Dr. Dado's kind demeanor slipped, and his face betrayed the rage, vengefulness, and madness underneath. He quickly hid his true self again, but it was too late.

A small cheer went up among the Makers, while some Rooster faces started to look a little hesitant. Even Dado fell silent at the mention of his father. Toby called out with "Preach, *hermano*," Texas snapped out of the downcast mood that Dado's words had put her in, and Min now squeezed Zavier's hand more gently while looking up at him with a proud smile.

"Those bankers in there are corrupt and power-mad, yes," Zavier continued. "But greatness lives inside anyone with the ability to create. Would you kill them too? Without that ability, the Oz is nothing and every element remains worthless. People have been saying for centuries that power corrupts; I think you even implied it in a couple of your history classes I took in my first years at the Academy."

"Power corrupts," Dado agreed. "And absolute power corrupts absolutely. That is why those within that ivory tower need to be cast—"

"And then it falls to who...*you*? Of course it does. You're not fooling anyone but yourself. Dado, your quest for this absolute power has already *absolutely* corrupted you. You are just as crooked as those behind me, and it's time to change that."

>>Z>>**Koj, I need it NOW!**<<

>>**Koj**>>**Just got it, Z! Executing command.**<<

A quick string of text followed across not only Zavier's textlens, but everyone else's in the squad—and possibly Zandrie's as well, judging from the surprised look on her face.

>>**Quantum Bank systems report: registering numerous non-functional devices. Internal VacGuard maps authorized for use. Vac cleanup of faulty Ozmium units initiated.**<<

As the report scrolled across their view, Min's expression went from loving and proud to one of pure horror. The grip she had on Zavier's hand suddenly tightened in anger.

"No, you can't!" she screamed. *"Don't!"*

Suddenly, the OzBots patrolling the battlefield suddenly stopped what they were doing and headed for a new selection of targets. A wave of them rose up behind the Ripper lines, then crashed down into the shores of their ranks. Suddenly, dozens of OzBots rushed directly toward the Rippers, with hundreds more speeding in across the horizon, doing what they were designed to do.

But the debris they now vac'ed up were the Ozmium units that the Rippers themselves used.

At first, the cries were ones of surprise as Ozes started to vanish off people's wrists. Then, Rippers began screaming as the OzBots—interpreting their bodies to be a part of each Ripper's Oz—also vac'ed up parts of the arms those devices were attached to.

Using the VacGuard maps, the OzBots flew through the ranks like torpedoes with a split second for each vac job that didn't even slow them down. Rippers fell by the score, screaming and clutching at smoothly vac'ed stumps. Some of them turned in panic and ran recklessly in every direction as they tried to outrun the unexpected assault.

Unfortunately, the janitors of the Ozmium Age were everywhere.

Dado's attention snapped in an instant, quickly taking in the situation. Beside him, the Viking and Manchester United woman had their weapons up, ready to take aim at the first OzBot that came near them.

And one did come at them. It vac'ed up the protective shield around them and their weapons, as well as their Oz units…plus the forearms they were attached to. Suddenly, they were falling to the floor of the platform while Dado stared in shock at the stump where his right forearm used to be. It all happened in a single quick pass as the bot coldly moved on to another target.

Hundreds of Rippers abandoned their weapons and devices as they fell to the ground screaming, their ranks decimated by robot custodians.

Min was paralyzed with shock for a moment, then released her grip on Zavier and savagely pounded her fists into his shoulder. "*This* was your plan?! How *could* you?!"

She shoved him to the ground and then ran off to the nearest fallen Ripper, quickly printing a medkit along the way.

The pending victory of the Rooster Rebellion had suddenly been turned on its head, with Zavier at the center of it all. Makers rushed out into the chaos to secure their new prisoners. Zavier slowly rose to his feet, looking up at Dado while the latter finally summoned up enough willpower to overcome the shock to his body and offer one last grandfatherly smile down to him.

"Well…done. You are indeed…my…prize student…"

Dado fell to the floor of his platform.

Celebratory messages exploded across Zavier's textlens from other Maker squads as they rushed out to clean up the mess. One message from Zandrie to Zavier nearly got lost in the cascade of messages.

>>Zandrie>>That was some seriously fluid thinking!<<

For a few minutes, he stood there. Maker Medics rushed out to wounded Rippers at the same time as others arrested the survivors, who at this point had no problem with surrendering.

Min was leading the charge of Medics, scrambling to save who she could. She was able to save some, staunching the blood then quickly printing a new arm before rushing onto the next. But there were many she could not get to in time.

Zavier tried to catch her eye with an apologetic look, and even sent a textlens message.

>>**Z**>>**Min, it was the only way.**<<

All he got in response, though, was a look of disgust before she hurried to the next victim. Zavier had found a way to win the war against the Rippers. But while he had saved billions of lives, he did it by betraying the one person he cared for the most.

CHAPTER 27

An Innovator is the embodiment of the phrase "stay fluid." As the nickname implies, an "Edge" must operate on the edge of all things to create the unimaginable solution.

Where others see a dead end, the Innovator must see possibility. To do this, the Innovator must cultivate a mind that is open to making connections between the seemingly unrelated. This is why the Innovator studies all the disciplines while specializing in none of them.

Being an "Edge" is learning how to both break the rules but keep the law. The challenge of maintaining that balance summarizes the opportunity—and burden—of the Innovator.

Global Maker Corp Innovator Handbook

The squad without a name sat in the officer's lounge near their quarters in the Maker Corps orbital facility. Several other squads rested and talked with each other as well. The lounge was decorated with a mixture of classic and post-modern styles, as well as a circle of zero-grav bag chairs around a large vidcube. The station was now finished, and was larger and more armored than before. A fleet of Maker vessels and drones kept up their patrols around it.

Kojo, Toby, Texas, and Zavier relaxed in the bag chairs, with Min notably absent. The central vidcube displayed a news report on one of the more popular programs.

"It has been three weeks since the Rooster Rebellion came to a dramatic end at the Quantum Bank, thanks to the efforts of the Makers, and one young squad in particular."

"Squad Vik," Toby said as he smiled. "I think that's a definite possibility."

"Squad Solomon has a better ring to it," said Zavier.

Kojo shrugged, grinning. "Hey, using the OzBots *was* your idea, after all."

"Sure," Zavier replied. "Blame me. You were the one who made it happen."

"The true leader of the Roosters, Dr. Eduardo Oliveira, known to many as simply 'Dado,' has been imprisoned along with the surviving Rippers after what turned out to be the fastest trial on record. They are now currently locked away in the L-four ultra-security facility, as distant from the Earth as the Moon. Food and such necessities are physically shipped to the L-four ultramax, as Ozmium units are prohibited. Dr. Oliveira is considered an extreme threat, so such precautions were deemed necessary."

"Thank goodness we don't have to listen to any more of his shattered speeches," Texas muttered.

"Must be pretty crowded in that ultramax," Toby remarked. "Z's clever maneuver took down every Ripper within range of an OzBot. Everywhere. Overkill, much?"

"I gave it a blanket order and the computer did the rest," Zavier said. "Without Kojo tapping into the Quantum Bank's mainframe, it would have been impossible."

"Overkill? Nah. Justice is more like it," Texas corrected.

"Lemme guess," Toby laughed, "Texas-style?"

"Actually, I was gonna say *Vik* style," Texas said with a slightly forced grin. The squad had been keeping up their usual lighthearted banter over the past few weeks, but underneath all their quick comments ran a thread of pain that still made it all feel forced. The trauma of war was something they were each struggling with in their own way, and the disappearance of Min hung particularly heavy over them.

"Some Rippers who managed to avoid being targeted by the Solomon OzBot Hack—as it is being called—remain at large and are currently being hunted down. It is expected that they will be arrested within the month."

Several Makers in the room cheered and gave Kojo a congratulatory thumbs up. He shook his head in embarrassment.

"How long did you have this idea brewing?" Toby asked.

"Zavier bounced it off me after one of our training sessions with the veterans," Kojo answered. "It seemed like a pretty brilliant way of cutting a battle short in an emergency. We just didn't have the computing power—or access—necessary to pull it off."

"Min gave me the idea with her VacGuard hack." Zavier paused, lost in a painful memory. "Min...didn't seem to think it was so brilliant, though."

"No one's seen her since we came back from the Moon?" Toby asked.

"She screamed at me at the dock, then turned and left," Zavier replied. "I don't know where to. She told me that her idea was designed to save lives, and said she could never forgive me and Koj for stealing it and turning it into a weapon of mass destruction. She has a point, but it...Well, we had to do something to save everybody."

"You did," Texas assured him. "Your idea saved billions of lives, Z."

"Did it? Maybe we could have found another way," Zavier countered.

"Z, even if Dado would have listened to you—which is doubtful—and kept the containment safeguards in place, do you actually think that he would have stopped?"

"You said it yourself, *hermano*," Toby added, "power corrupts, and Dado was corrupted by revenge. He would have simply used one excuse after another to seize that power for himself and use it to start eliminating anything he didn't like."

"How sure can you be of that?" Zavier asked.

"History," Kojo said. "The corruptible are the only ones that ever *want* to seize power, no matter how good their stated intentions. Dado would have made all of history's tyrants look like gentle kittens in comparison."

"I still wish there had been another way."

Zavier sighed, got up, and walked away from the squad. Nightmares of screaming and dying Rippers still echoed in his mind. His speech had given Kojo the time he'd needed, and Kojo had made it happen…but it had still been Zavier's idea. He had brought down the Rippers, yes, but that meant their pain was also his responsibility. Tens of thousands wounded, some of whom could not get medical attention in time. He was responsible for it all. His idea, his choice.

How would he ever be able to live with that?

Texas stepped next to him and touched his arm. "Dado would have vaporized everyone on both sides. It was the only way out. A few lives for billions. You're a hero, Z."

"Maybe. Do you want to try and get Min to believe that?"

Texas paused and shook her head. "I don't know what she's thinking right now. But she's a smart kid. I'm sure she'll come around sooner or later."

"I hope so…I really hope so."

The news had just finished up with the report on the Rippers when Kojo called their attention back to the program. "Here it comes."

Zavier looked up at the vidcube to watch, while Texas kept her hand on his arm.

"In related news, the revelation of OzTech's secretive practices has been brought before the Global Nations Alliance with charges of extreme invasion of privacy, insider trading, and market manipulation on a global scale. Hefty fines have been levied, and

safeguards have been installed to prevent any future such intrusions. Furthermore, a special oversight committee from the Global Nations Alliance has been selected to supervise all operations at the Quantum Bank, changes to begin immediately. As OzTech shares fell sharply, President Ryan Pedigrand and Chairperson Ci Xi submitted their resignations. After the announcement, OzTech's co-founder and former CEO, Helen Lo, issued the following statement to the press:"

Helen appeared on the screen. *"I believe I speak for all OzTech shareholders when I say that we are shocked and saddened by these developments. Clearly, our former leadership team overstepped their bounds. We are grateful to the Global Maker Corps for both protecting OzTech's Global Bank, and for exposing the heinous activities of two of our rogue executives. The privacy of every person is paramount in our minds, and we will comply with GNA oversight to ensure nothing like this will ever happen again."*

"Can you believe that?" Toby said. "She lies so smoothly."

"They still got off easy, if you ask me," Texas remarked. "Back home, we'd take them out back and—"

"Zavier, can I speak with you?"

He turned to see Zandrie standing a couple yards away, in full dress uniform with insignia medals pinned across her shoulders. Zavier immediately jumped to his feet and came to a salute. "Commander Vik, ma'am."

"Ease off," she told him, motioning him over. "I'm here as your sister."

"But the uniform—"

"They've got me going to another slagging medal ceremony Earth-side." She sighed. "Now, come over here, I want to speak with you before I leave."

Zavier glanced at his friends, who gave him a mock salute, then followed Zandrie across the lounge to a more private spot.

"This is the third ceremony this week," she complained once

they were alone. "I'd start ignoring them, but registration of new cadets is up three hundred percent as a result, and we really need the new manpower."

"You deserve the attention after all you've done to hold things together after the Rippers demolished this place, plus leading the defense of the Bank. I could never have done any of that. You deserve the acclaim."

"Zavier, that's what I wanted to talk to you about. I'm good at what I do, yes, but there are things that *you* do that I could *never* measure up to. Hacking the Oz units?"

"Kojo did the actual hacking."

"But it was *your* idea, Edge. How many other people could have thought up something so simple yet so devastating? Not even the techs at the Bank thought of that. Time and again, you have come up with ideas and suggestions that no one else would have thought of. You still lack discipline, but I understand it takes time to learn control. I never mentioned this, but I actually punched out one of my trainers when I was a cadet."

"What? You're kidding. Who was it?"

"Mr. Hyatt, the physical education instructor. Caught him by surprise and laid him right out."

"So *that's* why he constantly preaches about keeping your guard up…"

"The point is, everyone starts out somewhere, but it's where you end up that counts. And I'm pretty proud of where you're ending up. I know you've always worried about measuring up, but don't. Even *I* couldn't have stopped an entire Ripper assault-force with a single squad when I was your age."

Then, Zandrie did something that caught Zavier completely off guard. She snapped to attention and saluted him. "Maker Vik, it is my personal honor being your commander…but more especially, your *sister*."

Zavier returned the salute, still stunned. His sister then gave him a small grin and then grabbed him into a big hug. After a moment, she returned to her military demeanor for a final word.

"Things are peaceful enough right now," she said. "But our jobs as Makers are just beginning."

For the first time in his life, Zavier felt the warmth of accomplishment—and a glimpse of his own true worth. He felt proud not only of his sister and his squad…but himself.

EPILOGUE

Sweetheart,

Do not weep. I have lived a beautiful life, and greatest among the beauty I have seen is to know you, little one.

You desire to respect all life and protect others from harm, and at such a very young age you have already learned so much. What a clever, bright girl you are becoming!

You said you wanted to save me. And you shall. Learn to heal others, and every person you save shall be someone's grandmother, mother, sister, or daughter. They shall also all be me, and you will see my face in each of them. Do this, and I will always be with you.

You will change the world. I know this to be true.

Go with peace, dear Min.

Final letter from Hyun-Aw Yu to her granddaughter, 2159 (translated)

Min sat alone in the garden at a simple wooden bench, tinkering with a mechanical device that lay across the bulk of the table before her. A glass roof shielded her and her device from what little rain there was, two walls of the alcove open to the fresh scents of the garden and the soft plops of raindrops on the little pond beyond. Her usual blend of loud, defiant, yet oddly jaunty music played in the otherwise peaceful background. She was staying in her family's home, a simple house of traditional Chinese design, in Yanji of the Yanbian Independent Prefecture—what used to be North Korea and parts of China.

Min kept her thoughts to herself as she continued tinkering with the OzBot that sat in front of her. *I joined the Corps to save lives. My grandmother died of cancer before the tech was available to save her. I joined to save others like her, and what happens?*

She worked a tool into the OzBot, made an adjustment, then brought up a diagram on a portable vidcube to double-check something. *I get sucked into a battle between one set of vengeful people versus another. Just people wanting to control things. Elitists want to control the people, Rippers want to control the Elitists, and the Makers want to control the Rippers. But who gets stuck in the middle?*

She started poking at the OzBot again. *Everyone. Can't trust anyone…not even the person I…cared about. Now, technology…*

She went back to her display and started moving elements of it around with her hand.

…that you can trust. It's the people using it who are the problem.

After another few adjustments to her diagram, she pressed something on her wrist and a new set of components printed into the OzBot. *Oz technology is the core of it. To be able to change matter around as you please…manipulate starks…create or destroy at will. It's what caused the world to shatter into a thousand pieces, caused so many millions to die in the war.*

She reached back into the OzBot with her tool and made another adjustment, turning something while keeping an eye on the diagram floating in the vidcube. *It's what caused Zavier and Kojo to do what they did and shatter any chance Z and I had of being together. I thought my team had my back. I thought I'd found a true…*

The diagram shifted, interrupting her thoughts. She raced her fingers across a few icons at the bottom of the display, adjusting her engineering blueprint.

I'm better off on my own. No one's going to betray me, ever again. I won't let them. I'm more focused working alone, anyway—just me and my music.

Her adjustments made, she performed a last inspection of the OzBot's innards before reaching over for the panel to close it back up. *It's all so clear now. Oz technology didn't save anyone's life. It's not a blessing. It's a curse that ruined everyone's lives.*

The panel in place, she began sealing it shut. She used a tool carefully along the panel's edges, melding the two components together as if there had never been a seam.

Things used to be so simple, but it's like both Zavier and Dado said: power corrupts, and absolute power corrupts absolutely. Oz technology is about as absolute as you can get. It's the power of a god. It's time someone did something about it...

She put down her tool and leaned back for a final inspection of her work, double-checking with the diagram in the vidcube before shutting it off. Her friends—her former squadmates—would never have recognized the stern, unforgiving, stone-cold expression that came over her face.

It was final. She had made her decision.

Min stood up before her customized OzBot while the rain continued to trickle down and her music continued to play.

"None of it," she said through gritted teeth.

"*None* of it for *any* of us."

SPECIAL THANKS

Thank you to everyone who participated in bringing the world of the Maker Corp to life! Special thanks to:

- My son, Stratton, for the many discussions we had about battles, weapons, and characters. He also was the first true maker I met. So much of this book was inspired by his journey.
- My wife, Katherine, for both putting up with my endless talking about this imaginary world that was floating around in my head, as well as her polishing touches to make the book shine.
- My agent, Matt, who believed in the book enough to devote hours of his life to get it out to the world.
- My alpha readers Elijah W., Katlyn E., and Ashlynn K. for helping me shape the path of this book.
- My editor, Elizabeth B., for catching all the little things I missed.
- My interior layout and all-around helpful graphics guy, John Arce, who always makes my books look professional.
- Cover artist, George Sellas, for bringing the squad-without-a-name to life.
- Everyone who supported me and pushed me forward as I shared the ever-developing Maker universe with them. Thank you for listening!

SOUNDTRACK

I'm a fan of synthwave—often called retrowave—music. It's a cross between 80's synth and video game music and is possibly the nerdiest thing you could listen to. It's also a lot of fun and stirred my creativity for many of the chapters in this book. Whenever I felt a lag in my motivation to write, I would put on tracks like the ones listed below and then could easily imagine Zavier and his squad doing their thing.

This is only a beginning list of many of my favorite tunes. Please check out these artists, give them a listen, and if you like what you hear, tell them you heard about them from D. M. C. Shaw and *The Maker War.*

- "The Sector" by Sung, *Auto Ran - EP*
- "Legend of the Keeper" by Magic Sword, *Legend*
- "Beacon (feat. Dimi Kaye)" by Volkor X, *Desync (Original Soundtrack, Vol. 2)*
- "Fata Morgana" by Monomer, *Labyrinth*
- "Last Run" by Tokyo Rose, *The Chase: Last Run*
- "Breakout" by Daniel Deluxe, *Desync (Original Soundtrack, Vol. 1)*
- "Job for a Cowboy" by OGRE Sound, *195*
- "The Silence" by Stilz, *Quadrant 457*
- "Looking for Tracy Tzu" by Carpenter Brut, *TRILOGY*
- "Exit Music" by Lost Years, *Black Waves*

You can also find my entire, ever-evolving synthwave Google Play Music playlist at **MakerWar.com/music**.

SUPPORT THE MAKER CORPS

Thank you for reading *The Maker War*! If you would like to see more stories of Zavier and the squad-without-a-name, here's what you can do to make it happen:

1. **Leave a review on Amazon and/or Goodreads.** Every review makes a difference and will help more amazing people like yourself find the book.

2. **Share a post about the book on social media.** A quick post on Facebook, Instagram, or Twitter will help spread the word. (Coming soon: post a vidcube video!)

3. **Get free stuff at MakerWar.com.** I'll occasionally share updates on the progress of future books. Enter your email on my site, and I'll reward you with insider stuff like the timeline of the Maker Universe, short stories, and more.

Also, if you catch something that you think is a typo or error, please send me an email at **fan@makerwar.com** and I'll see if it should be fixed in the next edition. Please remember to be kind: a lot of love and work went into making this book come to life.

Thank you for your support!

ABOUT THE AUTHOR

D. M. C. Shaw grew up being enthralled by science fiction action and adventure movies. In fact, for many years he wanted to become the next Stephen Spielberg. He wrote many fantasy and science fiction short stories when he was younger and dreamed of a day when he would see his stories become reality.

Life took him a different, still wonderful, direction and he found a career in business consulting. His work allowed him to travel the world which helped him develop an appreciation for many different countries, cultures, and people. These new friends and experiences help shape the world of *The Maker War*.

He also started a family and, as his children began to grow, they helped him rekindle his desire to tell fantastic stories. After playing with the idea of his made-up sci-fi universe and characters for many years, he decided to finally bring Zavier and the Maker Corps to life.

D. M. C. has dealt with ADHD throughout his life, so the experiences of characters in this book reflect many of his own. Thanks to the help of caring therapists and doctors, he has learned how to find success in life, and how to "stay fluid." He regularly encourages those with similar issues to seek the same help.

He lives in the shadow of Utah's Rocky Mountains with his wife and three children. When he's not writing sci-fi books, he's still paying the bills with business consulting. And when he's not doing that, he enjoys spending time with his family, playing video games, and getting lost in sci-fi and adventure movies…just like he did when he was young.

Made in the USA
Middletown, DE
06 February 2020